A GODAWFUL SMALL AFFAIR

By J.B. Morrison

First published in Great Britain in 2020 by Cherry Red Books (a division of Cherry Red Records), Power Road Studios, 114 Power Road, London W4 5PY

A CIP Catalogue record for this book is available from the British Library.

ISBN: 978-1-909454-79-8

Layout by Nathan Eighty (nathan.eighty@gmail.com)
Cover design and Illustrations by Mark Reynolds.

BY THE SAME AUTHOR:

Fiction:

AS JIM BOB

'Storage Stories' and 'Driving Jarvis Ham'

AS J.B. MORRISON:

'The Extra Ordinary Life of Frank Derrick, Age 81'

'Frank Derrick's Holiday Of A Lifetime'

Biography/memoir:

'Goodnight Jim Bob – On the Road with Carter The Unstoppable Sex Machine'

'Jim Bob from Carter – In the Shadow of my Former Self'

In Loving Memory

David Jones 8.1.47 – 10.1.16

Jenny Morrison 12.8.29 – 10.1.16

'Tonight, Big Brother is watching you

And I am watching too

I will watch over you'

And God Created Brixton –

Carter The Unstoppable Sex Machine

ONE GIANT LEAP FOR BOYKIND

Nathan checked the equipment and supplies in his backpack. He'd already eaten the cheese sandwich and the Kit Kat, but he still had half a bottle of Coke Zero left, and he hadn't touched the Satsuma. There was a small Christmas cracker compass in the backpack and a notepad and pencil — he had originally packed a pen but remembered Zoe telling him that writing in zero gravity was like writing upside down. He'd packed a half-used disposable underwater camera and an old MP3 player. He'd found them both in Zoe's room. There were thirteen photos left on the camera and sixty-four songs on the MP3 player. The songs were mostly by groups of girls shouting and swearing, but Zoe's favourite David Bowie playlist was on there too.

Nathan looked up at the night sky. The stars didn't seem as bright as when his dad had first stuck them onto the ceiling. Zoe said that most stars were either dead or dying, maybe that was true with the plastic ones as well. On the morning after his sister went missing, Nathan woke up with Jupiter stuck to his forehead. Zoe would have told him that as it was falling from his bedroom ceiling it was a meteor and when it landed on his head, Jupiter became a meteorite.

Nathan unzipped the front pouch of the backpack and took out his Space Torch. He switched it on and shone the light onto the photo of his sister. Every police officer in London knew what she looked like because of the same picture. It was on the posters and leaflets and it was the profile picture on the *Where is Zoe Love?* Facebook page. The photo was the screensaver on Nathan's dad's laptop and there were plans to have it printed on the front of T-shirts. In the television appeal there was an enlarged copy of the photo on an easel. Nathan's dad's friend Craig said it looked like the police were auctioning a painting.

Nathan changed the setting on his Space Torch. He projected an image of a galaxy from eight million light years away, taken by the Hubble telescope, onto his bedroom wall. Nathan's own telescope was in the backpack, but it wasn't powerful enough to see into the flat opposite. He switched off the torch and put it in his backpack. He probably wouldn't need it where he was going. The bright light was the first thing that Zoe had talked about. For a while it was the only thing she would talk about. The light had been so bright that, for a week afterwards, she had to wear sunglasses indoors. Craig had called her Bono. To protect Nathan's eyes from the bright light, he was wearing his dad's tinted swimming goggles. And to stop him coming back from space with the same cuts and bruises as Zoe, he had skateboard pads on his elbows and his knees.

Nathan put the red Swiss Army knife into the backpack. The knife's two sharp blades probably contradicted the *We come in peace* slogan on the badge pinned to his bright orange *Mission to Mars* all-in-one astronaut costume. He didn't know if they even spoke English where he was going – there was a small dictionary in his backpack just in case. He'd written his name and address on the back of his hand: Nathan James Love, Brixton, London, England, the World, Earth, the Solar System, the Universe.

Nathan took one last look around his room before pulling the swimming goggles down over his eyes. He looked at the model rocket and the Lego Space Shuttle and the three Buzz Lightyear figures and the books on astronomy and his Dalek money bank and the Star Wars figures guarding it. He looked at the NASA patches on the sleeves of his *Mission to Mars* spacesuit and at his *Guardians of the Galax*y backpack and at the planetarium on his ceiling and he wondered if the aliens had gone to his sister's bedroom by mistake.

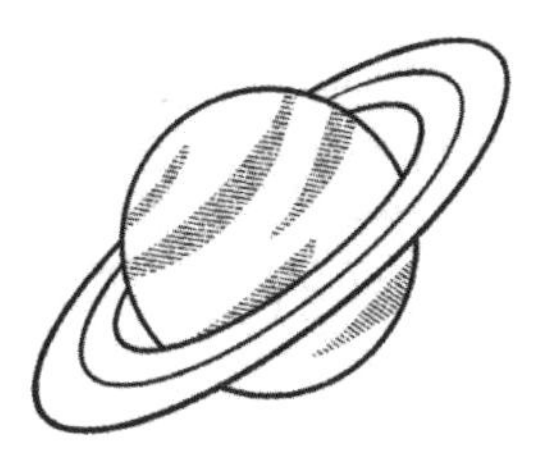

1

Zoe Patricia Love was fifteen when she went into town with her little brother to pay respects to their favourite singer on the first anniversary of his death. Before they left the house, Zoe painted a red and blue lightning bolt onto Nathan's face.

"Don't get it in *my eyes,*" Nathan said.

"I won't, if you'd just keep still."

When Zoe was finished, she gave Nathan a mirror and the album cover she'd been copying from. Nathan compared the record sleeve to his reflection.

"I could shave your eyebrows off too, if you like?" Zoe said.

Nathan put his hand and the record in front of his face, until Zoe swore on their dad's life and their mum's grave that she wasn't really holding a razor.

In spite of Nathan thinking his make-up looked cool, he moaned so much to his sister about not wanting anyone else to see it, that when the security light came on over his head the second he stepped out of the front door, like a spotlight pointing him out to the world, Zoe laughed and didn't stop laughing until the bus came.

Nathan zipped his parka right up to his chin and kept the hood pulled over his head, even when they were on the bus. The snorkel hood was so long that he couldn't see where he was going without turning his whole head. Zoe said he looked like a meerkat. When they got to the mural and Nathan saw he wasn't the only one with a lightning bolt on his face, he removed the hood. And when he saw the painting of David Bowie with the same bolt of red and blue, Nathan wanted everyone to see.

There were hundreds of messages for David Bowie, written on the mural and on the walls surrounding it. People had tucked postcards and scraps of paper underneath the square of see-through Perspex that protected the mural.

Messages were written on train tickets and till receipts, with different coloured pens, and with lipstick and eyeliner pencil. The messages were in English and French, Italian and German, and what Nathan thought was Japanese. One message was written on a Brixton ten-pound note – the one with David Bowie's face on.

The pavement in front of the mural was covered with candles. Decorative church candles in posh candlesticks, plain white power-cut candles planted in their own melted wax, and tea-lights in flimsy tin cups. There were a lot of flowers in front of the mural. Bunches of garage flowers still in their wrapping and single red roses poking out of wine bottles and beer cans. A star-shaped balloon anchored to the buckle of a gold high-heeled shoe swayed in the breeze. When the wind picked up, the balloon bashed against David Bowie's face.

After Zoe explained why somebody had left a Mars bar on the pavement, Nathan quickly worked out the reason for the box of Heroes chocolates next to it. Neither of them knew the significance of the three plastic bottles of milk.

A man played 'Five Years' on an acoustic guitar. Another man joined in on a school recorder and a group of girls sang, following the words on their phones. Zoe squeezed Nathan's hand, pumping it in time with the music. There were so many people with the same lightning bolts on their faces now that Nathan couldn't believe he'd ever tried to hide his. Zoe borrowed a lighter from a Japanese girl. She took a tea-light out of her pocket and lit it. Shielding the flame with her hand, Zoe placed the stubby candle on the ground. She took another candle out of her pocket.

"One from Mum," she said. Or it might have been one *for* Mum. She lit the candle and put it on the ground. When she stood up Zoe closed her eyes and Nathan thought she was praying or making a wish. She took a red felt pen out of the pocket of her green army jacket and she wrote on the wall next to the mural:

WE MISS YOU SO MUCH DAVID
NATHAN AND ZOE (THE GIRL WITH THE MOUSY HAIR) X

They stayed at the mural for almost an hour. When Nathan admitted he was shivering because he was cold, they walked home, letting buses pass them by. They sang David Bowie songs – 'Starman', 'Let's Dance' and Nathan's favourite, 'Kooks' – remembering the family sing-alongs on long journeys in their bright red car, with the noisy engine in the boot and their luggage under the bonnet at the front. People overtaking in their boring square and rectangle, round-the-right-way cars, looked at them as though they were a family from outer space. 'Kooks' was Nathan's favourite David Bowie song to sing in the car. Whenever it got to the bit about David Bowie throwing his son's homework on the fire, Nathan and Zoe would sing the line really loud. Zoe once asked their dad, if her homework ever got her down would he throw it on the fire and take the car down town. He said they didn't have a fire, but he promised to leave her homework by the radiator and turn up the central heating and see what happened.

They walked home from the mural, their journey captured on CCTV cameras outside chicken shops and banks. The camera on the wall of the library filmed them when they stopped to look at a huge picture of David Bowie, projected onto a bare brick wall that had the word *BOVRIL* painted on it. It was the first time Nathan had even noticed the wall was there, as though it had been built especially to project David Bowie's face onto. Zoe told him the wall had been there forever and that Bovril was a bit like Marmite.

They carried on walking, filmed by the security cameras outside Halfords, PC World and Sainsbury's. They passed the big pub on the corner and the wooden fence surrounding it, where soon their dad would stick a long row of posters, making it look like *HAVE YOU SEEN THIS GIRL?* was one of the bands playing at the pub. The remainder of their journey was filmed by CCTV cameras mounted to the walls of council estate blocks and the gated private community new-builds and by the cameras inside the Tesco garage, where they stopped to buy crisps and Cokes. The girl who served them complimented Nathan on his face paint. The police said the quality of the images from the garage's security cameras were of a high enough quality to say that when Zoe paid for the drinks and crisps, she looked happy.

2

When they got home, Zoe changed into her favourite black onesie – with the white star pattern on the hood and body. Nathan put on his *Mission to Mars* astronaut costume.

"It's Guantanamo Boy," Zoe said when he came into the living room in the bright orange boiler suit. Nathan asked who that was, and Zoe opened a Wikipedia page on her phone and gave it to him. She found a music video channel on the television and they listened to back-to-back David Bowie songs while they ate the crisps and drank their Cokes. Nathan said he was still hungry, and Zoe made toast, with Marmite because of the Bovril wall.

They took the toast into the living room and sat next to each other on the carpet with their backs against the sofa. Nathan pulled his knees up to his chest, copying his sister, and they watched *E.T.* on a movie channel. They'd missed the beginning, but Nathan knew the story off by heart. It was one of the films that came with an old home movie projector their dad had won in a card game when Nathan was seven and Zoe was eleven. Their dad would show the films in the living room, projecting the washed-out images onto the wall. He removed pictures, pulled out nails and filled in holes but he could never get the wall smooth enough or the room dark enough. In the years since, if Nathan ever saw *Close Encounters of the Third Kind*, *Raiders of the Lost Ark* or *E.T.* on television, he always expected there to be a break halfway through, when he'd help his dad change the reels of tape while Zoe and their mum made popcorn in a wok. He could see the ghost of the living room wallpaper pattern and the holes his dad had filled in when he watched the films on television, even though they weren't there.

"*Zo-ee,*" Nathan said. "Were your aliens like E.T.?"

Zoe gave him a sideways look. "*My* aliens?"

"The ones who took you."

Zoe looked at the television. E.T. was building a communication device out of old toys.

"You do know this isn't a documentary, right?" she said. "And they didn't ride BMX bikes or celebrate Halloween, if that's what you mean. And I'm sure I've told you this before, they weren't the aliens."

"What do you mean?"

Zoe sighed. She'd been answering Nathan's questions for ten months now. On and off, but predominantly on. At first she'd refused to answer them at all, and then she was reluctant, begrudging, but eventually her brother's persistence and enthusiasm wore Zoe down and she seemed happy telling Nathan what the spaceship looked like and how fast it went and where she thought it was going to and what it was like there when it arrived. Now though, after ten months of the same old questions, Zoe actually sounded bored by the whole thing. Nathan couldn't understand that. If aliens abducted him, he'd never tire of telling people about it. Sometimes he thought his sister didn't realise how lucky she was.

"You know like if you go to a foreign country," Zoe said. "It's you who's the foreigner? Well up there, *I* was the alien."

She pointed at the ceiling.

"So, are you still an alien then?" Nathan looked at her pointing finger, expecting it to glow.

Zoe shook her head.

"Why not?"

"Because I'm home now."

Nathan tried to hide his disappointment.

"Have they contacted you since you've been back?"

"Only in my dreams."

"What do you mean?"

"That's when they make contact. When you dream about them."

"I dream about aliens all the time."

"I don't mean dreaming about a film you've just watched. And you need to believe, of course."

"In what?"

"Their existence, for a start."

"The aliens?"

Zoe nodded.

"I do believe in their existence," Nathan said.

"I mean truly, properly believe."

"I do truly, properly believe."

"And you have to want them to contact you."

"I *do* want them to contact me."

"In that case," Zoe said. "They probably already have. You just haven't realised it. When they come for you, they'll wake you up."

"Is that what happened to you?"

Zoe nodded.

"Did you want them to take you?"

"I suppose I must have done. Otherwise they wouldn't have woken me up. People call it an abduction, but it's more of a two-way street."

"What does that mean?"

"They wouldn't take you if you didn't want to go. It's not a kidnapping."

"I want to go," Nathan said, looking at Zoe as though she might be able to fix that for him somehow.

"Hmmm," Zoe said, like she was considering it. She picked the blue varnish off her fingernails. Nathan hated the sound it made.

"Do you want them to take you again?" Nathan asked.

Zoe shrugged, as though it didn't make any difference to her one way or the other.

"What if they didn't bring you back this time though?"

Zoe shrugged again.

"What about school? You'd miss school."

"I hate school."

Nathan nodded. "So do I."

"No you don't. You love it."

"Well, what about your friends at school then?"

"What about them?"

"Wouldn't you miss them?"

"I doubt they'd miss me. Most of them are dicks anyway."

"Girls can't be dicks."

Zoe assured him they could.

"What about me and Dad then?" Nathan said. "*We'd* miss you."

"And I'd miss you too," Zoe said, messing his hair up like he was a puppy. He pushed her hand away.

Zoe got up and went over to the window. Nathan tipped his head back to look at her. She opened a gap between the curtains and looked out. Sometimes Zoe would sit at the window with her eyes fixed on the same spot in the sky for such a long time that Nathan thought she was asleep or in a trance. Now he wondered if she was homesick.

"If you go again," he said. "Me and dad could go with you."

"Maybe you could but definitely not Dad."

"Why not?"

Zoe closed the curtains and turned to face him.

"You really have to believe first, remember."

"I do believe."

"I know *you* do. But Dad doesn't."

Nathan muted the television. He got up from the carpet and knelt on the sofa. He put his arms on the back and rested his chin on his hands. He watched Zoe take a blue inhaler out of the pocket of her jacket. She shook the inhaler and took two long puffs. Nathan wondered if she wasn't fully human again after all and still needed some sort of artificial breathing apparatus to keep her alive. He waited for her to breathe out and then asked if he could have a go on the inhaler. She said no. He decided that's exactly what an alien would have said.

3

When Zoe was abducted by aliens, she was back in bed before anyone had the chance to notice she was gone. It was easy for her dad to believe she hadn't been anywhere at all and had woken up screaming in the middle of the night because she'd had a bad dream. When he noticed his fourteen-year old daughter had wet the bed and there were scratches and bruises on her arms and legs, he upgraded her bad dream to a nightmare.

In the days and weeks that followed, Zoe's dad found earthly explanations for everything. Her sensitivity to light he blamed on headaches caused by her reading in bed too late at night, and when the headaches worsened, he Googled 'migraine cures' and took her to the doctors. They gave her stronger pills. Zoe couldn't seem to remember what day or year it was anymore, or if it was summer or winter. Her dad said he could be forgetful himself. He called it an early onset senior moment. It was supposed to be a joke, but Zoe didn't laugh, and Nathan didn't get it.

When Zoe had been back for nearly a month and she forgot how to tell the time, her dad blamed her iPhone. The tapping, humming and scraping noises that no one else could hear were the fault of the loud music Zoe listened to and because of the earphones she constantly wore, even when there was no music playing. When Zoe started sleepwalking, her dad fixed a gate to the top of the stairs as though she was a toddler or a dog.

Zoe's dad refused to believe that toast popped up when it was still bread if Zoe was in the kitchen, or that the television switched itself off or changed channel when she walked into the living room. He said it was just a coincidence that light bulbs didn't seem to last as long anymore, and mobile phones lost their signal if Zoe was nearby. He said she was making everything up, and probably for her brother's entertainment. Nathan thought his sister was a superhero.

He watched her take another puff from her inhaler.

"Do you want to play a game?" Zoe said.

"What game?"

"A question and answer game."

She took a thick block of Post-it notes from the top of their dad's desk. The block was made up of three different coloured layers. The top and bottom layers were each an inch thick and both pink. The layer of notes in the middle was white and half as thick. Zoe peeled off the top pink layer and half of the white Post-it notes. She replaced the top pink layer and returned the now much thinner block back to the desk. It reminded Nathan of the time he'd caught her topping up a bottle of their dad's best wine with tap water when she was thirteen.

Zoe took the red Sharpie she'd used to write a message for David Bowie out of her jacket pocket and came over to the sofa.

"Budge up," she said.

Nathan shuffled along the sofa on his knees. Zoe wrote something on the top Post-it note and peeled it off. She reached her hand out and lifted Nathan's fringe. He pulled his head away.

"What are you doing?" Nathan said.

"Trust me."

Nathan sat round the right way on the sofa and let Zoe stick the Post-it note to his forehead. Her hand on his head reminded him of when their mum used to check his temperature when he was trying to get out of going to school. He went to remove the Post-it note to see what it said.

"Leave it," Zoe said.

She gave him the pad of Post-it notes and the red pen and told him to write a name down.

"What name?"

"Someone famous. And don't let me see."

Nathan looked at the small square blank page like it was homework.

"Anyone?" he said.

Zoe nodded. "Not one of your mates from school though. Somebody I would have seen on telly or at the cinema. And no footballers. Unless it's David Beckham or Wayne Rooney." Nathan went to write something down. Zoe arched her eyebrows. "*Not* David Beckham or Wayne Rooney."

Nathan sat back on the sofa. All he could think about was his sister in a spaceship and what the aliens looked like. Since Zoe had been back on Earth, that had been Nathan's most frequently asked question – what did they look like? He'd even made an Alien Guess Who? game to try and find out. Nathan had cut pictures of aliens out of comics, TV listings magazines and from the toy section of the Argos catalogue. He'd spread them out on his bedroom floor and asked Zoe if the aliens – *her* aliens – were green, and did they have eyes or beards, tentacles, antennae and so on, turning pictures over every time Zoe said no. When every single picture was turned over, Zoe had shrugged and said, "I suppose aliens don't look anything like aliens."

Zoe gestured at the still blank Post-it note in front of her brother. "Take your time," she said sarcastically.

"I'm *thinking,*" Nathan said. "Can he be from a film?"

"So, it's a he, is it?"

"Might not be."

"Yes, then," Zoe said. "He, *or she*, can be from a film, and stop chewing my pen."

Nathan thought again. Zoe picked at her blue nail varnish. He tried to block out the horrible sound.

"I've got one," he said. He turned his whole body away from Zoe while he was writing it down.

Zoe gathered her hair in her hand and tied it in a ponytail with a black scrunchy and Nathan stuck the Post-it note to her forehead.

"Don't look," he said.

"I can't see through my skin," Zoe said, and Nathan wondered if she really could. He put the lid back on the pen and gave it to her. She wiped his drool off on the arm of the sofa.

"What do we do now?" Nathan said.

"We ask each other questions about the name of the person written on our heads. But the answers can only be yes, or no. Shall I start?"

"It's like Alien Guess Who?"

"What's that?"

"You remember."

Zoe shook her head.

"Shall I go and find it?" he started getting up.

"Can't you concentrate on one thing for five minutes? Sit," Zoe said. "And stay," like he was that puppy again. "Right. Am I male?"

Nathan had forgotten what he'd written. He leaned closer to look at the piece of paper he'd stuck to his sister's forehead. "Yes."

"Your turn," Zoe said.

"Am I male?"

"It doesn't have to be the same question."

"Am I female?"

Zoe rolled her eyes. "You've already had your question. My answer to your first question is, yes, you are male. My turn now. Am I alive?"

"Yes."

"Am I in acting?" Nathan asked.

"Hmm," Zoe said. "Sort of."

"You said we could only say yes or no."

"Okay. No. You aren't in acting. Am I American?"

"No," Nathan said. "Am I black?"

"No. Am I a singer?"

"No. Am I a man or a boy?"

"Is that one or two questions?"

"Am I a boy then?"

"Yes. Do I play a sport?"

"No. Am I Elliott?"

"*Whoa,*" Zoe said. "Yes, you are."

Nathan peeled off the Post-it note. From the way he smiled, Zoe immediately knew what was written on the piece of paper stuck to her forehead.

"Am I E.T.?" she said.

Zoe folded the two Post-it notes in half and poked them through the slot of a fat pink piggy bank on the mantelpiece. In its time the piggy bank had been everything from a swear box to a phone money honesty box and their dad's 'tattoo fund'. Most recently the piggy bank had been raided to buy ice creams from the ice cream man. Now it was a bin for used Post-it notes. They both wrote more names and stuck them to each other's heads. Nathan asked the first question.

"Am I a famous singer?"

"Yes."

"Am I David Bowie?"

The speed in which they guessed each other's identities was like a magic trick. Some names were easier to guess than others. David Bowie was easy, of course, and Zoe got George Best because Nathan kept looking over at the picture of the footballer hanging on the wall. Zoe had allowed it, even though she'd said no footballers. After six or seven games the magic started to lose its power and more and more questions were required, clues had to be given to make the games end and twice Zoe gave up. The final game was as slow as *Monopoly* and ended with both of them giving up, even though Nathan suspected he was Taylor Swift but didn't want to have to ask, "Am I Taylor Swift?" And also because Zoe was never going to get Hugh Jackman as long as Nathan thought his name was Hugh Jackson.

Zoe put all the used Post-it notes in the piggy bank and

Nathan went upstairs to the toilet. He left the bathroom door open and aimed his wee at the sides of the toilet bowl and he didn't flush, in case the aliens used the noise of the rushing water to mask the sound of their spacecraft landing. Ten months after Zoe's abduction and Nathan still couldn't leave his sister on her own without thinking she wouldn't be there when he got back.

4

Nathan looked at his lightning bolt make-up in the bathroom mirror. There was a square patch of red missing, where the Post-it note had been, but it still looked cool. Nathan came out of the bathroom and walked along the landing to his bedroom. He pulled a large drawer out from under his bed. His dad had fixed the heavy drawer to castors so that Nathan could easily get to it and keep his room tidy. Once the drawer was full and pushed under his bed though, it rarely came out again.

Nathan looked through some of the toys and games in the drawer. Things he'd broken, grown out of or lost interest in, and yet he would never allow his mum or dad to give anything to the charity shop or sell them on eBay. He took the dried-up slime and hard Play-Doh out of the drawer and put them on the floor. He pulled out plastic dinosaurs, trading cards and Panini stickers, the Power Rangers ninja star blaster that was snapped in half, Spider-Man with one arm missing and three Action Man dolls.

Both the WWE figures in the drawer would never wrestle again. Stone Cold Steve Austin was headless and Dolph Ziggler's leg had been melted with a lighter by Nathan's friend Arthur. There were four board games at the bottom of the drawer – Battleships and Bingo, Snakes and Ladders, and a maths game he'd really hated – but he couldn't find Alien Guess Who? He did find his Space Torch though, and the notebook his dad had bought him from the National Space Centre. The cover of the notebook was red and made of plastic. Nathan had crossed out the words 'National' and 'Centre' with a black marker pen and added Zoe's name, so it said:

ZOE LOVE. Space Cadet.

Nathan squeezed the notebook into the one pocket of his Mission to Mars spacesuit that was real and tested the Space Torch. The batteries were flat. He threw everything except the torch and the notebook back into the drawer and pushed it underneath the bed. He went back downstairs, taking the steps two at a time. Halfway down, he could see into the living room. When Zoe wasn't there he panicked. He took the last three stairs in one big jump.

Zoe was on the other side of the living room. She'd switched the television off and was trying to close the door of their dad's overstuffed desk. She had a large roll of Sellotape hooked over her wrist and a thin wad of copier paper held between her teeth.

"What are you doing?" Nathan said.

Zoe said something that with the paper in her mouth Nathan couldn't understand. She pushed the sofa back, exposing a crime scene on the carpet beneath. Nathan picked up a tiny plastic ray gun, Spider-Man's missing arm and the head of a Bratz doll. He stuffed the ray gun and Spider-Man's arm in the same pocket as the red notebook. He pretended to bowl a cricket ball with the doll's head. It was hard to imagine Zoe had ever played with dolls. It was easier, in fact, to picture her decapitating the doll than it was to picture her playing with it.

"What are you doing?" Nathan asked again.

Zoe took the paper out of her mouth. "Making contact."

She laid four sheets of copier paper on the carpet to form one larger rectangle, and with the roll of tape still around her wrist she peeled off long strips and taped the paper together. She tipped her arm up and let the roll of tape slide down into her open hand. She put it on the sofa behind her. With the red Sharpie Zoe wrote the letter 'A' and continued writing the alphabet in an arched line across the centre of the paper. When she ran out of space, she started a second curved row of letters underneath.

"What is it?" Nathan said.

"The alphabet."

"*Duh,* I know that. What's it for?"

"I'm making a Ouija board."

"What's a Luigi board?"

Zoe laughed. "It's a device for speaking to the dead."

She was now writing numbers in a straight line under the letters, from zero to nine. Nathan sat on the carpet next to Zoe.

"Do you mean Mum?" he said. The only other dead person he could think of was their gran, their mum's mum, who he hadn't liked talking to when she was alive. She was always in a bad mood and he always felt like he was in trouble with her for no reason, until she forgot who everyone was, which was worse because she didn't even give him money from her purse anymore.

"This Luigi board isn't for speaking to the dead," Zoe said. "It's for speaking to life."

"What life?"

"Other life. On other planets."

"Mars?"

"Maybe."

"Cool."

Zoe wrote a large YES at the top of the paper and a NO at the bottom.

"Is it like the Post-it game?" Nathan said. "How does it work?"

"I don't know if it does yet," Zoe said. "It's a beta Luigi board."

"What's that?"

"It hasn't been tested yet."

"Is it like E.T.'s communicator?"

"If you like. It is a sort of intergalactic communication device."

Nathan said, "Cool. You can ask them to abduct you again and I can come with you this time. Can I come with you this time?"

Zoe didn't answer, which as far as Nathan was concerned was the same as a yes. She asked him if he had any glue. He thought there was some in the kitchen. He bowled another pretend cricket ball with the Bratz doll's head and went to get it. Zoe called out for him to bring a glass in too. When he came back, she was drawing the last of five stars around the edges of the Luigi board. Nathan gave her the Pritt stick and the glass tumbler. She breathed on the glass and polished it on her sleeve, then put it on the carpet next to the Luigi board. She popped the lid off the Pritt stick with her teeth and dabbed glue onto each of the five stars. She replaced the lid and gave the glue to Nathan.

"Pass me my jacket," she said.

Nathan went and got her jacket. She took two tubes of glitter out of the pocket. She gave Nathan the gold one and removed the lid from the silver tube.

"It was supposed to be for David," Zoe said. She sprinkled silver glitter onto each of the five Luigi board stars and replaced the lid. "I meant to make him a birthday card to leave at the mural." She put the lid back on the tube of silver glitter and gave it to Nathan. He handed her the gold tube. He pretended he was the nurse and Zoe was the surgeon. She sprinkled gold glitter on top of the silver.

"Stardust," she said.

"Ziggy Stardust," Nathan said, and Zoe congratulated him on his 'very clever joke'.

When there was a messy pile of mixed silver and gold glitter covering all the stars Zoe asked Nathan to hold one of the now empty tubes steady. She picked up the Luigi board, folded the corner into a spout and carefully poured glitter back into the tube. She put the Luigi board back down on the carpet. Nathan looked at it.

"*Sick*," he said, as though his sister had just invented the PlayStation.

Zoe put the two tubes of leftover glitter and the red Sharpie back in her pocket and threw the jacket onto the sofa behind her.

"Your hands are covered in stardust," Nathan said.

Zoe held her fingers up to the light. The glitter twinkled.

"Yours are too," she said.

Nathan moved his hands around, twisting and turning them.

"There's nothing," he said.

"Have some of mine," Zoe brushed her fingers across the back of his hand until it twinkled too. "Did you know our whole bodies are made of stars? Or nearly all of them."

"Why?"

"Why? Or how?"

"Both."

"Because we're made up of molecules and atoms. The atoms come from distant galaxies billions of years ago."

"How many billions?"

"I don't know. More than four."

"Five?"

"I don't have the exact figures to hand right now. You'll have to get back to me on that," she put her fingers to her ear. "Next caller please."

"You're weird," Nathan said.

"So I've been told. We're made of stars because all organic matter that contains carbon is made from stars."

"How?"

"The Universe was originally just hydrogen and helium. Carbon was made afterwards. That took billions – I don't know how many billions before you ask – of years. When the stars run out of hydrogen they die."

"How?"

"They explode. The explosion's called a nova. Massive stars exploding are supernovas. They're brighter than the sun. Billions of times brighter. It's always billions with space. The nova or supernova burns bright, and then it eventually fades. It's more complicated than that obviously. But basically, we are all made of stars."

"Am I made of stars?"

"Everyone is. We all come from stars and we'll all go back there eventually too. At least half the things in this room are made of stars as well."

"The telly?"

"Parts of it, definitely."

"The carpet?"

Zoe rubbed her hand on the carpet. "I expect so."

"Is the Luigi board made from stars?"

"The paper is."

"Are the stars on it made from stars?"

"I don't know," Zoe said. She picked up the glass and placed it upside down at the centre of the Luigi board, underneath the letters and numbers.

"Is that why you want to go back there?" Nathan said. "Because it's where you came from? From the stars?"

"I don't remember saying I wanted to go back," Zoe said. "Okay. Shut up now. Put your fingers here, opposite mine." Zoe put two fingers on the base of the glass.

"Is the glass made from stars?" Nathan said.

"Yep. And from sand."

"Shut up, is it? Are my fingers made out of stars then?"

"All of you is. All of us."

"Is Dad made from stars?"

Zoe nodded.

"Is Hitler?"

"From Dad to Hitler?" Zoe said. "How does your brain work, Nathan? Now stop asking stupid questions and put your fingers on the glass."

Nathan put his index and middle fingers on the base of the upturned glass opposite Zoe's. He asked her if she thought their mum had gone back to the stars.

"She *was* cremated," Zoe took her fingers off the glass to mime smoke rising. "So, yes."

"Do you remember when we sprinkled her ashes in the sea?" Nathan said.

Zoe smiled. "She wouldn't go, would she?"

"Dad said, 'She doesn't want to go to France?' "

"She did *not want to go* to France," Zoe said. "Right. Stop changing the subject. Are you ready?"

"What do we do?"

"We ask questions."

"Yes and no questions?"

"They don't have to be. If anyone's listening, the glass will move and spell out their answer."

"Other lifes?"

Zoe nodded.

"Aliens?"

Zoe said sshh. She closed her eyes and took a deep breath and then in a strange voice said, "Is there anyone out there?"

Nathan laughed at her weird voice. Zoe opened one eye and told him to take it seriously. "Move the glass to yes if you can hear me."

Nathan watched the glass.

"Nothing's happening," he said.

"Give it a chance."

Zoe asked three more times if anyone was there and the glass moved slightly, and then it snagged on the paper and toppled over. Zoe opened her eyes.

"Did you move it?" she said. Nathan shook his head.

Zoe picked up the glass and lifted the Luigi board and brushed toast and crisp crumbs from the carpet underneath with her hand.

"We need a smoother surface," she said. "Pass me some of Mum's records."

Nathan went over to the shelf beside the sofa.

"Which ones?" he said.

"It doesn't matter."

Nathan pulled out an album and gave it to Zoe. She looked at the cover.

"Good choice."

"I didn't choose it."

"I was talking to Mum."

Zoe put the T. Rex album on the carpet and asked Nathan

for three more records. He picked them at random and brought them over. Zoe examined the covers, as though she was considering buying them from him. She looked at the front of *Kings of the Wild Frontier* and said she would have to paint an Adam Ant white stripe across Nathan's face later. Nathan said cool. Zoe said he was lucky their parents had good taste in music, or he'd be made up to look like Victoria Beckham or Robbie Williams instead of David Bowie. She put the Adam and the Ants record next to one by Kate Bush and completed the square with the same copy of *Aladdin Sane* she'd used to copy Nathan's lightning bolt make-up from.

Zoe put the Luigi board on top of the square of records and replaced the upturned glass. She moved it around to test the new surface and seemed satisfied. She put her fingertips back on the base of the glass and Nathan did the same. Zoe closed her eyes.

"If you can hear me," Zoe said. "Move the glass to YES."

Nothing.

"Is there anybody there?"

Still nothing.

"There's probably too much interference," Zoe said. "All the crap in the house made from stars. The walls and the ceiling, the roof, the furniture, that picture of George Best. The piggy bank. You and me. The signal can't make it through."

"Let's try again," Nathan said. He put his fingers on the glass. Zoe didn't move and Nathan picked her hand up. She made it go deliberately limp. He straightened her fingers out for her and placed them on the glass. "Ask it," he said.

Zoe sighed. "Is there anyone out there?"

"Do the proper voice," Nathan said.

Zoe rolled her eyes. "If you can hear me, move the glass."

The glass moved.

Zoe stared at Nathan. "Are you doing that?"

Nathan shook his head. "Ask it something else."

"Where are you speaking to us from?" Zoe said, both eyes open and fixed on Nathan.

The glass moved again. Zoe called out the letters as it went to them. "A. S. P. A. C. E. C. R. A. R. F. T. I know it's you, Nathan," she said, "because your spelling is so atrocious."

Zoe took her fingers off the glass. She got up from the floor and sat cross-legged on the sofa. She switched the television on. *Casualty* or *Holby City* was on. After her abduction Zoe couldn't bear to watch anything set in a hospital or with any kind of medical procedure in. She said it was because of something that happened to her on the spaceship. Her dad insisted it was just a delayed reaction to the death of her mother. Zoe changed the channel. She didn't mind the surgery so much now. She just couldn't stand soaps. Zoe got up from the sofa and picked the glass up from the Luigi board. Nathan followed her out to the kitchen.

"Let's try it once more," he said. "I'll do it properly this time."

"Nope. It was just a stupid game anyway."

"It's probably just manmade interference stopping it."

"More like *boy* made interference."

She filled the Luigi glass with tap water and swallowed it in three gulps. She went back to the living room and folded up the Luigi board. She put it inside the sleeve of *Aladdin Sane,* as though that's where it was always kept. She sat on the floor in front of the sofa. Nathan took the National Space Centre notebook out of his trouser pocket and stood between Zoe and the television. He flipped open the red plastic cover of the notebook like a communicator in episodes of the old *Star Trek* his dad forced him to watch.

"Are you calling for back up?" Zoe said.

He looked at the first page. "Zoe Love. Where were you going on the twenty-third of April two thousand

and sixteen?"

Zoe looked at Nathan. "What the hell are you on about?"

"At one thirty-one a.m.," Nathan said. "You left the house and turned left. You returned at two forty a.m.."

"What is that?" Zoe reached out to take the notebook. Nathan held it behind his back.

"You'll tear it up," he said.

"I'm not five. Show me."

Nathan gave her the notebook and she read the cover: **ZOE LOVE. Space Cadet**.

"You do know what that means, right?"

"A person training to go into Space," Nathan said. "It's what Dad said you and Mum were."

Zoe shook her head and tutted. "Hmm," she said, reading the first page of the notebook. "Congratulations on *observed*," she said. "But you've spelled subject wrong." She held the notebook up to him.

23rd April. 1:31. The subjict was observed leaving the house. She turned left.

"I think that was the best night of the Lyrid meteor shower," Zoe said. "I was going to the park to watch it. Get my phone, Nath. It's in my jacket."

"I'm not your servant," Nathan said but he went and got it anyway. He sat on the floor next to Zoe. She turned the notebook pages, nodding to herself. She seemed to be comparing whatever she was looking at on the phone with what Nathan had written in the notebook. Last year, he'd recorded all the times he'd seen his sister sneaking out of the house late at night. He'd never shown the notebook to Zoe. He thought he'd lost it and then he forgot all about it.

"Why didn't you just ask me where I was going?" Zoe said.

Nathan said he didn't know. He did know that watching his sister sneaking out late at night had quickly turned into a game for him. If he'd told her about it, the game would have ended. He'd pretended he was a scientist, observing a human who'd met beings from another planet.

"I thought you were going to meet the aliens," Nathan said.

Zoe laughed and then she looked more serious. "Has Dad seen your little red book?"

Nathan shook his head.

"Best keep it that way, okay?"

Nathan nodded.

"I promised him I wouldn't do it anymore," Zoe said.

"Dad *knows*?"

Nathan hated that a secret he thought he'd shared with his sister for almost a year was actually common family knowledge. He'd always been jealous of Zoe. Because she'd been to outer space and he hadn't. Observing her was his consolation. If Zoe was the astronaut, he could at least be her Mission Control. He started looking forward to being woken up by her leaving the house and imagining where she was going. Even though he could never get back to sleep again, until he heard the chink of the chain being put back across the front door when she returned. He thought it had been their secret. A secret Zoe didn't even know they shared. And now it turned out their dad knew as well. Nathan was annoyed. He wished he'd never shown the notebook to Zoe.

She turned the pages, biting her nails and nodding to herself. She asked Nathan to get her red Sharpie and on the first page, underneath where Nathan had written:

23rd April. 1:31. The subjict was observed leaving the house. She turned left, Zoe added, "To the park. To watch the Lyrid meteor shower".

Zoe went through the rest of the book, adding where she was going and for what reason when Nathan had recorded her leaving the house. Sometimes it would be for a meteor shower or something called the transit of Mercury. Other times Zoe had gone out because of a clear sky or a full Moon.

"Is my sister a werewolf?" Zoe said, holding up the notebook page with Nathan's entry for May 22nd. "This one's the Perseid meteor shower," Zoe read aloud, "On 13 August at one fifteen a.m. the *subjict*...Do you want me to correct these spellings for you as well? The sub*jict* was observed walking away from the house...That was when I spent the night on the roof of the Rotunda."

"*The* Rotunda?" Nathan said. "*Our* Rotunda?"

Zoe nodded. "Do you remember last year when the council put the scaffolding up?"

She told Nathan that when she saw the scaffolding and the two ladders leading up to the roof of the circular community building at the centre of the estate, she couldn't resist. She'd spent most of the night of August 13, inside a sleeping bag staring up at the sky, watching 'the most amazing celestial display'. It was the best Perseid meteor shower for years, Zoe said. "Two hundred meteors an hour smashing into the Earth at thirty-seven miles a second. I couldn't miss that could I, Nath? There hadn't been that many Perseids since Space Camp."

"What's Space Camp?" Nathan said.

"I suppose you might have been too young to remember it. I was eleven, I think. I was just about to start secondary school. Or I'd just started. So, you must have been, what... six?"

Zoe turned her attention back to the notebook. Nathan tried to remember going to something called Space Camp.

"You know the flats where Gran used to live?" Zoe said.

Nathan nodded.

Zoe held the book up to show him. "That's when I went there."

"What for?"

"I wanted to see the supermoon. I used to see that rusty old door when we went to visit Gran. With the sign on it saying, *Roof. Authorised Access Only*. I always wondered what was on the other side of the door. The roof, obviously, but I wanted to see for myself."

"You never went up there," Nathan said.

Zoe nodded. "I know an extra eight floors wouldn't really have made any noticeable difference. And I was still as far away from the Moon as I was when I was on the ground floor, but once I got the idea in my head—"

"What's Space Camp, though?"

Not looking up from the notebook, Zoe said, "You know when we went to Cornwall—"

"Who did?"

"*We* did. You and me, Mum and Dad."

"When?"

"When I was eleven and you must have been six. We stayed in that big tent Dad bought. It had separate rooms—"

"I remember that," Nathan said.

"There you go, then. That was Space Camp."

"I didn't know it was *Space* Camp," Nathan said. "I thought it was just *camp*."

Zoe smiled.

"You did spend most of the time playing football with Dad. So, you might not have noticed. Or climbing trees. Doing your boy's stuff. I seem to recall Dad sneaking off to the nearby pub a lot, while me and Mum were up all night with the other nerds. Staring at the stars through Mum's massive telescope—"

"Our mum had a *telescope*?" Nathan said. He couldn't believe he'd been to something called Space Camp and not known about it or remembered it. And their mum had a telescope! A *massive* telescope.

"Where is it now?" Nathan said.

"The telescope? I think Dad sold it. We didn't use it anymore anyway."

"*I* would have used it," Nathan said.

Zoe told him more about Space Camp. They'd stayed for two nights, near a forest but away from trees. They weren't allowed to use any white light, and everyone had red torches. Their mum had made theirs by covering normal torches with red sweet wrappers. On the last night of Space Camp, Zoe and their mum sat in a circle with everyone – except Nathan apparently! – watching the Perseid meteor shower. Their car broke down on the way home and they had to finish the journey on the back of an RAC truck.

"I remember that!" Nathan said. "We have to go to Space Camp again. I'm going to ask Dad tomorrow."

While Nathan tried to remember Space Camp, Zoe filled in the details for the rest of the night-time destinations her brother had recorded in the notebook. She managed to match most of the times and dates to interesting or important events in the sky. There were seventeen in total. Nathan had first seen Zoe leave the house on April 23rd, a month after she'd returned to Earth, when he now knew she'd been in the park watching the Lyrid meteor shower. The notebook entries stopped on September 16th, when Zoe had gone to the flats over the road to be closer to the penumbral lunar eclipse. After that there was a three-month gap, when Zoe either didn't leave the house or Nathan had slept through it. And then on December 14th at 11:30, he observed her leaving the house and turning right. Even though it was the most recent entry in the notebook, Zoe couldn't remember where she was going or why.

"Must have just been a good sky," she said, closing the notebook.

"Can I have my book back?" Nathan said.

"Only if you promise not to show Dad."

"You said he already knows."

"Not in your Stasi-like detail," Zoe said. "Dad thinks I went out two or three times at the most. And he was *so* not happy about that. He thought I'd be snatched or something."

"You *were* snatched."

Zoe gave him a look. "A different snatched."

"We could go and look at the stars now," Nathan said.

Zoe shook her head. "Uh uh, no way. Dad would literally kill me."

"I won't say anything," Nathan said. "Not about any of the other times you went out either."

Zoe raised her eyebrows. "Are you trying to blackmail me, Nathan Love?"

"No."

"Hmm."

"*Please.*"

"No," Zoe said. "There won't be any stars tonight anyway."

"How can there not be any stars?"

"Because of all the streetlights and the illuminated tall buildings. That's why I used to go to the park—"

"We could go to the park now," Nathan said.

"Absolutely no way. Apart from anything else, it's closed. The gates will be locked." The more detailed Zoe's protests were, the more Nathan thought she was considering his request.

"How did *you* get in the park then?"

Zoe didn't answer. She looked at her fingernails. She used the edge of the notebook to scrape at the blue varnish. She stood up.

"Right," she said. "Ten minutes in the park. We'll look for stars and then come home. Okay?"

Nathan tried not to appear too pleased in case Zoe changed her mind just to annoy him.

"And it's not going in your little book either," Zoe said. "Space cadet indeed."

She tapped Nathan on the head with the notebook. He reached up to grab it and Zoe gently pushed him. He lost his balance and toppled over, with his legs bent and his knees on his chest and his hands hugging his ankles. It was the same position he'd found Zoe in almost a year ago, lying in her bed, covered in cuts and bruises, after being abducted by aliens.

5

When Nathan had been pleading with Zoe to go to the park, it had seemed like such a good idea. Now that it was actually happening and they were in the hall putting their coats on, he was having second thoughts.

"What about the gangs and paedos?"

"It's too cold for gangs of paedos," Zoe said.

"Not gangs of paedos. Gangs *and* paedos."

"It's still too cold. Now stop whining. What would have happened to E.T. if Elliott had such a defeatist attitude?"

"What's a defeatist attitude?"

"I'll tell you in the park."

"What if Dad comes home, though?"

Zoe looked at her wrist. She wasn't wearing a watch.

"Dad's out with Craig, and Craig doesn't like to leave a pub until somebody rings a bell and asks him to. We'll be back home ages before Dad. And how come I'm talking you into what was originally your idea? Do you want to go to the park or not?"

Nathan thought about it. "We should take the Luigi board," he said. "To try it outside."

Zoe sighed. "Go on then. And hurry up."

Nathan ran into the living room. He grabbed the David Bowie album with the Luigi board inside and gave the record to Zoe.

"David's coming too, is he?" she said.

She tucked the album under her arm, switched off the security sensor light and opened the front door. They both pulled their hoods up and walked through the estate. The hood of Nathan's parka was so far over his head that his coat looked empty. They walked quickly, keeping to the centre of the path between houses, so they didn't set off any of their sensor lights. There were no CCTV cameras on the estate. There'd be none in the park.

A metal railing fence separated the estate from the park.

Two of the railings looked like they'd been forced apart by a circus strongman in a leopard skin leotard. Nathan crouched down in front of the gap, one that had more likely been created with a car jack as an escape route for drug dealers. He put his head through the gap.

"What are you doing?" Zoe whispered. "Do you really want to be known on YouTube as *Boy with Head Stuck in Railings*?"

She dragged a tall green wheelie bin over. In the darkness it sounded like thunder. Everything was so much louder in the dark. Zoe held the bin steady and told Nathan to climb up. When he was on top of the bin Zoe said, "Are you going commando?"

"What's that?"

"Are you not wearing any underpants?"

Nathan lifted the back of his parka. There was a hole in his astronaut suit, exposing the flesh of his left buttock.

"I took them off earlier."

"Why did you… Actually, don't tell me. Jump over."

Nathan looked down into the darkness on the other side of the railings. He wished he'd put batteries in his Space Torch and brought it with him.

"What if there's dog shit?" he said.

"It'll break your fall."

"What do you mean *break* my fall?"

"Just jump," Zoe said.

Nathan hesitated. He heard a siren. He thought it was because of them.

Zoe took a puff on her asthma inhaler and exhaled, "*Jump*."

Nathan pretended he was a parachutist in the war. He rolled when he landed and stood up in one expert movement. That was how to go commando. He smelled his hands, spitting on them and rubbing his palms together.

"It's only mud," Zoe said, landing in the park next to him, not even bothering to parachute roll.

She immediately started walking along the path between the estate and the park as though she knew where she was going. Nathan followed her. The only light was behind them on the estate and from a nearly full, but dim, Moon. The sky looked dark brown, the colour of Marmite or Bovril. They walked as far as the ponds. Nathan heard animals or birds that he didn't recognise enough to be sure they were actually animals or birds. The park could be frightening enough in the daytime because of the gangs and the loose dogs and all the paedos who hid in the bushes. But it was twice as scary at night. It sounded like a Tarzan film. Nathan followed Zoe as she doubled-back on herself. She was acting like they were being followed and she was trying to throw who or whatever was following them off their trail. She circled the sand and water play area and walked through some longer grass. It was wet and Nathan wished he'd worn his older trainers but at least it was quieter now they were away from the ponds. Until he realised the silence made the darkness even scarier.

Nathan followed Zoe to the open ground at the centre of the park. It was where the air ambulance had landed last month after a jogger had a heart attack, or when a man was shot, depending on whose story Nathan believed – the newspaper's or his friend Arthur's. There was a large tree lying on its side. It looked completely out of place so far from all the other trees and bushes. It looked like it had fallen from the sky.

"What's she doing all the way up here?" Zoe said. She went over to the tree and stroked the bare, rough bark. "And where are her arms?"

"Trees don't have arms," Nathan said. "And trees aren't *shes*."

He knew ships were female and their mum used to call her VW Beetle 'she' and 'her', and eventually, not long before the council picked the red car up and took it away to be crushed, their mum named the car Sarah after the girl in

Labyrinth. Their mum had cried when the car was crushed. But trees weren't female. They didn't have girls' names. Nathan knew some French words were male and others were female, and he wondered if the tree was French. Trees definitely didn't have arms though. He was sure of that.

"This is my favourite tree," Zoe said. "She belongs down there."

Zoe pointed down the hill to a clump of trees in front of the building where the café was. The café was being renovated. A row of white vans was parked outside and scaffolding was up. If Zoe asked Nathan to climb the scaffolding to be closer to the Moon, he was going to say no.

Zoe walked the whole length of the fallen tree. Her favourite tree apparently, although it was the first Nathan had heard about that. Where it was once thirty feet high, the tree was now thirty feet long. Zoe put her arm around the thick trunk as though she was hugging it.

"There's a hole here," she said. "A hollow. I've never been able to reach it before."

Nathan walked over and Zoe showed him the large hole in the side of the tree. When the tree was upright it might have been home to a family of squirrels or a woodpecker. It was probably full of drugs. She told him to put his hand inside, but he said no.

Zoe stood up.

"How did she get up here?" She could make the most obvious and simple things sound like magic definitely had to be involved. "And why chop her down? Humans are terrible, Nathan." Not men with chainsaws. Not terrorists or murderers. Not even people. 'Humans'. As though Zoe was talking about a completely different species to her. Nathan wondered if perhaps she was. He even *hoped* she was.

"It might have a disease," Nathan said. "Our school tree got chopped down because it had a disease."

Zoe turned to look at him. "You have a *school* tree?"

Nathan nodded, unsure what was so unusual about a school tree.

"I've found her arms," Zoe said. She picked a small branch up from a large pile next to the tree. Nathan thought she might try and reattach it, but she returned the branch to the pile and sat down on the grass.

She put the David Bowie record on the ground next to her and lay down. Nathan looked at his sister and at David Bowie. Even the tree was lying down. Nathan felt exposed being the only one standing up. He sat on the grass first, and then he lay down. As long as he didn't think too hard about insects and worms, the park was actually less scary down low. He copied Zoe and made a pillow out of his clasped hands. He watched a blinking light in the sky.

"If it's the air ambulance, it might land on top of us," he said, trying to work out if the helicopter was moving closer or further away.

"At least we'll get to the hospital quicker," Zoe said.

Nathan laughed, stopping himself because it was so loud in the darkness. He watched the helicopter until it was far enough away that he couldn't even be sure it was moving, let alone in which direction. He could hear music coming from the estate or from a car stopped at the lights on the main road. Then the lights must have changed because the music went away.

"That's Venus over there," Zoe said, pointing to a vague white dot in the brown sky. "And that one is Jupiter, the fifth planet from the Sun and the largest in the Solar System."

"There aren't a lot of stars," Nathan said.

"I told you there wouldn't be. It's because of light pollution."

Nathan sniffed the air. Zoe gently punched him on the arm.

Nathan made a telescope shape with his loose fist and scanned the sky for more stars but all he could see were the lights at the top of cranes and on the tower blocks and skyscrapers in the distance. The tallest building was the Shard. The tip was lit up like a cigarette.

When their mum was in hospital, Nathan had been up high enough and close enough to almost reach out and touch the Shard. It was when their mum had been moved to a private room. Their dad had hated the busy ward she was on and was always asking the doctors if she could be moved to a room on her own. But when it finally happened, Nathan couldn't understand why his dad was so upset. The same thing happened when the doctors removed some of the tubes going in and out of his mum. Nathan's dad really hated the tubes being there, until the doctors started removing them.

Nathan and Zoe had left their parents alone and they'd gone to get some chocolate from the hospital vending machine. Zoe said she wanted to quickly look at something. Nathan followed her along corridors, turning left and right, getting further away from their mum and dad. He wanted to turn back, but he was so lost by then he had no choice but to follow his sister. They went through the revolving doors that led outside and crossed a road where the ambulances were parked and went into a different hospital building. Nathan followed Zoe to another lift. They were the only people in the lift who weren't doctors or nurses and Nathan was sure they'd get into trouble. A man in a white coat asked what floor they wanted, and Zoe said, "Top please," and smiled, as though she was on her way to conduct an important operation.

By the time they got to the top floor they were the only ones in the lift. Nathan followed Zoe to a large window with a view of London she called 'panoramic'. He could see Tower Bridge and the Tower of London and the funnels of a big ship and other smaller boats going up and down the Thames. There were trains below them that looked like models or toys and all around there were people in office blocks and high-rise flats. Rows of houses were laid out along streets, like in a game of Monopoly. And the Shard was right outside the window next to them. But Zoe didn't seem interested in anything the panoramic view had to offer. It didn't matter how high she went, she was always looking up.

Zoe named the clouds for Nathan: cumulus and cirrus, cumulonimbus, stratocumulus, lenticularis, noctilucent, altocumulus, and a cloud called mamma that only occurred when the sun was low. That was the day Zoe told Nathan there was a cloud in outer space called Sagittarius B2 that tasted like raspberries but was also poisonous. She also told him contrails were caused when planes flushed their toilets. Nathan looked at his sister to see if she was smiling, but she seemed quite serious.

"How come they're white then?"

"When you go up high enough your poo and wee change colour."

"No they don't."

"It's basic physics, Nathan. Ask your science teacher."

"I haven't got a science teacher."

"Well then."

"Well then what?"

Zoe turned away from the window and Nathan followed her back to the lift. They passed a toilet on the way and Zoe suggested Nathan should go in to see if they were up high enough for his wee to turn white. He said he didn't need to go to the toilet, which wasn't true, he was bursting, but he didn't want to find out that Zoe was just teasing him. Even before she'd been abducted by aliens, Nathan wanted to believe everything Zoe said.

As they walked through the revolving hospital doors and along corridors back to their mum and dad, Zoe tested Nathan on cloud names.

"No, Nathan," she said. "Columbus is not a cloud."

Their dad was waiting for them outside their mum's

room. His expression was so new to Nathan that it might not even have been his dad at all. His face seemed broken. He frowned and smiled and sighed all at the same time.

"She's gone," he said, and Zoe started crying, while Nathan couldn't help himself asking, "Where?"

Nathan turned his hand telescope into a Spock salute and then a Vulcan death grip. He chopped off the tip of the Shard with his fingers. He looked around the park for other landmarks. He thought he could see the darkened shape of the church spire next to the estate, and in the distance the Crystal Palace Tower that Zoe once made him believe was the Eiffel Tower.

"Did you know, if either of us ever have children," Zoe said, "they might live their whole lives without ever seeing a single star?"

"I'm not having children," Nathan said with certainty.

"You might one day."

"No, I won't," Nathan closed his hand telescope. "Miss Casablanca says that most children have never seen a cow in real life."

"Who the hell is Miss Casablanca?"

"My yoga teacher."

"Your *Yoga teacher*?"

"Yoga helps our posture and stops stress."

"Posture and stress? *You're ten*. And yoga? Seriously, Nathan? And you have a school tree? Where is this school? Hogwarts?"

"No," Nathan said. "Brixton. Which star did you go to?" He didn't want to talk about yoga or Miss Casablanca or even think about school right now.

"You mean which planet," Zoe said.

"What's the difference?"

Zoe told him it was too difficult to explain but basically planets appeared to move and stars didn't.

"And stars twinkle," she said.

Nathan looked at Venus, waiting for it to move or

twinkle.

"Which planet did you go to?" he said.

"You can't see it."

"Because of light pollution?"

"And unimaginable distance."

Nathan tried to imagine distance.

He heard a siren coming from somewhere on the other side of their estate, probably out on the main road. It changed from a woo-woo to a nee-naw and then dropped to a low honk, like someone was trying out the ringtones on a new phone. Nathan recognised it as the siren of a fire engine. He listened until it was loud and nearby, and then quieter, and far enough away, for him to know it wasn't their house that was on fire.

"Was it scary?" Nathan said. "When the aliens took you?"

"Of course it was scary."

"Scary horrible or scary fun? Like a fun fair ride?"

"I don't like fun fair rides."

"Yes, you do. I remember we were on that big wheel when it stopped, and we were right up the top. I was scared but you said you loved it."

"I like being up high," Zoe said. "It's the coming back down to Earth that makes me want to throw up."

Nathan made a pretend vomiting sound.

"Do you remember when we were going to be the first brother and sister on the Moon?" Zoe said.

Nathan said he did and when he asked her if she still wanted to go, Zoe said, "Yes. But let's go to a different planet. An undiscovered one. A planet without a flag stuck in it. We can be the first brother and sister on a planet that hasn't been named yet."

"*We* could name it," Nathan said. "Like we did with the star when Mum died."

"What would you call our planet?" Zoe said.

Nathan only needed a second. "David Bowie."

Zoe laughed and Nathan said *sshh,* which made her laugh even louder. He looked at her, shaking next to him, trying to contain her laughter. She had her eyes closed like David Bowie on the record cover on the grass next to her. Nathan said their names in his head like the start of a nursery rhyme: Nathan, Zoe and David Bowie. If they fell asleep now and dreamed, he was sure the aliens would take all three of them.

"We should go home," Zoe said. She stood up.

Nathan opened his eyes and looked up at her. "What about the Luigi board? We need to make contact."

"I forgot the glass," Zoe said.

Nathan stood. His bum felt wet. He wished he was wearing underpants.

"If the aliens do come tonight though," Nathan said. "How will they know where to find us?"

Zoe looked around her. "We could leave them a sign I suppose."

She took the leftover wad of white Post-it notes out of her jacket pocket and with her red Sharpie she wrote NATHAN on one note and ZOE on another. She stuck them to the side of her favourite tree.

"Give me a hand," she said. She put the Bowie album down and started picking small branches up from the pile next to the tree.

Nathan looked at her and she did her best *just trust me* face. He tried to make his face say *I do trust you.* He put his arms out and Zoe loaded him up with branches. When he couldn't hold any more Zoe took three branches back and placed them on the ground next to where she'd stuck the Post-it notes. She picked up the Bowie record and they started walking back to the estate. They took a more direct route, not walking around the ponds, Zoe stopping every few yards to lay more branches on the ground.

"How will they see them in the dark?" Nathan said.

"We could set them on fire I suppose?"

Zoe put her hand in the pocket of her jacket and Nathan tried to remember if she'd kept the lighter she'd borrowed at the mural. He was relieved when she took out the tube of mixed silver and gold glitter. She removed the lid, ran back towards the tree and sprinkled glitter on all the branches she'd left behind on the ground.

"Remember," Zoe said when they were almost back at the railings. "Don't tell Dad we were here."

She lifted the lid of a small metal bin attached to a pole near the railings and dropped the empty glitter tube inside. When she threw the Luigi board in the bin, Nathan scream-whispered, "That's the dog shit bin."

Zoe closed the lid. She said they could make another Luigi board.

With nothing to climb onto on the park side of the railings they had to risk getting stuck in the drug dealer gap and becoming YouTube stars. Nathan went first. Just in case he did get stuck and Zoe left him behind as a joke, or to film him and put it on YouTube herself. They both made it through the gap easily though. They stood for a moment on the estate side of the railings, looking back into the darkness they'd left behind. Even though Zoe had covered the branches in glitter Nathan couldn't see the nine arrows pointing from Zoe's favourite tree to their house. She reassured him that from space they would 'look like the Aurora Borealis.'

Zoe took her phone out and Nathan thought she was going to look up Aurora Borealis on Wikipedia for him. But instead she held the phone up to the sky and took a picture of Venus.

"It won't come out," she said.

In the morning when Nathan woke up, Jupiter had fallen from his bedroom ceiling and was stuck to his forehead. There was red and blue make-up on his pillow. He went along the landing to the bathroom. His dad was snoring in his bedroom like he always did after a night of heavy drinking. Nathan weed for ages and looked in the mirror at the lightning bolt smeared across his face. There was gold and silver glitter in his hair. He went to show Zoe, but she wasn't in her room. He picked the David Bowie record up from her bed, stood on a chair and put it back inside the open plastic frame on the wall where he'd taken it from the night before. He clicked the frame shut and went downstairs to the kitchen. His red National Space Centre notebook was on the table. He picked it up and put it in the pocket of his pyjama bottoms.

He fed Officer Dibble and poured himself a bowl of cereal and sat on the floor next to the cat listening to the saucer banging against the skirting board, and the snap, crackle and pop from his bowl of Rice Krispies. Otherwise the house was quiet. Just a boy with a smudged David Bowie face and glitter in his hair, a cat eating his breakfast, a man snoring upstairs and the hum of the fridge. Less than twenty-four hours later, there'd be a police helicopter hovering loudly above the house for so long that when it eventually ran out of fuel, Nathan would hear someone on the estate cheer.

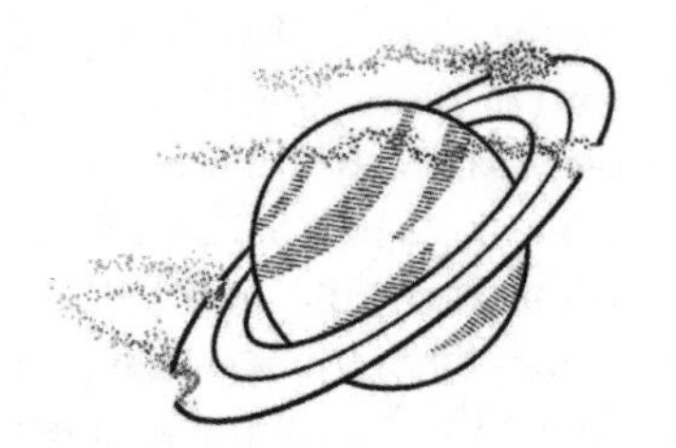

6

Before Nathan's dad called the police, he rang the two numbers he found in Zoe's phone.

"Where are all her friends, Nathan?" he said, while he waited for the second girl to answer. "And why didn't she take her phone with her? That's a good thing though, right?"

Nathan told his dad he didn't know. Both girls said Zoe hadn't been at school that day.

Nathan's dad rang his sister Maureen next and she suggested phoning the hospital. He phoned three, asking if a Zoe Love had been admitted, describing her by age, height and hair colour, just in case she'd been admitted with amnesia or unconscious or in a coma. Every time he presumed that he'd imagined the worst, Nathan's dad thought of something else that made him realise he hadn't even come close. When his dad was on the phone to the third hospital, Nathan said, "Zoe's hair colour's called mousy."

Like his dad, until he'd seen it written on the mural wall, Nathan had thought his sister's hair was light brown or dark blonde. And just like his dad on the phone to the hospital, Nathan wouldn't have been able to say for sure what colour Zoe's eyes were either.

After ringing the hospitals Nathan's dad phoned his friend Craig. Craig arrived almost immediately, his voice booming through the letterbox, like when he was advertising *strawbreees a paarrnd*, a *paarrnd yer strawbreees* on the market stall where he worked with Nathan's dad.

"It's *Craaig!*"

Nathan and his dad went with Craig to the main road at the front of the estate, where his van was parked with the hazards on. There was a card with 'EMERGENCY BUILDING WORK' propped under the windscreen.

"She's going to feel like a right Muppet when she sees all

the fuss she's caused," Craig said.

Nathan sat in the front of the van, between his dad and Craig. There was nothing to attach the frayed looking seatbelt to and he had to hold it across his belly. The van bounced in and out of potholes, jerking Nathan forward every time Craig forced the stubborn gearstick to change. The van smelled of potatoes.

Craig drove into town, following the same route the bus had taken Nathan and Zoe the night before. When they reached the short pedestrian street leading to the mural, Craig mounted the kerb as though it wasn't there. He switched his hazards on and waited while Nathan showed his dad where Zoe had left the candles and where she'd written on the wall. Until his dad saw the message for himself, Nathan could tell he hadn't believed it was there and Nathan had made it up for some unknown reason. They got back in the van and Craig drove them around Brixton for half an hour, Nathan's dad slapping the dashboard like a driving instructor to make Craig stop every time he thought he'd seen Zoe. Nathan had to grip the seat to stop himself from being thrown into the windscreen.

"Did you go anywhere else apart from to the mural?" his dad asked him.

"We went to the garage."

"Nowhere else after that?"

Nathan said no. He'd promised Zoe he wouldn't tell their dad they'd been to the park and he'd convinced himself it wouldn't make any difference if he did. The last time Nathan had seen Zoe was just before they both went to bed. It was over an hour after they'd returned home from the park and so telling his dad about it would only get Zoe – and himself admittedly – in more trouble when she came home. And while they were driving around Brixton in Craig's rusty old van, before the police had been called, before the helicopter and the dogs, before Zoe was even officially missing, Nathan was positive she would come home. Craig drove them back to the estate and Nathan's dad called the police.

"Do I ring 999? Or is it 101? Or is that the NHS helpline?" he said. "And what if she tries to ring while I'm on the phone?"

Craig googled 'Brixton police station' on his phone. He dialled the number and gave the phone to Nathan's dad. The police were there within half an hour. The older looking female officer introduced both herself and the other younger male officer.

"My name's PC Joanne Torres. And this is PC Joe Kari." Nathan wondered if he was the only one who noticed they were both called Joe.

PC Torres looked at Craig and said, "Hello Craig. Keeping out of mischief, I hope."

Craig smiled, "You know me, officer."

Nathan wondered what mischief the police hoped Craig was keeping out of and if mischief was even a crime. As far as he knew, mischief was the same as high jinks or monkey business, dropping a water bomb on a cat or putting a spoon in the microwave.

Craig turned to Nathan's dad and said, "I better get back to the stall. If you need me. Call. Twenty-four seven." Craig took hold of Nathan's dad's hand as though they were about to arm wrestle.

"I hope to Christ she wouldn't be gone that long," Nathan's dad said and the two men shoulder-bumped each other like rappers.

When Craig was gone, PC Torres asked if they could have a quick look around the house, as though Zoe was a mislaid door key or the remote control. They looked in the same easy-to-find places Nathan used to hide from his sister when they were younger, under tables and beds and behind the curtains. When PC Kari pulled the drawer out from under Nathan's bed, Nathan half expected Zoe to be hiding there amongst all his old toys.

The two police officers opened every single door in the house, including the small square mirrored door on the bathroom medicine cabinet, in case it was a TARDIS or a wormhole to another dimension. Nathan's dad stood and stared at Zoe's open wardrobe, trying to decide based on the clothes that weren't there, what she might be wearing.

"I know her green army jacket is gone," he said at last. "She always wears that."

He asked Nathan if he thought the space between Zoe's blue Converse and the cream pair meant she was wearing her red shoes. Nathan said he didn't know. He'd already told his dad and the police that Zoe was wearing her black and white star onesie when he last saw her. But the onesie was there, lying on Zoe's bed as though she'd been vaporised inside it or beamed up out of it. Seeing Zoe's onesie on the bed was the first time Nathan wondered if aliens had abducted his sister again. His immediate reaction to that possibility was jealousy, that the aliens might have taken Zoe again and not him. PC Kari put the onesie in a plastic bag with Zoe's toothbrush. He took the bag out to the police car and Nathan and his dad went back downstairs with PC Torres to find a photo of Zoe.

"As recent a picture as possible, Mister Love," PC Torres said. "One that shows her face clearly and preferably with her facing the camera, with a background that's not too busy."

She reminded Nathan of his mum when he had to get his photo taken for his passport.

"Face forward, Nathan," his mum had said. "And look at the camera. Keep your eyes open and your mouth closed. Try not to fidget. I realise how difficult those things might be for you. Are you ready? Stop smiling. And don't laugh. Stop making him laugh, Zoe."

"I'm not."

"Look at the camera, Nathan."

"I *am*."

"Try to look neutral."

"What's neutral?"

"Detached. Emotionless. Like your sister."

"*Thanks,* Mum."

"Right. Don't laugh, Nathan. Seriously, don't laugh."

"And don't laugh seriously, Nath."

"*Zoe.*"

"What time's our flight?"

"Shut up, Zoe. Ready, Nathan?"

"We'll have to leave him behind."

"*What? Mum?*"

"Ignore your sister. Maybe we'll leave her behind instead."

"Suits me just fine."

"Ready, Nathan? Are you still facing the front? Stop laughing. I can hear you laughing in there. *Zoe,* for God's sake, stop making your brother laugh."

Zoe said Nathan's passport photo made him look like a terrorist and it would be his fault when they were stopped at French customs. But in the end their mum was too ill to travel and then she died from what Zoe called 'Earth cancer'. A few weeks after her mum's funeral Zoe was abducted by aliens. 2016 had been what their mum would have called 'one thing after another'.

Nathan sat at the living room table while his dad went through the photos on Zoe's phone. He was reading a heavy hardback book he'd borrowed from the library, called *Moonmen*. Zoe had written (*and Women)* on a strip of paper and stuck it to the front cover. Nathan turned the pages slowly, looking at the pictures of astronauts and rockets. Through the living room window, he saw PC Kari walking back from the police car. Nathan thought the policeman was whistling. It seemed funny for a policeman to be whistling.

"Where are all her friends, Nathan?"

Nathan looked up from the library book. His dad

showed him the photo of the plain blue sky on Zoe's phone. He might have dismissed it as his daughter trying out the camera for the first time, if the second, third, fourth, fifth and sixth photos hadn't also been pictures of the sky.

Nathan said he didn't know. His dad resumed his search for a picture of Zoe, finding more and more images of the sky. The sky in the daytime and the sky at night, taken outdoors and through windows, in sunshine and rainfall.

"I think this one's taken from the top deck of a bus," Nathan's dad said. He gave the phone to PC Torres. "There's something scratched on the window. Can you work out what it says?"

PC Torres looked at the photo for a second. "I think it's just graffiti."

"Couldn't you use it to find out which bus it is?" Nathan's dad said.

"There are a lot of buses in London, Mister Love."

PC Kari came back into the room and PC Torres gave him the phone. The policeman studied the photo, pinching and stretching it to zoom in, until he reached the same conclusion as his colleague. It was just graffiti. PC Kari gave the phone back to Nathan's dad.

"Is it unusual for a fifteen-year-old girl to have no selfies on her phone?" Nathan's dad said, and PC Torres said it was as unusual as a fifteen-year-old girl leaving home without her phone.

"Unless she left it behind because she doesn't *want* to be found," PC Kari said.

PC Torres gave the younger officer a stern look.

"It's best not to jump to any conclusions. Maybe she didn't need her phone where she was going. Or she left in a hurry. Perhaps she simply forgot it. Let's concentrate on finding a suitable picture for now, Mister Love."

Nathan's dad went through the rest of the photos, moving quickly from one to the next. His hopes raised slightly when he found a picture of a park bench or a phone box – at least they weren't more photos of the sky. He also found pictures of road signs and drain covers, two bus shelters, and a dustbin with a pretty '21' stencilled on the side. He found four pictures of a tree that Nathan knew was probably Zoe's favourite tree, even though the tree was still standing. But apart from any passengers who might be looking out of the windows of faraway airplanes or from distant high-rise flats or offices, not a single person photo-bombed any of the pictures on Zoe's phone. Some of the photos were too dark to be recognisable as anything at all. 'It's very difficult to photograph stars,' Zoe had told Nathan in the park. 'They're like ghosts.' The final picture was so black it looked like Nathan's dad had accidentally switched the phone off. Nathan knew it was Venus. Zoe was right. It hadn't come out.

7

Nathan's dad went to the kitchen to get his laptop. He said there were definitely photos of Zoe on the laptop. Although, after looking at over two hundred pictures of sky and street furniture, he couldn't have sounded any less certain. When Nathan's dad was out of the room PC Torres asked Nathan if he knew why Zoe had taken so many pictures of the sky.

Nathan looked at PC Torres and at the other officer standing in the doorway of the living room as though he was guarding it. *Don't tell the feds nothing*. That's what Nathan's friend Arthur was always saying. *Snitches get stitches*. Arthur called the police the feds, five-o or the po-po. His brother was in prison for shanking someone and Arthur hated the police. But it wasn't Arthur's sister who was missing.

"She's looking for shapes in the clouds," Nathan said.

PC Torres smiled. "What, like animals do you mean? Sheep or polar bears, or cotton wool? That sort of thing?"

Nathan shook his head. "No. Spaceships. They can fly with the same density as clouds," he was quoting Zoe. "Sometimes you can see them change into solid shapes. You have to look closely though, or you'll miss it happening."

PC Torres nodded, as though it made perfect sense to her.

"I noticed a lot of Zoe's pictures were taken at night, though. I imagine it's impossible to see any spaceships in the clouds in the dark. What would Zoe be taking pictures of when it's dark, Nathan?"

"Stars," Nathan said. "And planets."

PC Torres got up and came over to sit on the chair at the table next to Nathan. He closed the *Moonmen* book. PC Torres looked at the piece of paper stuck to the cover with *(and Women)* written on it.

"Zoe did that," Nathan said, snitching on his sister. "It

comes off, though," he added, in case Zoe got into trouble for vandalising a library book.

"Does your sister go out at night a lot to take pictures of stars?" PC Torres said.

"She used to. She doesn't anymore."

Nathan's dad came back into the living room, carrying his laptop open in front of him like a tray of drinks. PC Torres turned to face him.

"Nathan's been telling me how Zoe likes to go out at night to photograph the stars, Mister Love," she said. "Or that she used to. That's right, isn't it, Nathan? Zoe doesn't go out at night to look at stars anymore?"

Nathan nodded. The back of his neck felt hot.

"She stopped all of that last year," his dad agreed.

PC Torres turned back to Nathan. "Did you know, Nathan, that every time you take a photo on your phone it sorts them into chronological order? Do you know what chronological order is?"

Nathan shook his head.

"It means we can tell what day and time each photo on Zoe's phone was taken. If we look at the last pictures on Zoe's phone will they tell us they were taken last night?"

Nathan looked over at his dad. "Am I in trouble?"

"Why would you be in trouble?" his dad said.

Nathan felt sick.

"It was only ten minutes," he said. "Just to look at the stars."

"She went *out last night*?" his dad said. He almost dropped the laptop.

"We just wanted to look at the stars."

"Wait," his dad said. "You *both* went?"

"Is that the big park behind where we are now, Nathan?" PC Torres said calmly.

Nathan nodded.

"What time would that have been?"

"After we watched *E.T.* and then after we played a

game." Nathan was talking about the Post-it notes name game. The Luigi board wasn't a game. It was an intergalactic communication device.

"Why didn't you just tell us this in the first place?" his dad said.

"I thought I'd get into trouble for climbing over the fence."

His dad threw his hands in the air. He was still holding the laptop. PC Kari ducked. "You *climbed over the fence?*" Nathan's dad said.

"The gates were locked," Nathan said.

"And what did you do in the park, Nathan?" PC Torres said.

"We looked at the stars but there weren't many, so we came home again."

"Did you see anyone else while you were there?"

Nathan shook his head.

"Not on the way to the park? Or on the way back home?"

"No."

"Right, Nathan," PC Torres said. "However unimportant it might seem to you now. Can you think of anything at all unusual? Either in the park or on the way there or back?"

"We couldn't see the planet Zoe went to. Because of light pollution."

Nathan's dad put his hand up like he was at school. PC Torres ignored him.

"When you say, the planet that Zoe went to," PC Torres said. "Which planet is that? Which planet was it that Zoe went to?"

"It hasn't got a name yet."

"And when did Zoe go to this planet?" PC Torres said.

Nathan's dad put his hand up again.

"One minute, Mister Love," PC Torres said.

"Just after my mum died last year," Nathan said.

"And how did your sister get to this planet?"

"The aliens contact you in your dreams."

"Oh, mate," his dad said, shaking his head.

"When they wake you up, that's when they take you."

"Is this really helping?" Nathan's dad said. "My daughter had some bad dreams last year. It was after her mum had just passed away. And... well...I feel ridiculous even having to say this out loud, but, my daughter did *not* go to another planet."

"So where did Zoe go to last year, Mister Love?" PC Torres said.

"Nowhere. She went nowhere. Literally, I mean. She didn't even leave the house."

"Did you report it?"

"*Report it*? Who to? Mulder and Scully?"

PC Kari bowed his head. Nathan thought the policeman was trying not to laugh.

His dad apologised for raising his voice. He asked if they could just concentrate on finding Zoe.

"That's why we're here," PC Torres said. "Perhaps Nathan could show us whereabouts in the park he went with Zoe. Do you think you'd be able to do that, Nathan?"

Nathan pictured the gap in the railings and the dustbin and the long grass leading to the open ground at the centre of the park where Zoe's favourite tree was and the tree branches and the glitter on the branches.

"We left directions," Nathan said.

"Directions?" PC Torres said.

"So that the aliens could find us."

His dad made a sort of growling noise. He said he was going to murder Zoe when she got home. Nathan didn't think it was the best thing to say in front of the police.

8

Nathan led his dad and the two police officers through the estate. PC Kari walked with Nathan and his dad followed behind with PC Torres. PC Kari took his torch out. He showed Nathan the three different settings, switching back and forth between them and naming them.

"Lowlight. Flashing. Spot. Flashing. Lowlight. Spot."

He gave the torch to Nathan, who expected it to be heavier than it was. It didn't weigh any more than his own Space Torch. On the side of the torch it said 'ALPHA ZULU'. Nathan asked what it meant and PC Kari said Alpha was A in the police alphabet and Zulu was Z.

Nathan told the policeman his Space Torch only had two settings but one of them was a picture of a distant galaxy. PC Kari said, "Cool." The word sounded as funny coming from a policeman as whistling. Nathan thought he must be the good cop. PC Torres was definitely the bad one. Nathan's dad had taught him about good cop, bad cop. When his mum was still alive she was usually the good cop, but sometimes she'd swap roles with Nathan's dad, to trick him or Zoe into doing their homework or to get Nathan into the bath. Arthur would have said all cops were bad.

"I got my torch at the National Space Centre," Nathan told PC Kari.

"That's in Leicester, right?" The policeman said his family lived in Leicester, but he'd never been to the National Space Centre himself. "I suppose it's like people who live in London all their life but never go to Buckingham Palace."

"I've been to Buckingham Palace," Nathan said.

"Inside?" PC Kari said. Nathan shook his head. The policeman whispered, "I have."

"What for?"

"I'm afraid I'm not at liberty to disclose that," PC Kari said in a jokey voice. He was definitely the good cop. "So, what sort of things do they have at the National Space Centre? Apart from a gift shop selling cool torches."

Nathan told him about the simulator he'd been on, where they had to save the ice moon Europa. He told him he had to stand on tiptoes to trick the Space Centre staff into thinking he was tall enough to be allowed on the ride. Nathan remembered his dad teasing Zoe, asking her if she was sure she'd be okay to go on the simulator, because of the warnings on the sign at the entrance saying it wasn't suitable for those with inner ear disorders, sensitivity to loud noises and bright lighting effects, or people who suffered from motion sickness. Zoe had complained of all those things after her alien abduction and her dad still didn't believe her. Nathan used to think that there were no adults who believed. He wondered if PC Kari might be different. PC Torres wasn't a believer that was certain. But maybe because he was still quite young, PC Kari would believe. Maybe even truly and properly.

Nathan told PC Kari about some of the exhibits at the National Space Centre. He told him about the Tranquility Base and the Planetarium and the Rocket Tower where the two huge rockets were kept.

"The Blue Streak and the Thor Able." Just saying their names out loud was enough to remind Nathan how dizzy he'd felt looking up at the rockets.

The trip to the National Space Centre was the first time they'd been away from home as a family since their mum had died. Nathan's dad had hired a car and they stayed at a hotel near the motorway. Their dad had booked two rooms, one for himself and one for Nathan and Zoe to share.

"What if she sleepwalks?" Nathan had asked his dad.

"As long as she doesn't sleep run, you'll be okay. I'll be in the room next door anyway. Just bang on the wall and I'll come and sort it out."

"Can't you lock us in?"

"Hotel rooms don't really work that way round, mate. You're thinking of prisons."

Nathan had reminded his dad about the two locks he'd fitted to the outside of Zoe's bedroom. She was convinced somebody, or something was trying to get into her room and her dad reluctantly agreed to fix the two small locks to her door. But he didn't lock either of them. He pretended at first, loudly pulling each bolt across and then quietly unlocking them again when Zoe was in bed.

Nathan showed PC Kari where they'd climbed over the railings into the park and the policeman wheeled the same dustbin over. They all climbed over the railings and Nathan led the way into the park, looking for the first arrow. PC Kari shone his torch on the ground in front of them, sweeping it from side to side. The other police officer hung back with Nathan's dad, who kept calling out Zoe's name as though he was looking for his dog.

"Has your sister always been a keen stargazer?" PC Kari asked Nathan.

"We both have," Nathan said but he knew that was like describing Jamie Oliver and the boy who tipped the chips into the fryer at Chicken Cottage both as chefs. Nathan may have had the library books, the fancy-dress astronaut costume and the stars on his ceiling but for Zoe it had always been different. Looking at stars seemed as ordinary and yet as essential as breathing to Zoe. Nathan found himself boasting to PC Kari about his sister. He told him they had a calendar showing when the International Space Station was due to fly over but Zoe didn't need it because she just knew.

"Zoe knows when lightning's going to strike as well," Nathan said. "And when fog is coming and when it's going to rain. She says she's like a cow lying down in a field. My dad doesn't believe her, of course," Nathan lowered his voice, in case his dad could hear him because of the amplifying powers of darkness. "He thinks she had a bad nightmare or made it up."

"Why would she do that?"

"Dad says for attention."

"Does your sister crave attention?"

"What's crave attention?"

"Does Zoe like being the centre of everything?" PC Kari said. "I've got a sister like that. It must have been difficult for your dad I expect, though. Bringing up two kids after you lost your mum."

Nathan liked the way the policeman spoke to him like he was an adult.

"They don't argue anymore," Nathan said.

The policeman shone his torch in Nathan's face. He apologised and aimed it back down at the ground. Nathan realised he still hadn't seen a single arrow.

"My mum and my sister used to argue all the time," PC Kari said. "I thought mothers and daughters were supposed to be best friends—"

"Zoe and my mum *were* best friends," Nathan said. "I meant my dad and Zoe used to argue."

They were almost at Zoe's favourite tree and Nathan hadn't seen any of the arrows they'd left. He knew everyone was going to think he was lying, especially his dad. He wondered if he could have possibly gone the wrong way or if the tree had been moved again. PC Kari shone his torch on the tree trunk and Nathan looked for the two Post-it notes. He hadn't told the police or his dad about them. If they found the sticky notes, one with his name on and Zoe's name on the other, he'd hardly be able to claim they were nothing to do with him. Nathan had hoped the policeman wouldn't find them, but when Kari shone his torch the length of the tree and even inside the hollow and found nothing Nathan started to panic. *Where were the Post-it notes and the directions*?

Nathan showed the police where he'd laid on the grass with Zoe. PC Kari got down on one knee and put his palm on the ground, like an Indian scout tracking the outlaws in a cowboy film. PC Torres shook her head as though she didn't approve. The two police officers walked about aimlessly for a bit, shining their torches as far as the beams would reach, until it looked like they weren't searching for Zoe anymore but were instead having a competition to see whose beam would reach the furthest. Nathan thought he saw PC Kari's torchlight hit one of the white vans parked in front of the café at least two hundred feet away. Arthur said he had a laser pen that was powerful enough to blind an airline pilot. Nathan didn't know why anyone would want to do that.

"There's a helicopter on its way," PC Torres announced, and they went back to the house.

On the way back Nathan looked again for arrows. It hadn't been windy enough for the branches to have simply blown away, and if somebody had swept them up, wouldn't they have also swept up the Red Bull can and the KFC box? All the rubbish Nathan remembered seeing the night before was still there. The squashed cigarette packet and the baby's sock, and a small pile of silver laughing gas canisters that last night Nathan had thought were bullets. It was only the directions they'd left for the aliens and the Post-it notes that were gone. If Nathan hadn't seen what looked like snail slime, caught for a second in the beam of PC Kari's torchlight, he might have wondered if he could have imagined or dreamed the arrows. When he looked again for the snail slime, which he knew was actually glitter, just like the branches, the Post-it notes and his sister, it was gone.

By the time they were back at the railings Nathan knew exactly what had happened. The aliens must have landed in the park. They found the first arrow and picked it up, following its trail to the next arrow and then the next, picking them up one by one like Hansel and Gretel picking up breadcrumbs, until they found the house, and found

Zoe. Nathan would have been pleased that he'd worked it all out if he hadn't also felt so envious. *Why her again? Why not me?*

Back at the house his dad looked for a photo of Zoe on his laptop. When he found the first one, he said, "Thank God," as though Zoe had just walked through the door.

"She hates having her picture taken," he said, rejecting the first photo because Zoe had her hand over her face. In a lot of the pictures on the laptop, Zoe either hid her face or had her back to the camera. Her dad skipped past those and dismissed any photos where she looked grumpy or she was doing her sarcastic '*cheese*' smile. "I don't want her to look like she'd be happier if she didn't come home."

In the photo he eventually chose and gave to the police, Zoe wasn't looking directly at the camera. Her eyes were half-closed, and her mouth was open, showing her braces. The photo wasn't all that recent and the background was far too busy. It wasn't really in focus. It would never have been allowed on a passport. Zoe would have hated it. But Nathan's dad said it was the best one available. He told the police he wanted a photo that people would look at and think, if she was their daughter, they'd want her back. He emailed the picture across the living room to PC Kari, who now had more photos of Zoe on his phone than she had on hers.

When the police were gone, Nathan prepared himself for a massive telling off. He wondered what his dad would be most angry about. Would it be him going to the park with Zoe or that they'd climbed over the fence? Or would he be most angry that Nathan hadn't told him about it all sooner? Nathan thought his dad would be especially annoyed with him for apparently making up a story about leaving directions that led to their house. But his dad was surprisingly calm. He didn't shout or swear. After the police left, he put his arm around Nathan's shoulder. He held him for a full minute. When he let him go there was glitter on his dad's hand.

Nathan was about to point it out, when his dad said, "I wish you hadn't told the police all that stuff about aliens. They're not going to search half as hard now."

9

Nathan couldn't imagine how the police could have searched any harder for Zoe than they did. The helicopter arrived and shone a bright stream of light down on the park and the estate, reaching further than any torch ever could. PC Torres and PC Kari came back to the house in the morning and other police came too. They searched the house again, taking a diary from Zoe's room even though it had nothing written in it. The police walked through the estate, knocking on doors and stopping people passing by, speaking to dog walkers and postmen and showing them the picture of Zoe. The police lifted the lids of wheelie bins and they parted bushes. They forced open the jammed door of a fly-tipped cooker in the adventure playground and found nothing.

The police looked under every car in the estate's underground car park, sticking their faces up against the windows, in case Zoe was asleep or hiding on the backseat. They walked around the whole park, crossing it from top to bottom and side to side, staring at the still water of the ponds and disturbing the flowerbeds inside the walled garden. The police checked the community greenhouses and walked through the sand and water play area. They searched the café and the stable block and spoke to the builders doing the renovation work there. The police looked for Zoe in the One O'clock club and all of the public toilets. They walked across the bowling green and tennis courts and searched the cricket nets. Nathan couldn't imagine how they could have searched any harder.

And there were just so many places to hide or to be hidden, so many places to stay and such a lot of ways to leave. There were hundreds of buses and night buses, the Tube and the Overground, black taxis and Ubers, unlicensed mini cabs and Boris bikes for hire. Everything that Nathan's dad said helped to make the area such a desirable place to live, and why the developers and the council were so keen for them to move out, so they could knock the estate down and build posh flats. Nathan's dad called it gentrification.

Nathan asked his dad if he could help the police search. He wanted to go back to the park to look for the arrows and the Post-it notes in daylight. His dad said there was absolutely no way he was leaving the house on his own.

"I'm not losing another one," he said.

In just a few days, the police had been at the house often enough for Nathan to learn some of their language. Zoe was a misper. A fifteen-year-old IC1 female missing person. The helicopter that flew above the estate and annoyed the neighbours was called India 99, and the Alsatian dog that barked at Nathan was a Delta. The two women who'd been at the house the most were called FLOs, which stood for family liaison officers. They dressed in normal clothes, usually black trousers and jumpers and they had their names on badges hanging around their necks, like the boys who worked in JD Sports.

The FLOs would be at the house so often that Nathan would almost forget they were the police. They already knew where the cups and coffee were kept and that the hot and cold taps in the kitchen were fitted the wrong way around. To Nathan, the two women looked and sounded so alike one another, he struggled to remember which FLO was called Janet and who was Anne Marie. Craig said that was why they always sat in the same places on the sofa – to make it easier to identify who was who, like Ant and Dec. Nathan didn't think there was a good FLO and a bad FLO. They were just FLOs.

Nathan learned the rest of the police alphabet. Filling in the spaces between Alpha and Zulu. He was November Alpha Tango Hotel Alpha November and Zoe was Zulu Oscar Echo. Their dad was Delta Alpha Delta, or Sierra Tango Echo Papa Hotel Echo November to everyone who wasn't Nathan or Zoe.

When Zoe had officially been missing for three days, the police filmed a television appeal. On the fourth day it was shown on the local news. There were so many family members and friends and random people from the estate in the living room to watch it on television, it felt more like Nathan's dad was about to be a contestant on *Britain's Got Talent*. Craig brought a box of beer and one of Auntie Maureen's workmates from Greggs brought cakes.

Nathan sat on the living room carpet next to Craig because there was nowhere left to sit. Nathan's gran on his dad's side of the family was knitting on the sofa behind him. He was worried he was going to end up with an ugly yellow jumper because of Zoe. He pictured his sister really laughing about that when she came back. And Nathan still believed she would be coming back.

With all the police in the living room and Maureen and her friends in their Greggs uniforms and even the vicar dropping by briefly, Craig said they were two cowboys and a pirate short of being at a fancy-dress party. The one person most obviously missing – apart from Zoe of course, and Nathan thought how brilliant it would be if she walked through the door when everyone was watching her appeal on television – was Nathan's dad. He'd gone upstairs to the toilet a long time ago and hadn't come back.

The appeal began and Maureen told everyone to be quiet. Nathan had never seen anyone he knew on television before. He never thought his dad would be the first. He was sitting behind what looked like a table for spreading paste onto wallpaper. There were two policemen sitting at the table with his dad. Nathan hadn't seen them before. There was a large picture of a police badge and a website address on the wall behind them and two microphones on the table in front. The enlarged picture of Zoe was on an easel next to the table. Craig whispered to Nathan that it looked like they were auctioning a painting. When the policeman sitting to the left of his dad said, "Her younger brother was the last person to see Zoe alive," Nathan thought it sounded like the policeman was investigating a murder instead of looking for a missing person.

"You know they film these things to look for crocodile tears," Craig whispered.

"What are crocodile tears?"

"Pretend tears. The police want to see if your dad's just pretending to cry."

"Why would he pretend to cry?"

"If he wasn't really sad about Zoe."

"But he is."

"Of course he is. But they have to find out. This is the quickest way."

Nathan looked at his dad on television.

"But he isn't even crying, though."

"I expect they're looking for that as well," Craig said. "Maybe they'd get more phone calls if he'd cried. People expect tears."

The appeal was really short, and Nathan was glad when it ended. Everyone in the room started discussing it. The clickety-clack of knitting needles started again. Craig finished his beer and shook the empty can, a signal for Nathan to get him a fresh one. Nathan took the beer can and went out to the kitchen. He dropped it in the bin and opened the fridge. His dad hadn't been shopping since Zoe had disappeared and the fridge was almost empty. Nathan had heard his dad telling the FLOs how guilty he'd feel, choosing between brands of baked beans or standing in a checkout queue, while his daughter was still missing. Nathan moved the slice of quiche Zoe had bought herself from Brixton Village to the back of the fridge and took out the last can of beer. He closed the fridge door and went back to the living room.

Craig had moved to a space on the sofa. He was looking at his phone and Nathan walked past and went upstairs to look for his dad. He found him in Zoe's bedroom, standing in front of her open wardrobe, staring at the space left by her red Converse. Nathan had seen his dad look at the gap on the bathroom shelf where Zoe's toothbrush should have been in the same sad way.

All the fairy lights in Zoe's bedroom had been switched on. The white ones draped around the headboard of her bed and chair, and the red, blue, yellow and green fairy lights inside long tubes that haloed the dressing table and framed the window.

"Do you remember what Zoe used to say about fairy lights?" his dad said, when Nathan appeared in the doorway. Nathan shook his head. "They're like dogs. Because they're not just for Christmas," he gestured at the can of beer Nathan was holding. "Is that for me?"

"It's for Craig."

"How many left?"

"Just this one."

His dad nodded. "He'll go soon then. How did I look on telly?"

"Craig thought you looked like a football manager who's just lost the Cup Final."

Nathan's dad quarter-smiled. He looked across the room at the window. The curtains were half open. It was raining.

"Does Zoe have an umbrella, Nathan?" he said. "I don't think she even owns a proper winter coat."

10

The police's search for Zoe may have been thorough but it was nothing compared to her dad's. Every day he repeated the same steps as the day before. He rang Zoe's friends, wishing there were just a few more numbers to call, thinking that if his daughter had been more popular, she would have been easier to find. He couldn't allow himself to dwell on that though. He told Nathan they had to stay focused. He rang the hospitals again, trying new accident and emergency departments in different hospitals further away from home. The woman who answered the phone at one hospital recognised his voice from the day before and he didn't need to say Zoe's name or try to describe her. In the short amount of time Zoe had been missing, her dad had already become a regular customer.

They went out in Craig's van again. Craig had a new van. The seatbelt worked and the gears didn't crunch. It already smelled of potatoes though. Craig drove them around Brixton again and also as far as Croydon in one direction and deep into the congestion zone in the opposite direction.

Using the photo that Nathan's dad had given to the police, he had two hundred posters printed. Nathan helped put them up on bus shelters and fences. They stuck posters in shop windows and pinned one up in the library. Nathan's dad had smaller versions of the poster printed and he stood outside the Tube, handing them out. He did the same on the green in front of the cinema and at the David Bowie mural.

Nathan had to show his dad where Zoe had left the two candles again. He waited while his dad read Zoe's message over and over, in case he was missing a clue to where she might be or why she was gone. His dad read the other messages on the wall too. He picked up pieces of paper, turning over postcards and opening tiny greetings cards left with the wilting flowers. To anyone passing by, Nathan's dad must have looked like the world's biggest David Bowie fan.

"Which candles are hers, Nath?"

Nathan shrugged. "I don't know."

"This one?" his dad picked up an empty tea-light holder.

"You shouldn't touch them." Nathan said.

"Which ones do you think they are?" his dad asked again, more urgently this time.

Nathan said he didn't know and saw how frustrated that made his dad, so he pointed to a random tea-light and another next to it. It didn't matter because his dad had already started scooping up handfuls of the candles and stuffing them into the pockets of his jacket.

"Dad," Nathan said. "Stop *it*."

Nathan wanted to run away. People slowed down to watch. He thought someone would call the police. He sort of hoped they would. When his dad had filled his pockets with tea-light holders they walked home in silence, his dad stopping to pick up discarded leaflets, smoothing out the creases in the paper and wiping footprints from Zoe's face.

Nathan had been embarrassed by his dad before, and he'd certainly been scared of him. But until he saw him scrambling about on the dirty pavement, stuffing other people's candles into his pockets, Nathan had never felt ashamed of him. And yet, he would have gladly taken that raging, shameful, manic version of his dad back, in place of the silent man staring blankly into the space between two pairs of shoes in his daughter's wardrobe right now. Nathan needed to comfort his dad somehow. He had to convince him that Zoe was all right.

"Dad."

"Yes, mate."

"I'm not ill, am I?"

"No, mate. You're not ill."

"And am I in any danger?"

"Of course you aren't. Why?"

"Well. You know when E.T. is dying?"

"In the film?"

Nathan nodded. "And so Elliott gets sick too, because E.T. is sick? Because Elliott 'feels his feelings'?"

"I think so, mate. Why?"

"That's how I know Zoe is okay. Because if she was sick or in danger, I would be as well."

For a moment Nathan was worried that instead of comforting and reassuring his dad, he was going to make him cry. His dad stared at him. He was breathing heavily and his lip had started to quiver. And then Nathan realised he wanted his dad to cry. So that he could call Craig and show him exactly how sad his dad was about Zoe.

11

Jupiter had fallen from Nathan's bedroom ceiling and the edge of Saturn's rings was stating to curl away. His dad was already a meteor and like Jupiter he might soon become a meteorite. The home planet was dying, and Nathan had to do something to save it. Once he'd decided where Zoe was, it didn't take him long to work out what that was. It wouldn't even be that difficult. It was after all, something he'd been training for in his dreams for most of his life. Neil Armstrong had needed Saturn V, the tallest, most powerful rocket ever built, to get him into space. He had all of Mission Control and over 400,000 engineers, scientists and technicians. All Nathan had to do was go to sleep.

The police could search every last inch of the Earth, but they would never find Zoe. She wasn't in a wheelie bin or a dumped cooker, she wasn't hiding on the backseat of a car in the underground car park. Zoe hadn't left on a night bus or taken the first Tube of the day out of Brixton. She wasn't in any of the places the police were going to have to add to their search list because of all the phone calls they were expecting following the television appeal. Zoe wasn't in any of the places the police had searched or anywhere they were likely to search in the future. They wouldn't find her under a bed or behind the curtains or in the community compost or the leaf mould box. The India99, the Deltas, the FLOs and the Joes and Nathan's dad, were all looking in the wrong place.

Nathan wished he could just tell his dad that the aliens had taken Zoe again. But he knew he wouldn't believe him, and it would only make him angry. And besides, it was Nathan's fault Zoe was gone. He'd talked her into going to the park and he was the one who made her write their names on Post-it notes and leave directions. Zoe wouldn't have made the Luigi board if Nathan hadn't asked her about making contact. Zoe was missing because of Nathan, and his dad was always telling him how important it was for people to take responsibility for their actions. Nathan knew what he had to do. He would get himself abducted by the same aliens who took Zoe. He would find his sister and bring her back home.

First though, he would try and make contact with her. To do that he needed a Luigi board. The chain was on the front door during the day and his dad had locked all the windows and hidden the little keys. If Nathan could have opened his window, he was probably close enough to be able to see – and even smell – the dog poo bin where Zoe had thrown the original Luigi board, the beta version, which Nathan had remembered as the *better* version. But his dad wouldn't let Nathan out in the back garden, let alone to the park. Twelve Apollo astronauts had been to the Moon and back and Nathan couldn't get to a dog poo bin less than a minute's walk from his house. He considered texting Arthur to ask him to go and get the Luigi board. He could picture his reaction. *Get something out of a dog shit bin? No way, man.* And even though Nathan would have loved to share his rescue plan with Arthur, he knew his friend was less capable of keeping a secret than he was himself. Nathan decided, for his mission to be successful, it also needed to be secret.

Nathan looked around his room for some paper to make a new Luigi board with. He could have taken some more from his dad's desk, but the risk of discovery was too great, and although Nathan was happy to keep a secret from his dad, he didn't want to tell him any more lies. There were four blank pages in *Moonmen (and Women),* two at the front and two at the back. He justified what he was about to do by telling himself because the pages were blank, they wouldn't be missed. Once, after a huge row with Zoe, she'd torn the last page out of the book Nathan was reading. He hadn't found out until he reached the ending of the story. Remembering how angry it had made him, he thought maybe he should cancel his mission and leave it to the police to find his sister.

Nathan looked at the blank pages and considered the best way to remove them without the library noticing or his dad hearing. He could tear the pages out slowly or pull them really quickly. Like removing a plaster his mum's way or his dad's. Nathan didn't like either method. He left his plasters on long after his wounds had healed, until they started to gradually peel away on their own. And then he'd soak the plasters in the bath until they dropped off.

Nathan couldn't soak the library book in the bath though, and he didn't have time to wait for the pages to fall out. He leaned his arm on the book like a ruler and slowly tore out the front blank page. He did the same with the second. The two pages at the back he pulled sharply, sneaking up on them and surprising them. He thought of Zoe trying to scare hiccups out of him. He coughed to cover the sound of the paper tearing.

He knew it was wrong to vandalise library books but even though it would be overdue soon he doubted his dad would return the book yet. *Moonmen (and Women)* was part of the Zoe Love Museum now. Ever since Zoe had gone missing, her dad had been trying to keep everything of hers exactly as it was when she left, so it would be waiting for her when she came back. The piece of quiche in the fridge that Zoe bought from Brixton Village was part of the museum, as was her crusty bit of artisan loaf, turning blue in the bread bin. The wonky angle she'd sliced the bread at. That was Zoe's too.

There was a paperback novel on her bedside table, bookmarked at page 136 with a Waterstones till receipt, and a Bikini Kill CD jammed inside the CD player. If it was plugged in, the disc would start spinning but it wouldn't play. They were all Zoe Love Museum exhibits now. As was the half-drunk bottle of Summer Fruits Oasis on Zoe's dressing table and the empty jellybean dispenser next to it. Every key ring and badge she'd collected, the two Ikea storage boxes piled on top of each other on the floor next to the wardrobe, and the teddy bears packed tightly inside the boxes. The fake cactus that used to light up but didn't anymore and the Caffè Nero cup on the dressing table were museum exhibits now. As were the sachets of sugar from Starbucks and Costa. Even the four stripes of paint in almost identical shades of pale blue, like four of her sky photos, on the wall behind the dressing table, waiting for Zoe to decide which colour she preferred so that her dad could paint the rest of the wall.

Moonmen (and Women) didn't actually belong to Zoe. And it was Nathan who'd chosen and pulled the heavy book down from the shelf in the library. He'd wiped the dust off the cover and taken it to the counter to be scanned and stamped. And it was Nathan who was reading the book. But Zoe had written and stuck *(and Women)* on the cover. She might as well have planted a Zoe Love flag in it.

Nathan put the blank pages he'd torn from the book on the carpet and looked for something to stick them together with. It wasn't until he'd peeled off the tape holding his WrestleMania poster on the wall and stuck it to the four pages of the library book, that he realised he could have used the back of the poster for his Luigi board instead. He lay the wrestling poster on the carpet in front of the wall where it came from, so he could say it had fallen off the wall if his dad asked.

Nathan tipped the pens and pencils out of his *London 2012* mug and tried different coloured felt tips on the back of his hand until he found one that worked. He wrote the alphabet across the centre of the paper, misjudging the amount of space he needed for the second row of letters. The X and the Y were squashed together and tiny, but they were probably the least required letters. He wrote the numbers under the alphabet and a big YES at the top of the Luigi board and a NO at the bottom. Using Zoe's two triangles method, he drew five stars. The stars looked rubbish, especially without any glitter on. But they would have to do. He added a thumbs-up emoji to his Luigi board, as a joke for Zoe because he knew how much she hated emojis.

Nathan placed the Olympics mug upside down at the centre of the Luigi board and put his fingers on its base. He tried moving the mug, but it was too heavy and it took the paper with it. Zoe had used their mum's records to make a smoother surface for her Luigi board. The only record upstairs was the David Bowie album inside the plastic frame on Zoe's bedroom wall. He could get that one at least.

Nathan crept along the landing to Zoe's room. He opened her door just enough to slip through the gap. His dad had forbidden Auntie Maureen from vacuuming the carpet or dusting in Zoe's bedroom and Nathan was aware he was disturbing Zoe's footprints with every step he took, smudging her fingerprints with everything he touched. One of his teachers had told him once that dust was made from human skin. He thought she'd only said it to scare him or to trick him into keeping his desk clean or something. But if it was true, Zoe's bedroom was covered in her skin, her mostly human skin, her Ziggy stardust.

Nathan took pigeon steps in a direct line to the album hanging on Zoe's bedroom wall. He'd just read how Neil Armstrong's footprints were still on the Moon because there was no wind. He looked up at the record, shut away inside the frame, and the chair he'd used to climb on to reach the picture frame before. Nathan didn't want to move the string of fairy lights draped over the back of the chair and risk disturbing the Zoe Love Museum. He decided that using a lighter mug or cup on his Luigi board would achieve the same results as having a flatter surface underneath it. He picked the paper Caffè Nero cup up from Zoe's dressing table, rearranging the surrounding sugar sachets from rival coffee shops to fill the space left behind.

He held the cup under his shirt and crept back along the landing. His dad was talking to the FLOs downstairs. He couldn't hear what they were saying. There were a lot of things they wouldn't talk about when Nathan was in the room. If he asked his dad about it his dad would tell him not to worry and that it didn't concern him. How could it *not* concern him? Yesterday Nathan had overheard the FLOs asking his dad about all the arguments he'd had with Zoe. Presumably because Nathan had told the policeman about it in the park. He felt like PC Kari had tricked him into telling tales on his dad. Arthur was right. He should have told the feds nothing. Nathan went into the bathroom. He removed the lid from the Caffè Nero cup and tipped the cold coffee down the toilet. He flushed it and went back to his bedroom.

Nathan sat on the floor and placed the coffee cup upside down at the centre of his Luigi board, and very quietly, in his best Zoe Love weird voice he said, "Is there anyone there? Move the cup if you can hear me."

The cup didn't move.

He asked again, this time with his eyes closed.

"Are you an alien again, Zo?"

Even upstairs there must have been too much interference blocking the signal – the ceiling and the roof and whatever was in between. He wondered how difficult it would be to climb up on the roof with the Luigi board. But the windows were locked anyway, so that was out of the question. Maybe the Luigi board didn't work with only one set of fingers on the cup. He thought about how rubbish *Cluedo* was when it was only him and Zoe playing. He turned the paper cup up the right way, dripping coffee on the paper. He wiped it off with his fingertip, tasted the cold coffee and sat with his back against his bed. He pulled his knees up against his chest and looked at the Luigi board. He'd only ever seen two Luigi boards but his was definitely the worst. Zoe's wasn't just better, it was the best.

Nathan thought about the time their mum was really ill in hospital, when she looked like she was asleep, but her eyes were still open, and their dad had told Nathan and Zoe they should talk to her. Even though she probably wouldn't reply or even look like she could hear them, it was still possible that she actually could. So, Zoe told their mum that she loved her and she told her what she'd been doing that day and even made some things up when she ran out of things to talk about. Nathan couldn't think of a single thing to say. He wondered if, maybe like their mum, Zoe could hear him now but couldn't move the cup to answer, even though it was only made of paper.

"There are police here every day because of you, Zo," Nathan said. "Everyone is looking for you. Me and Dad put up loads of posters with your face on. So, you're famous now. And you've sort of been on telly as well. Auntie Maureen is here every day. She says me and Dad would starve to death otherwise and we'd be wearing dirty clothes. I'd have to go commando all the time. Auntie Maureen didn't say that. That was me. Every time she offers to make Dad something to eat though, he says, oh, just something simple please, Mo. Move the cup to yes if you can hear me, Zoe, and if you want me to come and find you. Because I know where you are." Nathan stared at the cup, willing it to move. "If you don't move it, it doesn't matter because I've decided anyway. I'm coming to get you. Seriously though, Zoe. I've got hundreds of things to tell you. Since you've been gone it's been one thing after another."

12

Nathan adjusted the crotch of his orange spacesuit. It felt tighter than when he'd worn it to the park just a few nights ago. Zoe had already been gone long enough for Nathan to have grown. He double-checked the contents of his backpack. The compass and the telescope, the underwater camera and the MP3 player and the Swiss Army knife he'd taken out of the kitchen drawer when he was looking for batteries for his Space Torch. He ate the last Kit Kat finger and threw the silver foil wrapper at the bin in the corner of his room and missed. He pulled the swimming goggles on, adjusted the strap again and looked up at the stars. Even though all he had to do was go to sleep, he doubted he'd be able to.

He tried naming the fifty-three moons of Saturn. Like counting sheep. Aegaeon, Aegir, Albiorix, Anthe, Atlas, Bebhionn, Bergelmir, Bestla, Calypso Daphnis. What came next? Nathan knew three people with the same names as Saturn moons now. A girl in his class was called Pandora and the policeman who'd tricked him by pretending to be a good cop was called PC Kari. The other person was Arthur's Staffy cross, Titan, the name of Saturn's biggest moon and Brixton's ugliest dog.

Nathan chased an itch around his body. It ran across his belly and up and down his arms and into his hair like when someone talked about ants. He loosened the skateboard pad on his left knee and itched underneath. He felt so wide-awake. How had Neil Armstrong ever managed to sleep before he left for the Moon? It must have been like a billion Christmas Eves. Maybe it was dangerous for an astronaut to fall asleep in Space. If Neil Armstrong had a dream about aliens and the aliens woke him up, Apollo 11 could have ended up stuck in orbit forever. Nathan tried to empty his mind, like Miss Casablanca said he should do during yoga. Arthur always said, 'That won't take long.'

Every single time.

Nathan yawned. An encouraging sign. He adjusted his spacesuit again. He wondered whether the aliens would be tall like Chewbacca or short like E.T. Ever since Nathan had been able to stand upright, people had remarked on how short he was for his age. His parents had said it and so had doctors and teachers, even complete strangers in supermarkets. And they always made being short for his age sound so negative. Like having something wrong with his speech or being slow at reading. Whereas the boys in his class who were tall for their age were hailed as legends and heroes. They got picked for the basketball team even if they couldn't catch or throw to save their lives.

When the astronauts returned from the International Space Station, they were two inches taller. Nathan hoped that would happen to him. Perhaps on whatever planet or galaxy he was taken to, he'd already be the tallest one there. Apart from Zoe, of course. The sooner he fell asleep, the sooner the aliens would wake him up and he'd find out. He gave up trying to empty his mind or remember Saturn's moons and went through the police alphabet instead. Alpha, Bravo, Charlie, Delta, Echo, Foxtrot, Hotel...missed one, Golf, Hotel, India, Julia, Lima, Mike, November...

13

Nathan woke up. Still in Brixton, London, England, the World, Earth, the Solar System, the Universe. He went to the toilet, checking in the bathroom mirror for bruises or strange marks on his body, finding nothing except the rings under his eyes from the swimming goggles. He liked the way the rings made him look more like his dad.

Along the landing his dad's bedroom door was open and his bed was empty. Nathan imagined the aliens had taken his dad as well and that he was the last boy on Earth. For the three steps along the landing to Zoe's room Nathan was excited by all the adventures he was going to have on his own. By the time he knocked on her door, he was imagining the film *Home Alone* with the two robbers successfully breaking in and killing him.

Recalling a game that he used to play with Zoe, Nathan knocked on her bedroom door. In the game one of them would think of a tune and tap out the notes on a table or the wall with their knuckles. The other person would have to guess what tune it was. They both became so good at guessing correctly, that like the Post-it note game, to anyone else it would have seemed like it was a rehearsed trick. Zoe said that even though they were born nearly five years apart, they were more connected than identical twins.

Nathan knocked on the door five times. If Zoe had returned during the night — they always came at night, she'd told him — she would recognise the up-and-down notes from *Close Encounters of the Third Kind*.

A few seconds passed without response and Nathan opened the door. He checked the tripwires and alarms he'd set up the night before. The cotton bud still seesawed on the edge of the dressing table and the plastic beads were unmoved on the narrow windowsill, still forming the shape of a 'Z'.

He picked the snow globe up from Zoe's dressing table

and shook it, watching the snow falling on Neil Armstrong. The plastic astronaut was almost as big as the Moon he was standing on. He was holding an American flag like a golf caddy. Nathan hadn't read anything yet in *Moonmen (and Women)* about whether or not it snowed on the Moon. Zoe would know. When she came home, he would ask her. He'd also ask her to explain how astronauts weren't floating but falling. He'd read it over and over in the library book, but he couldn't seem to understand it. Zoe would make it all make sense to him. On the base of the snow globe it said: 'ONE SMALL STEP FOR MAN', which, everyone who knew anything at all about space knew, Neil Armstrong hadn't meant to say.

The snow globe was from the same National Space Centre gift shop as Nathan's torch and the stars and planets on his bedroom ceiling. His dad had painted the ceiling black and then he'd stood on a chair, sticking the stars to the night sky. Zoe said he looked like God on his fourth day.

When Zoe came back, or when Nathan *brought* her back, he would ask their dad if they could all go to the National Space Centre again. They could stay in the same hotel as before and Nathan would share a room with Zoe again. He would help her reacclimatise to life on Earth back among the humans. Her bones and muscles would slowly start to recover from lack of gravity, she'd find her voice again and they'd stay up all night talking. They'd make cups of tea with the hotel kettle that took forever to boil. Nathan would squirt milk onto the carpet again when he tried to open the tiny cartons and Zoe would have to creep out into the corridor to steal more milk from a trolley. She'd take two packets of biscuits from the trolley as well and they would lay awake for hours on their hotel beds, Zoe on the double and Nathan on a small bed on wheels, that the scary-tired-bored man from reception would pull out from under the bigger bed like a DVD tray.

With nothing but the light from the television to see her by, Nathan would watch his superhero sister picking at a new scab on her leg. He'd record it in a notebook he'd bought from the National Space Centre gift shop. He would ask her how she got the scab and Zoe would tell him, "I think there's an implant under my skin. So they can track my movements."

"The aliens?"

"Yep."

"Like an Oyster card?"

Zoe would look at him like *he* was the strange one in the family.

"Dad says the government can tell where you are because of your Oyster card," Nathan would tell her.

Zoe would roll her eyes again, because her dad was even stranger than her brother.

"Do you want to go out?" Zoe would say.

"Where?"

"Just outside. See if there are any stars."

"What about Dad?"

"He won't want to come."

"You know that's not what I mean."

"Come on."

Zoe would open the heavy hotel room door and hold it until it closed behind them and they'd walk along the corridor and go downstairs. They'd go through another heavy door and sneak past the scary-tired-bored man in reception who would see them anyway but wouldn't seem to care. Outside, most of the shops and services would be closed. There wouldn't be any people around, just lots of parked cars and vans. Zoe would say it looked like a film about the end of the world.

They'd walk to the same grassy area that reminded Nathan of the middle bit of their estate. The only light would come from the kind of short streetlights they have on the roads near airports to stop low flying planes crashing into them. They'd sit on the same concrete bench and tip their heads back, just as they'd done earlier on in the planetarium at the National Space Centre. Nathan would turn on his Space Torch and he'd project the galaxy from eight million light years away at the sky.

Zoe would say, "Don't do that."

"Why not?"

"You don't know what might happen. It might be like meeting yourself when you time travel. Or typing Google into Google. Something calamitous will happen. The sky will explode, or we'll all die in a huge ball of fire."

Nathan wouldn't believe her, but he'd switch the torch off anyway. Just in case. They'd stare at the sky without talking for a while. Nathan would steal glances at his sister, wondering what she could see up there that he couldn't, and Zoe would make the same joke as the last time they were there, "You'd think they would have built a National Space Centre somewhere with a few more stars."

On the way back to their room they'd get ice creams from the vending machine in the hotel's reception. Nathan loved that vending machine. It had a robot arm that moved over and sucked the ice creams out of the freezer. It was better than a lot of the interactive exhibits at the National Space Centre. He wanted to have a second go, but Zoe said no. She would steal more milk cartons and two more packets of biscuits from the trolley outside their room. Nathan would pocket a sachet of sugar and feel like Professor Moriarty.

The snow settled inside the snow globe and Nathan returned it to the exact same spot on Zoe's dressing table where he'd picked it up from. He tightened the lid on the half-drunk bottle of Oasis and felt the boobs on a glass perfume bottle in the shape of a woman with no head. He sprayed some of the perfume into the air and sniffed it. It was the only thing in the room that didn't remind him of Zoe.

Her bedroom was like the living museum Nathan had been to with the school. It was like a world stopped in time. At the living museum people in old-fashioned clothes with no make-up or hair products weaved baskets out of straw and made wooden furniture and pots without using power tools. Arthur had stolen a small stoneware pot from the museum and smashed it on the coach back to school. Humans were terrible, even if they were your friends.

Nathan sorted through a basket full of Zoe's pencils and pens and badges, looking for glitter. At the bottom of the basket there was a see-through wallet with eleven different coloured Sharpies inside. He stared at the space between the blue and the green pens and pretended he was the father of a missing teenager, trying to see what it felt like to be his dad. At least Nathan knew where Zoe was. And how he was going to get her back.

He took one last look around, what his dad called 'an idiot check'. He put a bottle of blue nail varnish in his pocket, promising Zoe he'd return it, and closed the bedroom door. He replaced the strip of Sellotape across the door and the door frame and went downstairs.

14

Nathan's dad was in the living room. He must have fallen asleep sitting on the sofa and had gradually slid down onto the floor in front of it like a silk scarf. His laptop had travelled with him and somehow remained balanced on his knees. Both dad and computer were asleep and Nathan didn't want to wake either of them.

He went into the kitchen and climbed on a chair to pull the top bolt across the back door to let Officer Dibble in. If he was quick enough, he could have probably gone out through the garden to the park and retrieved the Luigi board. He could have looked again for the arrows and the Post-it notes. But the thought of what his dad would do to him, and the knowledge of what thinking he'd lost 'another one' would do to his dad, was enough to stop him. He closed the back door and scooped some stinky meat onto a saucer for Officer Dibble and poured himself a bowl of Rice Krispies, keeping his hand over the bowl, in case the snaps, crackles and pops woke his dad. He sat on the floor next to the cat and opened *Moonmen (and Women)*. He found the chapter titled: 'Animals in Space'.

"Fruit flies were the first animals in space," Nathan said, reading to the cat. "They were launched in a V-2 rocket from the desert in New Mexico and travelled sixty-eight miles in three minutes and ten seconds."

When Zoe came back from space, she was allergic to cats. Nathan remembered her breaking the bad news to Officer Dibble. Zoe told the cat she wouldn't be able to stroke him or brush his stinky teeth with her old Disney toothbrush anymore. Officer Dibble, who'd been an indoors-cat since kittenhood, was going to have to be put outside at night like the bins. Perhaps Nathan was remembering it wrongly, but when he pictured Officer Dibble's face as Zoe told him he wasn't going to be able to sleep on the end of her bed and would have to take his chances with the rougher estate cats and weapon dogs from now on, Nathan was convinced the cat could understand. As if switching the television on and off with her mind and popping toast up just by looking at it wasn't enough, Zoe was also a Doctor Dolittle.

With one eye on the cat, Nathan continued reading to him, hoping for a similar reaction.

"In 1957, Laika was the first animal to go into orbit. The Russian…" Nathan whispered the word, "*dog*, left Earth on board the Sputnik 2 spacecraft. Laika was the first animal to go into orbit, although he didn't make it back as the technology hadn't been developed yet." Nathan turned the page and angled the book to show the cat a photograph. "That's Félicette Dibs. It's a French black and white cat that was sent into space in a special capsule on top of a rocket that launched from the Sahara Desert. The cat travelled one hundred miles in fifteen minutes and then the capsule separated from the rocket and came back to Earth by parachute. The capsule and the cat were both recovered safely. In Britain – that's where we live, Dibble – the newspapers called Félicette the Astrocat."

Officer Dibble carried on eating and ignoring Nathan, even when he told him that after Félicette returned to Earth, scientists had killed her so they could carry out tests on her body. Nathan closed the book and got up from the kitchen floor. He poured the last of the Rice Krispies into his bowl and topped the bowl up with milk. He boiled the kettle and rinsed out a mug. There were no clean teaspoons and he didn't want to put his arm into the sink full of cold murky water so he poured coffee into the mug from the jar. He hadn't left enough milk for the coffee and had to tip some out of his cereal bowl.

Nathan walked slowly along the hall to the living room, careful not to spill milk or coffee but managing to do both. He trod the spilled liquid into the carpet, until his sock was so wet he had to limp to the living room. His dad woke the moment Nathan walked into the room, catching the laptop just before it hit the floor. His dad yawned and hauled himself back up onto the sofa. After he'd stretched his back and his neck and pulled a few early morning faces, Nathan gave him the mug of coffee.

"Have we run out of little marshmallows?" his dad said. He smiled, picking a Rice Krispie from the surface of his coffee. And then he must have remembered Zoe was missing and his smile was sucked into the black hole she'd left behind. Everything good about the day would follow it.

Nathan sat next to his dad. He balanced the cereal bowl on the arm of the sofa, and in the time it took him to take his wet sock off and drop it on the floor, his dad had woken the laptop up and was collecting emails. He refreshed the Facebook page and counted the notifications before Nathan had taken the spoon out of his bowl. His dad read the new Facebook messages and comments and accepted friend requests. This was his morning routine. Nathan already hated it.

One of the FLOs had helped his dad set up the *Where is Zoe Love?* Facebook page and he was on the internet all the time now. He had a Twitter account too and every morning he searched #WhereisZoeLove. Zoe's dad had been on social media more often in one week than his daughter had in her entire lifetime. Zoe's lack of what PC Torres had called, 'her digital footprint', made it harder for the police to track her movements.

Nathan's dad had found some other photos of Zoe and he'd scanned them onto his laptop and added them to Facebook. At the top of the page there was a picture of the whole family together, all with identical skinhead haircuts. It had been Zoe's idea to support her mum when she was ill. She'd shaved Nathan's head and her own before telling their dad. Luckily, he was too moved to be angry and so Zoe shaved her dad's head too. In the photo, their dad said they looked like a cult.

Zoe's Facebook profile picture was the same one that was on posters all over Brixton. It had appeared in newspapers and on television. It was the picture Nathan was going to take it into Space.

The only other pictures of Zoe taken in the six months following her alien abduction were two that her dad had taken at the National Space Centre. In one she was standing in front of the two huge rockets with her head tipped back, as it so often was, staring up at the Blue Streak and Thor-Able. Nathan was standing next to her in the picture, but he'd been unable to look up at the rockets without feeling giddy. In the other photo of Zoe taken at the Space Centre, she had her head inside an astronaut's helmet and her body hidden behind the astronaut, so it looked like she was wearing a spacesuit. Nathan thought his dad should have given that picture to the police instead.

After he found Zoe's two friends in her phone, her dad had looked for more online. He began by searching for the two girls on Facebook, hoping to find Zoe in their photos and the photos of their friends, but she wasn't there. He told Nathan that without any recent pictures of her, he felt like Zoe had been gone for an extra half a year already. He said he was worried about forgetting what she looked like and only being able to remember her when she was six months younger than when he'd last seen her. Nathan promised his dad he would remember what she looked like and would remind him if he ever forgot.

Nathan's dad read out loud the latest theories and answers to the question posed by the Facebook page's title: *Where is Zoe Love?* Someone had seen her in a train station in Liverpool, another person was sure Zoe had asked them for directions on a high street in Glasgow. Zoe had been spotted as far away as Spain and America and in the duty-free shop at Gatwick Airport buying a bottle of brandy. Another Facebook post included a picture of a girl begging outside a pound shop in Cardiff. The girl's face was obscured by her hoody, but it was obvious she wasn't Zoe. Nathan's dad stared at the picture for ages anyway. Zoe had black hair now, someone commented, another said she dressed like a boy and worked in a charity shop less than a mile away from the estate she was missing from.

The FLOs had warned Nathan's dad that after the television appeal a lot of people would want to help. Even if they had no genuine information to offer, they might make things up just to feel involved. Yesterday someone suggested Zoe was buried in her back garden. *They* weren't trying to help. There would be a lot of people like that too, the FLOs said. The nasty comments on Facebook had more replies than any of the other well-intentioned ones. There was one particularly long thread of theories about where Zoe really was and how her family had invented the whole story to make themselves rich and famous.

"There are a lot of new posts because of the television appeal," Nathan's dad said. He sounded so pleased that Nathan worried he was starting to enjoy the attention.

"Can I watch cartoons?" Nathan said.

His dad passed him the remote control. He gestured at the address written on the back of Nathan's hand. *Brixton, London, England, the World, Earth, the Solar System, the Universe.*

"What's that for?"

"In case I get lost."

"We'll have to get it tattooed," his dad said.

Nathan looked at him. "Really?"

His dad nodded. "I'll get one done as well."

Nathan looked at the snake's head on the back of his dad's hand and the beginning of the snake's body on his arm. It continued under the sleeve of his T-shirt, across his shoulders and back down the other arm, where it ended with the snake's tail tattooed on his dad's other hand.

"Where?" Nathan said.

"I'm sure I can find a space."

Nathan couldn't think where that might be. His dad's body was literally covered in tattoos. There was a lion, a tiger, and a kangaroo wearing boxing gloves on his back. Elephants, polar bears and penguins filled half of his chest – Nathan's dad's tattooist paid no heed to the laws of geography. Some of his tattoos were bright and beautifully coloured in, while others appeared unfinished, they were black or grey and looked like he'd fallen asleep on a damp newspaper. On his right ankle there was a tattooed pair of hands. The little fingers were hooked around each other in a pinkie swear and the words: *South London Boys Forever 2013* were tattooed underneath. 'Never go near a tattoo parlour when you've had a drink,' his dad had declared before the tattoo had properly healed.

On his chest, over his dad's heart, there were three scratchy looking letters: 'KAT'. Kilo Alpha Tango. Nathan and Zoe's mum. Katherine. Their mum had five tattoos. Four black dots and one blue one. They were targets for the rays that were supposed to destroy her Earth cancer. Like when they'd shaved their heads to support her, the whole family had the same tattoos. Nathan and Zoe had drawn theirs on themselves with ballpoint pens.

Nathan's dad refreshed the Facebook page.

"We need to give out more leaflets," he said.

"Do I have to go?"

"Thirty-three million people go in and out of Brixton station every year, Nathan," his dad said. Somebody on Facebook had told him that. "What if one of them has seen Zoe?"

Nathan thought his dad must have noticed people were happier accepting leaflets from a man who had a small child with him. Nathan was like the well-dressed boys and girls who accompanied the religious people that knocked on their door every Saturday.

"We can go for a McDonald's after if you like," his dad said.

"I'm a vegetarian now."

Nathan regretted saying it so quickly. It sounded like he was making an excuse because he didn't want to help his dad. Because he didn't care about finding Zoe. But Nathan had decided he'd be a vegetarian last night. He thought, if he made himself more like Zoe, the aliens would be more likely to take him too.

His dad closed the laptop and Nathan prepared himself for a lecture about priorities. Instead, he said, "Then I suppose I'll have to be a vegetarian too."

15

Because it was Sunday it wasn't as busy in town as the day before, and Nathan didn't feel like he was going to be trampled to death or swept away in a tide of commuters flowing in and out of the Tube. He even handed out a few leaflets himself. When they'd run out of leaflets, Nathan and his dad crossed the road and went to the Subway for their first-ever vegetarian lunch together. The sandwich shop was almost directly opposite the David Bowie mural and Nathan wondered if his dad had only given up meat because it gave him an excuse to read Zoe's message on the wall again.

They both had Veggie Delite sandwiches. It was Zoe's favourite and Nathan asked for his sandwich with 'the works' like Zoe always did, even though he didn't know what the works were. They sat at one of the tables outside and ate their sandwiches while they watched David Bowie fans and tourists posing for selfies in front of the mural. Nathan's dad paid close attention to anyone who appeared to be reading the messages on the wall next to the painting.

Nathan pulled the lid off his Fruit Shoot, tipped his head back and squeezed the plastic bottle, aiming a squirt of the juice into his mouth. He squished it around like mouthwash. His mouth was on fire.

"You can pick the jalapeños out if you like," his dad said.

Nathan said he was fine. His mum used to say that if he ate something that he didn't like enough times, eventually his brain would teach his mouth to like it. Nathan's dad used to test the theory by bringing exotic, unusual fruit and vegetables home from the stall. Nathan and Zoe would eat starfruit and lychees, yams and butternut squashes, and other fruit and vegetables that didn't look like real food at all.

Nathan used to love watching his dad at work on the stall, juggling fruit and spinning the paper bags to seal them. He'd call out the names of fruit and vegetables in a voice he didn't use at any other time, except maybe at the football. "You got your eeeeasy peelers...*Nanas! Three for a parrrnd!*" his dad would shout while trains rattled across the railway bridge overhead. Nathan wondered what Zoe might be eating now. How weird must alien fruit be, and how many times would Zoe have to taste it before her brain taught her mouth to like it?

Nathan's dad was staring at a girl reading the messages on the wall opposite. Nathan wanted to tell him it wasn't Zoe.

"Are you going back to work?" Nathan said.

His dad didn't answer until the girl had walked away. "I can't even think about that yet. You *are* going to have to go back to school though."

"Why do I have to go if you don't?" Nathan said. "I want to help you find Zoe."

"I know you do, mate. But no one's going to miss me at work. They'll get their apples from Sainsbury's or—"

"Craig said half of Brixton will get scurvy if you don't start selling them fruit again," Nathan said. His dad shook his head and did his, *tsk, Craig eh* face. Nathan asked him what scurvy was.

"It's something to do with biscuits," his dad said. "It's what sailors used to get...I think...You see, Nathan. That's exactly what I mean. If you don't go to school, you'll end up thick like your dad. You'll never be a doctor or a lawyer if you don't go to school—"

"I don't want to be a doctor or a lawyer."

"What do you want to be?"

Nathan didn't need any time to think about it. "An astronaut. Or work with you on the stall."

"Blimey, Nath," his dad said, almost spitting his food out. "There's got to be something in-between astronaut and greengrocer."

"Like what?"

"I don't know...*everything*? Sorry, mate, but you've got to go back to school. And isn't that astronaut day coming up soon? You were really looking forward to that."

Nathan was surprised his dad had remembered about the *Space and Science Far Beyond Infinity Workshop*. The letter from the school about it had been stuck to the fridge door since before Christmas. In the last week though, the letter had been gradually shifted along and then down the fridge door. It was now almost completely hidden under Zoe leaflets, police business cards, scraps of paper with phone numbers on and flyers for three separate private investigators that had been posted through the letterbox.

It was true, Nathan had been looking forward to the 'fun, scientific and out-of-this-world unforgettable space experience' that the letter described. An astronaut was going to 'touch down' in Nathan's classroom and spend the whole day with the students, taking them on 'the intergalactic journey of a lifetime'. The day would include interactive HD videos and a quiz, and everyone would get the chance to see and touch actual items from space. They would also be able to try on an astronaut helmet and launch a rocket. But with Nathan's sister in real space, on a genuine intergalactic journey of a lifetime, seeing and touching actual things that weren't just from space, but *in* space, it all seemed a bit silly.

Nathan tipped his head back and squeezed the last of his fruit juice into his mouth. The sun was in his eyes and he sat up straight and angled his chair away from it. It was just coming up to midday but there was a moon over H & M.

"Have you got any fruit?" Nathan said.

His dad patted his pockets, both real and imaginary. "Not on me. Why?"

"Zoe showed me how there can be a sun and a moon in the day and at the same time. She used fruit. The orange was Earth and the grapefruit was the Sun. The Moon was a tomato. I think."

"Sorry, mate," his dad said.

"We could go to the stall and get some off Craig."

Nathan's dad looked at his phone for the tenth time since they'd sat down for lunch. "We should probably get back," he said. He'd already started to get up.

"Can't we stay a bit longer?" Nathan said.

"Not today. The police are coming around."

"Again?"

Nathan hadn't meant to sound so selfish. He just didn't want to be searching for Zoe *all* the time. He stood up and followed his dad. When he paused to read Zoe's message for the zillionth time, Nathan looked at the Moon. It was more like a pickled onion than a tomato. It reminded him of the silvery grey lychees his dad brought home from work once. It seemed so out of place in the midday sky above H & M that Nathan wondered if it was actually a hot air balloon, tied to the roof of the shop to advertise jeans.

There were fewer leaflets on the ground on the way to the bus stop. They ran for a bus but missed it. And then the driver opened the doors for them at the traffic lights, which never happens. And best of all, the Oyster card reader wasn't working and the journey was free. His dad said it was his favourite thing in the whole world. Nathan could think of one thing to top it but didn't say anything. It was only a short bus ride home, but they went upstairs and sat at the front. They talked about football and video games and his dad didn't mention Zoe once.

16

Nathan ran a bath deep enough for water to spill out onto the floor when he climbed in. He pulled the swimming goggles over his eyes, took a huge breath and pinched his nose. He slid down the bath until his toes touched the tap and his face was under water. He started counting: one Mississippi, two Mississippi. His record for holding his breath was fifty-two Mississippis and he was determined to beat it. The Apollo astronauts had sophisticated spacesuits and helmets and boxes of oxygen strapped to their backs when they trained for space travel. There were pictures in *Moonmen (and Women)* of the astronauts training in a huge empty swimming pool and in the middle of the ocean. They had a team of frogmen and medical staff standing by in case they got into trouble. All Nathan had was a bath, some tinted swimming goggles, and his lungs.

Everything sounded different underwater. Not louder like in the dark but more like his ears were selecting a few things for him to listen to. Like putting a shell to his ear. He could hear the water rushing through the pipes as the tank refilled and he heard either his heartbeat or drum and bass music in a car. After sixteen Mississippis the house phone rang and less than two Mississippis after that he heard his dad's muffled voice. He waited for footsteps on the stairs, either running with good news, or if it was bad, a zombie dawdle. Twenty Mississippis passed. Nathan couldn't hear his dad's voice anymore but there were no footsteps on the stairs. He thought of all the times Auntie Maureen had told his dad that no news was good news and how that so obviously wasn't true.

Nathan wondered what it would feel like if Zoe was dead. How would he react to the news? When his mum died, he just remembered being confused. It felt more unfair than sad. Like they had unfinished business. But even though everyone had been expecting her to die for a long time and his dad had tried preparing Nathan for it, the actual moment was impossible to prepare for. When their dad told him and Zoe, it sounded like a mistake, or even a joke. The worst April fool's joke ever.

The water tank was almost full again and the pipes were quieter. The drip from the bath taps had slowed down. Nathan could feel the cold drip on his big toe. He would have to breathe like an astronaut if he wanted to beat his record. He cheat-counted his seconds faster. Brixtons instead of Mississippis. Forty-one Brixtons, forty-two Brixtons, forty-three. When it was time to resurface, the Navy or the Air Force would pop the hatch on the capsule, and he'd climb into a dingy. Fifty-two Brixtons, fifty-three. He'd be out of breath and the air tanks would be so heavy that they'd have to pull him into the dingy. Fifty-six, fifty-seven. An all-new Nathan J Love record. A new personal best. His PB. His Papa Bravo. Nathan counted down. Ten, nine, eight. Like David Bowie on Zoe's favourite ever song. Seven, six. Ground Control to Major Zoe. He wondered how Zoe managed to breathe in space without a helmet, or without a box on her back, especially with her asthma. Nathan had seen her gasping for air when she couldn't find her inhaler, and it had terrified him. He thought his sister was going to die. Four, three. Two. He sat up suddenly, sending a wave of water onto the floor. He climbed out of the bath, coughing up swallowed water. He pulled his pyjama trousers on, almost tripping over and falling headfirst into the bathroom door. *Less haste more speed, Nathan,* his mum used to say. He never knew exactly what it meant but he knew it applied to this sort of situation.

Still pulling his pyjama trousers on, he hopped along the landing, leaving single wet footprints on the carpet that would have confused detectives. He went into Zoe's room, snapping the Sellotape across the door, setting off the alien alarms. The cotton bud fell off the dressing table. Only the plastic beads remained in place on the windowsill, still forming the shape of the initial of his asthmatic sister.

Nathan sat on Zoe's bed. He pulled his pyjama trousers up and opened the drawer in the bedside table. He took the inhalers out and shook them one by one. First the three pale blue inhalers and then the brown one. PC Torres had said it was unusual for a fifteen-year-old girl to leave home without her mobile phone, but what about a fifteen-year-old asthmatic girl leaving home without her inhaler? Nathan went along the landing to the top of the stairs. He leaned over the banisters and called out, "*Dad*. Zoe forgot her puffer."

"What?" his dad called back from the kitchen.

Nathan repeated himself, louder and more urgently, picturing Zoe gasping for air with every second, turning blue, dying. "Zoe forgot *her puffer*."

His dad came out into the hall below. He looked up at Nathan.

"I know," he said calmly.

"Shouldn't you tell the police?"

"They know too, Nath," his dad tilted his head to get a clearer look up the stairs. "Why are you wearing swimming goggles?"

Nathan pulled the goggles off the top of his head.

"I didn't want to get soap in my eyes."

"Okay, mate. Don't forget to let the bath out."

Nathan walked back along the landing, stepping into his single wet footprints, hopping from one to the next. He pulled the plug out of the bath and watched the water until it started to gurgle and then he went back to Zoe's room. He sat on her bed and looked at the inhalers on the bedside table. He put the brown one and two of the blue ones back in the drawer and closed it. Aliens would obviously be more advanced than humans. They could hide their spaceships in clouds. They could sneak into bedrooms unnoticed, like Father Christmas. Zoe wouldn't need a stupid human inhaler. Nathan pictured her hooked up to a machine, full of beeps and blinks and flashing lights. There'd be tubes going into her and coming out again, feeding Zoe and emptying her, refuelling her, making her comfortable and keeping her alive, like their mum in hospital. It was when they removed the tubes, when they took Zoe to a nice private room on her own. That was when Nathan needed to worry.

He shook the blue inhaler. He breathed out and then in and put the puffer in his mouth and pressed. He was instantly lightheaded and thought he was going to be sick, like when Arthur made him smoke half a cigarette. Astronauts had to try hard to not puke in Space, because the sick would float around and might end up in another astronaut's mouth. Nathan lay down on Zoe's bed and waited for everything to stop spinning.

Before he went back to his own room Nathan took a Kwell tablet from the packet in the bathroom cabinet. There were pictures of a car, a plane and a ship on the front of the box. He didn't know whether the pills would work for space travel, but he put the tiny pill on his tongue and swallowed it anyway. He placed three cotton buds in the shape of an arrow outside his bedroom door and went through the contents of his backpack. Every night he was adding something new. If Zoe didn't come home soon, he'd have to get a bigger bag. Tonight, he would take the snow globe and the blue nail varnish. He sat on the edge of his bed and painted both his thumbnails blue, shaking and blowing on them like Zoe did. If he made himself more like her, the aliens would be more likely to take him too.

17

Brixton, London, England, the World, Earth, the Solar System, the Universe. Nathan's dad had gone out early on his own and Auntie Maureen was on guard duty. Nathan tried his luck and asked her if he could go to the park and she said categorically no, which she told him meant no times a thousand. The chain was on the front door and both bolts were pulled across the back. As his dad was the only one who knew where the window keys were hidden, Nathan told Officer Dibble, if there was a fire, they would both burn to death.

Maureen made Nathan a full English breakfast, with Linda McCartney sausages and two eggs, sunny side up, because that's how Zoe had hers. Nathan sat with Maureen at the table in front of the living room window. Up until a week ago no one in the house ate their meals at the table. They always sat on the sofa or the armchair with their plates on their laps, usually watching television or looking at their phones. With Maureen in charge of mealtimes the living room had quickly turned into a restaurant. Knives on the right, forks on the left. Placemats in the middle and a tablecloth underneath. Maureen held up two sauce bottles, a brown one and a red.

"Daddies?" she said. "Or Aunties?" Nathan couldn't decide. "I'll leave them both and let you choose." Maureen said.

Nathan poured tomato ketchup onto his plate and shook the bottle of brown sauce. He slapped it on the base like his dad did, firing a huge dollop onto the plate. He mixed the two sauces together with his knife. He'd expected the tomato ketchup to disappear into the darker brown sauce, but the opposite happened.

He asked his aunt if she was going to get sacked from Greggs because of all the time she was having off work. She said no because they owed her a lot of holidays. Nathan said she was having a really rubbish holiday and Maureen laughed. She said at least no one in Brixton would get scurvy because she wasn't selling them cakes, and Nathan knew his aunt and his dad had been talking about him. After breakfast he asked Maureen if she had any glitter.

"Not on me," she said, patting her pockets.

Nathan wondered if saying 'not on me' and patting your pockets when someone asked you for something that you didn't have was a family joke handed down to his aunt and his dad from their aunts and dads. It occurred to Nathan that his dad and his aunt had the same dads and aunts as each other. It hadn't been long since he'd realised Maureen was his dad's sister. He always knew she was his aunt, but he hadn't made the connection.

After breakfast Maureen went to look for more things to wash. Nathan could hear her in the kitchen, humming along with the radio or the washing machine. His dad told him a joke once: Why do bees hum? Because they don't know the words. Nathan didn't think Maureen even knew she was humming all the time. And unlike a bee, she sang as well. If a song she knew came on the radio or was played in the middle of a television programme, Maureen couldn't help joining in. It could be quite annoying at the end of a film. Nathan didn't think he'd heard his aunt singing since Zoe had been missing though. Or at least not when his dad was in the house. It was funny how, because Nathan's sister wasn't there, his dad's sister never seemed to leave.

Nathan watched cartoons and read *Moonmen (and Women)*. There were new facts to share with Zoe when she came back. Moon dust was soft as flour but sharp as broken glass. It smelled and tasted of burned gunpowder and gave the astronauts lunar hay fever.

He rested his hand on his dad's laptop on the sofa next to him. He felt for warmth, like a detective feeling the bonnet of a car. He remembered how PC Kari had done the same thing to the grass in the park. The laptop was cold.

Nathan listened for the sound of his aunt, still humming in the kitchen. He lifted the laptop lid and touched the Z key. Before the screen was fully awake, seventeen emails arrived with a loud ping and the Twitter bird was jumping up and down in the dock at the bottom, trying to catch his attention. Nathan quickly closed the lid.

He listened again for his aunt in the kitchen and then opened the laptop again. He turned the sound down and looked at Twitter. There were thirteen new Tweets mentioning Zoe. Nathan opened the *Where is Zoe Love?* Facebook page. Ignoring the twenty-nine Facebook notifications, he scrolled down his dad's timeline. Every two or three posts there was an advert or a sponsored link that somehow related to missing, kidnapped or murdered teenagers. There were YouTube recommendations for videos of suspicious men in white vans idling outside schools that the internet thought his dad might also like. There were sponsored links to private detective agencies, solicitors and second hand vans, and an Amazon promotion for DVDs of *Gone Girl* and *Gone Baby Gone*.

Nathan was careful not to open any of the unread Facebook notifications or messages, even though he wanted to. If there was good news, Nathan would love to be the one to break it to his dad. He imagined telling him that Zoe had been found alive and well, knowing how that would make his dad feel. Nathan would even have preferred that to bringing her back from space. He looked at a few of the Facebook comments his dad had already read.

'Is this her?' one asked, above a picture of a girl who was about Zoe's age. She did actually look like Zoe, but from the clothes the girl was wearing and the old-fashioned cars and shops in the background, it was obvious the photo had been taken at least twenty years ago. Nathan followed a long thread of Facebook replies back to the comment that started the thread: 'Spoiler alert. Face it. This girl is dead!'

Nathan leaned over to the arm of the sofa and picked

up the house phone. He pressed the button and listened to the dialling tone. He put the phone back in its cradle, repositioning it to make sure it was definitely recharging and then he checked the dialling tone again, pretending to be the father of a missing teenager.

The house phone had rung more times since Zoe had been away than it had in the entire ten years they'd had it. The loud ring made Nathan and his dad jump every single time and his dad would practically throw himself across the room to answer it, as though the phone might explode or – far worse – stop ringing if he didn't reach it in time. Almost every call was someone asking if there was any news. Nathan's dad told them all the same thing. As soon as he heard anything, they would be the first to know.

The sound of his dad's mobile was more familiar and so it was less of a shock when it rang. But the ringtone was too chirpy and upbeat. Nathan knew his dad could have changed it easily enough or Nathan could have shown him how. But as Zoe had chosen the ringtone, 'Shrill Frog Song' was now part of the Zoe Love Museum.

Nathan looked at the photos of Zoe on his dad's laptop. Relatives had shared some of their pictures, taken when Zoe was younger than Nathan was now, and some from before he was even born. Nathan looked at those and at the two hundred or so pictures of the sky and street furniture that his dad had insisted on copying onto the laptop before allowing the police to take Zoe's phone away. Nathan zoomed in on the incidental tower blocks and office buildings in the distance or on the edges of the photos. The bigger he made the images, the more impossible it was to see any detail.

He took the laptop over to the window and held it up to the glass and compared the thread pattern on the curtains in one of the photos to the real-life living room curtains. Zoe had obviously taken the photo from there. Apart from the curtains, everything else in the picture had changed.

The sky was long gone.

Nathan worked out which other skies had been photographed from the living room window and which pictures Zoe had taken from the kitchen and from the bedrooms and the bathroom upstairs. He zoomed in on the edges of rooftops and aptly named Sky dishes. The majority of Zoe's indoor sky photos had been taken from her bedroom. Nathan wondered what she was looking at when she sat for hours at her window. Was it really just clouds and stars or was she feeling homesick? Did Zoe wish she was an alien again? *They wouldn't take you if you didn't want to go*. She'd told him. *It's not a kidnapping*.

He flattened his nose against the window and followed the slow movement of a wispy puff of cloud across the sky. He followed it for so long he didn't want to look away or even blink, in case that was the moment the cloud morphed into the Starship Enterprise. He couldn't remember if clouds actually moved or if it was the sky behind or both, and he'd forgotten all the names Zoe had taught him. All he could remember was Columbus wasn't a cloud.

Nathan knew the Earth was moving. Maybe the aliens had brought Zoe back and her house wasn't where they'd expected it to be. There were no arrows to lead them to it. Zoe could be on the other side of the world now. Nathan watched the wispy cloud until it was almost over the house. Before it disappeared, he waved. Just in case.

He went back over to the sofa and looked at the photos Zoe had taken that weren't of the sky. His dad had stared at each one a hundred times, hoping to find some significance in his daughter's random, uninhabited photos. Who was it that had last made a call from the empty phone box before Zoe took the picture, and who caught a bus from the deserted bus stop? Nathan's dad had stared at the drain covers and at the traffic island and the swimming pool, wondering who had just crossed the road or last swam in the empty blue water of the lido. Whose body was about to break the surface of the water? What was the deeper meaning in the photo of the rubbish skip? Who did the mattress sticking out of the skip belong to? Who had slept on it?

Nathan mimicked his dad, enlarging the picture of the empty park bench, trying to read the name on the brass plaque on the back of the bench, but just making it blurrier. It was like Zoe was playing a cruel joke on her dad. Leaving clues behind for him. All of them just out of his focus. What did the stencilled number on the grey dustbin mean? What was so special about the number twenty-one? Nathan thought Zoe just liked how the stencil looked pretty on the side of such a plain and ugly bin, and so she took a photo of it. But he couldn't tell his dad that. His dad needed it all to be a solvable puzzle, or else how would he be able to go on?

Nathan closed the laptop and returned to his library book – the edge of the known Universe is forty-six billion light years away from the Sun. Astronauts scratch their noses on Velcro inside their helmets. He read aloud to Officer Dibble, purring on the sofa next to him.

"On the first American human spaceflight, electrodes were stuck onto the astronauts' bodies, Dibs. To measure their heart rates and calculate the amount of air in their lungs. And look," he held the book up to show Officer Dibble the picture. "They've got tattoos like my mum had. So that the NASA doctors knew where to stick the electrodes on the astronauts."

Nathan put the book down and lifted up his shirt. He searched his skin for the dots Zoe had drawn on him when their mum was alive. He wished Zoe had used permanent ink like the time she'd helped him draw his own snake tattoo. Nathan had managed to draw the end of the tail on his left hand and he'd drawn the snake's body up his arm as far as his shoulder, but he couldn't reach any further. Zoe offered to help. Nathan gave her the pen, and starting with the head, she drew on his hand and up his arm, right across his shoulders until the two halves of the snake met on his back.

When Nathan went downstairs to show his parents his tattoo, his dad laughed and his mum said, "Oh for Christ sake, Zoe." Nathan's mum was bad cop that day. She took him up to the bathroom and told him to stand in front of the mirror. His mum went into her bedroom and came back with another mirror, which she held behind him like a hairdresser and he saw: 'GULLIBLE BROTHER' written on his back. It took three weeks of baths to completely wash it off.

Nathan thought about times like that when he really thought he hated his sister. He thought about her flossing her teeth and dropping the disgusting dental floss on his shoulder for him to discover later. Or when they played hide and seek and it was Nathan's turn to hide and he'd be in their parents' wardrobe behind the coats, or outside in the tiny shed, while Zoe sat in the living room, watching television, or in the kitchen making herself a sandwich, not counting to a hundred and with no intention of doing any seeking.

When Nathan was five or six, Zoe taught him to say swearwords, hoping he would one day repeat them in front of their mum and dad. When he eventually said fuck, their mum didn't tell Nathan off but instead explained calmly that it was a 'bad word'. A few days later when their dad stubbed his toe and swore, Nathan had put his hand over his open mouth and said, "Fuck's a bad word, Dad." Everyone couldn't stop laughing, especially Zoe. Nathan was the last to laugh, because he didn't really get the joke. Realising he might never be pranked or annoyed by his sister ever again made Nathan feel so anxious he thought he was going to throw up.

He listened to Officer Dibble purring next to him and his aunt humming to herself in the kitchen. He imagined they were both robots. He stroked the cat, combining the stroke with a search of his fur, to see if there was an implant under the cat's skin. Officer Dibble had been a missing person once. A misca. No one had called the police or made posters or filmed a television appeal. There were no India99s or Deltas. Nathan supposed the Deltas might have eaten Officer Dibble. Nathan's mum and dad had just waited for the cat to return, which he eventually did. Strolling through the back door into the kitchen, looking for his saucer, as though he hadn't been anywhere at all.

The cat stopped purring. His ears twitched like radar. He was staring at the empty doorway out into the hall. Nathan heard the front door. It would only open as far as the chain would allow and the door slammed against the chain. Maureen came out of the kitchen. Nathan got up and went out to the hall. His aunt spoke to somebody through the gap. She unhooked the chain and opened the front door.

It was Nathan's dad. He was out of breath, as though he'd been running. He put his hands on his knees for a moment until he got his breath back. Nathan thought about getting him a paper bag to blow into, like Zoe did once when she lost her inhaler. She told Nathan afterwards that it wasn't her asthma. She was having a panic attack. Nathan wondered if his dad was having a panic attack. When his dad stood up straight, he was almost too excited to speak.

"The police have found some more photos on Zoe's phone."

18

The geeks – that was what Anne Marie called the Hi-Tech Crime and the Digital Capability units – had recovered nineteen deleted photos from Zoe's phone and from the Cloud. Anne said the geeks were incredibly pleased with themselves for being able to say they'd found photos of clouds hidden in *the* Cloud. Zoe had probably deleted them from her phone because they were so badly out of focus. The geeks also found two blurred images that looked like accidental pocket photos. They discovered another empty phone box picture and a photo of Zoe's favourite tree, still standing and down at the bottom of the park where it belonged. When the FLOs brought the deleted photos to the house to show Nathan's dad however, it was the last picture they were especially keen to share. Nathan thought either the FLOs or the geeks had rearranged the order of the pictures, so they could save the most dramatic until last. It was a photo of a boy. A human boy.

The police didn't know who the boy was. They'd hoped Nathan's dad could help. He couldn't, and now he was searching for two teenagers instead of one. He asked the FLOs if he could post the picture on the *Where is Zoe Love?* Facebook page. The FLOs talked about correct procedure and data protection, but after failing to get through to a senior officer on the phone for advice, they said something about resources and needing all the help they could get, and they told Nathan's dad to go ahead. He posted the photo on Facebook with two questions: 'Do you know who this is?' and 'Is this you?' It didn't take long for the usual theories, jokes, accusations and arguments to mount up. The comments under the photo were soon so far off topic that Nathan's dad had to repost the picture and start again.

In the afternoon he went to Zoe's school and stood outside the gates showing the picture of the mystery boy to any girls coming in and out of the school, until a parent complained and a teacher asked Nathan's dad to leave. He gave a copy of the photo to the teacher and she promised to show it to the whole school at the next assembly.

The photo of the boy fitted all the requirements for a passport or a missing poster. He was looking directly at the camera and the background was simple, too simple to work out where the picture had been taken beyond it being somewhere outdoors. Nathan's dad wondered if the boy was somehow connected to the all the other objects and places photographed by Zoe. He could be the missing piece of the jigsaw she'd left behind. Maybe the mystery boy caught a bus that left the bus stop before Zoe took a picture of it. Was he making a call from the phone box? Was he calling Zoe? Had the boy crossed any of the roads in Zoe's photos or swam in the empty pool and sat on the park bench, maybe even next to Zoe?

"He looks all right, doesn't he, Nath? Do you think? He looks like a nice kid. Don't you think?"

It was like the mystery boy had asked for Zoe's hand in marriage and her dad was considering his suitability. The boy did have a nice smile, Nathan agreed. His dad was sure the boy was smiling because of Zoe, either because she made him happy or because she'd asked him to smile and he wanted to please her. Nathan's dad speculated on the boy's age and even his name. Nathan agreed he was maybe a little older than Zoe. He needed even less time to think of a name for the boy than when he'd named a planet David Bowie.

"Alex," Nathan said, so quickly that his dad thought Nathan must know who the boy was after all. It took him a while to convince his dad he just thought he looked like an Alex.

Maureen warned Nathan's dad about making something out of nothing. He told her nothing was all he had. Maureen rolled her eyes.

"I'm just glad there was someone who Zoe thought was

worthy of taking a picture of."

All Nathan could think of was that his sister might have gone into Space with someone else instead of him.

"I wonder why she deleted the photo," Nathan's dad said. "Do you think it was because of me?" he looked to Nathan for an answer. "Because she thought I would have scared him away?"

Maureen told her brother to stop torturing himself.

When the geeks recovered the deleted photos, they also knew the time and date each one had been taken. There was nothing on Zoe's phone relating to the time or day the picture of the boy was taken. And apart from the default national and religious holidays and a few family birthdays, there were no entries whatsoever in the calendar on Zoe's phone. Nathan's dad checked the International Space Station calendar as though that might hold the answer and he found last year's kitchen calendar and looked at that. Nathan suspected his dad had only kept the kitchen calendar because it had Nathan's mum's handwriting on. There was a Katherine Love museum too.

The date that Zoe – presumably it was her – took the photo of the mystery boy did seem familiar to Nathan for some reason. He just didn't know what it was. When Nathan and his dad were alone watching TV, it came to him. He went upstairs to his bedroom, tipped the yellow plastic bucket of Lego out onto his bed and picked his red National Space Centre notebook out from amongst the bricks. He went downstairs and gave the notebook to his dad.

"What is it?" his dad said, reading the cover but not taking the notebook.

"Look inside."

His dad took the book and opened it carefully, as though it might be a practical joke and a snake might fly out. He read the first few pages, unsure what any of it meant, recognising Nathan's handwriting and visibly excited by Zoe's notes in red. It looked like she was marking her brother's homework. And then his dad realised what he was reading.

"We're going to have to show this to the police," he said. He reached for the phone.

"No, but look though, Dad," Nathan said. He leaned over and turned the pages to show his dad the three-month gap, between 'the subjict' leaving the house and turning left, and three months later leaving the house and turning right. The night Zoe said she couldn't remember where she was going, other than to look at 'a good sky'.

"Can't you see it, Dad?" Nathan said. His dad looked blankly at him. "December 14th. It's the same date *as that picture*."

"Oh my God," his dad said. "She was with that boy."

Before calling the police, Nathan's dad scanned every page of the notebook onto his laptop. He told Nathan he was worried the police might lose it, and Nathan knew he wasn't talking about the notebook. His dad didn't want to lose Zoe's handwriting. The notebook was part of the museum now.

19

Zoe had officially been a misper for a week. The anniversary brought more people to the house than usual. Every time the doorbell went Nathan had to go downstairs to meet someone new. He thought his dad was worried people might start to believe some of the things written about him on social media. He wanted everyone who came to the house to see that Nathan was there, both alive and well.

Because it was an anniversary people brought flowers and 'thinking of you' cards. Maureen had to buy more vases from the charity shop. The living room smelled like fabric conditioner. When the FLOs came to take Nathan's notebook, his dad showed them a bunch of mixed yellow flowers, still wrapped in cellophane.

"These came last night," he said. "There was an envelope with fifty quid in it but no note. Do you think they might have been left by whoever's got Zoe? Or by someone who knows where she is and feels guilty about it? Maybe they're from Alex?"

"Who's Alex?" Janet said.

"The boy in the photograph. We made up a name."

Janet looked at Nathan's dad as though he was an idiot. Even Nathan thought it sounded daft. He should never have told the FLOs about giving the boy a name. Janet took the flowers and pulled five cashpoint fresh ten-pound notes out of the envelope.

"Shouldn't you be wearing gloves?" Nathan's dad said.

"You can't dust flowers for prints, Steve," Janet said. Nathan thought she was lying. He thought the FLOs were growing fed up with his dad. When he gave them Nathan's notebook, they didn't seem particularly excited by it. They were more annoyed with Nathan for not giving it to them sooner.

At lunchtime Maureen arrived with news that 'WHERE IS ZOE LOVE?' was spelled out in plastic letters on the front of the Ritzy, as though it was a film the cinema was showing. And then three girls from Zoe's school came to the house. They were wearing *Where is Zoe Love?* T-shirts they'd made in their art class. They'd made shirts for Nathan and his dad too and they both had to put them on so the girls could take selfies with them. They took a lot of photos. With Nathan and his dad and then just with his dad and then just with Nathan. One of the girls ordered everyone about like she was an official wedding photographer. Nathan's dad showed them the photo of Alex and they all shook their heads and apologised. Nathan wasn't convinced they even knew who Zoe was.

He didn't recognise any of the girls and they hadn't been to the house before. They weren't either of the two numbers in the contacts on Zoe's phone. Nathan thought they only made the T-shirts because they wanted to feel involved, like the people who rang the helpline after the television appeal and who posted time-wasting lies on Facebook. When Zoe came back – not if, *when*, Nathan still knew that – she would be more popular than before she left. Nathan knew that would annoy Zoe as much as it did him. The three girls reminded him of people who only became David Bowie fans after he was gone and didn't know any of his songs except for 'Let's Dance' and 'Heroes'. Zoe really hated that. Nathan thought the girls might be the dicks she'd mentioned. When they left Nathan went back up to his room. He closed his bedroom door and sat on the floor next to his bed. He opened *Moonmen (and Women)* and tried to concentrate. He could already hear new voices downstairs and waited for his name to be called out again.

He pulled the drawer out from under his bed and took his Space Torch out of his backpack. He pushed the library book under the bed and rolled in after it. He had to push a crumpled cardboard box away with his feet to give himself enough room. He lay under the bed and pretended he was in quarantine after coming back from the Moon.

In *Moonmen (and Women)* he'd read about the returning Apollo 11 astronauts spending twenty-one days in a specially converted trailer called the Mobile Quarantine Facility, to stop them spreading space flu. In the picture in the library book, the silver 'MQF' (Mike Quebec Foxtrot) reminded Nathan of the caravan Zoe had bought them crepes from at last year's Lambeth Country Show. He wondered what would happen if his sister wasn't home in time for this year's show.

For a weekend every summer, the Lambeth Country Show took over the park behind their estate. It was mostly the same stuff there every year. There were jousting knights on massive horses and a dog show and birds of prey displays. The same farm animals were there every year. When Nathan's yoga teacher had said most children in London had never seen a cow before, she obviously hadn't been to the Lambeth Country Show. Nathan always saw his teachers there. Zoe said they had to pretend to be pleased to bump into pupils, when what they really wanted to do was get as far away from work as possible at weekends and in the school holidays.

Last year at the Country Show one of Zoe's teachers had come over to say hello. She said that she looked forward to seeing Zoe at school next term. The teacher said it like she was joking, because she thought it was so unlikely. Zoe had been off school so many times, either because of her sensitivity to light and sound or with her headaches, her migraines or her asthma. Nathan was surprised the teacher had even recognised Zoe because she was at school so rarely. Zoe told Nathan that was *how* the teachers recognised her. She said she was 'conspicuous by her absence'.

Zoe had been back on Earth for two months when they went to last year's Country Show. She must have been almost fully human again by then. She might even have forgotten she'd ever left the planet if Nathan didn't keep reminding her about it. Even at a Country Show he found excuses to bring the subject up. Like when he went on the space rocket ride at the fair or saw a moon-shaped lamp for sale on the Oxfam stall. Any excuse. Yoda constructed out of cauliflowers and cabbages in the vegetable sculpture competition. A man dressed as Mister Spock handing out flyers and balloons for British Gas.

Zoe still had some symptoms left from her alien abduction then. She could hear tapping sounds that no one else could. Tinnitus her dad said. And she was still predicting (*guessing*, her dad said) weather. She hadn't walked in her sleep for a while though and her eyes weren't sensitive to light anymore. The sunglasses she wore to the Country Show were because of the sunny day. And she'd stopped hiding the cuts and scratches on her arms under long-sleeves. Zoe had told Nathan before that she was proud of her space scars. She compared them to their mum keeping her radiation tattoos after her treatment was over. Zoe called her cuts and scratches, and their mum's tattoos, 'badges of honour'. Souvenirs from the journeys they'd both been on.

They sat on the grass at the Lambeth Country Show, watching a group of African drummers and some boys from the posh school in Dulwich demonstrating touch rugby, and then they went to the fair. Zoe stood with their dad while Nathan went on the rides on his own. Every time a ride spun past his sister and his dad or if he caught sight of them when he was halfway down the inflatable Mega slide, he wondered what they were talking about. Did Zoe tell her dad more about her alien abduction than she told him? Nathan had always thought their dad knew nothing about Zoe sneaking out at night. Now he knew that wasn't the case. Maybe his dad knew more than anyone.

They left the fair and the four of them (their dad had won a massive Smurf toy by hooking ducks on the end of a pole) went into the longest, hottest tent at the Country Show, the one with the vegetable sculpture competition in.

Their dad shrugged off the potato dinosaurs, pineapple parrots and pop stars made from carrots and onions, describing it all as 'a bit of a busman's holiday'. Afterwards he went to find a toilet and left Nathan and Zoe queuing at the silver crepes van. Nathan couldn't decide to have sweet or savoury and eventually chose sweet – Nutella and banana – while Zoe had cheese and spinach, which Nathan immediately wanted too. They sat under the shade of a tree with their crepes and waited for their dad. Nathan asked Zoe what a busman's holiday was.

"It's a saying. It means when you go on holiday and end up doing something there that you'd normally do when you were at work."

"I don't get it."

"If you're a busman, or *bus woman,* and you go on holiday, and then while you're there you spend your time going on bus trips. That's a busman's holiday."

Nathan tried connecting Zoe's explanation to what his dad had said in the vegetable sculpture tent.

"I get it now," he lied. "Do you think they're watching us?"

Zoe gave him a confused look. "The busmen?"

"No, silly," Nathan said. "Aliens."

"Do you ever think about anything else?"

Nathan shook his head. He didn't know how *she* could ever think about anything else.

"But *do* you though?" he said. "Do you think they're up there watching us?"

"Us generally or us specifically?"

"I don't know what either of those are."

"Do you mean are they watching all of us earthlings, or just me and you?"

"Just me and you."

"Right now?"

"Yes."

"I don't know."

"But if they were, would they need a telescope to see us or would their eyes just be mega powerful."

Zoe sighed. "Do you ever relax? Do you ever stop asking questions? Try not speaking. Go on. See if you can. Get your mates to sponsor you. Give something back to society."

Nathan held his breath.

"You don't have to hold your breath to stop talking."

He puffed his cheeks out and let out a big breath. He rolled over onto his back, looking up at the sky, searching for spaceships.

"At school," he said, "we had to name something you can see from space. Did you know you can see the Pyramids, the Great Wall of China and the Grand Canyon?" Nathan knew what two of those were.

"You can see loads of other things too," Zoe said. "Cities and mountains, rivers and motorways, the Greenhouses of Almería."

"What's that?" Nathan said. He closed one eye and watched a plane. He could see the orange EasyJet on the tail. He wondered where it was going or where it had been, who was on it and if they were watching a film or eating lunch. Who was in the toilet causing the thin white cloud that followed the plane across the sky?

"There are thousands of these enormous plastic greenhouses in Spain," Zoe said. "In Almería I presume. It's where all Dad's Spanish vegetables come from. And a lot of the stuff in that tent we were just in. John Lemon, the Tower of Onion, Potato Modern and all the other *hilariously* named vegetable sculptures. They were probably all grown in the Greenhouses of Almería."

Nathan watched the contrails of another plane. It crossed over the others already in the sky, forming an almost perfect Union Jack.

"Can you feel that?" Zoe said. She sat up straight and took her sunglasses off.

Nathan sat up. He looked around. "What?"

"The Earth spinning."

"I can't feel anything."

"Don't you feel dizzy?"

"No. Do you?"

"Like I'm seasick. Like I'm trapped in a washing machine."

Nathan sat really still. He pressed his open palms into the grass by his sides, like Zoe.

"I think I can feel it now," Nathan said.

"It's stopped," Zoe said. She put her sunglasses back on and lay down in the shade of the tree.

Nathan tried to feel the Earth beneath them spin. He closed his eyes and held his breath, hoping it would make him feel dizzy.

"Did you know that's where Dad met Mum?" Zoe said.

Nathan opened his eyes. Zoe was sitting up. She was watching their dad, walking towards them, alongside the row of charity stalls, looking at old books and knitted animals. He was holding two yellow balloons.

"Where?" Nathan asked Zoe.

"His fruit and veg stall," Zoe said. "Mum was a customer. Dad used to say she came for Brussel sprouts and left with his heart."

"That's madness."

"Other people would say it was romantic."

Nathan watched their dad approaching. He was wearing a grey Lonsdale vest top, displaying both ends of his spectacular snake tattoo. His Elvis shades were on top of his head. Keeping the sun off 'his napper'. One day Nathan would have muscles like his dad.

"Do you miss Mum, Zoe?" Nathan asked.

Zoe yawned. "Like you wouldn't believe."

"Why wouldn't I believe?"

"It's a saying, you fool."

"Like busman's holiday?"

Zoe pushed her sunglasses down her nose and looked over the top of them. They both watched their dad, walking towards them with the yellow balloons.

"Hello, you two," their dad said. He gave them both a balloon. Zoe told him she was nearly fifteen but took one anyway.

"What did you buy?" she asked.

Their dad held up a carrier bag with the same 'Hands off our Homes' message printed on it as the balloons.

"Info," he said.

Nathan and Zoe got up and they all walked back home. Nathan tried leaving the Smurf behind, but Zoe said, "Don't forget your new friend, Nathan." And he had to go back and get it.

And then Zoe let her balloon go, she claimed accidentally, but Nathan knew it was deliberate, so she could watch the balloon float high into the blue sky, higher than the contrails and the EasyJets. Nathan watched the balloon as well, until his neck was stiff and the sun hurt his eyes and he couldn't look anymore.

Later on, they ate their dinner in the garden. They could hear the reggae and steel band music coming from the main stage in the park. Their mum said once that it was like living next door to Glastonbury Festival.

20

When Nathan realised Zoe might not be back in time for this year's Country Show he felt sick and panicky. He started to think about what else he'd miss. What if there was no Christmas this year because of Zoe? He couldn't imagine his dad buying him an Easter egg or making them pancakes on Pancake Day. It was one of the only days of the year his dad really enjoyed cooking. And there wouldn't be any firework displays while Zoe was still missing. No Halloween or holidays, no last-minute strolls across the park to the Lido with his dad on the first hottest day of the year. There'd be no Father's Day if Zoe wasn't back. Nathan was sure of that. His dad would never allow himself his own special day. He'd heard him say to Maureen and to the FLOs what a terrible father he was for coming home drunk and not checking his daughter was in her room before he went to sleep.

Nathan had been underneath his bed now for half an hour and his dad hadn't been to check on him. He'd heard people arrive and leave but his dad hadn't called out his name. He wondered how long he could stay under the bed before his dad noticed he was missing too.

Since the police had found the deleted photos, and especially the picture of Alex, Nathan's dad was like a dog with a bone. He'd completely forgotten about Nathan going back to school. He didn't seem so bothered about him becoming a doctor or a lawyer anymore. Nathan hadn't left the house for two days. He wasn't allowed to go to the shops or to play on the estate or to go to Arthur's house, and he definitely wasn't allowed anywhere near the park. He was starting to think the only way he'd ever leave the house again was if the aliens came and took him away from it. He might have believed his dad was worried about him and didn't want to risk losing him, but Nathan thought that, really, what his dad didn't want was for the

Zoe Love Museum to be disturbed. Just by being Zoe's brother, Nathan was another exhibit. He was no more or less important or significant than a half-drunk bottle of Oasis or the dust on Zoe's dressing table. Nathan's dad was so focused on finding his daughter he'd forgotten he had a son as well.

Nathan's quarantine lasted uninterrupted for nearly an hour. It ended when someone knocked on his bedroom door. At first, he thought the five knocks was Zoe, using their secret *Close Encounters* knock. Then the door opened and he saw Craig's black Levi's, the same kind of jeans he always wore. Different pairs, but always Levi's and always black. He saw Craig's espadrilles too. Black. No socks. Nathan didn't think Craig ever wore socks. Even if it was raining or snowing.

"Hiding from someone?" Craig said, bending down and lifting the edge of the quilt.

"I'm in quarantine."

"What from?"

"I've been to the Moon. I don't want to give everyone flu."

"Makes sense. How long does it last?"

"What? Moon flu?"

"The quarantine."

"Three weeks."

"I better keep my distance till then then."

Craig stood up and sat on the bed. The bed springs creaked under his weight and the bed sagged. Nathan worried he might be squashed. Nathan's dad and Craig used to be as twin-like as Nathan and Zoe. As alike as two FLOs. There was a photo of them on the mantelpiece in the living room, both wearing matching black bomber jackets. Nathan's dad said they looked like nightclub bouncers. But Craig didn't go to the gym anymore. He ate and drank too much, and with every second helping and 'one for the road' Craig looked less like his twin.

"Left or right?" Craig said. He held both his closed hands down over the side of the bed. Nathan worked out which fist contained the best, or at least the largest, prize. He thought the swallow tattoo between Craig's right thumb and forefinger was larger than usual and the ink thinner because the skin beneath it was stretched.

"Right," Nathan said.

"Sure?"

"Definitely."

Craig opened his hand, revealing a Kinder Surprise. He held it there until Nathan reached over and took it. Craig closed his hands and pulled them away out of sight. He sat back on the bed, making the springs creak again. Nathan could see the top of the *South London Boys Forever 2013* tattoo on Craig's ankle.

"You can change your mind if you want," Craig said.

"It's all right, thank you."

"No wonder greengrocers are going out of business," Craig said. Nathan heard him biting deliberately noisily into some kind of fruit.

"Is it a plum?" Nathan said.

"Good guess."

"It wasn't a guess."

"Well, you're right anyway. It is a plum. And a particularly juicy one. It's too late to change your mind now though you realise?"

"That's okay." Nathan unwrapped the Kinder Surprise.

His dad always used to come home from work with the smell of whatever were the freshest or most popular items on the stall that day. Sometimes he'd come home smelling of potatoes or bananas. Nathan didn't like the banana peel smell because it reminded him of cheesy feet or going past a farm with the car window open. He preferred it when his dad came home smelling of strawberries or peaches. It usually meant he had some with him. Nathan thought Craig must have sold a lot of cherries today. He also smelled like he'd drunk a lot of alcohol.

Nathan rolled the Kinder Surprise foil into a ball and flicked it out from under the bed. He asked Craig where his dad was.

"He's gone outside to think for a while."

Nathan broke the Kinder egg into two halves and put the plastic pod containing the surprise on the cover of the library book by his side.

"What was the book you were reading?" Craig said as though he could see through the thick mattress he was sitting on.

Nathan moved the Kinder surprise so that it obscured the *(and Women)* sticker. He didn't want to have to explain what it meant and, more importantly, who'd stuck it to the front of the book. Every conversation couldn't be about Zoe.

"It's about astronauts and the men who went to the Moon," Nathan said.

"What's that rocket on the cover called?"

"Saturn Five."

"Is that a good one?"

"It's the tallest rocket ever built. Higher than the Statue of Liberty and Big Ben." Nathan bit into the chocolate.

"Where's it off to on the cover?"

"It's taking Apollo Eleven into orbit."

"Houston, we have a problem." Craig's American accent was bad. It made Nathan laugh.

"That's Apollo Thirteen," Nathan said.

"My mistake."

Nathan really hoped he had a friend like Craig when he was older. Someone to go to the football with and share identical tattoos. Craig was always there for Nathan's dad – *twenty-four seven* – but he didn't ask him how he was all the time. Craig didn't say 'any news?' or ask how Nathan's dad was coping or if he was holding up. He did say a lot of inappropriate things, and he could make Nathan's dad lose his temper with his poor taste jokes sometimes. Like last night when Craig came to the house on his way home. He was in the kitchen, eating the huge bunch of grapes he'd brought from work for Nathan's dad as though he was recovering from an operation. Craig looked at the picture of Zoe on the leaflet stuck to the fridge and asked Nathan's dad when he thought the police would use age-progression software to show how Zoe might have changed. Nathan's dad threw his *World's Best Dad* mug at the wall. He just couldn't bear thinking of Zoe being gone for long enough to look any different. Nathan wanted to tell his dad that time moved slower in outer space and Zoe probably wouldn't have changed at all.

Craig shifted his weight on Nathan's bed. The springs creaked like a pirate ship.

"Perhaps the rocket people should have skipped straight to Apollo Fourteen," Craig said.

"Why?"

"Thirteen is unlucky, isn't it? They should have jumped from Apollo Twelve to Apollo Fourteen. Was there even an Apollo Fourteen?"

"Alan Shepard, Stuart Roosa, Edgar Mitchell," Nathan said proudly.

"Who are they?"

"The Apollo Fourteen astronauts."

"You should go on *Mastermind*. I suppose you know all the names."

"Yes," Nathan said. He hoped Craig didn't test him almost as much as he hoped that he did.

"Do you want half of the Kinder egg?" Nathan said. He was relieved that Craig knew enough about ten-year-old boys to say no. Nathan stuffed the last piece of chocolate in his mouth.

"I used to think they were called kinda eggs," Craig said, pronouncing the 'i' with a 'y' sound.

"How can eggs be kinder?" Nathan said with a mouthful

of chocolate.

"Not *kinder*. I don't mean like nicer eggs. No. I mean, I thought they were *kind of* eggs. You know, like eggs but only kind of?"

Nathan laughed. He popped open the lid of the Kinder surprise pod with his teeth. He took out two halves of a plastic Hot Rod car and clicked them together. He opened the library book on the floor next to him and put the car on the surface of the Moon.

"Okay," Craig said. "Your two minutes begin now. How many men went to the Moon altogether?"

"Twelve," Nathan said. He picked up the hot rod and closed the library book, so Craig didn't think he was cheating. "There were six lunar landings altogether."

"Who's the geezer who played golf on the Moon?"

"Alan Shephard and two golf balls are still there."

"On the Moon?"

"Yes."

Nathan told Craig there were twenty-eight different objects that astronauts had left on the Moon. He'd been awake last night trying to memorise them all, like the names of the seven dwarfs or the French hens and turtledoves in 'The Twelve Days of Christmas'. He thought it might help him fall asleep where counting sheep and the moons of Saturn had failed. Twelve cameras, six flags, three lunar roving vehicles, two pairs of flight suit trousers, one pair of gloves, two golf balls and twelve pairs of space boots. When Nathan told Craig about the hundred bags of poo, wee and sick, Craig made a *Mastermind* beeping noise and told Nathan his time was up.

"What was the surprise?" Craig said.

"A hot rod car."

"Mine just had a stone in it," Craig said. "That's not even a *kind of* surprise."

Nathan laughed. He opened the library book again and wheeled the Kinder car across the Moon. He thought about the three lunar rovers the astronauts had left there. Even when they went to a different planet, humans had to leave their rubbish behind. Golf balls and cars, movie cameras and towels, the empty packaging from the space food they'd eaten or the flags they stuck in the ground to claim the Moon as their own.

Craig had gone so quiet that Nathan thought he might have fallen asleep. He pretended Craig was Richard Nixon, visiting him in his Mobile Quarantine Facility. There was a picture of the American President talking to the Apollo 11 astronauts in *Moonmen (and Women)*. They watched from a window while the President spoke to them through a microphone on a stand. He looked like he was singing them a song.

"Craig," Nathan said.

"Yes, Nathan."

"Do you believe in aliens?"

"I think I've met a few in my time."

"My sister has."

Craig didn't answer.

"I mean for real," Nathan said. "She really met them."

"I remember that," Craig said. He sounded tired, or sad.

"Do you think they could have come back? To take her away again?" Nathan said.

Craig didn't answer. Nathan wondered if he was one of the adults that believed. Perhaps he could ask Craig to go with him on his mission. Craig could get his own *Mission to Mars* spacesuit and *Guardians of the Galaxy* backpack and they could go and find Zoe together.

Nathan rolled out from under the bed until he could see Craig. He was lying on his back on the bed, staring up at the ceiling.

"The stars don't come out until the lights are off," Nathan said.

Craig looked down at him and forced a smile.

"I better get back down to your dad. Make sure he

doesn't do anything daft," Craig sat up on the edge of the bed and then stood above Nathan, like one of the rockets in the tower at the National Space Centre. He put his hands behind his back. "Left or right?"

Nathan chose left this time and Craig bent down and placed a sticky, wet plum stone in Nathan's hand.

"Eeurrgrh," Nathan said, throwing the stone on the floor and rolling back under the bed.

"Enjoy the rest of your quarantine," Craig said. He zipped his Harrington up over his beer gut, causing a bulge that made it look like he was shoplifting a frozen chicken.

Nathan listened to him walking down the stairs. Halfway down he heard Craig call out, "Get the kettle on, Stevie boy. If you haven't broken all the crockery, chucking it at the wall."

21

When Zoe had been missing for ten days Nathan and his dad were invited onto a breakfast television show. A car was coming early in the morning to take them to the TV studio and the FLOs would follow behind in their own car. Nathan asked why they couldn't all travel together, imagining a fast ride in a police vehicle with flashing blue lights.

"I'm sure the car the telly people are sending will be preferable to us all squashing into our old jalopy," Janet said.

"What's a jalopy?"

"I think it's a Peugeot," Janet said and both FLOs laughed. They were in good spirits. They seemed to be looking forward to the television show. Certainly more than Nathan's dad was. The two women looked like they'd been to the hairdressers and were wearing more make-up than usual. Nathan's dad, meanwhile, although he'd washed and shaved for the first time in ages, was dreading it. He was pacing the living room and going to the toilet a lot. Nathan heard him being sick.

A text message pinged on both FLO phones to say the car was waiting for them. Nathan's dad put the front door on the latch in case Zoe came home without her keys while they were out, and they walked through the estate to the main road.

The television car was as long and shiny as the FLOs' jalopy was short and covered in a layer of dust with *clean me* written on the bonnet. Their car looked like it had been dumped. The driver of the TV studio car got out and opened the door for Nathan and his dad like they were the Queen. When the engine started Bhangra music played, and the driver apologised. He turned it down and changed the station to a phone-in show about the news. Nathan hoped they didn't start talking about Zoe. The car was so quiet he thought it was electric or at least a hybrid. The engine's silence reminded him of the noise his mum's Beetle used to make. Nathan's dad used to say he could hear it coming when it was still in Streatham or Camberwell.

The TV car got stuck in traffic before they'd even left Brixton and Nathan's dad saw the opportunity to show Zoe's picture to the driver. He also showed him the photo of Alex, who people on Facebook were referring to as 'Zoe's boyfriend'. The driver said he didn't recognise the boy and he only knew Zoe from reading about her in the paper.

"I feel your pain, boss," he said. "I had a teenage daughter myself."

The traffic cleared, the car moved silently forward, and Nathan's dad sat back in his seat. Nathan guessed he was wondering what the driver meant when he said he *had* a teenage daughter. Was it because she was missing as well or because she dead? Nathan thought the driver's daughter was probably just twenty now and so not a teenager anymore.

Nathan checked behind to see if the FLOs were still following. The shiny leather car seat made a fart noise when he turned around on it, and so he checked for the FLOs at regular intervals. There was a box on the parcel shelf almost blocking his view. It was gold and shiny and decorated with a swirly pattern and looked like it contained something more valuable than tissues. Nathan thought they'd lost the FLOs and then he saw them two cars back. He was pleased with himself for guessing that because Anne Marie always sat on the right, she would be the driver.

When they got to the television studios Nathan's dad and the FLOs signed their names in a large book and they were all given ID badges, including Nathan. He pinned his to the waist of his school trousers. It was the first time he'd worn his school uniform since before Zoe had gone missing – or at least half of the uniform. He had his trousers and blazer on but wasn't wearing his school shirt and tie because his dad wanted them both to wear their *Where is Zoe Love?* T-shirts. His dad had a long-sleeved sweatshirt under his T-shirt to hide some of his tattoos. When he'd finally watched himself on a recording of the television appeal, the first thing Nathan's dad had said was that he wished he'd kept his hands off the table. He thought he looked like 'a thug'. Nathan had worried his dad might have made him wear his school cap, so he'd hidden it in Zoe's room. There was no way he was wearing a school cap on television. He didn't even really properly hide it. He just placed it on Zoe's dressing table as though it belonged there. His dad would never disturb a Zoe Love Museum exhibit.

A man called Oliver came out to the television studio reception. He shook everyone's hands, commenting on Nathan's 'pincer grip', and took them all through a pair of glass saloon gates to the 'green room', which wasn't green.

"Can I get you anything?" Oliver said. "Coffee? Tea? Water?" The FLOs said yes to coffee, Nathan's dad said no to everything. "How about you, Nathan? Gin and tonic?"

Nathan laughed. "No, thank you."

"I can get you a Coke out of the machine, if you like?" Oliver said.

"Coke Zero, please."

Oliver rolled his eyes. "I'll *see* what I can do, Mariah Carey," he winked at Nathan's dad. "I'll be back in a tick to take you through to make-up."

Nathan's dad looked horrified. "We won't need make-up, will we?"

Oliver studied his face for a second. "I'm sure you'll be fine."

Nathan's dad had shaved for the first time in over a week and he'd washed his hair. He'd had a shallow bath, but only after Maureen had insisted, as though he was seven years old. He was only in the bath for about five minutes and he kept his mobile phone on the window ledge with the shampoos and shower gels, as though the phone could never leave his side, like a gunfighter's six-shooter. Nathan was disappointed when Oliver didn't inspect his face. If he'd been allowed make-up, he was going to ask for an Adam Ant stripe.

Oliver left and Nathan's dad and the FLOs talked quietly, as though they were in a library or a church. The FLOs reminded Nathan's dad what he needed to say and told him not to be nervous. Nathan looked at his phone. His belly was rumbling. He hadn't eaten breakfast and really wanted one of the pastries piled high in a basket on the table at the centre of the room or even an apple (the only actual green things in the room) from the bowl next to it. He didn't know if he was allowed or if the food was even real. Auntie Maureen used to have plastic fruit in a bowl in her house. Nathan always thought it was mad, considering her dad and her brother were both greengrocers. Nathan's dad made a joke once about Maureen getting her plastic fruit from a plastic greengrocer. It reminded him of his dad's other joke about the paper shop blowing away.

Oliver came back with the drinks. He gave Nathan a glass bottle of Coke with a paper straw.

"I couldn't find any ice and lemon I'm afraid," he said, and winked again.

The producer came in and told Nathan's dad what to expect and how it would be painless and over before he knew it had even begun. A different woman clipped tiny microphones onto their T-shirts and put battery packs in the back pockets of their trousers. She asked them to make sure their phones were switched off and for a moment Nathan's dad looked like he might refuse, until Anne Marie offered to look after his phone. Nathan gave her his as well. He told her it had a good *Minions* game on it.

Oliver led Nathan and his dad through a large area full of people, typing on computers and talking on phones.

When they went past the make-up room Nathan saw a woman sitting in a chair and he was sure it was Beyoncé. There were television screens everywhere, some showing the news and others with yesterday's sport on. When half of the screens changed to a big picture of Zoe, even though Nathan and his dad had seen the same picture a million times, it startled them both.

Oliver showed them to a long sofa next to a desk where a man in a grey suit and a woman in a red dress were sitting. Nathan was so distracted by seeing his sister's face on television he immediately forgot the two presenters' names. Zoe was replaced on the screens by a competition to win a holiday. All you had to do was answer the question: Is Barracuda a country, a type of cheese or a fish? Nathan was only ten and he knew it was a fish. Somebody said, "Stand by," and a man behind a camera counted down and Nathan saw his dad on television, pulling the sleeves of his sweatshirt down over his tattooed hands. Then he saw himself and then it was the picture of Zoe again. The male presenter introduced a video. Zoe would have hated the way he pronounced David Bowie, with the Bow like cow instead of snow. 'It's *Bowie,*' she used to say. 'Like *Zoe*'.

Nathan had watched the same YouTube video with his dad, more times than any movie or cartoon. The last time they'd watched it to see if they could see Alex in the crowd. It was like a game of *Where's Wally?*

The sound on the video was turned down and replaced with a woman's voice, describing Zoe's last known movements. Even though there was no sound, Nathan knew everyone at the mural was singing 'Five Years'. Zoe was easier to spot than usual because there was a red circle drawn around her. When she stepped forward to put the first candle on the ground the red circle went with her as though she was about to score a goal on *Match of the Day*. Nathan saw himself for about two seconds. He didn't have a red circle around him. On television though, his make-up looked sick and he wished it was a weekend or half-term so his friends could see him on television. Arthur would be the most jealous. Arthur was going to be a famous rapper one day. He was going to have his own YouTube with a billion subscribers. But he'd never been on television.

The video finished and the female presenter asked Nathan's dad to describe the type of girl Zoe was. If they asked Nathan, he would have wanted to say 'weird', but his dad lied and said she was a normal fifteen-year-old girl. Zoe would have hated that. She could be a handful sometimes, his dad said, but they loved her, and they just wanted her back. That wasn't a lie.

The female presenter nodded and looked like she might cry. Everyone seemed so much sadder about Zoe than her dad did, but Nathan knew that wasn't true. He wished his dad would just break down or cry, to prove his sadness to everyone. Like the police and everyone on Facebook and Twitter who didn't think he was deserving of the *World's Best Dad* mug he'd smashed against a wall.

The male presenter said, "It's got to be an incredibly stressful time for you," he looked at Nathan. "For *both* of you. If it's okay, Steve, can I take you back to when you first realised Zoe might be missing. What time was that?"

"About half-five."

"In the morning?"

"In the evening. When she didn't come home from school."

The man seemed baffled by that. "You didn't notice she wasn't there the night before? Or the next morning before she would have ordinarily left for school?"

Nathan's dad looked down at his shoes. His wedding shoes, his funeral and birthday shoes, and now his breakfast television shoes. Nathan was wearing his best trainers. He'd hidden his school shoes in the Zoe Love Museum with his cap. He had considered putting the shoes in the space left between her Converse, because it seemed funny, but he'd put them toes-first under Zoe's bed instead. That was when he'd found an old grey cardboard folder with the Alien Guess Who? pictures inside. The police must have missed the folder or seen it and considered fifty or so pictures of aliens unimportant. Nathan couldn't believe Zoe had kept Alien Guess Who? He hid the folder under his mattress.

"I'd been out for a drink with some friends," Nathan's dad told the two TV presenters. "And I woke up late," he reminded Nathan of himself, making excuses when he'd forgotten his homework or his P.E. kit. "Because it was my day off," his dad said. "I should have checked her room and I didn't."

"You mustn't blame yourself, Steve," the female presenter said, tipping her head at a sympathetic angle.

"You do though, don't you?" Nathan's dad said.

"Zoe didn't take her phone with her," the male presenter said. "Isn't that unusual nowadays? And apparently she wasn't on social media?"

Nathan didn't like the way he said *apparently*, as though he thought his dad was lying.

"I know it makes her sound a bit strange," Nathan's dad said. "But she's not…she's…she's just a bit different I suppose." He half-smiled. Nathan thought he was thinking about how good Zoe being a bit different could be.

"And you lost your wife recently too," the woman said. "That must have been tremendously upsetting, especially for Zoe. A young girl losing her mother."

It was upsetting for a boy to lose his mother too. Why did everyone think only Zoe could be sad about it? And their mum wasn't lost anyway. She was dead. Nathan knew exactly where she was. They'd sprinkled her ashes in the walled garden in the park when no one was looking. Zoe had wanted to fire their mum into space in a rocket, but it was too expensive, and their dad suggested naming a star after her instead. They didn't do it officially or pay for a certificate. They went out into the back garden and chose a star. It took less than a minute. "That's Mum," Zoe had said, and she sounded so sure about it that there was no need for further discussion.

"Is there anything you'd like to say to Zoe, Steve?" the female presenter said. "If she's watching right now? Into that camera if you can." She pointed at the camera in front of them.

"If you're watching, Zoe," Nathan's dad said. "Please, please get in touch. Or leave a message, send a text, anything. Me and Nathan need you back."

Nathan knew how much Zoe hated the kind of television programmes that were on in the morning, and it was possible this was the one she hated the most. Even if the aliens had Freeview, Nathan was sure his sister would *not* be watching.

"And I believe the police have found a photo of a boy they need to identify?" the male presenter said. Nathan's dad nodded and the picture appeared onscreen. "If this is you or if you know this boy or if you think you recognise him, please get in touch," the presenter said. "The number is on the screen and there's a website link. And of course, everything will be on our website too."

"Yes," the female presenter said. "If anyone watching knows anything, however unimportant or trivial it might seem, please don't hesitate to get in touch. Let's get your sister home safe, Nathan."

Nathan's attention had drifted. Maureen had ironed sharp creases down the front of his school trousers. He'd tried smoothing them out in the posh car without success. He was positioning his legs so the creases were perfectly straight next to each other and he was thinking about his dad, always straightening pictures, not just at home but in other people's houses and in shops and restaurants. Zoe used to move the pictures at home ever so slightly. She'd tilt them back at the angle their dad had just straightened the pictures out of, as though the house was on a hill. Nathan almost laughed remembering it. Typically, their dad assumed Nathan was responsible, of course, which only encouraged Zoe to keep on doing it. Nathan didn't realise the female presenter was talking to him. He looked up to see her smiling at him. His face was on TV.

"You never really get used to seeing yourself on telly, Nathan," she said. "I think we should see if we can get Zoe home safe and well, don't you?"

"I'd know if she wasn't safe or well," Nathan said, irritated by the suggestion the woman could miraculously achieve what his dad and all the different police had so far failed to do.

"Nathan has a theory," his dad said. He looked at Nathan. "Because you're E.T. and Zoe is Elliott. That's right, isn't it, mate?"

"Zoe is E.T.," Nathan said. "*I'm* Elliott."

"I must admit I'm a little confused," the male presenter said.

"Nathan can probably explain it better than me," his dad said.

Nathan looked up at his dad and then at the man. His dad gave him a 'go ahead' nod.

"You know when Mike goes to the bald spot in the forest to look for E.T.?" Nathan said. "And Mike finds E.T. dying next to a river and he brings him home?"

"Mike is Elliott's brother," Nathan's dad said, helpfully. He looked to Nathan for confirmation.

Nathan nodded. "And when Mike brings E.T. home, Elliott is dying as well and so his mum gets scared and then the government come to their house in spacesuits, to stop them getting space flu like when Neil Armstrong went into the Mobile Quarantine Facility—"

"I'm afraid you've completely lost me too, now," the woman said. Everyone was looking at Nathan.

"It's where the astronauts went when they came back

from the Moon," he said. "It wouldn't have worked properly though, because there was a hole somewhere and Buzz Aldrin said he saw some ants walking through —"

"I think what Nathan is saying," his dad said, "is because *he* feels okay, Zoe must be okay as well."

The female presenter looked at Nathan. Her whole face said, *Aww*. "I see, Nathan. So that's how you know Zoe is all right?"

Nathan nodded. "I don't even think she'll have any cuts or bruises when she comes back this time, because she was more prepared for —"

"I'm afraid Nathan has a bit of a vivid imagination," his dad interrupted. He rested his hand on Nathan's knee. Nathan looked down at the head of the snake. His dad turned to face him, looking him squarely in the eye, and he said something to Nathan that he must have said a hundred times before. As far back as last April and as recently as three days ago. He'd just never said it on national television before, "Your sister has *not* been abducted by aliens."

The two television presenters shifted uncomfortably behind the desk. The cameraman smiled. The male presenter put a finger to his earpiece. The woman sitting next to him had tipped her head so far on its side, it was almost resting on her shoulder. She looked at Nathan as though he was a video of an animal doing something cute. And then the man said they'd be right back and an advert for soup came on.

Nathan's dad tried to speak but Oliver was there at his side, gesturing for him and Nathan to follow him. They walked back past the make-up room. Nathan looked for Beyoncé but she was gone. He'd wanted to get a selfie with her to show Arthur. Oliver took them back to the green room and the woman removed their microphones and battery packs.

"Well, they got what they wanted," Nathan's dad said to the waiting FLOs. "What a disaster."

"It wasn't that bad, Steve," Janet said. "The important thing is you've got the message across to a huge audience."

"Who now all think I've harmed Zoe somehow."

Anne Marie said, "We will need to talk about that, Steve," she mouthed, "The *cuts and bruises,*" as though Nathan didn't know how to lip-read.

Oliver walked with everyone back to the reception desk. They signed out and returned their name badges. Oliver said Nathan could keep his. Everyone was quiet on the walk back to the car park. Just the clip-clop of the FLOs' high heels on concrete and the sound of Tweets arriving on Nathan's dad's phone. In the green room before the interview Janet had said it might be best to not read anything online for a day or two because some of the comments, possibly even the majority, would be negative. She probably hadn't realised quite how negative. On the way to the car park Nathan's dad held his phone up to show the FLOs.

HAS ZOE BEEN ABDUCTED BY ALIENS?

He also showed them something on Facebook Nathan didn't understand:

Out of the mouths of babes and sucklings. Matthew 21:16

The FLOs went off to get their jalopy and Nathan and his dad walked a short distance to their car. The driver didn't get out to open the door this time. He played loud music on the radio all the way back to Brixton. When they were almost home and stuck in the same traffic as earlier, going in the opposite direction, Nathan's dad asked the driver if he had any cigarettes. The driver gave him a packet with two left in it and Nathan's dad asked him to drop them by the Tube. The driver pulled the car over. He didn't get out to open the door for them or say goodbye. Outside the Tube Nathan's dad asked a busker for a light and he smoked his first cigarette since Nathan's mum had died from Earth cancer. He lit his second from the end of the first and Nathan thought he might never stop. His dad didn't say it, but Nathan knew it was his fault that he was smoking again. His mission was more vital and urgent than before. He couldn't wait to go to bed.

22

Nathan was woken by a light in his room. He was too scared to move and he thought he might be paralysed. That's what happened to Zoe about a week after she came back from space. She had to get out of bed to go to school but she said she couldn't move. "I'm paralysed, Nathan," she said. Her dad dealt with this latest symptom of his daughter's alien abduction by tickling Zoe. She didn't laugh. She screamed at her dad and told him he was a fucking big child. But she did move though. So she wasn't paralysed. *"Not anymore!"* Zoe had shouted at her dad when he pointed that fact out to her.

Nathan watched the light as it swept across his bedroom, travelling through the galaxy on his ceiling, like a spaceship, passing Venus and Mars, Pluto and Mercury. The light made the glow-in-the-dark planets disappear into the black as it lit them up. The light wasn't anywhere near as bright as Zoe had described. There were actually two or three different lights now. White lights and blue lights. Nathan thought he might be dreaming, but it felt nothing like a dream. Maybe the dream the aliens woke you up from didn't feel like a dream.

The lights separated and dropped down the wall, the brightest one settling for a second or two on Nathan's backpack. He'd been feeling around for it but now he remembered he hadn't packed the bag and it was over on the other side of the room. He wasn't wearing his orange spacesuit either and he hadn't taken a Kwell. There was no address written on the back of his hand. If they took him now, they wouldn't know where to bring him back to. He was unprepared and he was incredibly frightened. Why had he thought he wouldn't have been frightened when they came?

He lay as still as he could and held his breath, using his bath time training, trying to recall Zoe's answers to

Alien Guess Who? – Did they have ears? Did they have eyes? Could they hear him or see him? Nathan's nose was itching. He wished he had a helmet on with Velcro inside. Why *was* he so terrified now? Wasn't this what he wanted? Hadn't he been preparing himself for over a week and maybe even his whole life for this exact moment?

He wanted to call out to his dad but didn't want to give himself away. He had the feeling that if he opened his mouth no sound would come out anyway. He imagined aliens small enough to fly inside his open mouth, like the giant cockroaches and chinches Arthur said crawled into your mouth in Sierra Leone when you were asleep. Nathan put his lips together as tightly as he could. If he did call out to his dad, what if his dad ignored him? He might still be sulking because Nathan had told the whole television-watching world about Zoe's cuts and bruises.

The lights in his bedroom reminded Nathan a bit of PC Kari's Alpha Zulu torch – Lowlight. Flashing. Spot. Flashing. Lowlight. Spot. The aliens must be searching for him. They probably had a beam that could reach across the Universe and into the past. A telescope so powerful, it would make the Hubble telescope look like a cardboard toilet roll tube. Nathan heard footsteps running past his window and voices as well. He'd asked his sister so many questions about what the aliens looked like, whether they were friendly, what type of spaceship they had and how fast it travelled, but he couldn't remember if he'd ever asked her what they sounded like. They didn't have mouths, he remembered that from Alien Guess Who? How did they speak?

The lights suddenly disappeared, and Nathan was in total darkness. But he was still too scared to move. A crack of light appeared as his door slowly opened. He closed his eyes as though it would make him invisible. They'd think he was still asleep and they'd leave him alone. Three Mississippis passed.

"It's okay, mate. Go back to sleep."

Nathan opened his eyes and saw his dad in the doorway. He sat up, relieved to discover he wasn't paralysed.

"Did you see it, Dad?"

"It's nothing to worry about, Nathan. Go back to sleep."

"The lights, though, Dad. Did you see them?"

His dad came into the room. "They've gone now, mate."

"You *saw them*?"

"Outside. Yes. But they've all gone now. Go back to sleep."

"Have they brought her back?"

"No, mate. They're looking for someone else."

"Did you see the lights as well though?"

His dad nodded. "I think they're searching the park."

"For Zoe? Did they find the directions?"

His dad sat on the bed. "What directions, Nathan?"

"In the park."

"What? No. Come on. Go back to sleep." He tried to tuck Nathan in but he resisted.

"Who are they searching for then?" Nathan said.

His dad sighed. "A kid's been stabbed."

23

There was no India99, either that night or in the morning. The police did send a drone up to search for the weapon. They were experimenting with drones as a cheaper alternative to helicopters and they didn't have a nickname or a call sign yet. Arthur's brother got his drugs delivered to prison by a drone.

"I know it sounds terrible," Nathan's dad said the following afternoon. "And it's tragic that kid's in hospital fighting for his life," he shook his head. "Fourteen years old. Kids have to grow up so young these days. But at least his parents know where their child is."

Nathan was trying to read but his dad wouldn't stop talking.

"It's the not knowing isn't it, Nath? It sounds like a cliché when you hear other people say it. But it is sort of true, you know, the lack of closure."

Nathan looked over the top of his book. He was lying on his back on the carpet in front of the television. His dad was sitting at the living room table, staring out of the window. Nathan wasn't even sure his dad was actually talking to him. He was like President Nixon talking to a window through a broken microphone.

"You know what the worst thing is, though? When I heard that boy hadn't died," his dad said. "I was relieved. But not because I was thinking of him or his family," he turned away from the window to look at Nathan. "I mean I was relieved because I thought if the police had a murder to investigate, they wouldn't have so much time to look for Zoe."

His dad turned away again, as though he was ashamed of himself. Nathan lowered the library book and let it rest on his face like a roof. He pressed his open palms into the carpet, hoping he'd feel dizzy because the world was spinning so fast.

He heard his dad get up and go out into the hall. There were voices, at least one of the FLOs, and a Joe as well, PC Torres, maybe PC Kari, too. Nathan sat up. He closed the library book that was now overdue and that both he and Zoe had vandalised. He hid it under the sofa.

His dad came into the living room and got his phone. Nathan looked at PC Torres and PC Kari in the hall. They were both holding their caps under their arms. The undertakers did that at Nathan's mum's funeral. He thought Zoe must be dead. His dad said he was going to talk to the police in the kitchen and Nathan should stay with the FLOs. They were both there. They came into the living room and closed the door. They'd been at the house enough times now to know to lift the door a little, so it didn't snag on the carpet.

Janet told Nathan to sit down at the table. She gave him a colouring book and a small box of crayons. Nathan was now certain Zoe was dead. People in authority had used colouring books to distract him or shut him up before – flight attendants and babysitters, cancer nurses and a train guard on a long journey once, and now the police. He looked down at the picture of the smiling giraffe on the cover of the book and it made him incredibly angry. If thinking that colouring in stupid looking cartoon animals was suitable for a ten-year-old boy wasn't already insulting enough. Thinking it would comfort Nathan when his sister had just died really made him angry. He wrote 'fuck' along the trunk of an elephant.

He could hear his dad's voice in the kitchen. It was muffled but his dad occasionally raised his voice enough for Nathan to hear part of what he was saying. He sounded very angry. Maybe the police had given his dad a colouring book too. Nathan heard the kitchen door open and his dad's voice spilled out into the hall. Nathan coloured a hippopotamus in. What else was he supposed to do? The living room door opened, and Maureen came in. Nathan hadn't heard her arrive. She said hello to Nathan and to the FLOs and took her coat off. She was wearing her Greggs uniform. Nathan knew she wouldn't be selling any cakes today because Zoe was dead.

"What's wrong?" he asked her.

"Best wait for your dad."

His dad came in a minute later and Nathan looked for the same blank and yet busy expression from when he'd told him and Zoe that their mum had just died. He waited for the same two words: *'she's gone'*. Nathan already knew Zoe was gone, but up until now he thought she was coming back.

"Is Zoe dead?" Nathan said.

"Oh, mate," his dad said. He crouched down next to Nathan and awkwardly hugged him.

"She's dead, isn't she?" Nathan said. He was crying.

"Oh, Nath. Of course she isn't. I just have to go to the police station. That's all."

"What for?" Nathan sniffed loudly. He wiped his eyes on his sleeve.

"The police just need to clear a few things up. It's easier for them if I do it there. That's all. Mo's going to stay with you till I get back. Oh, mate. Stop crying. You'll set me off."

Why don't you cry then? Nathan thought. That was what everyone wanted, wasn't it? Innocent people cried. But Nathan knew his dad couldn't cry. There just wasn't enough time. And crying would be a release. A signal that he'd given up. While everyone talked about golden hours and diminishing returns, likelihoods and unlikelihoods, worst case scenarios, Nathan's dad had to stay positive, even if it was deluded or hopeless to do so. Without Nathan's dad as their cheerleader, the FLOs and the Joes and all the other feds, the five-o, po-po and everyone on social media would give up. Nathan's dad wasn't allowed that luxury yet. Even now, when, as far as Nathan could tell, his dad was being arrested, he had to stay strong.

"I won't be gone long," Nathan's dad said. "Okay?"

"How long?"

"Not long."

"Not long compared to what? A journey to Mars? A sneeze? Ten years, six seconds? Be *more precise*, Dad."

His dad couldn't help laughing and Nathan laughed, too, even though he hadn't finished crying yet.

"I'll be gone an hour or two at the most I expect," his dad said. He looked at the police for confirmation.

"Let's hope so," PC Torres said.

His dad picked up his sheepskin jacket. He put his right arm in the sleeve but couldn't seem to manage the left. It looked like he'd picked up a similar jacket belonging to someone smaller than him by mistake. At any other time, Nathan would have found it funny. In the end his dad gave up. He took the jacket off and slung it over his shoulder. He slow-motion jabbed Nathan on the chin and told him not to worry.

Nathan said okay and the police left with his dad. He watched them from the living room window. PC Kari had put his cap on, presumably to free the space under his arm for the clear plastic bag he was carrying, containing Nathan's dad's laptop. PC Torres had a bag too. Hers had some of Nathan's dad's clothes in. It looked like she was collecting them for charity. The bag was see-through, and Nathan saw a pair of his dad's trainers, some jeans and a white T-shirt.

Maureen put her arm around Nathan's shoulder. To comfort him, but also, Nathan was sure, to stop him from running after his dad. And he really did want to run after him. He wanted to see if the police were waiting until they were away from the house before they put the handcuffs on. He imagined PC Kari placing a hand on his dad's head to stop him banging it as he climbed into the back of the police car. The neighbours would all come out to watch. They'd stand there with their arms folded, smugly nodding to themselves because they'd known it was him all along.

24

It was almost seven-thirty in the evening when Nathan's dad finally came home. When the feds took Arthur's brother to the police station, he still hadn't come back almost three years later. Nathan had been sick with worry that the same would happen to his dad. He couldn't eat the pasta Maureen had cooked and now he was hungry, so Maureen had made him some tomato soup. It had enough garlic in it to kill Dracula. Nathan sat at the table making loud slurping noises and letting his spoon bang and scrape against the bowl because the house had been so quiet without Zoe, and now his dad was gone too. Maureen wasn't even humming. He thought she might be broken. They both kept looking out of the window for Nathan's dad. Maureen tried to pretend she wasn't looking, so as not to worry Nathan any more than he already was. When he saw his dad walking towards the house, he had to stop himself from rushing out into the hall to hug him. He didn't want to act as though he was relieved or even surprised that the police had let him go.

"I've left you some dinner. It just needs heating up," Maureen said.

Nathan's dad removed his sheepskin jacket without any of the trouble he'd had putting it on earlier. Arthur said his brother lost loads of weight in prison, but Nathan didn't think his dad had been gone long enough for that.

"Did anyone ring?" his dad said.

Maureen said no, but Nathan's dad picked up the house phone and checked for a dialling tone. He looked around the room for something, then sighed, no doubt realising his laptop and mobile were at the police station. He looked exhausted. His skin was almost grey. He looked like the police had used age-progression software on his actual face.

Maureen went home soon after that. She told Nathan's

dad there was soup in the fridge and a bowl of pasta in the microwave. He just needed to press start. He thanked his sister in a way that told her he had no intention of eating anything, and Maureen went out to the kitchen and pressed start herself. A couple of minutes later, the microwave pinged and Nathan and his dad both looked around for the laptop, thinking it was an email.

Nathan's dad took the pasta out of the microwave and sat on the sofa next to Nathan. He looked down at the bowl a few times, surprised to see it there, as though he'd felt the warmth on his legs and thought it was his computer.

"What did you do today?" his dad said.

"Reading and watching telly."

"Anything good on?"

Nathan shook his head.

His dad looked at the bowl of pasta again.

"Shall we order a takeaway?"

Nathan went and got the menus from the kitchen. When the food arrived Nathan's dad dished it up, discovering more gaps in the house left by Zoe – no vegetable Balti, no Peshwari naan – and they ate from trays on their laps. Nathan's dad told Nathan he would do his best to explain what had happened at the police station. It seemed easier for him if he made it sound like a riddle in a school maths test.

"There are thirty-five CCTV cameras on the way from the mural to our house and after you and Zoe turned into the estate there are no more cameras. We're apparently lucky we live somewhere there's no need for CCTV. Because every home on the estate overlooks at least one other home and we're all supposed to look out for one another," his dad paused for the first of many deep sighs.

"The last time Zoe was seen, by anyone else apart from you, was just after you both left the Tesco garage. Someone from the flats over the road has just given the police some grainy CCTV footage. It's really out of focus and Zoe's only recognisable because of you skipping along by her side," his dad gave him another affectionate slow-motion punch to the chin. "The police have managed to track down and speak to everyone else on this new CCTV film. They've spoken to everyone going in or coming out of the estate after you and Zoe went in. The last two people were me and Craig at about two in the morning. So, basically, the police think Zoe must have left the house again, when you were asleep, either after I came home, or possibly before that. Why didn't I check her room, Nath?" his dad shook his head and took a long pause. "Because there's no CCTV of Zo leaving the estate, the police think she could have returned to the park. But there are no cameras in the park either, and so there's no film of her coming out of any of the twelve entrances… or e*xits*. It's like she vanished, mate."

His dad put a whole onion bhaji in his mouth. To stop himself from talking, Nathan thought.

"Why were you shouting at the police?" Nathan said when his dad had finished the bhaji.

"When was I shouting?"

"In the kitchen, when the police came."

"I wasn't really shouting...was I? They wanted to take my phone and my laptop, and I didn't want them to. In case Zoe tried to ring."

"Why did they want your phone and your laptop?"

"In case it could help them."

"How?"

"I don't know, mate."

"Is that why they arrested you? Because you wouldn't give them your phone?"

"They didn't arrest me, Nath. They just wanted to ask me some questions—"

"You were there for so long though."

"They had a lot of questions."

"When the feds took Arthur's brother, they didn't let him go at all."

"The *feds*?"

"That's what Arthur calls them."

"Well, the feds have let me go, haven't they?" he looked at Nathan. "You're not satisfied with that explanation, are you? I can tell," his dad moved closer. He smelled of what Nathan imagined a police cell would smell like. "When bad things happen to kids, a lot of the time it's someone from their own family who's responsible and the police have to eliminate them from their enquiries."

"What does that mean?"

"Eliminate? It means to…cross off their list."

"What list?"

"Those closest to Zoe."

"Will they have to cross me off their list, too?"

"No, mate. Of course they won't. Can we talk about something else now? I'm knackered," he pointed at the last onion bhaji. "Half each?" He broke it into two pieces.

"Is it because you didn't cry on television?" Nathan said. "Is that why they think you're a suspect?"

"Didn't I?" his dad said. "I felt like I cried," he shrugged. "I suppose I was trying to keep it together. Be the big man."

They finished the food and Nathan took the plates and trays out to the kitchen. Nathan knew it was his fault the police had taken his dad away. Because he'd told everyone about the arguments and about Zoe's cuts and bruises.

"Maybe we'd be better off if the council did evict us," his dad called out from the living room. "We could move into a gated community with hundreds of cameras and a concierge."

"What's a concierge?" Nathan called back.

"A bloke in a uniform who stops your kids from running off."

Nathan scooped the curry into the kitchen bin. He put the little bag of salad that they never ate in the fridge, with the pot of leftover cucumber raita. He closed the fridge door and wiped his greasy hands down his Adidas three stripes.

Nathan was scared his dad was going to prison. He knew he hadn't done anything wrong, but Arthur said that didn't matter. The feds could send anyone to prison if they wanted. They did it all the time. If they couldn't solve a case, they could just arrest someone and blame them for it. Nathan needed to find Zoe and bring her home, to prove that she was all right. He had to make contact. All he could think of doing was finding a way to get to the park to retrieve the original Luigi board. With the real Luigi board, he'd be able to make contact.

He moved the letter from the school about the *Space and Science Far Beyond Infinity Workshop* to the top centre of the fridge door where his dad would see it. He held it in place with an extra fridge magnet in the shape of a map of Hayling Island, and then he repositioned the letter so it was at a slight angle. His dad would never be able to leave it like that. When he straightened the letter, perhaps, like Nathan had just done, his dad would notice the date of the Space Workshop was tomorrow.

25

Nathan put his school uniform on, brushed his teeth and checked his dad's bedroom was empty. He reset Zoe's alien alarms and went downstairs. He fed Officer Dibble and made his dad a cup of coffee. On the fridge door the letter from the school had been straightened. He removed it and replaced it with a Zoe leaflet and went along the hall to the living room.

When his dad opened his eyes, he saw Nathan standing there with a cup of coffee in one hand and the letter in the other. His dad looked suitably ambushed. Nathan needed to act fast.

"Can I go to school?"

"What?" His dad looked around, presumably searching for his laptop and phone. Both still with the police.

"The astronaut is coming to school today," Nathan said. "Can I go?"

Before his dad had time to sit up straight, Nathan gave him the letter. His dad blinked deliberately, trying to make his eyes work. Nathan gave him his reading glasses.

"I thought you didn't want to go," his dad said, taking the glasses but not putting them on.

"I changed my mind."

His dad looked at the letter, still not reading it. "I can't leave the house empty."

"I can go on my own." Nathan did his best to sound grown up and safe and not another person about to go missing.

"That's out of the question," his dad said.

"Can't someone else take me then? Craig or one of the neighbours?"

"No."

His dad lifted the sofa cushion. Could he still be searching for his laptop and phone?

"But it's an astronaut, Dad. '*The intergalactic journey of a lifetime'.*"

His dad gave him a look suggesting that might be the one line of the letter he'd managed to read. He put his glasses on.

"I made you a coffee," Nathan said.

His dad took the coffee. He sighed. "I suppose maybe I could ask Maureen—"

Nathan could see there might be a way out of the black hole after all. He sat on the sofa next to his dad.

"It's going to be an out-of-this-world, unforgettable space experience," he said. His dad raised his eyebrows over the top of his reading glasses and Nathan realised he might have overdone it.

26

Maureen walked so slowly. She held Nathan's hand when they crossed the road, like he was six, and she insisted on waiting for the green man, even when there were no cars. When there were cars, she squeezed his hand until they passed. If Nathan's dad saw Zoe everywhere, his aunt saw her killers and her kidnappers.

When they got to the school Maureen took a pink plastic lunch box out of her bag. It had an equally pink lid with pictures of unicorns and rainbows on. She gave it to Nathan and said, "Lunch". Nathan thanked her and stuffed the lunchbox into his bag before anyone saw it and he got his head kicked in.

"I'll be waiting right here at the end of the day," Maureen said, pointing at the pavement, possibly at a precise spot. She tried to kiss Nathan goodbye and didn't seem to want to let go of his hand. When he was safely inside the school gates, Maureen stood in the street until the bell went. Nathan told Arthur she was a fed.

Everyone wanted to know about Zoe. Nathan's friends crowded around him, asking the same questions newspapers and people on Facebook asked his dad every day. At first Nathan enjoyed the attention and he told them about the FLOs and the Joes and the Deltas and the India99 and the drone, even though it had nothing to do with Zoe. He boasted about how many likes his sister's Facebook page had and he gave everyone leaflets. Two girls asked him to autograph theirs and they took selfies with him. Everyone thought it was cool that he'd been on television.

Christian Sandel said everyone knew Nathan's dad was lying about Zoe. Nathan asked him how he knew that, and Christian said his mum had told him. Nathan told him to fuck off. If Nathan had been worried that missing a week of lessons would have left him behind the rest of his class, he soon realised he needn't have worried. Everyone seemed just as stupid as they were when he'd last seen them.

That was why Nathan didn't tell anyone he knew where Zoe was or that he was going to bring her back. They wouldn't have believed him anyway. They would have teased him or laughed at him. Or even worse, his friends would take him seriously and they'd tell a teacher or his dad or they'd ask if they could go into space with him. Nathan decided it was best for his mission to remain a secret. He did feel bad for not telling Arthur, but if he was going to tell a blabbermouth like Arthur, he might as well tell the whole school.

The day seemed to last forever. Lessons and break times dragged and even the *Space and Science Far Beyond Infinity Workshop* that Nathan had waited so long for couldn't end soon enough. It had only really been an excuse to get him out of the house anyway, to get to the park and find the Luigi board before his dad was arrested for something he hadn't done. After school Nathan would go to the park. He'd get the Luigi board out of the dog poo bin and leave new directions for the aliens just in case they didn't know where to return Zoe.

The park gates would be locked 'Fifteen minutes before dusk'. In the winter that was about 4:15. If Zoe had gone missing in the summer, Nathan would have had another three hours to get to the park. But if he was quick enough, he could still easily make it. The one thing he wasn't sure of was how to get past Auntie Maureen when she came to collect him. Towards the end of the day Astronaut Buzz lined up his plastic rockets at the front of the class and prepared them for launch. It was the grand finale of the *Space and Science Far Beyond Infinity Workshop* and it would give Nathan his escape opportunity.

So far, the *intergalactic journey of a lifetime* had been rubbish. Astronaut Buzz got everything wrong. He really needed to read *Moonmen (and Women)*. He wasn't even a real astronaut. His spacesuit was less convincing than Nathan's own Mission to Mars fancy-dress costume. His helmet was made from a plastic so flimsy that he had to pull it back into shape every time anyone tried it on. The 'portable life support system' he had strapped to his back looked like a cereal box covered in white wrapping paper. Nathan could see the Sellotape peeling away. Buzz claimed it provided him with enough oxygen for a half-mile spacewalk and also removed dangerous carbon dioxide. It monitored his heart rate and had a built-in two-way radio, with a signal strong enough to hold a conversation between Earth and Mars. When Arthur asked if he could have a go on the radio, Astronaut Buzz said the battery needed charging.

The 'actual items from space' that Nathan had been looking forward to, ever since reading about them in the letter, included a piece of Moon rock and some freeze-dried space strawberries and ice cream. The strawberries and ice cream were okay, but Nathan had seen real Moon rock at the National Space Centre. People hadn't been allowed to touch their Moon rock either, but that was because it came from the Moon. The only reason Buzz didn't want anyone to touch his Moon rock was because they'd find out it was just a lump of modelling clay from Poundworld.

The only really good bit of the Space Workshop was the end. Astronaut Buzz lined up six foam rockets on the floor and asked for volunteers to step on a sort of half a basketball launchpad. The launchpad would pump air through a tube and send the rockets up towards the ceiling. Arthur volunteered, of course, and he jumped so high and landed so hard that he hurt his ankle. The workshop had to be stopped and Arthur was taken to hospital. It was so funny. Even Arthur, who was in agony, couldn't help laughing. The unexpected sudden end to the workshop also presented Nathan with a way past his aunt, as the class was allowed out of school ten minutes early.

Nathan rushed out of the building and when he saw his aunt wasn't waiting for him, he crossed the busy main road. He turned up a side street and started walking a way he knew Maureen wouldn't come. He could always say he must have missed her. He took Zoe's MP3 player out of his bag, put the earphones in and found the David Bowie playlist and turned it up loud. If Maureen called out to him from across the street, he'd pretend he hadn't heard her.

By the time the playlist was on its third song, Nathan had taken so many left and right turns, he didn't know where he was. When he saw the big church at the end of the road, he at least knew he was heading in the right direction. He'd stood outside the church a week ago, while his dad removed the screws so he could lift the glass front of the noticeboard and pin a poster to the green felt board inside.

Almost every street Nathan had walked along had at least one poster for his missing sister. Either stuck to a lamppost or pinned to a tree or fencepost. There were more pictures of his sister in Brixton than there were of David Bowie a week earlier. If their dad could have arranged it there'd be a Zoe Love mural opposite the Tube. If he hadn't sold his old film projector there'd be an enormous picture of her face filling the Bovril wall.

Nathan stopped outside the church. The poster was still there among the notices for pet blessings, Holy Communion and pilates. But it was different to all the other posters he'd walked past. Underneath Zoe's picture, where it said: 'Zoe Patricia Love (15) has been missing for 2 days', the '2 days' had been crossed out with a black pen. The poster now said Zoe had been missing for '13 days.'

Nathan carried on walking, seeing posters wrapped around signposts and bollards and one stuck to a glass-recycling bin. Every poster had been altered. Nathan couldn't think of anyone other than his dad who could be responsible. He wondered if he'd changed the posters because of what Craig had said about the police using age-progression software. Updating the number of days Zoe had been missing on the posters was his homemade age-progression software.

Nathan's phone rang as he walked into the big estate. He took it out of his blazer pocket, forgetting two things his dad always told him – *don't use your phone in public* and *don't walk through the big estate.* The phone call was from an unknown number, but Nathan knew it must be Maureen. He let the phone ring out before switching it to silent and hiding it down the front of his underpants. A trick Zoe had taught him to avoid getting robbed. He hoped it wasn't just another one of her jokes. He took his school tie off, zipped his coat up to hide his blazer and, doing his best to look like he belonged there, walked through the estate.

27

There were two tall blocks at the centre of the estate, the wider block on the left with the flats inside and a thinner block on the right where the stairs and the lifts were. A gap between the two blocks, about the width of a car, was the shortest route through to the other side of the estate and the quickest way to get to the main road where Nathan lived, and where the park and the Luigi board were. Five or six boys were standing in front of the gap. They'd dropped their bikes on the ground, like a roadblock or a border that Nathan was going to have to cross. He knew there was bound to be a toll.

The boys hadn't seen him yet, and if he turned back now he could take a different, longer route home. He'd have to forget about going to the park. There wouldn't be time. He considered his options. The MP3 player was still playing. He needed to stop that first. When he pulled the earphones out, David Bowie sang *Turn to the left*. It was as though he was trying to help Nathan by showing him the safest way through the estate. But it was too late to take his advice as one of the boys had seen him. He quickly stuffed the earphones and the MP3 player into his pants with his phone and carried on walking.

The boys shuffled about, zipping up their jackets and spitting, preparing themselves for Nathan's arrival at their makeshift border crossing. They were older than Nathan, maybe twelve or thirteen. He thought he knew what school they were from, even though they were all wearing dark coats or jackets, zipped up to their chins, hiding their uniforms. One of them had covered his face with a yellow scarf. Another had a plastic fork in his mouth. When Nathan was just a few feet away the boy removed the fork. He put his hand out like a stop sign and asked Nathan where he was going and, more crucially, where he was from. Nathan lied to both questions, "Here." He looked up at the two blocks that towered over them like the Blue Streak and Thor Able rockets. He felt just as giddy and twice as sick.

"You're getting taxed," the boy said. He dropped the plastic fork on the ground and put both his hands in Nathan's coat pockets.

"I haven't got anything," Nathan said.

The other boys surrounded him. Someone pulled his bag off his shoulder. Plastic fork boy counted a handful of loose change and studied Nathan's travel pass as though he was checking his passport. He gave the pass back and for a moment Nathan thought they were finished with him. But the boy with the scarf over his face said, "What's this?"

Nathan couldn't remember putting the fallen ceiling Jupiter in his school bag. The boy waved the rubber planet about, making it flap like a drowning fish.

"It has to be dark to work," Nathan said.

"What?" the boy said. He spat on the ground. If he was aiming for Nathan's shoes, he missed by a mile.

"It only glows in the dark."

The boy threw Jupiter on the ground. Nathan wished the real planet would fall out of the sky and land on him. Two of the other boys were playing tug-of-war with Nathan's school bag. He watched his homework and his *Star Wars* pencil case fall out. When his lunch box fell out of the bag, Nathan thought the lame pink unicorns on the lid would get him murdered, but no one seemed to notice it. One of the boys threw a plastic alien with a parachute on its back into the air. The parachute failed and the alien crashed to the ground. The scarf-faced boy picked up the head of the Bratz doll and turned it around in his hand like a rare diamond.

"It's my sister's," Nathan said, and the boy threw the doll's head in the air. He tried dropkicking it but missed and the others laughed at him. Nathan nearly laughed himself, thinking the best way to stop being the victim was to join the bullies.

"This is that girl what's missing," fork boy said. The others leaned in to look at the poster in his hand.

"I know her," one said. "Her dad killed her, isn't it?"

"No, he didn't," Nathan said, luckily too quietly to even register as a sound.

He couldn't remember whether he'd seen any posters on the big estate. If his dad hadn't updated them yet, he might be here right now. Nathan could call out his name. His dad would really mess these boys up.

"She's run away. I know," the boy with the scarf mask said. He read aloud from the poster. "Zoe Patricia Love has been missing for two days—"

"Thirteen," Nathan said. They ignored him.

"Nah, man. She's dead."

"She's fuck ugly."

"Gis it."

Nathan prayed for a supernova a billion times brighter than the sun, to explode and fall onto the boys and their bikes and their stupid shitty flats. If he had the Swiss Army knife with him, he definitely would have used it. He felt a strange sensation in his trousers. He thought he was wetting himself, but it was just his phone vibrating in his underpants. *Not now, Auntie Maureen*. He wondered what time it was. The sky was a sort of off-white, like slush or ruined snow. Neither night nor day. Was that what dusk was? Soon the man from the council would be driving around the park in his car with the lights flashing to warn everyone it was about to close.

Nathan watched the boys fighting over the poster, wishing a meteor as big as the one that crashed into Russia, that Zoe had watched so many times on YouTube, would hit Brixton now. No, not a meteor. It was a meteoroid. The memory of Zoe correcting the man on the news like he was an idiot almost made Nathan laugh out loud. He really had to get to the park and find the Luigi board so he could speak to his sister. He couldn't let a few stupid boys stop him. What would have happened to E.T. if Elliott had such a defeatist attitude? What would happen to Zoe?

The boys were playing a violent game of pass the parcel with the poster now and they seemed to have lost interest in Nathan. Zoe would have called it their 'short attention span'. While they were distracted, Nathan picked up Jupiter, the lunchbox, his pencil case and the doll's head. He put them in his school bag and stepped over a silver mountain bike. He entered the gap between the two tower blocks without any of the boys seeming to care. They were too busy fighting over the picture of his sister. In a way Zoe had saved him. He had to save her in return. About halfway through the gap, Nathan realised he shouldn't have said that he lived in the flats. If he didn't get in the lift or go up the stairs, it would be obvious he'd been lying.

Without stopping to think, he started running. He jumped over a low bush and almost tripped in a pothole. It wasn't easy running fast with a phone and an MP3 player in his pants. The phone was vibrating again, and the earphones had started to slide down his thigh. He carried on running, not looking back until he reached the main road, and then he still kept running. He only stopped when he was on the other side of the road where there were more people about.

He bent over with his hands on his knees and waited for his stitch to unpick itself. He took the MP3 player and the phone out of his pants. There was a text message from the same unknown number as the other calls. Nathan knew how difficult it would have been for Maureen to write the simple *Nathan where are you??* text. She was obviously worried about him and it should have been enough to make him go straight home. But he thought he could still make it to the park before it closed. He sprinted up the road next to the big pub and went through the entrance to the park. Just inside the gate there was a poster on the noticeboard. It hadn't been updated yet and Zoe had only been missing for two days. It was like stepping back in time.

28

Zoe's favourite tree had been cut into two, and one half was already covered in tags. Zoe was right. Humans were terrible. Nathan didn't recognise any of the squiggles or swirls as those belonging to any of his friends or anyone he knew on the estate. He put his hand on the graffiti to see if the paint was dry. He looked at his fingers and thought he saw glitter. But when he looked again it was gone. There was no sign anywhere of twigs or branches that might once have formed the shape of an arrow. He searched the two halves of tree trunk for the Post-it notes that Zoe had written their names on. So much had happened since then and it felt like such a long time ago.

Apart from an old man in running shorts jogging down the hill towards the Lido and a woman walking Digby, the biggest dog in the world, along the path between the park and the estate, the top of the park was deserted. Nathan couldn't see the man driving around telling everyone it was time to leave yet.

He leaned over the tree and looked inside the hollow, but it was too dark. The Post-it notes could have fallen further inside. He should have brought his Space Torch with him. He took a deep breath, closed his eyes, and put his hand in the hole and felt about inside. His face was squashed against the bark. He pulled his hand out, stood and shook it and brushed it against his coat, convinced it was covered in insects even though he couldn't see any.

Nathan took a poster out of his bag. His dad had given him six that morning to put on the school noticeboard, but he'd forgotten. He'd been too preoccupied thinking about how he was going to avoid Maureen and get to the park. He folded the poster in half and put it in the hollow of the tree. He was about to leave when he stopped and took the poster out again. He found the best pen in his school bag and changed the number of days on the poster from 2 to 13.

He wondered if he should have brought a picture of 'Alex' as well. But he didn't even want to think that Zoe might have gone into space with someone instead of him.

He heard a car. He could see it down by the café, the lights flashing to announce dusk and time for the park to close. Nathan put the poster back inside the tree and arranged three short branches in the shape of an arrow on the grass next to it. He collected as many more branches as he could carry and picked up his school bag. He walked towards the estate. When he was almost at the dog poo bin, there were six arrows behind him, leading from the tree and the picture of Zoe to the house she'd been taken from.

The dog poo bin hadn't been emptied since the other night. It was so full the lid wouldn't shut properly. But people had continued to throw bright blue and black bags into the overflowing bin and onto the ground beneath it. There were a few plastic bags trapped between the bin and the lid.

Nathan put his school bag down. With one of the two branches he had left, he lifted the lid. He wedged it open with the other shorter branch, and holding his nose he started poking around inside the bin with the first stick, lifting and separating the sea of bagged dog mess. The first thing he saw was the empty glitter tube. He was going to have to let go of his nose to reach into the bin to retrieve it. He turned his head away and took a deep breath. One small step. He reached into the bin. The thought of the dog shit, as much as any actual smell, made him gag. When he had the glitter tube between his fingers, he pulled it out at arm's length. He pushed his hip out and expertly dropped the tube into his trouser pocket.

The car with the flashing lights had stopped next to the row of white builders' vans in front of the café. The driver of the car got out and was talking to the builders. Nathan used his stick to root around in the bin again. There was a nappy in there and a Lucozade bottle. Humans are terrible.

He moved a few more bags about, and then he saw the unmistakable twinkle of Zoe's Ziggy stardust on the corner of the Luigi board. He had to flick two poo bags out of the bin to reach it. The dull sound they made when they landed on the grass made him gag again.

He poked the branch under the Luigi board and managed to lift it free. He had it almost the whole way out of the bin when everything seemed to happen at once. What his mum would have called one thing after another. First, the surprise of his phone vibrating in his pocket made him knock the branch holding the bin open. The lid slammed shut, not with the loud clang of metal on metal like the other night but with a dull thud as it landed on a cushion of dog shit. The Luigi board fell on the grass, and when Nathan bent to pick it up he saw the lid of a red Sharpie pen. His phone was still vibrating so he took it out of his pocket to cancel the call. He expected to see Auntie Maureen's unknown number again or another badly typed message, but the display said: DAD. Before he had the chance to consider how much trouble that meant he was in, a boy wearing a skull balaclava and riding a Boris bike snatched the phone out of his hand and sped off down the hill like a seagull with an ice cream cornet.

29

Nathan's dad wasn't about to risk losing a single second of what so many people had told him was the golden hour that followed a person going missing this time. When Nathan walked through the front door his dad was already on the phone to the police. Maureen came out of the living room. "Thank God," she said and pulled a tissue out from the sleeve of her cardigan and loudly blew her nose, like a trumpet fanfare announcing her nephew's safe return.

"It's all right," Nathan's dad said into the phone. "He's here. I'm sorry to have wasted your time. Yes, don't worry. I'll definitely be doing that," he hung up the phone and glared at Nathan. "Where the *hell* have you been?"

Nathan dropped his bag in the hall by the coats.

"The Space Workshop finished early, and I walked home with Arthur."

"Is that right?" his dad said, and Nathan quickly realised that if his dad was phoning the police, he might have already made the same series of phone calls he'd made when Zoe went missing. Presuming he made them in the same order, before calling the police he would have phoned the hospitals and before that his dad would have rung Nathan's school and spoken to his friends or their parents. From the satisfied look on his dad's face Nathan knew he'd spoken to Arthur's mum. She would have told him that Arthur had spent the afternoon in A and E getting his ankle X-rayed.

"I suppose you've noticed your sister is missing?" his dad said. Nathan recognised it as one of his famous rhetorical questions. He wasn't expected to answer it. If he stood still and looked sorry for long enough, the storm would pass.

"You must have been aware of a heightened police presence? All the people in uniform in the house? The helicopter? All those leaflets we've been giving out?

The posters? The television appearances—"

"You changed them," Nathan said, forgetting the rule with rhetorical questions.

His dad stared at him. Blinking like he'd woken up with the sun in his eyes. "What?"

"I saw the posters you've changed."

His dad thought for a moment and then waved his hand dismissively.

"Why weren't you answering your phone?"

There was a chance that if Nathan told the truth about his phone and about the boys on the big estate, it might not be too late to turn himself into the victim. His dad could never be angry with Nathan if he'd just been mugged. He might even get a new phone out of it, one with better games and more memory. Nathan looked at his dad's face and the house phone still in his hand, his thumb poised over the nine. He thought about having to go to the park with the police, to show them where his phone had been stolen. Everyone on the estate would see him and know he was a snitch.

"I lost it," Nathan said.

"You lost it? Jesus Christ, Nathan. How? Where?"

"At school."

"How did you lose it at school?"

"I just lost it."

"Where?"

"I don't know," that's what lost means, he really wanted to say.

His dad shook his head, turned his back and went into the living room, presumably to put the only remaining phone in the house back in its cradle. Because it didn't matter what else was happening in the world. His son could be mugged, there could even be a war going on. Nathan's dad wasn't going to forget to keep the hotline to Zoe open and fully charged.

"It's not my fault she's gone missing," Nathan shouted.

His dad came back out of the living room so quickly that Nathan stepped backwards and put his hands up in front of his face. His dad stepped back as well.

"I'm not going to hit you, Nathan. Jesus. Is that what you think? When have I ever hit you?"

Nathan shrugged, which was unfair because his dad had never hit him.

"Nathan can have my old phone," Maureen said.

"It's all right, Mo," Nathan's dad said.

He looked like he was about to say something else to Nathan, but he couldn't seem to find the words. Nathan recognised his expression from the last time he'd lost his phone. Zoe had called it 'exasperation'. His dad turned and looked like he was about to go back into the living room, but he stopped.

"You know how important looking after your phone is, don't you?" he said. "I must have said it a hundred times this week." Nathan could tell his dad was about to make it all about Zoe, as usual. "If Zoe had taken her phone with her...Or if she'd just ring to say she's all right. I don't care where she is. I just want to hear from her."

Nathan bent down and opened his school bag. He reached inside and pulled out the filthy Luigi board. He stood up and held it out to his dad.

"What's that?" his dad said, looking at the grubby and damp clump of paper.

"It's why I went to the park."

"You've *been to the park*?"

"I'm *trying to tell you,*" Nathan said. "It's Zoe's." It was the magic word for getting his dad's attention.

"What is it?"

"It's a Luigi board."

"A what?"

"He means a Ouija board, Steve," Maureen said. Nathan's dad turned to look at her and then back at Nathan.

"Why have you got a Ouija board?"

"Zoe left it in the park."

His dad unfolded it. The paper had stuck together in places. Nathan's dad watched specks of glitter fall onto the hall carpet like shooting stars.

"That was supposed to be for David Bowie's birthday card," Nathan said. "But Zoe forgot and most of it's rubbed off now."

His dad looked at the letters and what was left of the stars. He had glitter on his hands.

"I just don't understand why you'd be playing with a Ouija board," his dad said.

"We weren't playing."

"Do you think your sister is dead, Nathan?"

"It's not for that. It's a different one. We were trying to make contact."

"Who was?"

"Me and Zoe."

"Why? What do you mean make contact? Who with?"

Nathan didn't know why his dad couldn't seem to understand something so simple. "It didn't work indoors because of interference," Nathan said. "So we took it to the park, but Zoe forgot to take a glass."

"Please tell me you don't mean the other night?" his dad said.

"I thought we could try again now. Me and you, Dad, and Auntie Maureen. I think it needs more fingers on the glass to make it work," he looked at Maureen. "Three people's fingers might make it work. We can contact Zoe with it. You said you wanted to hear from her." Why wasn't his dad getting it? "Because she's an alien again. Like when we went to France."

His dad glared at him. "Zoe isn't dead, Nathan."

"I *know*. I didn't say that."

His dad said something under his breath and then screwed the Luigi board up and started along the hall towards the kitchen.

"What are you doing?" Nathan said.

"This sort of nonsense is not good for you."

Nathan's dad walked past Maureen. "Steve," she said and then, "Nathan," as he followed his dad into the kitchen. His dad walked over to the bin. He put his foot on the pedal to open the lid.

"Don't," Nathan said.

"It's nonsense." His dad dropped the Luigi board in the bin.

"No!" Nathan shouted. He tried to reach the bin but his dad stood in the way.

"Steve," Maureen said.

Nathan's dad took his foot off the pedal and the bin lid slammed shut.

"I wish she *was* fucking dead!" Nathan screamed. He ran past his aunt into the hall. He grabbed his bag and stamped up the stairs to his bedroom. He slammed the door closed and then slammed it three more times in case his dad hadn't heard it.

He threw his bag on the floor and sat down hard on his bed, making the springs creak. He kicked his trainers off so they crashed into his wardrobe door and lay on his bed. He pulled the hood of his parka over his head, tightening the drawstring to make the opening as small as possible. He wished the aliens didn't only come at night. He wanted to go right now and never come back. He felt in his coat pocket for his phone so that he could text Arthur about his phone being jacked. When he realised why that was impossible he turned his head around inside the hood of the coat and screamed into the material.

He lay like that for ten minutes. He'd expected his dad to chase after him. For swearing and for wishing Zoe was dead, for the Luigi board, for going to the park to get it, for losing another phone, for making Zoe go to the park with him in the first place, for snitching to the police and to the breakfast television presenters, and who knew what else.

Five more long minutes passed. Nathan wasn't going to be the one to back down. He'd stay in quarantine inside his parka forever if he had to. His dad had destroyed the only means of communication with Zoe. And it was something Zoe had made. The Luigi board should be in the Zoe Love Museum, not in the kitchen bin covered in cold curry.

He put his hand in his trouser pocket. He poked his little finger inside the red Sharpie lid and thought about the last time he'd seen Zoe using the pen. She'd written on the wall next to the mural and used it again when they played the Post-it notes game. After that Zoe had used the pen to write the letters and numbers and draw the stars on the Luigi board. And she'd written in Nathan's Space Cadet notebook. The last time Nathan had seen the red pen was when Zoe wrote both their names on Post-it notes and stuck them to her favourite tree. Nathan clearly remembered Zoe replacing the lid and putting the pen in her jacket pocket after that. He remembered because he'd waited to hear the lid click firmly into place because of all the times Zoe had told him off for not putting the lids back on her pens properly. He couldn't imagine she would have made the same careless mistake herself. The arrows were gone and the Post-it notes were gone, but the pen lid was somehow in the park. None of it made sense. And where was the actual pen?

Like the police, Nathan thought Zoe must have gone back to the park when he and his dad were asleep. But not to look at stars. There weren't any that night. Because of light pollution. Because of the streetlights and tall buildings. Zoe must have gone to the park for another reason. To leave a message for the aliens or maybe for him. As soon as he got the chance Nathan would go back to the park and find the message. He'd start by looking on Zoe's favourite tree. That was the most likely place. At the very least he'd find the pen and replace the lid before the ink dried up.

Nathan sat up and took his parka off. He pulled the grey cardboard folder out from under his mattress and tipped the Alien Guess Who? pictures out on his bed. He got the version of the Luigi board he'd made out of library book pages down from the top of his wardrobe. He opened it out on the carpet next to his bed. He took the glitter tube out of his trouser pocket, poking his little finger inside to scoop out any leftover glitter. He wiped the few specks onto the Luigi board's stars. He placed the glitter tube with the Sharpie lid, the blue asthma inhaler, the head of Zoe's Bratz doll, the ID badge from the television studio and the rubber Jupiter that had fallen from his ceiling around the edge of the board like Monopoly pieces. He put the upturned Caffè Nero cup at the Luigi board's centre.

Next, Nathan arranged the Alien Guess Who? pictures in five rows on the carpet next to the Luigi board. When he was ready, he asked the same questions he'd asked Zoe last year when he'd made the guessing game. This time though, instead of asking whether the aliens were green or if they had tentacles, he asked *are* they green and *do* they have tentacles? He had to imagine Zoe's answers, of course, but she said no to all of them. When Nathan had turned over every single green man, bug-eyed grey and tall white, when he'd discounted mutants and reptilians and a number of celebrity aliens that included Marvin the Martian, Mr. Spock, Darth Vader, Jar Jar Binks, a Klingon, two Doctor Whos, a Dalek and a picture of David Bowie with no hair or ears, there was only one picture that remained face up on the carpet. It was the same picture Nathan's dad had given to the police and posted online and stuck on to walls and to street furniture all over Brixton. It had been on television. Twice. It was the same picture that Nathan was going to take into space.

Nathan collected all the alien pictures together and put them back in the folder. He poked his little finger into the red Sharpie lid and flicked it in and out, making a satisfying popping sound. He held the lid up to his mouth and pretended it was a microphone, a walkie-talkie to Space.

"I don't know how much you can see what's happening on Earth, Zoe, but Dad threw the Luigi board in the bin. I took it out of one bin and he threw it straight into another one. How funny is that? I found your pen lid in the park, so I think you must have written me a message with it somewhere."

Nathan could hear his dad and Maureen arguing downstairs, probably about him. His dad was probably working out how to punish him. Nathan couldn't think of anything. He couldn't take his phone away or ban him from leaving the house. Nathan didn't care about television anymore, or toys. And there'd be no birthdays or Christmases until Zoe came back anyway.

"Dad hates me, Zoe, because I didn't wait after school for Maureen and because I had my phone snatched in the park. It nearly got taken in the big flats, but I hid it in my pants like you told me to do before. It was only a cheap Nokia, with a broken screen and no memory or proper internet and it had a rubbish camera, but Dad acted like I'd lost contact with the Apollo Lunar module. I read about that in that fat library book. I'm going to show you it when you get back. Did you know a boy got stabbed right outside our house? He's not dead but he nearly was. Dad's smoking because you're not here but mainly because I think I made him look bad on telly. You know that programme you hate? We were on it."

Nathan reached across for the ID badge. He held it up above the Luigi board.

"See? So, you should come home before Dad gets Earth cancer. I don't want to live with Maureen if he dies. She puts spices and pepper in everything, even though Dad keeps saying he only wants plain food. We're both vegetarians now, Zoe. I haven't eaten one animal since you went.

Auntie Maureen says Haribos have got animals in, but I think she's just saying it because she can't cook anything vegetarian. I'm going to keep on eating Tangfastics until you come home and tell me if they're for vegetarians or not. Did I tell you I found the lid off your pen? I think I did. Anyway, if you don't come back soon, the ink is going to dry up. And is that boy your boyfriend or something? Is he called Alex?"

30

Nathan had never been so grounded. When he did leave his room the atmosphere downstairs was so tense, he didn't want to stay for long. He ate his meals quickly in silence and went back to his room, only coming out again when he heard the front door opening and saw his dad leaving the house to hand out leaflets or update the posters again.

Nathan sat in his room, reading *Moonmen (and Women)* and staring out of his window at clouds, trying to remember all the names Zoe had taught him.

On the second day of this latest quarantine, when his dad went out, Nathan went downstairs and looked in the kitchen bin for the Luigi board, but the bin had been emptied. He said hello to Maureen and stole some Blu Tack from the living room desk. On his wall where the wrestling poster had been, Nathan stuck all his Alien Guess Who? pictures. He rolled the wrestling poster up and put it in the drawer under his bed. While the drawer was pulled out, he tried playing with some of his old toys, but they didn't seem to interest him.

He picked up one of the three Action Man dolls and pulled its khaki trousers down. During last year's summer holidays Arthur had drawn huge willies and balls on all three soldiers with a permanent marker. Nathan had hidden the Action Men under his bed, so his dad didn't find out. The dolls had belonged to his dad when he was a child. When he gave them to Nathan, he'd told him they would have been worth a fortune if only he'd kept the boxes. Nathan had the feeling his dad didn't really want to give up his toys and would rather have kept them for himself.

Nathan had been so angry with Arthur when he drew on the dolls, which had only made Arthur laugh more than he already was. Nathan pictured him, rolling around on the floor in hysterics, like it was the funniest thing ever. When Nathan started aggressively rubbing at the indelible penises with his spit-soaked thumb, he thought Arthur was actually going to die laughing.

He wished he'd told Arthur about his mission now. He hadn't heard from his friend since he'd broken his ankle – or 'just twisted it' as 'Astronaut' Buzz had kept insisting. When Nathan was eight, he'd broken his arm falling off a wall and Arthur wrote *ARTHUR'S BITCH* in huge black letters the whole length of his purple cast. Nathan didn't want to miss out on writing something rude on Arthur's cast. He wondered what colour cast he'd chosen. He hoped the only colour they had left was pink.

Nathan imagined going into space with Arthur. He pictured him floating around in zero gravity, trying to force out farts to make himself go faster, and finding it so funny, because the smell lingered for longer in space (there was a short chapter in *Moonmen (and Women)* about farting).

Nathan would have had to find a replacement for Arthur when he injured his ankle. When John L. Swigert caught measles, he was replaced on Apollo 13 by Ken Mattingly. Nathan couldn't think of anyone he'd want to replace Arthur. Thaddeus Kosto or Aaron Price maybe, and Joshua Alexander was good at football and running but he was an annoying show off. Nathan knew Joshua's sister, Kesha, would have volunteered. But Nathan didn't want to go into Space with Kesha Alexander.

At the start of Nathan's third day of quarantine the house was very quiet. He crept out onto the landing and made his usual checks for signs of life, signs of *other* life, but all the rooms upstairs were empty. Nathan walked slowly down the stairs.

His dad was in the kitchen. He was standing in front of the sink with his back to Nathan. He couldn't tell if his dad was still angry with him or if he'd forgiven him or, more likely, forgotten he even existed. When his dad turned around, he didn't ask why Nathan wasn't wearing his school uniform or why he was up so late. He probably thought it was the weekend. Or Christmas. One day was much like any other to his dad now. Every day was Zoeday.

"We need milk," his dad said, as though there was anything Nathan could do about that. If he offered to go to the shops his dad would have only said no. "If I buy you a new phone," his dad said. "Will you promise not to lose it?"

31

They walked into town and went to Argos where Nathan's dad bought a pay-as-you-go phone for Nathan and a cheap tablet for himself. The police hadn't returned his dad's laptop yet and using the remote control to navigate the internet on their smart TV was unbearably slow and frustrating. After leaving Argos they went to Subway. While his dad was ordering the Veggie Delites – without the works this time – Nathan unpacked his new phone on a table outside, almost breaking his fingernail prizing the thick plastic packaging apart. Nathan managed to eventually free the phone. He put the instructions booklet to one side on the table and switched the phone on. Then he remembered what his dad had told him about not using his phone in public and he switched it off again. He put it back in the box and hid the plastic packaging under the table.

Nathan watched his dad through the Subway window. He'd taken his jacket off and was pulling at the sides of the *Where is Zoe Love?* T-shirt he'd been wearing like a uniform ever since the dicks from Zoe's school had given it to him. Nathan's dad looked hopefully at the man behind the counter, as though he was expecting him to reveal his own T-shirt bearing the answer to the question written in colourful gel pens on the front of his own shirt – *Where is Zoe Love?* The man shook his head and did the same when Nathan's dad showed him the picture of Alex. Nathan's dad smiled and thanked the man and came outside with the tray of food. Nathan moved his phone out of the way to make room on the table for it.

"Aren't you going to open your phone?" his dad said, taking the sandwiches and drinks off the tray.

"I was waiting for you."

His dad put the empty tray on the table next to them and sat down.

"Can I open it now?" Nathan said.

"Of course."

Nathan took the phone out of the box. His dad shielded his eyes, pretending to be blinded by its bright yellow colour.

"At least you won't be able to lose it so easily," his dad said.

Nathan switched the phone on and put it on the table while it sorted itself out. He unwrapped his sandwich and they both ate their food while playing with their new toys. Nathan looked to see what games he had on his phone and his dad searched the internet for Zoe. Apart from looking at the *Where is Zoe Love?* page, he searched the rest of Facebook and Twitter for any mentions. He also typed Zoe's name into Google. Every day he looked he found more results than the day before. Sometimes Zoe would be mentioned in a story about a different missing teenager or she'd be tagged in an unrelated post about David Bowie or Brixton, or any number of other things. Online at least, the longer Zoe was missing, the easier she was to find.

They both looked up from their screens to watch a tourist taking a selfie in front of the mural opposite. Nathan had noticed there were no flowers or candles in front of the mural. He hoped his dad wouldn't notice. If people had forgotten about David Bowie what chance did Zoe have?

"Dad?" Nathan said, to distract him.

"Yes, mate."

"What colour is mousy?"

"It's sort of dark blonde. Or light brown."

"But mice are white though."

"I would have said they were more browny grey."

Nathan tried to picture what mice looked like. "Mickey Mouse is black."

"That's just Disneyfication."

"What does that mean?"

His dad gestured out at the busy high street. "Like what

they're doing to Brixton. Making it too nice."

"How can it be *too* nice?"

"When people like us can't afford to live here anymore."

Nathan nodded, pretending he understood. "What colour's your hair then?"

His dad rubbed his hand across his head as though he could feel colour, like Zoe said she could when she came back from Space before.

"My hair is what people call salt and pepper," his dad said. He came close to a laugh. "More salt than pepper lately."

Nathan presumed the specks of grey were the salt.

"Is that because you're old?"

His dad shrugged. "I have probably aged about a year this week, that's for sure."

"What colour is my hair?" Nathan said.

"Yours is…" his dad looked at Nathan as though he'd never considered the question before. Maybe a father wasn't expected to know the colour of his children's hair until they have to report it to the police or write it on a poster. "Brown, I suppose," he eventually said.

"That's too *boring*," Nathan said.

"Chocolate then."

"Which chocolate?"

"What's your favourite?"

Nathan considered his answer carefully, convinced that whatever chocolate he chose his dad would end up buying for him on the way home. He didn't want to rush his answer and end up with something small, like a Chomp or a Fudge.

"A Toblerone."

His dad started singing a funny song. He said it was from a Toblerone advert that used to be on television. Nathan hadn't heard music anywhere near his dad for such a long time. Nathan didn't know why, but the silly song about triangular honey and triangular bees almost made him cry.

"I didn't even ask you about the spaceman at your school," his dad said, as though the song had somehow reminded him. "How did it go?"

"It was all right I suppose."

"Until Arthur hurt his ankle," his dad said.

"That was the best bit."

They both laughed. "I mean, how did he even manage that?" his dad said.

"He jumped too hard on a rocket."

His dad nodded. "That'll do it every time. What was the astronaut like?"

"He was all right I suppose. His name was Buzz," Nathan said.

"*Buzz*? Do you think that was his real name?"

"I heard Miss call him Alan."

"I suppose Alan's not quite as astronauty as Buzz is it."

Nathan didn't tell his dad about Alan Shepard on Apollo 14 or Alan Lavern Bean on Apollo 12. His dad seemed in a good mood and Nathan didn't want to spoil it. He wondered if Subway or the sandwiches they sold were magic. Both times he'd been there with his dad he'd seemed a lot happier.

"Did we ever go to a place called Space Camp?" Nathan said.

"We did. Years ago."

"Can we go again then? I can't remember it."

"Of course," his dad said. "When Zoe's back."

He really didn't need to say that.

"And you won't just go to the pub this time?" Nathan said.

His dad raised his eyebrows.

"That was one unfriendly pub," he said. "They weren't keen on Londoners. I remember I asked for lager and I thought we were going to get lynched. They didn't like you being with me either. They might have had a sign outside saying children were allowed, but it didn't mean they were welcome."

"Dad," Nathan said. "Is it true you and Mum met when she was one of your customers?"

"You're all questions today, aren't you? On the stall you mean?"

Nathan nodded.

His dad smiled. "Who told you that? Zoe again?"

Nathan nodded. "She said that Mum came for Brussel sprouts and left with your heart."

His dad smiled again, either because it was true and he liked the memory of meeting his wife, or because Zoe told the funniest lies. Nathan thought it was more likely the Zoe memory. No one else stood a chance right now.

"Actually, I think it was runner beans," his dad said. "Not Brussels."

"Dad?"

"More questions?"

Nathan nodded. "Have you heard of the Greenhouses of Almería?"

"I don't think so, mate. What are they?"

"Zoe said it's where all your vegetables come from and you can see them from space."

"What are they called again?"

"The Greenhouses of Almería," Nathan liked the sound of the word Almería. He pronounced it like he imagined he would if he was Spanish.

"Is it anywhere near Battersea?" his dad said. "That's where most of our stock comes from."

A tweet arrived on Nathan's dad's tablet. He read it and typed something. He sat back in his seat and stared off into the distance. He seemed to be deep in thought or memory.

"I wish I believed aliens had her, Nathan," he eventually said. "I really do. I wish I thought I could speak to Zoe using a piece of paper with some letters on."

"Why don't you then?"

"I don't know, mate."

"What *do* you believe then?"

"About what's happened to Zoe?"

Nathan nodded.

"In a way, I hope she's with that boy," his dad said.

"Alex?"

His dad nodded. "Even if it's because she'd rather be with him than me. I'd rather she thought I was a terrible father than...Ah, I don't know, Nathan. I just want her to be safe."

"So do I, Dad."

"I know you do, mate."

"What would you do if you did believe she was with aliens though? Would you try and rescue her?"

His dad sighed.

"What if I could do it then?" Nathan said.

"I couldn't think of anyone I'd rather have rescuing her from aliens than you."

Nathan took a bite from his sandwich. His dad had hardly touched his.

"I'm sorry if I got you in trouble with the police," Nathan said.

"What makes you think you did that?"

"Because you were annoyed I said about Zoe's cuts and bruises on television."

"You were just telling the truth. It doesn't matter. It's only television. People will have forgotten all about it by now."

His dad looked over at the mural. He turned back to face Nathan. "It's hard to explain, Nathan, Zoe's cuts and that. But some people hurt themselves because it makes them feel better."

"That's stupid," Nathan said.

His dad shrugged. "And I wasn't annoyed with you. I was more annoyed with the programme."

"I didn't like the man," Nathan said.

"He was a bit of a nobber, wasn't he?"

Nathan laughed. He didn't know if nobber was officially a bad word.

His dad was distracted by something. He was staring at the mural again, or at the wall next to it. He'd stopped smiling.

"You've got to be kidding me," he said.

Nathan couldn't see what his dad was looking at. There was no one there other than the people walking by. His dad stood up, pushing his metal chair backwards. It scraped loudly on the pavement and almost fell over.

"What's wrong, Dad?"

Nathan looked at the mural and the empty pavement beneath it. Maybe it was the lack of candles and flowers that his dad was so upset about.

"Come on," his dad said.

"Where?"

"Just come on."

Nathan picked up his phone and the rest of his sandwich.

"You've forgotten your new iPad—"

"*Come on,*" his dad said.

Nathan picked up his dad's tablet and followed him. His dad walked over to the mural and then went straight past it, stopping in front of the wall where ten or eleven days ago Zoe had written her message to David Bowie. For a second Nathan couldn't see what his dad was looking at. He couldn't understand why he was so distraught. Nathan smelled it before he saw it.

Fresh white paint.

32

Nathan's dad refused to accept something that should have been as obvious to him as it was to his ten-year-old son. Somebody had painted over Zoe's message. It was gone. Or rather, it was still there, but it was hidden under a thick layer of white emulsion. But Nathan's dad grasped frantically at alternative straws, desperate for another explanation for what he was seeing, or not seeing.

He looked up and down the wall, and on the wall next to it, walking as far as the David Bowie mural in one direction and then back again, all the way around the corner, where the glass front of Morley's department store began. He scratched his head, perplexed, wondering if Zoe's message was in a different place on the wall to the one he'd remembered, or if it had managed somehow to slide down the wall. Had the wall itself moved? Anything but accept the awful truth.

He touched the wall and checked his fingers for wet paint. He sniffed his fingers. Maybe it wasn't too late to rescue what might be Zoe's last ever words with a damp cloth. When he found the paint was bone dry Nathan's dad started picking at it, scratching and scraping at the wall with his fingernails and making Nathan wince. And then his dad punched the wall, so hard that Nathan said ouch. He hit it again. Nathan screamed, "*Dad!*" Passers-by must have wondered if this could be the same man they'd seen before, going through all the postcards and scraps of paper left in front of the mural. The same man they saw there practically every day, a man they'd mistaken for the world's biggest David Bowie fan, when in fact the opposite was the case.

"Who would do this to her, Nathan?" he said.

Nathan said he didn't know.

His dad clenched his fist. There was a cut on his knuckle from punching the wall. It looked like the snake had bitten its tongue. Nathan thought his dad was going to punch the wall again, but then his anger seemed to suddenly leave him, and he sat down on the ground.

"Why would they do this to her, Nathan?"

Nathan didn't know how to answer. He wanted to comfort his dad, but he was a ten-year-old boy. Where would he even start? All he could think of was to be closer to his dad. He sat down on the pavement next to him.

"What is the matter with people, mate?"

They sat in silence with their backs against the wall, long enough for a woman to stop and crouch down next to them and ask if they were all right. She had her hand inside her bag and Nathan thought she was about to offer them money.

"They've painted over it," Nathan's dad said to the woman. "Can you believe it?"

"Have they?" the woman said. She couldn't possibly have known what he was talking about. She spoke to Nathan's dad like he was a baby.

"I need to make a phone call," Nathan's dad said. He asked Nathan for his phone and stood up. Nathan stood with him. The woman was now crouching on the pavement on her own.

"Come on, Nathan," his dad said, ignoring the woman.

They walked home. Nathan had to jog to keep up with his dad. All the way back he was on the phone to different people at the council. Every new person he spoke to gave him the number of somebody else to call. They were like kidnappers leading his dad to where he should leave the ransom. Outside the cinema his dad was put on hold. He took the phone away from his ear because the classical music was so loud.

When they got home, Nathan was relieved that Maureen was there. She'd know what to do.

"Can you believe it, Mo?" Nathan's dad said, holding Nathan's phone away from his ear, hold music spilling into the hall. "Why would anyone think that was acceptable?"

Maureen followed her brother into the living room.

"What's happened, Steve?"

He switched the mobile to speakerphone and put it on the arm of the sofa. He picked up the house phone and dialled the number he'd written on his palm on the way home.

"Why would they do it, Mo?"

"*Who*, Steve? Who's done what?"

A thin woman wearing a green tabard stepped out of the kitchen. She lived a few doors along, and Nathan's dad used to hate her because she was such a gossip. But he'd quickly learned how important gossips could be when your teenage daughter was missing.

Maureen turned to Nathan. "What on Earth has happened, Nathan?"

"They've painted Zoe's wall."

"Zoe's wall? What. Seriously? Who has?"

"The council," Nathan's dad said. He had two different phones connected and ringing now, Nathan's yellow mobile playing the same bit of looped Mozart over and over.

"I mean, I presume it's the council," Nathan's dad said. "Why the fuck would anyone else do it?"

The woman in the green tabard winced at Nathan's dad's swearing.

"Is it just Zoe's message?" Maureen said.

"What do you mean *just* Zoe's message?"

"Have they just painted over *Zoe's* message? Or all of them? Oh, not the lovely painting too?"

"Hello," his dad said into the house phone.

"It's just what's written on the wall," Nathan told his aunt.

The woman in the green tabard poked her head through the door and whispered, "I'll leave you all to it."

Maureen walked her to the front door. Nathan heard

it close. He wondered how long it would take this latest gossip to spread.

His dad hung up his mobile and walked over to the window. His whole body was shaking. Maureen put a hand on his shoulder. "Why don't you sit down for a bit, Steve? Ring them when you've at least calmed down."

"Hello," his dad said into the house phone. "I was given this number to speak to someone who's in charge of painting walls." He listened to whoever was on the other end of the line. "I don't know. Whoever paints over things written on a wall. No. No. It's not graffiti. Yes. Yes, it was written on the wall, but no, it's not graffiti. Yes, I'll hold."

Maureen took Nathan out to the kitchen. She closed the door but he caught the louder bits of his dad's phone call. "Well, can I speak to whoever is in charge of desecrating public monuments? No. *Desecrating.* D.E.S.C.R.... I don't know if it's council property. Did I take a photo? I've got loads, mate. That's all I have got photos of. That and the sky. Yes, the sky. Unless you've painted over that, too. It wouldn't fucking surprise me. No, you're not listening to me. I think you're missing the point. It's not the writing on the wall that's the vandalism. It's the painting over it. The vandals are probably in your building somewhere right now. You better hide any works of art you've got. Before they paint over them. If it was a Banksy you'd be protecting it, wouldn't you? What if they're my daughter's last words? And that message was evidence, you realise. You've destroyed police evidence. You know that, don't you? I'm not shouting. Ok, maybe I am shouting. That's because I'm fucking angry. Yes. Yes. I know. I'm sorry. I know it's not *your* fault. Can you put me through to whoever's fault it is? Yes, I'll hold."

Nathan's dad swore at a number of people on both phones and threatened to go to the Town Hall and speak personally to whoever was responsible. Nathan stayed in the kitchen with his aunt, listening to his dad shouting and the sound of glass breaking and what sounded like furniture being tipped over. Nathan tried to remember if there was anything breakable of his in the living room.

And then everything went quiet. Maureen suggested they wait a while before returning to the living room. She made Nathan's dad sound like a lit firework that hadn't gone off. Maureen made a cup of coffee and put three sugars in it for some reason. His dad didn't take sugar in his coffee. Maureen opened a box of Jaffa cakes and put everything on a tray. It was Nathan's job to take it into the living room to his dad, which hardly seemed fair.

His dad was sitting at the table, taking deep and deliberate breaths. Nathan wondered if he should get a paper bag. The house phone was off the hook on the sofa and Nathan's brand-new mobile was on the floor in front of the television in two pieces. A vase was broken, and flowers lay in a puddle of water and glass on the carpet under the television. Nathan stood in the doorway of the living room with the tray, scared to go all the way in. Maureen appeared behind him with a dustpan and brush. She looked at the mess.

Nathan's dad said, "I'll do it in a bit, Mo. Please."

Later, after Maureen had taken the bus home to West Norwood, Nathan's dad fixed the mobile phone and wrapped the flowers in newspaper with the larger pieces of broken glass. Nathan stood on the sofa directing his dad to any bits of glass he'd missed. His dad swept the carpet with a dustpan and brush and then he vacuumed. He told Nathan not to walk around without his shoes on for a while.

33

Nathan soon realised it wasn't just the vase that was broken. He'd seen his dad go through all kinds of emotions since Zoe had been missing. He'd seen him angry and resentful, bitter and short-tempered. His dad had scared him when he was stealing candles from the mural and Nathan had worried about him sometimes because he looked so sad. But not at any time had his dad been any less determined to stick to his cause. Even after feeling humiliated on television or when he spent almost a whole day being questioned by the police like a criminal. Nathan's dad had never looked like he was giving up. Until now. It was like the council had painted over Nathan's dad as well.

For the next two nights he slept in his own bed. He didn't stay up until three a.m. refreshing the internet or waiting for rolling news to change. He did still check Facebook and Twitter when he got up in the morning, but it wasn't with his usual frantic urgency. And he wasn't constantly online. Even when the FLOs returned his laptop and he could stop using the cheap tablet that took such a long time to load.

Yesterday, the house phone rang four times before Nathan's dad answered it, and at the end of the call he didn't put the phone back in the cradle. Nathan had to do it. The posters hadn't been updated and there were no leaflets left. In spite of everything Nathan's dad had said about the importance of not giving up, it was exactly what he appeared to be doing.

Zoe had been missing for eighteen days now. Nathan had finished *Moonmen (and Women)*. It was the biggest book that he, or possibly anyone, had ever read. He'd skipped a few of the longer parts but he was still proud of himself. He had a lot of new knowledge to show off to Zoe. The last things he learned were that a rocket would need so much fuel to get from Earth to Mars that it would be too heavy to take off, the building where NASA assemble their rockets is so big there are clouds inside, and if he was ever going to be an astronaut, Nathan would first have to learn how to fly a jet plane, speak Russian, get a university degree in science or maths and be quite a lot taller.

There'd been no visitors at the house since yesterday morning. Maureen was working extra hours at Greggs to catch up on all the time she'd taken off looking after Nathan and his dad. The FLOs hadn't been round with any updates. Even Craig hadn't been to the house with grapes or Kinder eggs or inappropriate jokes.

After a dinner of beans on toast, which they ate on their laps, Nathan and his dad shared a three-litre bottle of Coke and split a grab bag of cheese and onion crisps. Two days ago, Nathan's dad might have considered anything other than Ready Salted crisps too decadent. Flavour was a guilty pleasure he couldn't allow himself while his daughter was still missing. They went through the television channels, looking for something to watch but couldn't find anything. They browsed Netflix, iPlayer and Amazon Prime but nothing seemed to fit the mood they were both in.

"I'm sorry if I've been a bit of a rubbish dad lately," Nathan's dad said. "And I'm sorry if I scared you the other day. I'm just so terrified of losing her. And I know it's just a bit of writing on a wall. But I suppose I can't bear losing anything of hers either. She's left so little behind, Nathan."

Nathan told him he wasn't a rubbish dad. He was actually still the best dad.

"I'll have to get a new mug," his dad said, managing a smile.

Nathan scraped the final crumbs from the inside of the crisp bag. He sucked his fingers clean one at a time.

"Did you know, Dad, that the footprints of the first astronauts to walk on the Moon are still there?"

"Is that so?"

"It's because there's no wind on the Moon. There's loads of other stuff left on the Moon as well."

"Is that in that book you're always reading? *Moonmen*, is it?"

"And Women," Nathan said. He went and got the book and showed the cover to his dad.

"Did Zoe write that?"

Nathan nodded. If his dad wanted to peel off the sticker for his museum collection, he'd let him.

"I've just remembered something else," Nathan said.

He went over to the mantelpiece and picked up the pink piggy bank. He brought it over and pulled the rubber plug out of the belly. He held the pig over the sofa and slapped it as hard as he could until the folded up Post-it notes fell out.

"What are they?" his dad said.

Nathan unfolded the pieces of white paper and told his dad about the game he'd played with Zoe the night she disappeared. He arranged the pieces of white paper into two separate piles.

"These ones are Zoe's," Nathan said, pointing to the left-hand pile. "And I thought of all these names for her to guess."

His dad read all the names, smiling and looking sad at the same time. He picked up a Post-it note up from the pile on the right that Nathan had written *DAD* on.

"How long did she take to guess me?" his dad asked.

"Ages."

"I don't know if I should be flattered by that or not," his dad stuck the Post-it to his forehead. "In case I forget," he yawned and sat back on the sofa with his hands behind his head. "So, what did the astronauts leave on the Moon apart from their footprints then?"

"They left twenty-eight different things," Nathan said, sitting closer to his dad. "Space probes and golf balls, nail clippers—"

"Nail clippers?"

Nathan nodded. "And hammers and rakes and trousers and toothbrushes and toothpaste and bags of their sick and poo and used wet wipes. It weighed one hundred and eighty thousand kilograms altogether."

"How heavy's that in old money?"

Nathan shrugged. "I don't know. You should, though. You have to weigh vegetables all the time."

"Maybe that's why we're going out of business. Because of my lack of maths skills."

"I thought you said it was because of gentrification."

"I did, didn't I?"

"And Disneyfication."

"Have you been taking minutes?"

"How can you take minutes?"

"Different kind of minutes," his dad said. "I wonder what people from other planets think of humans when they see all the mess we've left behind up there."

"I thought you didn't believe in people from other planets."

"I'm not too sure I even believe in humans, to be honest."

"Zoe says humans are terrible."

His dad smiled.

"What is it?" Nathan asked.

"I'm glad you still use the present tense."

"What do you mean?"

"You always say Zoe *says* and not Zoe *said*."

"Because she's coming back, you mean?"

His dad put his arm around his shoulder. "We haven't given up, have we, mate?"

"Never, Dad."

"Because other people will, you know," his dad yawned again, stretching his arms wide apart and releasing Nathan. "They'll stop coming round with flowers and T-shirts, and they won't offer us money anymore or invite us onto their TV programmes. We're going to have to work a bit harder to take up their slack. Me and you." He adjusted the cushion behind his head and closed his eyes. "Tell me what else us terrible humans left on the Moon. You can check the book if you want."

"I don't need to." Nathan pushed the book away with his foot.

He named everything he could remember. The twelve cameras, the six flags, three lunar roving vehicles, two pairs of flight suit trousers, one pair of gloves, two golf balls, twelve pairs of space boots, one hundred bags of toilet waste, a watch strap, a falcon's feather, electrical cables, blankets and towels and so on. When he reached the last two objects – the gold olive branch and an eight-and-a-half-centimetre aluminium sculpture of an astronaut – Nathan realised his dad was asleep.

34

Nathan's dad still had his name stuck to his forehead when the police arrived. Both FLOs were there but no PC Torres, just PC Kari. He had his cap under his arm again. Nathan felt sick. He was sure his dad wouldn't be coming back if they took him away again. The FLOs followed his dad into the living room.

"Hello, Nathan." Janet sounded different. More serious. More like a normal police officer than a FLO. Nathan thought she was Anne Marie at first because she was standing on the wrong side.

"There've been a couple of developments," Anne Marie said to Nathan's dad. She looked at the space on the sofa next to Nathan. "You might want to sit down, Mister Love."

Nathan thought that calling his dad Mister Love instead of Steve was an even worse sign than PC Kari holding his cap. And Anne Marie's suggestion to sit down was like hypnosis to Nathan's dad, as he seemed to lose the feeling in his legs and he suddenly *had* to sit down.

"What's happened?" he said.

"A witness has come forward," Anne Marie said. "It appears this gentleman saw a girl—"

"Zoe?"

"We don't know that yet. But the gentleman in question saw a young girl. It was dark, so he couldn't give an accurate description."

"But it was Zoe, wasn't it?" Nathan's dad said. "That's what you're saying, isn't it?"

"All we *can* say right now is the gentleman believed the girl was," she hesitated. "She was about Zoe's age."

"Who is he?" Nathan's dad said. "The witness."

"I'm afraid we have a slight problem with drug users in the park at the moment," Anne Marie said. She sounded so apologetic, as though the slight drug problem in the park was all her fault. "It's the reason the gentleman didn't come forward sooner. He thought he'd get himself into trouble, and also…Well, I suppose there's a sort of criminals' code, isn't there? And it's not the done thing to talk to the police." Nathan thought of Arthur. *Tell the feds nothing. Snitches get stitches.* "But it seems that after seeing you both on television…" she looked at Nathan. "Apparently, the gentleman has a young lad himself. After he saw you on television, he decided to speak to us."

"When was this?" Nathan's dad said. "When did he see…the girl in the park? Was it definitely the other night? What time? Was Nathan with her?"

"No," Anne Marie said. "The gentlemen is certain of that. He says the girl was definitely alone. It was the night Zoe went missing, but this would have been a number of hours later. More like two or three in the morning. The gentleman…" she made it sound like she was talking about James Bond or the Three Musketeers rather than a problematic drug user. "The gentleman thinks the girl in the park was collecting firewood."

"Those were our *directions*!" Nathan said. "I *told* you. Dad, I told you, didn't I?" Nathan was almost shouting. "It's my fault, isn't it? Because I made her leave directions in the park so the aliens could find her. She even put glitter on them to make them easier to see because of me. It's my fault Zoe hasn't come back, isn't it, Dad?"

Nathan couldn't catch his breath. He was crying. His dad hugged him and rubbed his back like he had trapped wind, telling him it was okay. But it wasn't okay. It obviously wasn't anything close to okay.

"Perhaps Nathan would like to go out to the kitchen with Joe," Anne Marie said to Nathan's dad, "so that we can have a chat in private."

Nathan's dad didn't seem to hear her. He rocked Nathan in his arms.

"Steve," Anne Marie said. She placed her hand on his shoulder. He turned his head and relaxed his hold on

Nathan. His dad must have realised – as Nathan would much later – that Anne Marie had said there were a *couple* of developments.

"Probably best if we speak alone," Anne Marie said. She looked down at Nathan and smiled. "PC Kari was telling me how you went to the National Space Museum—"

"Space *Centre,*" Nathan corrected her. He wiped the snot from his face with the back of his hand and sniffed.

PC Kari smiled at Nathan like they were great friends. "I thought you could tell me some more about it." He moved an inch to one side to show the open doorway.

Nathan looked at his dad. "Dad?"

"It's all right, mate."

Nathan went to the kitchen with the policeman. One of the FLOs shut the living room door behind them. She forgot to lift it over the carpet. The noise it made was horrible. In the kitchen, Nathan asked PC Kari if he could have a drink of water, as though it was the policeman's house they were in.

"Where do you keep your cups?" PC Kari said. He started opening and closing the same cupboards he'd opened and closed two weeks ago when Zoe first went missing. He took a glass tumbler out of the cupboard above the sink. Nathan wondered if it was the original Luigi board glass.

The policeman filled the glass from the tap and gave it to Nathan. He sat down and sipped the water. PC Kari asked him about the planetarium and what he enjoyed most at the National Space Centre. What was his favourite thing there? All Nathan could think of was the Rocket Tower, but he'd forgotten the name of one of the rockets. He drank the water slowly, to avoid having to speak. He couldn't hear anyone talking in the other room. *Thor Able,* he remembered. And the Rocket Tower wasn't really his favourite thing. It wasn't the planetarium either or saving the ice moon Europa. It was staying up all night in the hotel room with Zoe afterwards. Getting ice creams from the vending machine and making cups of tea with the tiny milks that Zoe stole from the trolley. It was going outside to look at the stars with his sister.

Nathan looked at the kitchen clock. The hands were moving so slowly he thought it was broken. PC Kari asked him what his favourite planet was, which was such a stupid question and he almost told him so. It was definitely Saturn though. The second largest planet in the Solar System. It had at least sixty-two moons. Fifty-three of them had names but he could only remember one of them right now and that was only because it was the same as the name of the policeman in his kitchen. Nathan thought he heard his dad shout. It was more of a stifled scream. Titan was the name of Saturn's biggest moon, Nathan remembered. The same name as Arthur's dog. He wondered how Arthur's ankle was.

Janet knocked on the kitchen door. Two knocks. Not enough for a song. She opened the door and nodded a secret police signal to PC Kari. Nathan was certain that because he'd failed to bring Zoe back, his dad was going to prison. He followed the police back to the living room. His dad was sitting on his own at the table, looking down at his clasped hands, massaging the head and tail of the snake as though he was trying to rub the tattoos off. He didn't say anything when Nathan came in. He looked like he was about to say something, or he tried his best to say something, but he couldn't find his voice or the words that he really needed to say. He turned his face back to his hands instead.

They all sat together in silence apart from the occasional crackle of the police radios until Auntie Maureen arrived. Nathan would have to live with her forever now. He'd have to eat spicy food at the table with a knife and fork while his aunt hummed like a fridge. The FLOs spoke quietly to Maureen in the hall and then the three police officers left. Without Nathan's dad. Maureen asked Nathan and his dad if they wanted a hot drink. Nathan's dad shook his head and Maureen said she would make him one anyway. She said he didn't have to drink it if he didn't want to.

"Nathan," she said. "Perhaps you'd like to help me make it."

Nathan looked at his dad. He was staring at nothing now. Not his hands, not out of the window. Nathan realised that Maureen had been asked to come to the house because the police didn't want to leave his dad on his own. Nathan thought he knew what Craig had meant when he said he was worried about his dad doing *anything daft*.

"Will my dad be all right?" Nathan asked Maureen.

Maureen looked at her brother. "Steve?"

Nathan's dad looked up and managed a single nod.

In the kitchen, Maureen filled the kettle and switched it on. When it started to boil, with her back to Nathan and leaning heavily on the sink, she told him, "They've arrested Craig."

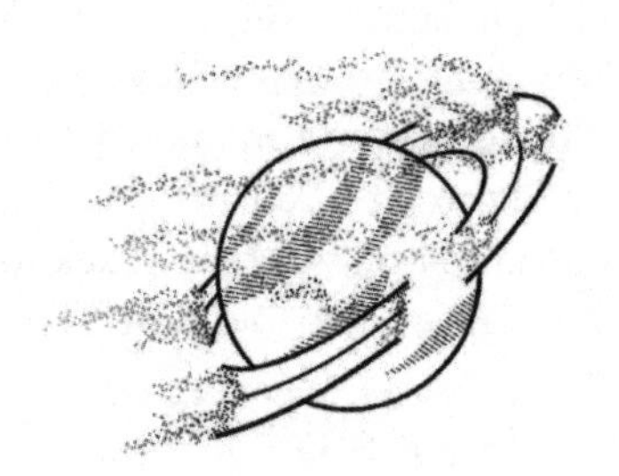

35

Nathan tested his Space Torch. The light flickered. He shook the torch, then unscrewed the end, removed the batteries and rolled them between his palms and replaced them. He tested the torch again. It was better but the beam was weak. He switched the torch off and put it in his backpack. He rested the Christmas cracker compass on his open palm and moved his hand around until the needle pointed north. He put the compass in his backpack. He packed the notepad and pencil, the underwater camera, the MP3 player, the pocket dictionary and the photo of his sister. He put the empty glitter tube in his backpack and also the Sharpie lid, Zoe's blue asthma inhaler and the doll's head.

There hadn't been time to get any food from the kitchen. All he had to eat was the ice cream and strawberries he'd stolen from Astronaut Buzz's display table and the remainder of his Subway sandwich. He'd taken Zoe's half bottle of Oasis out of her bedroom. The space ice cream had been in his backpack for almost a week and it still hadn't melted. It was no more real ice cream than the apples and oranges in Auntie Maureen's fruit bowl were real fruit. The Subway sandwich was stale and falling apart and he wished he'd asked for the works because that was Zoe's favourite. He pulled the longest blade out of the Swiss Army knife and trimmed the crustiest bit from the end of the bread. He dropped the crumbs on the carpet next to the fifty-six alien pictures and the wreckage of the Kinder Hot Rod.

There was a high-pitched scream outside. Nathan held the Swiss Army knife like a weapon. He opened the curtains just enough to see two foxes, playing with a chicken wing on the outdoor Ping-Pong table. No matter how many times Nathan heard foxes on the estate, he always wondered what creature could be responsible for such a noise – Velociraptor? Dragon? – before realising it was just a fox. They never seemed to make the same sound more than once. Something startled the foxes and they jumped down from the Ping-Pong table. Nathan watched them trot away into the darkness.

He sat back on his bed, opening and closing the tools of the Swiss Army knife. He stroked the sharp edge of the longest knife blade against his skin. He wanted to cut himself. If he was more like Zoe, the aliens might take him too. He touched the tip of the blade with his thumb, imagining what it would feel like to stick it into Craig.

Nathan pushed the blade back into the knife and put the knife in the front pouch of his backpack. He zipped the pouch closed. He lay on his back, hugging his backpack close to his chest, watching the night sky through the gap between his curtains. There seemed to be a lot of stars. He took the snow globe out of his backpack, shook it and waited for the snow to settle.

Holding his hand up to the estate light spilling in through his window, Nathan admired how well he'd painted his fingernails this time. He'd even managed to do the nails on his right hand. He'd drawn a snake's head on his left hand and coloured it in, using all of Zoe's eleven remaining Sharpies, listening to the lids click back in place a total of thirty-three times to be sure none of the pens would dry up. There was no room left on his hand to write his address, but he wasn't sure he wanted to come back home again, and his name was on the ID badge from the television studio anyway. He'd pinned it next to the *We come in peace* badge on his *Where is Zoe Love?* T-shirt. He was wearing the T-shirt over his orange spacesuit. He didn't bother with the swimming goggles or the skateboard pads.

When it stopped snowing on the Moon, Nathan put the snow globe in his backpack, placing it carefully at the bottom of the bag so it didn't break, like Maureen did when she was packing eggs at the supermarket. He checked his new phone was on silent, or as silent as anything such a bright yellow could be. He closed the curtains and stood up, slung the backpack over one shoulder, eased his bedroom door open and crept out onto the landing.

It was quiet enough to hear the house breathe, the central heating complaining and water rushing through the pipes at such great speed, he thought somebody must have got up to use the toilet. Nathan walked along the landing, checking rooms. Maureen was in his dad's bedroom. Even when she was asleep Maureen was humming, like she wasn't really asleep but on stand-by.

Nathan's dad was asleep in Zoe's room. He was lying on top of the covers, still dressed. Nathan presumed his dad had fallen asleep by accident, unable to physically stay awake any longer. He was snoring and Nathan wanted to turn him over or pinch his nose. He stood in the doorway and watched him sleeping, thinking of all the times his dad had stood in his bedroom doorway watching him sleep, or pretending to. Nathan was great at pretending to sleep. He didn't make it look too obviously fake by snoring loudly or yawning and his dad would stand there for ages, thinking he was fast asleep. Nathan liked it. He felt safe. Protected and loved. Lots of his friends didn't have dads, or they never saw them. Nathan watched his dad sleeping and wondered if he was dreaming. He hoped he wasn't. *Why didn't I check her room?*

Nathan went downstairs, avoiding the steps that always creaked when his dad stood on them, in case the backpack was heavy enough to make the stairs creak for him too. From the living room Officer Dibble watched Nathan. The cat could have no idea of the tragic events that had led to him finally getting his night-time spot back on the sofa. Nathan went into the living room and sat next to Officer Dibble. He stroked him until he was purring and struggling to keep his eyes open. Nathan almost sent himself to sleep too.

He reached over the cat for the television remote control. He took the back off, removed the batteries and swapped them with the ones in his Space Torch. He held the end of the torch against his hand and tested it. The beam was brand new. Nathan's dad claimed Zoe used to make the remote controls stop working by putting dud batteries in them. Nathan still preferred to believe she had superpowers.

He picked up his dad's laptop. There was a crack on the lid through the centre of the apple, where the police had dropped something on it. Nathan opened the laptop. There were eighty-nine unread emails. He daren't look at Facebook or Twitter. He opened his backpack and squeezed the laptop in as far as it would go, pulling the drawstring as tight as possible. He stood up and tested the bag for weight. The fact it was now almost too heavy to carry made it seem more important. The backpack felt like an actual portable life support system rather than a children's toy.

Nathan went out to the hall. He lifted his dad's sheepskin jacket off the hook by the front door and pulled his parka out from underneath. He returned his dad's jacket to the hook and put his parka on. He zipped it up and put his phone in the pocket. And then he paused. He took the phone out again and put in the pocket of his dad's jacket. He carefully lifted the chain off the front door. He disabled the security light and hauled his bag onto his back. It was almost heavy enough to topple him over. In space, the backpack would be so light that if it wasn't strapped to his back it would float away like a balloon at a country show. He opened the front door and looked back into the house. One last idiot check. Officer Dibble had come out into the hall. Probably hearing the door and expecting to be fed. Nathan looked at the cat and mouthed the words, "Don't tell Dad."

36

Outside it was as cold as the Moon. It could be as low as minus 173 degrees at night on the Moon and as hot as 100 degrees during the day. The material of Nathan's spacesuit was thin, and the T-shirt didn't provide much added warmth. It was too late to go back upstairs for a jumper. He gently closed the front door and looked out on the deserted estate and the jet-black sky. He'd never seen so many stars. *Like Oscars night,* Zoe had said to him when describing one of her secret nights out under the sky. There were too many stars to count. An astronomer in America once counted more than nine thousand stars without using a telescope. Nathan had asked Zoe how anyone could tell the astronomer was telling the truth. Zoe shook her head. She said she was disappointed with his scepticism, "and at such a young age too."

When Nathan saw the star-filled sky, his gut instinct was to go back inside and tell Zoe. *Look, Zoe.* Look what you're missing. The knowledge that he would never again be able to do that, almost paralysed Nathan and he thought he might collapse on the spot.

The backpack was pulling at his neck. He turned around and rested the bag's weight against the side of a dustbin while he adjusted the straps until it felt slightly more comfortable. The dustbin had been outside their house since Friday. The binmen had been but they hadn't emptied it. Nathan wondered if it was because his dad had been so rude on the phone to everyone at the council. He stood on his tiptoes and looked inside the dustbin. The stink knocked him back on his heels and combined with the weight of his backpack, he almost went 'arse over tit', as his dad liked to say. Nathan had seen a terrapin at the zoo once. It had managed to flip itself upside down and couldn't right itself. Zoe had ignored the warning signs to not tap on the glass until the terrapin turned himself upright again. "We probably saved that stupid terrapin's life," Zoe had said.

Nathan recovered his balance and took a deep breath and looked again in the dustbin. He reached his hand inside and tugged at the paper until it broke free from the rest of the rubbish piled on top of it. The paper was stained with curry and with egg yolk and tomato sauce. It looked like a T-shirt in an advert for washing powder. There was a big piece torn away from the corner and only three stars remained intact. Nathan stuffed the manky Luigi board into his coat pocket, wiped his hands on his sleeves and headed towards the park. His legs were already tingling and itching from the cold.

Nathan didn't know if he was running away from home or if he was looking for Zoe or for aliens. And he didn't know why he'd felt the need to bring so much useless stuff with him. Maybe he would leave it all in the park, like the cigarette packets and baby's socks that were already there. Or the 180,000 kilograms of litter left on the Moon by twelve highly-trained but still terrible humans. He walked along the centre of the path between the houses and flats, careful not to set off any security lights. He saw somebody had sprinkled table salt on the threshold of one of the houses. It was probably to stop the ground turning to ice, but it could also have been to keep evil spirits away. Auntie Maureen used to do that in every doorway of her house when she was upset after Uncle Sean left her.

Nathan pushed his backpack through the drug dealers' gap in the railings and climbed in after it. He didn't stop to think about getting himself or his bag stuck or to wonder if the boy who'd been chased through the estate was stuck in the same gap when he was stabbed. If Nathan had considered any of that he might not have had the courage to go any further.

When he was safely through the gap, he started walking towards Zoe's favourite tree. In the park it was a lot darker, so he stopped and took off his backpack. He found his Space Torch and Zoe's MP3 player. He switched the torch on and put the earphones in and pressed play. 'Life on Mars?' started. The torchlight and David Bowie's voice made him a little less frightened. He hooked the backpack over his shoulder again and carried on into the park. When he found his first arrow, he picked up the three short branches and threw them as hard as he could into the park. His second arrow he kicked apart and the third arrow he couldn't find. When he got to Zoe's tree, he found the first arrow that he'd left. The folded poster was gone from inside the hollow of the tree.

He picked up the three sticks and threw them in three different directions into the park. He put his backpack down on the grass next to the tree and stretched his arms out, pushing his shoulder blades together and turning his head from side to side, like his dad warming up or cooling down at the gym.

One half of the thick tree trunk had been cut into about ten smaller pieces. They were laid out in a row like stepping-stones across a stream. He sat down on one of the upturned logs and stared up at the night sky. He would have to go to Antarctica or Scotland or travel back in time a billion years to see so many stars. He didn't expect to ever see a sky like it over Brixton. It was like being at the planetarium or staring at his bedroom ceiling. If he changed the setting on his torch and shone the distant galaxy at the sky, maybe Zoe was right and something calamitous would happen.

'Life on Mars?' finished. He turned the volume up as far as it would go so that he could hear the end of the piano and the phone ringing and the swearing. Zoe had played the end of the song over and over, trying to work out what was being said after it was finished. Once she found out what it was, she couldn't wait to tell Nathan. No doubt hoping that he would repeat the swear words in front of their parents.

Nathan stopped the MP3 player and removed the earphones. He took his dad's laptop out of the backpack and put it on another of the upturned logs. Opening the laptop in the darkness of the park was like lighting a fire in a cinema. The screen was bright enough to be seen from Space. He half-closed the lid and pressed the key to dim the screen. He opened the photo library and went through Zoe's pictures to see if she'd captured a sky as spectacular as the one above him now. Even Venus was twinkling like it was a star. Unless it was his tears. Nathan hadn't realised he was crying.

An email arrived on the laptop. The pinging sound was so unexpected and so loud it made him jump and he knocked the computer off the log. He picked it up and read the subject of the email.

This is the money button!! Try it you self. Click here and win win win big $$$$!

If Nathan was an adult, he would definitely have clicked on the link and every other link like it. He hadn't thought it was possible to pick up Wi-Fi in the park and he wondered if the email had been sent by some other means, one as yet undiscovered by earthlings, spam from deep space.

He muted the laptop's sound and quit the email and the web browser. He created a new folder on the desktop and named it 'DAD' and started dragging all the desktop documents and folders into it. Every single archived webpage with reports of sightings and all the blurry iPhone jpegs of vans parked outside schools. Some of the pictures had been enlarged and cropped so his dad could read the number plates. They were so blurry they didn't even look like vans anymore. Nathan dragged them all into the 'DAD' folder.

He put the photo of 'Alex' in the folder and all the PDF guides about how to search for missing children and how to best use the media to your advantage and how to raise campaign funds and so on. Nathan put a desktop folder that his dad had named 'red herrings and timewasters' into the 'DAD' folder and finally the folder titled 'Space Cadet', with the scanned pages of Nathan's red notebook inside. Nathan dragged the full 'DAD' folder into the trash so that the only thing left on the desktop was the wallpaper picture of Zoe. He angled the laptop so she could see the stars. He imagined her eyes in the photo, not half-closed but half-open, waxing not waning, as she gazed in wonder at Orion's Belt and its two brightest stars, Betelgeuse and Rigel. Zoe's mouth was open in awe. Her braces shone like Ziggy Stardust.

Nathan took the dishevelled but still beta Luigi board out of his coat pocket and unfolded it in front of him on a different upturned log. He had to pull the paper apart where it had stuck together. The B, the L and the P were completely torn off. He wiped away tears and snot on the back of his hand and put the snow globe on the Luigi board to stop it from blowing away. He thought about Zoe telling him that the Luigi board was normally *a device for speaking to the dead*. All the time when he'd been trying to make contact with alien Zoe, he'd been speaking to ghost Zoe.

He took everything out of his backpack. The glitter tube, the lid from Zoe's Sharpie, her asthma inhaler, the doll's head and the Christmas cracker compass. Nathan looked at it all, laid out in front of him like E.T.'s Speak & Spell, coat hanger, record player, fork, umbrella and buzz saw blade. He felt if only there was some way to connect it all together, he would be able to make contact. Zoe would still be okay.

He heard a voice. At first he was sure it had to be Craig, escaped from the police and coming for him too. There was another voice though and then a third. And they were much younger voices than Craig's. Boys. In the darkness they could have been as far away as Herne Hill, but they felt very close by. Nathan tried to work out if the voices were getting louder or quieter, moving closer towards him or further away. They were definitely growing louder. The boys were swearing, threatening each other but laughing too. Nathan thought of the boys on the big estate. If it was them, this time they'd definitely kill him. He wondered if the boy who had his phone was there. The boys didn't seem to care about being heard. They either had no fear or were too scared to admit to it in front of each other.

Nathan thought about running. He looked at everything he'd taken out of his backpack and didn't want to leave it. If he put it back in his bag, the heavy backpack would slow him down. Even if he was willing to lose the Luigi board and the other components of his E.T. Communicator, he thought about how badly his dad had reacted to Zoe's words being painted over on the mural wall. He could never leave the laptop in the park with all of her photos on it.

Nathan still wasn't sure exactly whereabouts in the park the boys were. They might be between him and home, and if he ran, he might run right into them. He thought about the boy getting stabbed. The gap in the railing wasn't an escape route at all, it was a trap. Nathan shut the laptop and tried to put it in his backpack but it wouldn't fit. He did his best to remain calm. *Less haste more speed, Nathan.* He needed to be more like his mum, not like his dad chasing the sleeve of his sheepskin jacket like a dog trying to catch its tail. He was still crying. As long as he didn't sob. He wiped his nose on the sleeve of his coat to stop himself from sniffing.

Nathan forced as much of the laptop into the backpack as he could and wrapped everything else up inside the Luigi board and stuffed it all into the bag. He put the backpack down on the ground behind the longer section of tree trunk. He pushed it up against the tree and the backpack disappeared into the hollow. Nathan wondered if the hole was big enough for a small boy. He pushed his bag as far in as he could and rolled his body in after it. He hoped he didn't roll straight out of another hole on the other side of the tree.

It stunk inside the tree. He thought there might be something dead in there. Instinctively, he started counting to take his mind off it. One Mississippi, two Mississippi. Was the beat of his heart as loud to others as it sounded to him? He held his breath. Three Mississippi, four Mississippi. He'd trained for this, in the bath and in bed, underwater and under the covers. The voices of the boys were really loud now, and there were more of them. He thought he could smell weed. Arthur said skunk got its name because it smelled the same as a skunk. He thought there might be a skunk inside the tree with him, dead or alive.

He should get up now and run. It might be dark enough to disappear into the park and hide until the boys were gone. He could go home and his dad would never know he'd been away. He would find him in bed, cold and crying and presume he'd had a bad dream. Nathan knew his dad was probably right. There was no such thing as aliens. Zoe had made it all up. For attention. Or because she was grieving. Because of their mum. And because she was a teenager. She was going through a phase. Because it made her feel better.

The boys' voices were right next to him. He tried counting them. As many as seven or eight, maybe nine, and all talking at once. No one listening. He reached inside his backpack. His fingers traced the white cross on the side of the Swiss Army Knife. He took the knife out of the backpack and pulled out the tools until he felt the long sharp blade. He turned his body around. He wasn't completely inside the tree and could still see the sky. He held the penknife against his chest, with the point under his chin, like a knight buried with his sword. And then the sky exploded with light. His scream of surprise was drowned out by the most deafening of bangs. There were four more loud bangs and the fireworks turned the sky Aurora Borealis green and red. Every firework lit Nathan up too. Rockets whizzed and whooshed, in quick succession across the sky. When the third firework went off, Nathan thought he saw Zoe.

Smoke wafted above him. Moon dust smelled like gunpowder. Eugene Cernan had said that; Eugene Cernan from Apollo 17, the last man to walk on the Moon.

There was another almighty explosion and for a second or two there were no stars in the sky, just one enormous bright manmade light. And Nathan saw Zoe again. He reached his hand across and pulled the poster towards him. He lay still, waiting for the next explosion, or for the boys to drag him out and cut him up. He held the picture of Zoe close to his chest, with the penknife over it, singing the names of Saturn's moons in his head. Aegaeon, Aegir, Albiorix, Anthe, Atlas, Bebhionn, Bergelmir, Bestla. When he got stuck, he thought about the cameras and lunar vehicles, the golf balls and flags. The Moon was a tomato, the Earth was the orange and the grapefruit was the Sun. Zoe explaining the Universe with fruit. Meteors becoming meteorites. Asteroids and comets, stars that twinkled, planets that moved. Novas and supernovas, dwarf planets and supermassive black holes. Poison clouds that tasted of raspberries. Cirrus, cumulus, cumulonimbus, stratocumulus, lenticularis, mamma. *No, Nathan. Columbus is not a cloud.*

Hundreds of Mississippis must have passed since the last firework. It was dark again and so cold. Nathan pulled the hood of his parka all the way over his head and tucked his body further inside the tree. He was shivering too much and he was far too cold to fall asleep, but he was dreaming anyway. He dreamed he was weightless. He could feel his body floating and the Earth spinning and turning as he rose above it.

He opened his eyes and looked up at the stars, expecting to be in amongst them. He watched them move across the sky like planets and yet they were twinkling too. Like hundreds of India99s, looking for all the missing girls and stabbed boys. The mispers and the murdered. The stars seemed to bounce.

Nathan followed the zigzags and the curls, and the lines on the snake's body where it disappeared up the sleeve of his dad's T-shirt. The snake was covered in goose bumps because of the cold, and because his dad was only wearing a T-shirt – his sheepskin jacket wrapped around his bitterly cold son. Nathan rested his head against his dad's chest. He was still holding the poster with the picture of Zoe tightly in his hand. He must have dropped the knife. He hoped the boys didn't find it. He didn't want someone getting stabbed because of him.

Nathan's shivering had slowed. It was almost in time with his dad's heart, beating like a drum beneath the tattoo that said 'KAT'. He could already see the estate and an oblong of light filling the open door where Maureen was standing, crossing herself, thanking God. Nathan looked at the railings between the park and his house and at the narrow gap that him and his dad and the heavy backpack that appeared weightless when his dad was carrying it, were going to have to somehow squeeze through. But Nathan wasn't worried. He knew his dad would find a way.

37

In the days, weeks and months that followed, if Nathan's dad had a Mobile Quarantine Facility, he would have locked Nathan inside. He'd failed to protect his daughter from the worst horrors of the world, but he could at least try and protect his son from the details of those horrors. His dad turned newspapers over in shops, changed television channels and the password on his laptop. Nathan wasn't allowed to answer the phone and his dad wouldn't speak with the FLOs when Nathan was in the room.

But even if his dad bought all the newspapers and burned them, if all the paper shops really did blow away, if he disconnected the phones and cancelled the Wi-Fi, the news would have made it through. Like the line of ants that Buzz Aldrin had seen walking through the Mobile Quarantine Facility. Nathan would have found out what had happened to Zoe one way or another. From his friends at school or overhearing a woman in a green tabard on the estate. Their stories would be unreliable and full of hearsay and rumour. Facts would be exaggerated or made up and no doubt even more horrific and unbearable than the truth already was.

And so, Nathan's dad had to tell him himself. He tried to make it sound as much like a riddle as he could, as though he was talking about another girl and not his daughter. He told Nathan that Craig had walked into the police station and told the desk sergeant, that after watching his best friend and his best friend's son on breakfast television, he could no longer live with himself and the terrible thing he'd done. It was actually Nathan, talking about Elliott and E.T., that really got to Craig – just as it had moved the witness who'd seen Zoe collecting firewood to break the criminal code and go to the police. And as the stars and fireworks fought it out for dominance of the skies over Brixton, Craig was down below in a windowless interview room, completing the second of his police interviews.

Craig told the police how on the night Zoe went missing, he'd left the pub with her dad and they'd walked together back to his house. After talking and drinking in the living room for a while, Nathan's dad had gone to bed, leaving Craig alone in the living room. He was going to sleep on the sofa until it was time for him to walk into town and take his turn opening the stall. Up until Craig had told the police any different, they – and Nathan's dad – believed that was exactly what had happened. They'd all watched Craig leaving the estate at five a.m. on the blurry CCTV images, filmed by the same cameras that captured Craig and Nathan's dad staggering into the estate a few hours earlier.

But Craig couldn't get to sleep on the sofa. He was too tall. And the sofa was uncomfortable. The metal studs were digging into his side and when he removed the cushions, the broken spring in the base of the sofa was even worse. As Nathan's dad told Nathan the story, he frequently paused to blame himself – If only he'd fixed the spring in the sofa like he kept saying he would. If only it had been his turn to open the stall. If only he'd had one less drink.

Craig told the police that at three in the morning, he heard someone moving around in the hall. He heard the front door open and had the sensation of cold air entering the house. He got up from the sofa and went out to the hall just as the front door was closing. He put his shoes on and went outside and saw Zoe walking in the direction of the park. He went back to the living room to get his jacket and he followed her.

When the police asked Craig why he didn't just ask Zoe where she was going, he told them she used to sleepwalk. Everyone knew it was dangerous to wake sleepwalkers, didn't they? He said he would have told her dad he'd seen her, but he didn't want to wake him either. Craig told the police he didn't think it was a 'big enough deal' at the time.

He decided to follow Zoe until she woke up of her own accord and then he would bring her safely back home.

Craig followed Zoe and watched her climb over the railings. *In her sleep?* Nathan thought. Craig said he was very drunk. It was something he would say a lot in his interviews, telling the police he knew it was no excuse, while repeatedly blaming everything that happened on alcohol. Craig climbed over the railings and followed Zoe into the park, where she immediately started picking up sticks. He watched her carry them over to a tree lying on its side, where she added them to a pile. Craig watched her from a distance, but he said he wasn't hiding exactly. Not for sinister reasons anyway. He confessed he was curious. He wanted to know what she was doing. Craig told the police he then realised how cold it was and decided he would have to wake Zoe. He approached slowly and quietly. He wasn't *sneaking* up on her, he said. He was still wary of startling her. He'd heard about people having heart attacks and going into comas because they'd been woken up when they were sleepwalking.

But when Zoe saw Craig, she must have thought he was someone else. It was dark, Craig said. And she panicked. Craig said he only put his hands on her to calm her down. He wanted to reassure her that it was only him. It was just Uncle Craig. But she wouldn't stop struggling, and then she slapped his face and he had no choice but to tighten his grip on her. He just wanted her to stop struggling. That was all. He told the police she was like a caught fish. He asked them if they'd ever held an eel before. A policeman later told Nathan's dad that Craig had smiled at that point. It was one of the details Nathan's dad tried to keep secret from Nathan. There were things about that night his dad wished he didn't know himself. Everything would make its way down the grapevine to Nathan eventually.

At some point when Zoe was struggling to free herself from Craig's arms she blacked out. Craig said that was when he was the one who was panicking. He told the police he wasn't thinking straight. He sat on the grass with Zoe for a long time, waiting for her to wake up so he could take her home, but she didn't wake up. He lost all track of time. He picked Zoe up, intending to carry her home but for some reason he walked in the opposite direction. He was confused. He thought he might be in shock. One excuse after another.

Craig carried Zoe away from the estate, further down into the park. He told the police he was looking for a safe place and somewhere warm to leave her. He laid her down inside a thicket of small trees and bushes close to the clock tower. He covered her with his jacket and a thick sheet of plastic he found on top of a pile of bricks that must have been there for the work being done to the café and stable block.

Craig then went back to the estate. He planned on waking Zoe's dad, but he panicked again. He walked past his friend's house and kept going until he was filmed by the CCTV camera on the wall of the flats opposite, leaving the estate and walking out onto the main road. The images were of such poor quality that none of the police who watched the film seemed to notice that Craig wasn't wearing the green Harrington jacket he'd arrived in earlier. If Nathan's dad had looked in Craig's wardrobe, he might have seen the space left between the brown and navy jackets. Like the space between the Converse shoes in Zoe's wardrobe.

Craig walked back to the pub where he'd left his van. He sat in the van for a while, trying to clear his head. When the park was open, he drove through one of the largest of the twelve gates. His was just another white van entering the park, presumably as part of the building work. When he drove out again with Zoe in the back, Craig told the police he actually found himself in the middle of a short convoy of white vans.

Nathan's dad couldn't bring himself to tell Nathan anything that happened after that. He had to wait until he read it online or heard it at school. The thing that would upset Nathan the most when he found it out, something that would haunt him in his dreams for a long time, was that when they were driving around Brixton in Craig's van looking for Zoe, and when Craig pulled the van onto the kerb outside the Body Shop and put his hazards on so Nathan could show his dad where Zoe had written on the wall, and then on the journey back to the estate, taking diversions up and down side streets looking for Zoe, until they were back at the estate where Craig parked illegally with the hazards flashing and 'EMERGENCY BUILDING WORK' under the windscreen, and while they waited for the police to arrive, and when the police came and exchanged friendly banter with Craig about keeping out of mischief. For that entire time, Zoe had been in the back of the van, hidden amongst the potatoes and the carrots, underneath a carpet of green astro turf used for displaying tomatoes and oranges on the stall.

Later, Craig took the police to the forest where Zoe's body was hidden. Arthur showed Nathan a picture in the newspaper. Craig and the police were so tiny in the picture. It looked like it had been taken from space. But they'd probably just used a drone. Arthur said the forest looked like Center Parcs.

Craig pleaded guilty. He said he didn't want to put Zoe's family through any more suffering, as though he was some kind of hero for that. He was sentenced to Life, which only really meant twenty-three years, and everyone thought it wasn't long enough. Arthur said he could get his brother to stab Craig up in his cell, but Nathan told him they weren't in the same prison.

There was a drawing in the newspaper of Craig when he was in court. Because he'd kept his head bowed the whole time, the court artist had drawn him like that. It looked like he was going bald. Nathan was glad.

He would never understand how Craig had managed to appear so concerned or how he'd helped search for Zoe when he knew where she was. When he thought about Craig watching the appeal, drinking beer and making jokes, especially when Nathan thought about Craig giving him Kinder eggs and pretending to be interested in the Moon landings and being President Nixon, when all the time he'd murdered his sister. Nathan just couldn't understand it.

The FLOs, who months later still came to the house now and then, bringing news on court dates and the sentence and so on, said that Craig was only ever concerned about being found out. He was looking out for himself, no one else. He joined in the search for Zoe to conceal his guilt. That was all. Craig was, according to Janet, 'hiding in plain sight.' Like Nathan's school cap and his shoes in Zoe's bedroom. The cap was still there. Nathan's dad had found the shoes. Anne Marie called Craig a wolf in sheep's clothing, but Nathan thought he was more like a crocodile. Craig had pretended everything.

After Craig was sentenced there were fewer stories in the papers and nothing at all on the television, apart from a reference in a question asked on a daytime talk show: 'Have you ever been betrayed by your best friend?' The online chat, the speculation, hunches and conspiracy theories continued for longer, but people eventually lost interest. The notifications from Facebook, reminding Nathan's dad that he hadn't posted anything on the *Where is Zoe Love?* page, would presumably stop too at some point.

On the first day without a single post or email about Zoe, Nathan thought the internet was broken. His dad was relieved. He said, "I think the media circus has left town, Nathan." The publicity his dad had welcomed and encouraged when Zoe was missing had quickly become a curse when she was just gone. He had his closure, but it hadn't quite lived up to its name.

Nathan and his dad thought about Zoe every single day. His dad said he looked forward to only having good memories about her. Nathan knew his dad couldn't help himself from thinking that Craig hadn't really followed Zoe because he thought she was sleepwalking and that he'd known exactly what he was going to do. Maybe he'd been planning it for years, thinking about it every time he came to the house and saw Zoe. Nathan knew his dad must have had such thoughts because Nathan had them too. It was hard to picture Craig at the house without imagining him looking at Zoe as his first victim. Or even his next. His latest. What if there were other victims? Nathan's dad said the only way to not allow a never-ending stream of imagined worsts to destroy him was to accept Craig's version of events as the truth.

There was one thing, however, that even Craig couldn't explain. Why had Zoe gone back to the park in the middle of the night to move the branches? In the end, Nathan and his dad came up with their own reason. They were in the garden one evening, waiting for the sun to go down on the first day of summer and for the stars to come out, when Nathan asked his dad, "Are trees female?"

"How so, mate?"

"Like ships are called she. And Mum's car was female."

His dad laughed. "Mum's car was temperamental enough to be female," he put his hand on his heart. "Sorry, Kat."

"What does temperamental mean?"

His dad thought for a bit. "Moody. Was this tree a bit of a moody tree?"

Nathan laughed. "How can a tree be moody?"

Nathan told his dad how upset Zoe was that her favourite tree had been chopped down and dragged to the top of the park and that it had its branches cut off.

"She called the branches the tree's arms."

"That does sound like Zoe."

"I was thinking," Nathan said, "that what if she went to the park to carry the tree's arms back home down where all the other trees were? Like they were its family, the tree's family."

Nathan's dad nodded. "Maybe. Do you know what I think though? I think she was getting rid of the directions she left for the aliens because she didn't want to go anywhere after all. She'd realised she was happy where she was. She decided she wanted to stay on Earth with her family, with her brother and her dad."

"And Officer Dibble," Nathan said, looking at the cat, down on the grass shadow-boxing a wasp.

"With her brother and her dad, and Officer Dibble," Nathan's dad said, "Who she loved just as much as they all loved her."

Nathan nodded. "That's the best reason."

38

Nathan was eleven now and at big school. He was the second smallest person there. On his birthday he went to MacDonald's with his dad, but he felt guilty eating a burger and didn't finish it. It was difficult to do virtually anything without thinking of Zoe. All the special occasions he'd worried about not happening when Zoe was missing, now that she was gone, Nathan dreaded them. Birthdays, Pancake Day, Easter and Firework Night, Halloween and Christmas, none of them would be quite the same without his sister.

Zoe would have been sixteen now. On her birthday Nathan and his dad chose a star for her.

"How about that one?" Nathan's dad said.

"That's a planet."

"How do you know?"

"It's not twinkling. And it wasn't there yesterday. Stars don't move that much."

"Which star is the one we chose for your mum?" his dad said.

Nathan screwed up one eye and pointed. His dad followed the aim of Nathan's finger. "That one."

"How can you tell?"

"I remembered it."

The truth was Nathan couldn't tell. But it didn't matter. Not to either of them.

"How about that one next to it?" his dad said. "Could that be Zoe's star?"

They both watched the star for a minute, to check it twinkled and to be sure it wasn't going anywhere and it wasn't a helicopter or a drone, and they agreed to name the star Zoe Love. They lit the candles on the cake that Maureen had made. It was shaped like a half moon. Waxing or waning, Nathan had forgotten again which was which. They sang 'Happy Birthday' quietly in the garden and blew out the candles. They each made a wish. Nathan was sure it was the same wish.

They ate big slices of the cake and Nathan told his dad that NASA had programmed the Curiosity rover to sing 'Happy Birthday' to itself on the anniversary of the day it landed on Mars. He'd meant it as a happy story, but it made his dad sad. Nathan said he was sorry, and his dad told him not to be. They were going to be sad sometimes. A few days later his dad saw a child's glove hooked over a garden fence and started crying. Not crocodile tears either. Nathan thought he would never stop.

Nathan's dad got a job at the council. Even after all the awful things he'd said to them on the phone. Nathan thought that was so funny. His dad couldn't work on the stall anymore because he'd always associate it with Craig. When the developers tried to move all the stallholders out to build flats though, his dad was right there protesting with the other stallholders. He was also more involved in the campaign to save the estate now. There was a banner hanging from the bottom of the living room window with 'HANDS OFF OUR HOMES' painted on it. In the summer, it was Nathan's dad standing behind the table beneath the gazebo at the Lambeth Country Show, giving out the balloons and asking people to sign the petition.

Nathan had expected his dad would never have wanted to go to the park again, but he said they needed to 'reclaim it', 'like a bad word'. They walked through the park to the Lambeth Country Show and to the Lido on the first hot day of the year. His dad wore a verruca sock when they went swimming. Nathan knew he didn't have a verruca and was hiding the *South London Boys Forever 2013* tattoo on his ankle. In the winter his dad had the tattoo lasered off, but there was still a ghost of the crossed fingers and he rarely saw his dad without socks on. Around the same time, Nathan's dad took his black bomber jacket to the charity shop. He went all the way to Camberwell before handing it over to a charity shop there, as though it was a mouse he'd caught, and he didn't want it to come back to the house as soon as it was released. He threw the mantelpiece photo of himself and Craig wearing the same jackets in the bin.

When Nathan and his dad went swimming, they took the disposable underwater camera and they finished the film, taking pictures of each other counting Mississippis underwater. When his dad collected the developed photographs, Nathan had to look at them first. His dad was worried how he might react to seeing pictures of Zoe that he hadn't already seen before. Watching Nathan react to them first, made his dad feel less anxious about it.

The mystery boy who Zoe had taken a picture of eventually contacted the police. His name wasn't Alex. It was Lucas. He was two years older than Zoe. He was Dutch and lived in Utrecht. That was why he'd missed seeing his picture on television and in the newspapers in the UK. Nathan's dad spoke to Lucas on the phone. Lucas told him he met Zoe when he'd asked her for directions to the windmill in Brixton. Lucas hadn't believed his friends when they told him there was a windmill right in the centre of Brixton and he wanted to see it for himself. Zoe was outside the Ritzy when Lucas asked her for directions. He said she was the friendliest looking person he saw and that was why he'd asked her. Zoe had drawn Lucas a map. He said he thought it was cool that she hadn't just showed him on his phone. Zoe and Lucas had ended up chatting for a while. They sat on a bench in Windrush Square with the *BOVRIL* wall behind them, and Zoe recommended places to go and things to see for the remaining week of Lucas's holiday. They arranged to meet the next day for coffee in Brixton Village. Lucas had joked that he couldn't believe there was a village in the centre of Brixton as well as a windmill.

The night that Nathan had seen Zoe leave the house, she was going to meet Lucas for a third and final time. The next day he was returning to Holland. They went for a walk together, to look at – what else – stars.

Nathan's dad said he was glad that Zoe had met someone she thought worthy of photographing – a human who wasn't terrible – and when the police finally gave Nathan's red notebook back, he completed his final unfinished entry:

December 14th. 11:30. The subjict turned right to meet a friend.

Nathan's dad had been on television again. He was interviewed about the campaign to save the estate. It wasn't the same programme or on the channel he'd been on with Nathan. There were no name badges, make-up chairs or green rooms, and no pastries or free Coke Zeros. The television channel was only a local one, watched online by a handful of viewers, but even so, Maureen said her brother would lose his job at the council if they ever saw what he was saying about them on television. Nathan told his aunt she should have heard him when the council painted the wall next to the mural, forgetting that she had. Nathan was glad his dad had found things that he felt passionate about, whether it was saving their home or some old market stalls. It helped take his mind off that awful year, when it had been one thing after another.

Nathan hadn't put on his orange spacesuit or packed his backpack since the night his dad found him in the park shivering and freezing inside a tree, when his dad had carried him home in his arms like Elliott's brother, Mike, rescuing E.T.

If Nathan looked at the clouds now, he just saw clouds. Maybe a sheep or Arthur's mum after she'd had her hair done. But he didn't wait for spaceships to appear. He wondered if his dad had been right all along and Zoe had made everything up and she hadn't been taken away from Earth after all and that she only kept up the pretence for his benefit, for the amusement and entertainment of her brother. As long as Nathan enjoyed her stories, Zoe would have kept on telling them. Adding details when he asked, making things up to please him. But sometimes when Nathan was in bed, on the cusp of sleep, he did think, tonight might be the night the aliens came for him.

Whenever there was a supermoon on the calendar or if a meteor shower was forecast or somebody talked about a comet or the International Space Station on television, of course Nathan thought of Zoe and how excited she would have been and how infectious that excitement was for him. In August there was a solar eclipse and he remembered when Zoe made him a pinhole projector out of paper plates. She might be gone but Zoe Love was everywhere. If Nathan ate a crepe or saw the 'V' on a takeaway menu or when the batteries in the remote control ran out or if toast popped up or if he took the lid off a pen or saw the contrails of an airplane or an alien on TV, or if he thought it was going to rain and it did, or whenever he ate Marmite on toast or walked past the *BOVRIL* wall, Nathan would think about Zoe. He would never be able to hear a David Bowie song without thinking of his sister.

On the anniversary of the night Zoe became a misper – even though her dad had identified her body and even though they'd both cried their hearts out at her funeral, they would always think of her as missing – Nathan went upstairs to Zoe's room to get the face paints.

Nothing much had changed in her room in the past year. The carpet had been hoovered and her bed was made, but otherwise it was business as usual at the Zoe Love Museum. Her dad wasn't ready to close it just yet. Nathan picked up the plastic box of face paints from the dressing table and put them in the pocket of his tracksuit bottoms. He pulled the chair over and climbed up to reach the clip that opened the plastic frame on the wall. He didn't need to stretch or reach up as much as he had a year ago. He lifted the record out of the frame and climbed down from the chair. As he did, he felt something on the back of the album cover. He turned it over and looked at the picture. It was the same picture of David Bowie as on the front of the sleeve but there was no lightning bolt. No facial features at all in fact. It was just the outline of David Bowie's head and shoulders, drawn in red on a plain white background.

If Zoe's Sharpie had been yellow or green, or if she'd taken the pink Post-it notes out of their dad's desk instead of the white ones, Nathan might have noticed it before. He might not have picked the record up from her bed, early in the morning almost exactly a year ago and turned it around the right way, before shutting the record away inside the frame on Zoe's bedroom wall. He might not have missed something that he'd been searching for ever since.

HELLO SPACEBOY
IN CASE YOU WAKE UP BEFORE
I'M BACK. I HAVE DECIDED TO
STAY ON EARTH WITH YOU AND DAD.
GONE TO PARK TO REMOVE
THE ARROWS AND BOTH OUR
NAMES. JUST IN CASE.
DO <u>NOT</u> LEAVE THE HOUSE.
AND DON'T TELL DAD
Zx (THE SUBJICT)

Nathan slumped down on the chair and read the Post-it note again. His dad was right. Zoe *had* gone to the park to get rid of the directions because she wanted to stay with her brother and her dad. Only Officer Dibble was missing from Zoe's note.

It had taken Nathan a long time to not believe Zoe had died because of him. Even when his dad had made up the story about why she'd gone back to the park, Nathan hadn't been able to get finding the lid of her pen out of his head. He'd been back to Zoe's favourite tree many times to look for the missing Sharpie or for something written with it. The tree had changed with the seasons. Someone had carved cute animals into the longer section of trunk – a smiling caterpillar, a snail and a frog. Then, just before the Lambeth Country Show, that section of the tree was cut into small logs too. The logs were arranged in a circle like Stonehenge and a hog was roasted at the centre. Hipsters lit barbecues at the centre of the circle of logs all through the summer. Nathan could smell the cooking meat from his bedroom. He was glad Zoe wasn't there to smell or see what had happened to her tree and what it was used for.

When Nathan looked at the message Zoe had written to him on the Post-it note and stuck to the back of the album cover, he decided she hadn't replaced the lid on the pen properly before leaving the house again for the park. She must have dropped the lid by the dog poo bin by accident. The pen could be anywhere. Nathan looked at the note. If he'd seen it when he was supposed to, could he have saved his sister?

His dad called out from downstairs, "Hurry up, mate."

Nathan peeled the Post-it note away from the record sleeve, slowly, like he was removing a plaster from David Bowie's face using his mum's method. He rolled the small square of paper into a thin tube shape and put it in the zip pocket of his tracksuit bottoms. He went downstairs and gave the David Bowie record and the face paints to his dad. His dad read the song titles on the back of the record sleeve, chuckling and sighing to himself at the memory of the songs and what they in turn reminded him of.

"Do you actually know what this is?" his dad said.

"A record."

"But have you ever heard it, I mean? Have you *seen* a record play?"

Nathan shook his head. He'd seen records on shelves and shut away in frames. He'd watched them being used as flat surfaces for Luigi boards and he'd seen them used to copy make-up designs from. But he'd never actually seen a record doing what it had been designed and made to do.

"We should get a record player," his dad said. He looked at the track listing on the back of the sleeve again. "'Prettiest Star', that's what your mum used to call Zoe, just after she was born." He flipped the album over between his fingers, like he was making a pizza base. He looked at the picture on the front, at the lightning bolt on Bowie's face. "Oh well," he said. He passed the record and the face paints to Nathan. "Do your worst, Picasso."

39

There weren't as many people at the mural as there were the previous year, and no one sang while Nathan and his dad were there. His dad lit three candles and left one in front of the mural and the other two on the ground in front of the wall where Zoe's message was. It was Nathan who'd pointed out to his dad that although they couldn't see them, Zoe's words were still there underneath all that ugly white council paint.

Nathan almost gave his dad Zoe's Post-it note message when they were at the mural. He even thought about unrolling it and sticking it on the wall and pretending to find it there. But showing it to his dad wouldn't really change anything. It would only confirm a story they'd both already accepted to be true. And Nathan didn't want to spoil the day by needlessly upsetting his dad. He decided to keep the note somewhere safe until one day when he thought his dad was ready, and then Nathan would give it to him. He hoped though, that he'd forget all about the Post-it note, or his dad or Maureen would wash his trousers with it still in the pocket. It would make it easier to stay true to Zoe's last words:

DON'T TELL DAD.

When they got home from the mural, they ordered a takeaway and watched television for a while and then Nathan's dad climbed on a chair and stuck Jupiter back on Nathan's bedroom ceiling. He switched the lights off and made sure there was no gap between the curtains and they both lay down on Nathan's bed, looking up at the newly restored galaxy. Nathan told his dad where Orion's Belt was and which dot on the ceiling was the pole star.

"Venus should be over there," Nathan said, pointing at a blank black space on the ceiling.

"I can move it if you want?"

"It's okay."

"Maybe tomorrow then," his dad said. "The sky could do with repainting too. Which star do you think is the one we named after your mum?"

Nathan searched the sky. "That one."

"So that would be Zoe next to her?"

Nathan nodded. He was making it up, of course, but it didn't matter.

"And there's David Bowie," Nathan said.

"And whereabouts in the sky are we?"

"We're not there."

"Where are we then?"

"Down here."

"Brixton?"

Nathan nodded and they said it together, "London, England, the World, Earth, the Solar System, the Universe."

For the next ten minutes they lay close together on Nathan's single bed while he named the planets. Venus and Mars, Jupiter and Pluto, Uranus, Mercury, Saturn and all its moons. He showed his dad the stars, too, all the ones with names – his mum and David Bowie, and his sister, of course. If anyone ever asked now: Where is Zoe Love? Even if it was the middle of the day or if the sky was hidden behind a thick cloud of light pollution, Nathan would be able to show them the exact point in Space that was named after her. And it would always be there, because it was a star and not a planet.

❖

HARVEY KING UNBOXES HIS FAMILY

By J.B. Morrison

Thompsonn GP23X PhotoBoss All-in-One Desktop Printer

Harvey_King351 cut through the Sellotape and opened the box. He took out the power cable, the USB lead, instruction manual, installation CD and the four ink cartridges. All the time he was talking to the video camera, explaining each step of his latest unboxing, to a potential audience of more than three billion, but more likely in the tens or very low twenties.

Like a lot of people on TV or in the movies, Harvey hated watching his performances back once they were in the can. He couldn't bear the sound of his voice for a start. It lacked confidence or authority, he mumbled and had a stammer. And Harvey really hated the way he looked. His left eye would sometimes wink uncontrollably, and when he concentrated on unpicking tape or removing a cable tie, he licked his lips. And Harvey was overweight. Should he ever forget that fact, there were plenty of people ready to remind him. It was the adjective that appeared in almost all the comments underneath his videos.

"Speak up fat man."

"This fat guy stutters bad."

"I thought the camera is supposed to add 10 pounds not 100. #FATT!"

Harvey lifted the heavy printer out of the box and removed the two blocks of protective white polystyrene packaging. He peeled off the thick strips of plastic tape that held the printer lid in place and did the same with the tape on the paper input and output trays, and across the threshold of the ink access door. Harvey cut the cable ties from the mains lead and the USB cable, he plugged the printer into a four-way extension block and connected the USB lead to his computer. He loaded the ink cartridges and inserted the software installation CD and went through the printer's set-up steps. This was the least photogenic part of the process, and before putting the video online, Harvey would edit it down to a tight six or seven minutes, with smooth transitions – Cube or Page Curl, or a simple Dissolve.

Harvey loaded about twenty sheets of paper into the printer, switched it on and pressed print on his computer. The printer whirred and clicked, and Harvey watched the family tree, gradually emerging from the printer, as though it was growing before his eyes, in reverse, from the top down to the roots.

Harvey's second or third Canadian cousin, Megan, had posted the family tree online. It had then been sent to him from the genealogy website they were both signed up to. Megan's family tree was tall and wide, with an abundance of leaves and blossom, and delicious looking fruit growing on every branch. There was even a bird perched at the end of one of the branches. It was an unnecessarily elaborate family tree, far more decorative than any genealogical chart really needed to be. Megan's glorious Canadian Redwood made Harvey's own family tree look like a diseased English twig in a drought. There were fewer branches on his undernourished sapling, and no leaves or fruit, no blossom or birds. No decoration at all, in fact. It was just a simple chart, more of a family stump than a tree. Names were misspelled on Harvey's family tree, and half the dates were missing.

Information was missing from Megan's family tree too. Harvey wasn't on it, and neither were his mother, his mother's sister, Cathy, or Cathy's daughter, Sally. Harvey's father *was* on both family trees. On Harvey's version, his father had been dead for twenty-six years. While on Megan's family tree, up until just four months ago, he was still alive.

There was something about Megan's attention to detail – the choice of fonts, the colours, the intricate pattern of the bark, the curves and twists of the branches, the knots where the branches joined the trunk, and the ribs and the veins on the leaves, even the direction of the wind, that could be determined by the sway of the tree and the way the feathers of the bird parted ever so slightly. It was all that detail, all the time and effort that must have gone into creating Megan's family tree, that made it hard for Harvey to believe it was her, and not him, who would have made such a simple mistake with the date of his father's death.

HARVEY

1

The five turrets of The Castle appeared at the side of the road, poking through the trees like upturned Cornettos. There was a blimp moored to the nearest turret, swaying in the breeze twenty feet above it like a Pink Floyd pig, with the words 'HUGE SALE NOW ON' stamped across its torso. In the seven years Harvey had worked at The Castle, balloon or no balloon, the sale had always been HUGE and always very much ON.

It was autumn and more of the pink pebble dashing of the turrets, the ramparts and the battlements was visible than at other times of the year, more even than the day before. It was as though the building was ever so slowly rising up from the ground like a giant spaceship, beginning its journey back to the home planet. Passing motorists who'd not been on the road before, or only when there was more tree cover, would be wondering how on earth the unusual structure had got there. The Poundland Pyramids, the boot sale Stonehenge, with its 'thirty open plan departments selling 280 thousand discounted products at bargain prices, a miniature steam railway, boating lake, children's fun fair, eighteen holes of adventure golf, a maze and over twenty outdoor food concessions.'

The shuttle bus slowed, while the drivers of the cars in front gawped up at the blimp and the car crash of a building beneath. Harvey yawned and looked at his phone. There were now four comments underneath his printer unboxing video.

"Not this fat prick again." – Escosidebar33

"What's a p-p-p-printer?" – Splatterfish

"They shouldn't let fat people film theirselfs." – Killzit_101

"Leave him alone, you morons." – Jess86

If Harvey hadn't just discovered his father had come back from the dead, only to immediately die again, somebody sticking up for him on the internet might have been the last thing in the world he ever would have expected to happen. He gave Jess86's comment the thumbs-up and took Megan's family tree out of the pocket of his parka. It had slipped through a hole in the pocket of the coat and was caught in the lining. Like so many things bought from The Castle, Harvey's parka had a built-in obsolescence and its time was up. The zip was forever getting stuck and Harvey often had to remove the coat by pulling it over his head like a jumper. When he'd bought the parka earlier in the year, Harvey had hoped it might make him look like Bear Grylls or Sir Ranulph Fiennes, and not quite so much like an overweight lead singer from The Undertones.

When he'd freed the sheet of paper from the lining of his coat, Harvey unfolded the family tree and held it against the bus window. The early morning sun shone on the glass and the tree seemed to come alive, like in a Disney cartoon. If the bird perched at the end of the branch that bore the mystery of his father's death had given a little whistle, taken off and flown around the bus, Harvey wouldn't have been all that surprised. He took his hand away from the family tree and it stayed stuck to the bus window, like a party balloon on a jumper.

Last night, after he'd found the family tree, or rather, after it found him, arriving on his computer with a ping, like a solemn-faced policeman ringing the doorbell, Harvey thought, at long last the genealogy website had sent him something that wasn't just clickbait. The 'member of the King family' who wanted to share their information appeared to actually be from the same King family as him. Megan was the daughter of the sister of the wife of Harvey's father's brother. Harvey's second or third cousin, or his first cousin twice removed or something. At first Harvey was pleased. He could merge Megan's area of outstanding natural genealogical beauty with his own half-arsed blot on the landscape, print the combined results and present the family tree to his mother, taking all the credit.

And then Harvey noticed the discrepancy with the dates beneath his father's name. He thought it must be a mistake at first. And not his mistake. It was Megan who had obviously got the date wrong, either accidentally or deliberately, although Harvey couldn't think of any reason why she would have would gone to the trouble of faking a family tree and sending it to him. If it had been malware, clicking on the link would have been enough to infect Harvey's computer. There was no need for all the detail, no need for birds and flowers, no need for a family tree at all. If anything, it was his own scrawny effort that looked like the fake family tree.

Harvey rested his head on the shuttle bus window. He was very tired and wished he'd stayed at home. The unexpected death of a parent was surely the perfect excuse for taking a day off work. Stacking shelves seemed disrespectful. It didn't feel like a day for reaching.

The bus left the A-road and turned onto a narrow, winding B-road and The Castle disappeared and appeared again behind the trees, like it was playing peek-a-boo with a baby. The road widened and straightened out, and The Castle was gone.

Harvey closed his eyes. He could still see the branches and leaves and all the names and dates on the backs of his eyelids, like the ghost of a watched light bulb or the falling aliens or Tetris blocks he'd usually see after a long night of online gaming. Ordinarily, he'd sleep it off at the back of the warehouse, behind the out-of-season display Father Christmases, snowmen and reindeer. Forty winks in the basement didn't feel like it would be enough today.

In spite of his tiredness, Harvey's thoughts were racing. He had the sense of his whole world having been turned upside down, like he'd woken from a coma to discover a virus had wiped out half the population, and the apes or the Venus flytraps were in charge. He was unable to pinpoint the exact nature of how he was feeling though. He was reminded of the morning he'd switched on the television and learned that Princess Diana had died. Harvey's father was dead. Again. Why hadn't he cried? He'd been more upset when Disney had bought the rights to *Star Wars*.

2

The first time his father died, Harvey wept like a Beatles concert. He was eleven years old, sitting in the living room watching the children's programme *Why Don't You Just Switch off your Television Set and Go and Do Something Less Boring Instead?* The young presenters were demonstrating how to make a water bomb, when Harvey's mother came into the room, and, apparently without any intended irony, she switched the television off and did something less boring instead.

"I've got some bad news about your father."

Harvey stopped folding the piece of paper on his lap, still keeping one eye on the television, wondering when his mother would turn the TV back on, not wanting to miss any important folds. She sat down on the sofa next to Harvey and told him his father had had a heart attack. She pushed Harvey's fringe out of his eyes, something she'd probably seen in a soap opera. Maybe she was clearing a path for his tears. Because once Harvey realised his mother hadn't said *Art Attack* – another children's television programme he watched – and when it was obvious that his dad wasn't going to leap out from behind the curtains shouting, 'Surprise!', it must have seemed to Harvey's mother that her son's tears would never stop. He wept and he wailed, making alarming noises, like foxes mating and bagpipes bursting, blowing snot bubbles from his nostrils.

"Can I make you something to eat?" Harvey's mother said.

That was Harvey's year zero, when his mother couldn't think of any other way to stop him from crying other than to feed him. She made him fish fingers, peas and chips, and put a lemon meringue pie in the oven. She opened a huge bottle of cola. And then she went to the sweet shop. It would be the start of a sugar rush that, twenty-six years later, was still going strong.

Harvey's mum was rarely out of the kitchen that summer, baking jam tarts and roly-polies, building elaborate trifles, mashing and roasting potatoes, deep-frying thick-cut chips and filling pies with meats and fruits. Every morning the kitchen table looked like the breakfast buffet in a hotel foyer. There was always a bag of sweets or a huge tin of chocolates open on the sideboard. The summer that Harvey's father died the first time was a bit like Christmas. No, your mum is an enabler.

After six weeks of being fattened up by the witch in Hansel and Gretel, it was time for Harvey to leave the gingerbread house and start his first term at a new secondary school.

"You look so grown up," his mum said, probably meaning Harvey looked so much older in his new St. Peter and Paul Community College uniform. But Harvey was physically larger, too. He'd already outgrown the blazer his mother had bought him just a few months earlier.

"Do I have to go to school?" Harvey said.

"You can get some sweets on the way if you like."

His mother's weapons of mass distraction.

They walked together as far as the gates of the school, where Harvey's mother said goodbye and tag-teamed her son over to the headmaster. Mister Spencer escorted him through the empty playground, the swing doors and corridors, until they reached Harvey's new classroom. They waited outside the classroom while Harvey's new teacher, Miss Clark, explained to the rest of the class that a new boy was about to join them. She said that 'poor little Harvey' had been through a very difficult family trauma and asked them to be tactful and considerate. For almost a year, before Harvey became 'One and a Harvey', and then later, 'Two and a Harvey', he would be known by the whole class, and gradually the rest of the school, including one or two teachers, as 'poor little Harvey'.

"How's your dad, *poor little Harvey*?" a boy named Craig

Lyon asked him in the playground on his first day.

"He's dead," Anthony Lyon said.

"Is that true?" Craig said. "Is your dad dead?"

"*Poor little* Harvey."

"Is he dead?"

"Poor little Harvey. Is daddy dead?"

"Poor little fat Harvey's Daddy is dead."

Anthony and Craig Lyon were identical twins, with matching skinhead haircuts and angry faces. Skin like wood-chip wallpaper. They were their own gang. They never left one another's side. Nowadays, they'd be known as Craigthony or Cranthony. And when Harvey arrived at the school, they found their muse. Poor little Harvey would be the one and only school project they didn't find '*boring*'. He couldn't even find sanctuary in the dinner hall, a place where Harvey was amongst friends – the beef burgers and the sausages, the steamed puddings, the rhubarb and custard and all the dinner ladies. But lunchtimes at St. Peter and Paul were a living nightmare for Harvey. Craigthony would stand next to him in the queue and invite him to play 'the Circle Game'. One brother would hold his hand down at his side, in the shape of a circle. If Harvey looked at the circle, the other brother would be licenced to hit him. If Harvey refused to play, they would hit him anyway. And because he was now the child of a one parent family, Harvey was eligible for free school dinners. This only made the bullying worse. The Lyon twins didn't pay for their school dinners either, but that didn't seem to make any difference.

Harvey had never blamed anyone other than Craig or Anthony for his horrible time at school. Maybe Miss Clark bore some responsibility for being naive enough to think that a group of eleven-year-olds would know what tact or consideration was. And Harvey could have made more of an effort to stand up for himself. He'd *always* blamed himself. But since the discovery on Megan's family tree,

Harvey was re-evaluating his entire life. He wouldn't have been eligible for free school dinners for a start. How many dead legs and knuckle raps would that have saved him from? Harvey needed to find out what it was that made his mother tell him such a terrible lie that summer, before fattening him up and literally throwing him to the Lyons.

3

Harvey was woken by someone pushing gently on his shoulder. It felt nice at first, like he was dreaming he was having a massage, and then Harvey opened his eyes and saw the big, round Captain Pugwash face of the shuttle bus driver staring down at him. For a second, Harvey thought, *who's driving the bus?* Then he realised it wasn't moving. There were no passengers other than him. No engine noise or music playing on phones. Just the gentle sound of conditioned air overhead, and the bus driver's heavy breathing.

Harvey had never seen the driver standing up before. It was like seeing a newsreader in the supermarket or the postman at the swimming pool. He was an incredibly big man, a lot bigger than Harvey. The short walk from the front of the bus seemed to have exhausted him.

Whenever Harvey saw someone in worse physical shape than he was, he had conflicting feelings. On the one hand, Harvey realised that he needed to make some drastic lifestyle changes soon, or he would end up equally large and unfit. But on the other hand, Harvey would think, you know what, compared to this out-of-breath bus driver, I really don't need to worry about things too much just yet.

"Doughnut?" the bus driver opened a white paper bag and held it out in front of Harvey.

"No, thanks," Harvey said, knowing that doughnuts would now be his food ear worm and he wouldn't be able to stop thinking about them until he ate one. More likely two or three. He was already thinking about who sold the best doughnuts at The Castle – the Food Court of King Arthur or one of the outdoor food concessions?

The driver took a doughnut out of the paper bag, bit into it and licked his lips. Harvey licked his too. How alike we are, he thought. The bus driver was quite a bit older, maybe in his early sixties. He was like a warning from Harvey's future. The ghost of Christmas diabetes and narrowed arteries.

Harvey wondered if his dad had looked like the bus driver. The kind of man who ate jam doughnuts at eight-thirty in the morning. It was funny what he could remember all these years later. What he was watching on television when he'd learned about his father's supposed heart attack, for instance. And yet, Harvey couldn't seem to remember what his dad looked like.

Since last night, when his distant cousin (4,691 miles, he'd Googled it) had made him think about his father, his image had instantly started to fade. For years he must have taken his face for granted, not needing to think about it, but knowing it was always there, ready and waiting should that need ever arise. But now that time had come, Harvey's father seemed to be vanishing. He was like a shipwreck, perfectly preserved at the bottom of the sea, until it's hauled up to the surface, where it immediately starts to disintegrate.

"There was an actress on the television," the bus driver said. "She traced her ancestors all the way back to Jesus."

Harvey looked at the large man standing next to him. Perhaps the shuttle bus driver *was* his father.

"What?" Harvey was confused. "What actress?"

The bus driver pointed at Megan's family tree, still stuck to the bus window. Harvey quickly removed it as though it was a picture of the bus driver's wife in a bikini that he'd printed off Facebook. He stuffed it into his coat pocket and started getting up. But the bus driver sat down in the seat next to him, blocking his exit. He looked as out of place sitting in a passenger seat as he had standing up.

Harvey tried not to look at the bus driver's legs. His trousers were so tight that Harvey couldn't imagine – and he was really trying hard not to imagine – him ever being able to take his trousers off. They were so tight that his flesh was bunched up in speed bumps up his thighs.

Harvey looked down at his own legs instead. He'd undone the top button of his jeans and opened the fly a little when he'd first sat down on the bus. If the man next to him had noticed, he didn't say anything. The first rule of Fat Club.

"Isn't it funny how on the television, when they do their family trees, everyone somehow manages to trace their ancestry all the way back to royalty?" the bus driver said. "Or even Jesus. When I did my family tree, it was all bloody carpenters." The driver looked Harvey in the eye and winked. Harvey was clearly supposed to be in on a joke. "My name is *Carpenter*," the bus driver said, and then added, like a West Country 007, "*Bob* Carpenter."

Harvey had been on the same shuttle bus hundreds, maybe thousands, of times. But he'd never taken the trouble to learn the name of the man driving it. He'd heard people call him driver before – thank you, driver, see you later, driver, see you tomorrow, driver, slow down, driver, I need to go to the toilet, driver – but Harvey had never thought 'Driver' might be his actual name.

Bob held out his hand and Harvey shook it. There was a transfer of doughnut sugar, and he fought the impulse to lick his fingers. The bakery concession, near the steam train station. They sold the best doughnuts.

"I expect there must be quite a few kings on your family tree?" Bob Carpenter said, gesturing at the name badge on Harvey's work fleece.

Harvey looked down at the badge: 'Harvey King: Stock Replenishment'. He expected his twice dead father would be turning in both of his graves if he knew what his son's job was. He probably would have considered Harvey a mug for paying tax and national insurance and wearing a dumb uniform every day. His father would have been prouder of Harvey if he took things off the shelves instead. He couldn't actually recall ever seeing his dad steal anything. But he did remember he used to buy and sell things in pubs, cigarettes and stereo equipment, watches and jewellery, perfume and aftershave. No, your dad is Derek Trotter.

Another shuttle bus pulled up in the car park and Bob Carpenter said he'd better let Harvey go, as though he'd been holding him captive. The driver stood up and adjusted the crotch of his trousers. Harvey stood too, quickly zipping up his jeans. Anyone passing might have wondered what depraved sex-show they'd just missed. Harvey followed Bob down the aisle of the bus. The driver almost filled the space between the seats and bumped his hips a few times causing the vehicle to rock slightly from side to side. Harvey managed to avoid doing the same. Compared to Bob, he was still a work in progress. Bob sat down in his driver's seat. The newsreader back behind his desk, the postman back in his uniform.

"I've just realised," Bob said, "Jesus was a carpenter." He sounded like a vicar making a profound point at the end of a sermon.

Harvey faked a laugh and said goodbye. He left the bus and joined three sets of passengers from the other shuttle buses, heading through the car park towards The Castle. He was close enough now to see the many different coats and shades of pink paint on the wall of the building. The paint was dirty and weathered and the pebble dashing beneath was cracked and peeling. Like with a great painting, you had to step back to fully appreciate The Castle's beauty. Up close it looked like a dropped cake.

Harvey crossed the drawbridge, which was no more a real drawbridge than The Castle was a real castle, or the moat that ran beneath the drawbridge was an actual moat. A short queue of early morning customers had formed at the main entrance to the huge store. At the front of the queue a man was carrying a garden spade. The price label was still stuck to the wooden handle and there was a line of earth along the spade's sharp edge. In his other hand he held a till receipt. A security guard opened one side of the glass doors and Harvey followed the other staff members into a large foyer area, where it was no longer the Middle Ages. There was a toy spaceship with flashing lights and a smiley-faced helicopter, both of which children could be rocked back and forth on for a pound. There were two vending machines – one dispensing fizzy-drinks, and the other crisps and chocolate – and between the vending machines was a set of wheels and cogs inside a glass case that would crush a penny into the approximate shape of a castle.

Harvey walked through the foyer and onto the vast shop floor. Apart from the chatter of arriving staff, it was relatively quiet. Very soon, a cacophony of different infomercials would be switched on on the twenty or so televisions spread around the store. A pop song would be playing in the CD and DVD department and a film would be showing on a huge screen. The Bontempi organs would be powered up in the Music department and some show-off kid would be playing 'Chopsticks' on a piano keyboard. The in-store radio station would begin broadcasting, playing the same collection of recent hit records, interrupted every couple of minutes by intercom staff messages and customer service announcements.

Knowing the godawful racket that was coming, Harvey made the most of the peace and quiet. For now, at least, there were no beeping tills, no barcode scanners, no wannabe rock stars trying out drum kits or teenagers setting off the talking toys, programming swear words into teddy bears and opening all the singing birthday cards. As Harvey walked through a swing door at the rear of the store, the first jingle of the day played. Sung to the tune of 'Greensleeves' – *The Castle, The Ca-astle*. Harvey heard John Chalmers' deep voice joining in as usual from the downstairs warehouse – *Stick it up your ar-ar-arsehole.* John's rich baritone filled the stairwell, luring Harvey down into the basement like a foulmouthed siren.

Harvey took the goods lift instead of the stairs. He savoured the last moments of peace and quiet while the lift travelled the short distance between floors. In the basement, Harvey hung his parka on a hook. John Chalmers gave him a list of products – lipstick and flowerpots, bird food and rolls of wallpaper, paint pots and jigsaw puzzles – and he started putting them onto shelves.

4

After work Harvey bought Chinese food in the village's only takeaway restaurant, where they also sold fish and chips, kebabs, fried chicken, pasties and pizzas – none of which appeared to be the chef's specialty. The restaurant was called the Bay of Bengal, but they didn't serve Indian food. The girl working behind the counter was from Lithuania. She was new to the restaurant and Harvey felt she was judging him for the size of his food order. She was eyeing him up in the same way doctors did. As though she was about to ask him to jump up on the scales. He wanted to tell the girl that half the food was for his mother, even though he knew that would have been a lie.

While he waited for his order Harvey looked out of the restaurant window at the pub opposite – the Fusilier. He'd been thinking about some of the take-your-son-to-work days he'd been on with his dad. They used to go to the White Hart and the Pig and Whistle, and to the big hotel near the bypass that was now the largest ball pit and children's soft-play centre in the South West. They definitely spent the most time in the Fusilier. Harvey would sit on his own at a pub table, with a Coke and a bag of crisps, while his dad went about his business. He'd watch him gesturing and gesticulating to a small audience of men in the lounge or the saloon bar, perched on a high stool, working the room, tic-tacking like a bookie, selling people things they hadn't yet realised they wanted.

The business meetings might then move to a quieter corner or to the snug, where his dad would seal the deal, usually in hushed tones, punctuated by nods and winks and concluding with sudden loud bursts of laughter and firm handshakes. When he left the pub with his dad, Harvey often had a new toy or a game. People were always giving his dad things in pubs and hotels, as though he was a visiting dignitary. The majority of Harvey's birthday and Christmas presents came from men in pubs, already unboxed, stuffed into dirty carrier bags, or wrapped in a jumper or a towel. There were never any cable ties to unwind, no instruction manuals or warranties. No tiny packets of silica gel to keep out moisture.

There were two old men standing outside the Fusilier smoking. They were probably about the age Harvey's dad would have been when he died for the second time. It was strange to think that even if Harvey could remember what his father looked like he might not have recognised him because he would have been so much older than when he'd last seen him.

Harvey's phone pinged. It was an email informing him of new activity on his video channel. He clicked on the link. Beneath his recent unboxing of a pair of headphones, there were now seven comments.

"These headphones are crap." – Skunkheadx

"Tinny sound. Waste of money!!" – Tomas sic

"Where's the hate button? Lol." – L00Llol

"What are h-h-h-h-headphones FATSO?" – Splatterfish

"He needz stutter cancelling headfones" – L00Llol

"And fat cancelling ones." – Tomas sic

"STFU. M.O.R.O.N.S." – Jess86

Jess86 had stood up for Harvey twice now.

"Are you a troll hunter?" Harvey typed into his phone.

"No. I'm an Early Years practitioner."

The reply was so quick and unexpected that Harvey thought Jess86 must have had their answer already written and ready to post. It was a little unnerving. Harvey felt like he was being watched. He looked around the restaurant. There was nobody there other than him and the fat shaming Lithuanian girl behind the counter. Was she Jess86? Obviously not.

"Is that like a teacher?" Harvey replied, his fingers shaking when he considered the possibility, however distant, that Jess might be short for Jessica.

"Yes, that's correct. Like a teacher." Jess86 replied even faster than before, following immediately with another comment, "Hey! Where are the italics I put around the word 'like'?"

"Italics don't work on here," Harvey replied.

"So how am I supposed to be sarcastic?"

"Asterisks."

"Bless you."

Harvey laughed out loud. The girl behind the counter looked up. Harvey smiled apologetically. The girl gave him a look that made him feel like he was some sort of pervert.

He stared at his phone. The profile picture beside Jess86's name was just the default blue silhouette. Forgetting about the Jess part for a minute, Harvey focussed on the number 86. Jess could be eighty-six years old or born in 1986. They might simply be the eighty-sixth Jess to join YouTube. Jess86 might be a bot – the eighty-sixth model of the Jess web robot. It was an idea that excited Harvey as much as the fact he might be having a conversation with a real-life female.

"You can use asterisks instead of italics. Like *This*," Harvey typed, and then put his phone away because his food was ready. When the girl passed him the brown paper bag across the counter, their hands briefly touched. Harvey blushed. He sensed the girl was physically disgusted. He thanked her and left the restaurant. He was disappointed with his brain for making him think about touching Bob Carpenter's sugary hand earlier in the day. He also thought these accidental moments across bus seats and food counters might be the only physical human contact he would ever experience.

Harvey walked through the village. Everything he'd managed to ignore for the past twenty odd years reminded him of his father. It was like being on a sightseeing tour based on his life. The pub where he'd conducted much of his business, the hairdressers where he had his haircut.

What Harvey would give for a peek into that hairdresser's mirror now. To see his dad sitting in the chair next to him, while they both had Saturday haircuts. He stopped outside the florists, ate a spring roll and read the wreaths in the window – *'IN LOVING MEMORY, RIP, MANDY* – Was Mandy real? Or was she a sort of 'Show deceased'?

Not only did Harvey not know where his dad had been in the years between his two deaths, he also had no idea where he was now. Was his father buried in the ground somewhere or in an urn on someone's mantelpiece? Whose mantelpiece? The thoughts were never ending. Was it an ornate mantelpiece in a huge house, or were his dad's remains in an old Nescafé jar on a filthy shelf in a damp bedsit? Harvey may have been angry with his father for his parental neglect and apparent deceit, but he still hoped he hadn't died alone.

He tried to think of a more noble send-off. A bugler playing the 'Last Post' on the deck of a ship, while a smartly-dressed sailor pushed a coffin overboard, until he was left holding nothing but a flag as though he'd just performed a magic trick. Harvey imagined a televised state funeral, attended by actual kings. A twenty-one-gun salute and applauding members of the public throwing flowers onto the road in front of a slowly passing hearse.

Maybe his dad's body had been fired out of a cannon into outer space or turned into diamonds. There could be an annual national holiday somewhere in the world to commemorate his father's passing. Anything was possible, because Harvey knew nothing. Was there a star in the sky named after his father, and if so, by whom? And why hadn't it been Harvey who'd named it? Why wasn't his dad in a jar on Harvey's mantlepiece? Who was wearing a ring, inset with a diamond, made from the carbon of his dad's cremains?

Harvey walked past the house where he'd once lived with his mother and father. The windows had been replaced and the outside of the house was painted white. The front garden was paved over and was now a carport. Harvey had helped his day lay the grass in the garden. He remembered him unloading the turf from the back of an estate car. He'd rolled it out like carpet, stressing to Harvey how important it was to not walk on the grass. And then when the turf was all laid out, his dad put a long plank of wood on it and invited Harvey to stamp up and down on the grass like Godzilla.

Harvey walked as far as the 'THANK YOU FOR DRIVING CAREFULLY THROUGH WHYNOT ST. PETER' sign. After that, there were nothing but fields and farmland until the 'WELCOME TO WHYNOT ST. PAUL, PLEASE DRIVE CAREFULLY' sign. The countryside between the two signs was shrinking in size with every new-build estate and barn conversion, and the council had to keep digging up the two signs to move them closer together. The last original building in Whynot St. Peter was the Wildways care home. Harvey pressed a button next to the iron gates and they slowly opened. When the gap was wide enough, Harvey slipped through. He was sure he had to wait for a wider gap than when his mother had first moved into the care home eight months ago.

He crossed the small car park and typed a code into a metal box. He opened the front door and went inside. There was no pen next to the visitors book again, and Harvey made a mental note of the time. He would borrow a pen from his mother or from one of the lounges and sign in and out when he left. He looked at the visitors book to see who else was currently visiting. Michael and Karen had signed in to see Granny Alice forty-five minutes ago, and Grant had been to visit Ella and left again just thirteen minutes later. Harvey would definitely stay with his mother for longer than Grant. Grant was a terrible son. It was probably Grant who stole the pen.

Harvey went into the empty dining lounge. There was

no cook on Sunday evenings. Sandwiches would already have been left in the residents' rooms for their dinner. Harvey picked up a clean plate from a pile and put a knife and fork in the pocket of his parka. He put the plate in the carrier bag with his laptop and the headphones. He took a small roll-on deodorant out of his coat pocket, lifted his fleece and gave himself a quick bed bath. He combed his hair with his fingers, breathed onto his wrist and sniffed, as though he was sampling his own perfume. Hold your head up, he told himself. Don't slouch and don't mumble. Articulate, enunciate clearly and speak slowly. Don't rush to speak without first considering what you're about to say and consider where those words might lead you.

Harvey had learned to set his words up like a snooker player setting up their shots. He'd think not just about what he was saying but also what he was going to say next or after that. He needed to remember his stutter triggers and be aware that when he was tired, he was more prone to stammering. And Harvey was very tired.

He picked up the brown paper takeaway bag and the bag containing the laptop and headphones and walked along the corridor, sucking in as much of his belly as possible without passing out. The office door was ajar. He could see Asha, sitting behind the desk, staring at her phone. Harvey slowed down. Asha looked up and smiled.

"Hi there," she said.

"Hello." Just a small stutter. Breathe. Reset. Slow. "How is she today?"

"Oh, she's absolutely fine," Asha said. "Although, I'm afraid she won't use the stairs again. I found her yesterday, halfway up the stairs, with her eyes closed and her hands cupped over her ears, refusing to go further up or to come back down."

"Should I do something?" Harvey said.

"Hmm," Asha said. "I think we're just going to have to wait for her to come down of her own accord." Asha made his mother sound like a cat stuck up a tree.

Harvey looked along the corridor, in the direction of the stairs.

"Oh. Don't worry," Asha said, with a small laugh. "I didn't leave Margaret stuck on the stairs. I managed to get her up to her room eventually. But she is quite adamant that from now on, she will not, or *can* not, under any circumstances whatsoever, use the stairs."

Harvey couldn't remember the last time his mother had been so eloquent. He presumed Asha was exaggerating for effect.

"I would have phoned you," Asha said. "But I knew you'd be in today."

Asha *knew he'd be in today*.

The first time Harvey's mother had refused to use the stairs at the care home was so soon after she'd moved in that Harvey thought it was a protest, aimed at him for sending her there. The doctor had said his mother's fear of stairs was an ear infection. Or vestibular neuritis, Ménière's disease maybe, benign paroxysmal positional vertigo, a migraine, or possibly a combination of all five. Harvey might as well have Googled her symptoms. There was a lift at the care home, of course, but Harvey's mother had always refused to use lifts.

"What's today's film?" Asha said, looking at The Castle carrier bag Harvey was holding behind his legs.

"*Shrek*," Harvey said.

Asha nodded. "She'll like that. And what's your latest film?"

"My film?"

"What will you be taking out of a box for your mum today?"

"Oh, just some headphones," Harvey said. Embarrassed that Asha knew about his unboxing videos. At least he didn't stammer the word 'headphones', as he'd managed to do repeatedly when filming the video. "I thought they might help with her tinnitus."

"Perhaps they'll help her to use the stairs again as well," Asha said, which made no sense. "Anyway, I better let you go. You don't want your food to get cold."

She was looking at the other bag Harvey was holding. Bringing hot meals into the care home wasn't allowed. He hoped Asha didn't make him leave the Chinese food in the office or force him to eat it all before he was allowed upstairs.

"She's a bit like a Dalek, your mum, isn't she?" Asha said. "The way she can't use the stairs." She smiled and turned her attention back to her phone.

Harvey walked along the corridor. He went past an activity room where nothing was going on and a large communal lounge with nobody in. He had the song 'Brimful of Asha' in his head again. He knew Asha only spoke to him because it was her job. Or because she was like the women on the shuttle bus who said hello to him every morning – Hola, Harvey, Cześć, Harvey, Salut, Harvey. They didn't think of him as a threat, and certainly not a potential date.

Harvey wished he was brave enough to talk to Asha for longer, and about something other than his mother. He could ask her what time she finished work and invite her out for a drink at the Fusilier or for a meal in the Bay of Bengal. Asha would laugh, because the Bay of Bengal was close to where her family originally came from, and Harvey would quip, "What, the takeaway restaurant?" And they'd both laugh about their funny misunderstanding. And it wouldn't be awkward or racist, because of all the amazing chemistry between them. Harvey would love to be able to spend more time talking to Asha. He'd start by telling her that Daleks had been levitating up and down stairs since 1987.

5

Harvey's own phobia of stairs was more a fear of exercise and he took the lift up to the first floor, where his mother's room was the last of eight rooms at the end of a long corridor. There were four rooms on either side of the corridor. An A4 sheet of paper, with a photograph of the room's resident on, was stuck to each door. There were two men. If either man had been Harvey's father, he was sure he wouldn't have recognised him.

The photo on his mother's door had been taken when she first moved in to the care home. Her expression could be interpreted as joy, bemusement, sadness, horror or pain, almost depending on the angle Harvey looked at it. It was like one of his *Doctor Who* hologram trading cards.

Thinking about how the version of his mother waiting for him on the other side of the door might dictate what he was going to say to her, and how what he had to say might affect her, made Harvey want to turn around and run away.

Would he need to be good or bad cop? Should he offer his mother a cigarette or hit her with the *Yellow Pages*? She might refuse to speak at all, of course, pleading the fifth, whatever the fifth was, or saying nothing other than 'no comment' over and over again like in the cop shows. How many times had Harvey's father said 'no comment' since he'd last seen him?

Ever since Megan's bombshell of a family tree had dropped on Harvey, he'd been playing Dad Cluedo. Wondering whether his death had been a natural one or not. Had he passed peacefully in his sleep or was he hurtling towards a mountain at a thousand miles an hour in a flaming Jumbo jet? When Harvey was restocking the shampoo shelves earlier, he'd found himself picturing his dad dying in prison. He saw him falling from the roof of D block during a daring escape attempt or getting shanked in the showers with a sharpened toothbrush.

Harvey took his shoes off and placed them on the carpet beside his mother's door. He put his ear to the door. Every other room he'd walked past was blaring out a loud late afternoon television programme. His mother's room was silent. He knocked twice, opened the door and went inside.

The room was empty. If his mother's handbag hadn't been on the bed, Harvey might have panicked. But she never went anywhere without her bag. She took it to the dining lounge at mealtimes, and to the treatment room when she was having her hair done or her toenails trimmed. Up until recently, when his mother had refused to travel in the care home's minibus because she didn't trust the driver, she'd taken her handbag to the garden centre, the beach, the Tesco superstore and the House of Marbles. She was like the Queen in that respect. If the handbag was there, so was Harvey's mother.

He walked over to the bathroom and put his ear to the closed door. He listened for running taps or other sounds he really didn't want to hear. He heard his mother's voice, chatting away to herself, and the hum of the extractor fan. She liked to sleep with the bathroom light and the fan on, with the bathroom door slightly ajar. She said the persistent drone of the fan helped with her tinnitus and the light helped her sleep. Sometimes she left the television on all night, with the sound turned down. The mere thought of Noel Edmonds or Terry Wogan on old repeats of game shows would help her sleep.

Harvey's mother's room was a bit like a budget hotel room. There was a single bed, a chest of drawers, a small armchair, a second smaller chair, a wardrobe and an en suite bathroom. No minibar or trouser press. If Harvey ran a care home, there'd be a minibar and a trouser press in every room. Whenever the residents went out for the day, he'd place tiny squares of chocolate on their pillows for when they returned. There'd be a cinema and a swimming pool, and proper cash prizes at the Bingo, instead of the tombola leftovers of talcum powder and pocket diaries that they gave away on the first Thursday of the month in the downstairs lounge. If Harvey ran a care home, there'd be a games room with one-armed bandits and coin-pusher machines. A basketball hoop and pinball. It would be the Google offices of care homes.

Harvey cleared a space on top of the chest of drawers. He piled up two yoghurt pots and three teacups, all untouched and full of cold milky tea. There was bright red lipstick on the rims of two of the cups. He hoped his mother hadn't put her make-up on. He was already thinking of her as some kind of supervillain. The last thing he needed was her looking like the Joker. He put the bag of takeaway food and the borrowed plate on top of the chest of drawers. He ate a prawn cracker.

The toilet flushed and the bathroom door opened. Harvey coughed deliberately to let his mother know he was there, in case his presence alarmed her and, more importantly, in case she wasn't dressed. That was an experience he didn't want to repeat any time soon.

"I thought you were out at the park or the zoo or something," Harvey said.

"No. I was in there," his mother pointed back at the bathroom. "I was going on the toilet."

"Too much information, Mum." Harvey walked over. He switched the bathroom light off and closed the door on the en suite hum. "Shall I take your coat, madam?"

He helped her out of her winter coat without touching her, not really helping her at all. Under the coat she was wearing a dressing gown and a grey silk scarf with a long, frayed fringe.

"Are you wearing all your clothes?" Harvey said.

His mother didn't answer. She sat down slowly on the bed. Harvey held out his hands, in the same useless way he'd helped her take her coat off. Using the Force. His reiki.

He hung his mother's coat on a hanger in the wardrobe and walked over to the window beside the bed. He felt the radiator. It was switched off and the window was slightly open.

"Aren't you cold, Mum?"

"The rain helps with the loud."

Harvey knew she meant noise. His mother had difficulty expressing herself and also understanding the speech of others. It was called aphasia. Or aphonia. Ironically, Harvey could never remember which. Wet might mean rain, lunch might be dinner, swim might be fish, stepping was walking, mister was man. Today, loud was noise, and because Harvey didn't correct her, that was what it would be from now on. They were gradually creating a new language, that only they understood. His mother's new language, and the gradual loss of her old one, was one of the many reasons Harvey was dreading asking her about something she'd said to him twenty-six years ago.

"It's stopped raining now," Harvey said. "Shall I shut the window?"

His mother put her hands over her ears, as though she was expecting a balloon was about to burst. Harvey closed the window. When she took her hands away, Harvey saw there were two pieces of pink toilet tissue stuffed into her ears.

"Was that there just now?" Harvey said.

His mother pulled the tissue out of her ears.

Harvey winced. "I hope nothing else comes out," he said. "It's not one of those magician's handkerchief tricks, is it?"

"Do you want it?" His mother held the tissue out to him.

Harvey screwed his nose up. "Want is not the word I'd use."

With the tips of his fingers, Harvey took the tissue and dropped it in the bin next to the dressing table.

"Shall I be mother?" Harvey had made the same joke

every Sunday for the past eight months. Routines and patterns were good for his mother Asha had told Harvey.

He unboxed the Chinese food, taking the silver foil containers out of the brown carrier bag and removing the greasy white paper bags, containing the spring rolls, the dumplings and the prawn crackers. He scooped some of the food onto the plate he'd borrowed from the dining lounge.

His mother tilted her head. "Harvey. The television, please."

Harvey moved to one side, so she could see the television.

He was always relieved to hear his mother say his name, to know today wasn't the day she wouldn't know who he was anymore, the day he became a stranger to her, an intruder in her room. He finished dishing up his mother's food and carried the plate over to her. She held it while Harvey picked up a wooden tray from under the bed. He opened the two short legs of the tray and put it on her lap.

"Ready?" he said.

His mother put the plate down on the tray and Harvey took the knife and fork out of the inside pocket of his parka. He gave them to his mother and produced a glass bottle of soy sauce from another pocket, just as she was about to ask him for it. He flipped the lid of the bottle open with a one-handed movement. He was reminded of his father doing a similar one-handed trick with his cigarette lighter. He gave his mother the soy sauce, waiting until he was sure she had a firm grip on the bottle before letting go. It was a system they'd perfected together over many Chinese Sundays. Harvey unfolded a newspaper and put it on the bed, open at the crossword page.

"I've left the difficult clues for you."

The exact same jokes every Sunday. Patterns and routines. He picked up last week's paper and two magazines. On the cover of one it said: 'I Ate a Rat to Survive!' and 'My Imaginary Friend Slept with his Son'.

"Who brings you this rubbish, Mum?" Harvey said.

His mother flooded her food in soy sauce.

"They're magazines," she said.

"I know they're magazines, but who gave you them? They're horrible."

"The girl did."

"Which girl, Mum? The Girl on the Train? The Girl from Ipanema?"

"The girl. You know, with the thing."

"What thing. Mum? The dragon tattoo? The pearl earring?"

"The *thing*."

"The tea trolley?"

His mother nodded. Harvey had no idea how he could tell which girl his mother was talking about so easily. He just could. He'd known before he'd started joking about it.

He went over to the chest of drawers and took his laptop out of the carrier bag. He cleared a space next to the takeaway containers and located the HDMI cable that was hanging out of the back of the television. He plugged it into the laptop. He took a red felt pouch out of the carrier bag, unzipped it and removed the large pair of white headphones. He plugged them into the socket on the side of the television, turned up the volume and checked it wasn't too loud. He took the headphones over to his mother, making sure the long lead didn't snag or pull the TV over. He held the headphones open. His mother reached her hands up to stop him putting them on her head.

"They're just headphones, Mum. They might help with your tinnitus. They cancel noise out. By up to ninety per cent," he said, remembering his patter from the unboxing video. "Memory foam pads for supreme comfort."

His mother lowered her hands and Harvey placed the headphones carefully on her head. He gently closed them over her ears. There was a white streak of poliosis that ran from the front to the back of her hair, like the middle line of a road that needed repainting. Most of the women in his mother's family had it. Her sister, Cathy, had the same stripe and so did their mother.

Harvey reached over and switched on the noise-cancelling mode. A blue light circled one side of the headphones. It matched the curtains. He decided he'd ask her about his dad after dinner. After his video. After *Shrek*. He sat down and pressed play on his laptop.

6

Auraltastics H2Au Loud But Quiet Noise-Cancelling Around Ear Headphones

"Today I'm going to be unboxing the Auraltastics H2Au Loud But Quiet Noise-Cancelling Around Ear Headphones. They reduce environmental noise by up to ninety per cent, with memory foam pads on the earpieces for supreme comfort. There's a lead in there and a mini jack plug. There's also a larger jack adaptor."

Apart from when Harvey was editing the videos, these Chinese Sunday premieres were often the only time he watched a lot of his unboxings. He cringed, watching himself on his mother's television, cutting through the Sellotape and opening the box. The only sound from his mother's television was inside her headphones, but Harvey remembered every word that his onscreen self was saying, as he took the red felt pouch out of the box, unzipped it and showed the headphones to the camera.

He turned the plastic packaging, containing the headphones lead, the battery and the plug adaptor, around and around in his hand, his tongue nipping in and out like a lizard's, as he searched for a way into the thick moulded plastic.

He wanted to shout at the television, at Harvey_King351: *Get some scissors, you prick! Put your tongue away, you ridiculous looking fool! And hurry up! This is incredibly boring! For the viewers' sake! Get. On. With. IT!* He almost cheered when he watched himself finally pick up a screwdriver and force an opening into the packaging. But he knew the batteries were going to fall out and roll away out of sight. *Over there, you idiot! Over there! No! Behind you!!*

Harvey watched his mother. If it wasn't for the look of pride on her face every Chinese Sunday, he might have stopped filming the videos by now, or at least stopped uploading them to the internet like virtual 'kick me' signs.

On TV, Harvey_King351was balancing the headphones on his open palm, checking the weight, squeezing and stroking the padding around the earpieces as though he was buying a sofa. Real life Harvey felt like trolling his online self.

"There's a volume slider control. And you can turn the noise-cancelling on and off. They don't feel too tight. But not too loose either. I'm going to experiment with the volume to see if there's any sound leak. This is with the volume about halfway up. A little bit more volume now. About seventy-five per cent full volume now. You can probably actually hear this."

Don't nod. Please don't nod your head in time with the music.

"And this is one hundred per cent volume. Pretty loud now. I'm probably shouting. Quite loud. And that completes the unboxing of the Auraltastics H2Au Loud But Quiet Noise-Cancelling Around Ear Headphones."

Thank God.

The next video automatically cued itself up, the thumbnail image of Megan's family tree emerging from the printer, like a pop-up ad, reminding Harvey what he needed to do. The longer he put it off, the harder it was going to be. He was already wondering whether it was worth the inevitable hassle. His mother wasn't the same person she was when she told him his father had had a heart attack. She was barely the same woman in the picture pinned to her door less than a year ago. When his mother watched Harvey unboxing things on her television, she thought her son was famous.

There was a strong chance she wouldn't remember what she'd told him such a long time ago. If Harvey was struggling to recall what his dad looked like, how would it be for her? What damage had all the migraines and the vertigo, the aphasia, the tinnitus, mini strokes and small vessel disease, done to his mother's memory? And who would actually benefit if his mother told him the truth now? It wouldn't bring his dad back. That's what they always said in films. It wouldn't bring him back. And then Harvey remembered his dad *had* sort of come back.

After they'd both finished their Chinese food and watched the rest of *Shrek*, Harvey helped his mother remove the headphones.

"Mum," he said, casually. "Do we have any family in Canada? Any aunts or uncles, or cousins?"

His mother didn't reply. She stared at the blank television. Harvey disconnected the laptop and put the quiz and game show repeats channel back on. He went into the bathroom and washed the plate and cutlery in the sink.

"Mum," he called out from the bathroom, still trying to sound casual. Just chatting. "Do we have a relative named Megan? A second or third cousin, I think. Maybe from Dad's side of the family?" Harvey came out of the bathroom, drying the plate with a bath towel. "I need to talk to you about Dad."

"He's very busy."

Harvey looked at his mother.

"Who is, Mum? Who's very busy?" He put the plate on the dressing table, in case she said something that made him drop it.

"My brother can't come," Harvey's mother said, her eyes fixed on the television quiz.

"What brother?" Harvey said. "You haven't got a brother, Mum. Do you mean your sister can't come? Auntie Cathy? She's in New Zealand. But I'm talking about Canada. Megan from Canada?"

He put the empty takeaway containers in the brown paper bag. Deliberately standing between his mother and the television.

"I found something out. About Dad. About Terry." Harvey thought he caught a change in his mother's expression when he'd used his father's name. "Terry was your husband, Mum. Do you remember him? My dad?"

His mother moved her head to try and see around him. He took half a step sideways, standing at the end of the bed, blocking her view of the TV. She looked at the remote control in his hand. He put it out of sight in the back pocket of his jeans.

He took his phone out and found the picture of the family tree.

"I was sent this," he said. He squeezed and pinched at the screen, to make the image on his phone as large as possible without pruning too many relatives. He walked over to the side of the bed and held the phone close to his mother.

"I don't know what that is," she said, without actually looking. "Is it a phone call?"

"No, Mum. The picture, look." Harvey gave her the phone. She held it but was still looking up at him. "Look at the picture on the phone, Mum."

He waited, until his mother at last looked at the phone. She turned it on its side. The picture of the family tree spun. Harvey gestured for her to turn the phone back around. She looked at it for a moment and then held it to her ear.

"Hello," she said.

Harvey was determined to not let this be funny.

"No, Mum," he said. "*On* the phone. There's a picture. Look at the family tree picture, Mum."

She looked up at him, confused. Harvey pointed at the phone. She stared at his finger, like a dog or a baby would. He put his finger on the screen of the phone.

"There's nothing," his mother said.

Harvey sighed. He took the phone back. The family tree was gone. His mother had managed to open the web browser. Harvey tried closing it, but the screen was frozen. His mother had somehow discovered a secret combination to completely change the entire display. She'd hacked his phone.

Harvey switched it off and back on. It took forever. He reloaded the photo app, scrolling through all the pictures he'd taken of his mother since she'd been at the care home. Every Sunday, Harvey took another photo and added it to a slideshow of his mother looking happy and sad, amused and confused, pleased and disappointed, sometimes during the same visit.

Harvey swiped through the photos of his mother as though he was using a dating app in a nightmare, until he found the jpeg of the family tree. He resized it and zoomed in on the dates beneath his father's name. He held the phone out to his mother again. He didn't know if the picture was too close or too far away for her to see. She'd stopped wearing her glasses and she hadn't had an eye-test for years. How did you even test the eyes of someone who couldn't reliably recognise letters anymore? Why hadn't Harvey just brought the print out of the family tree with him? He thought about plugging his laptop back into the TV and showing his mother the video of the family tree coming out of the printer, but he decided it would still be far too small and impossible to read.

He handed his mother the phone.

"Now please, Mum. Try not to press anything this time."

She stared at the phone.

"Just read the dates, Mum."

His mother held the phone out to him.

"The dates, Mum. *Please* read the dates."

She looked from Harvey to the phone and back again. She was completely lost, scared. Harvey had only asked her a few simple questions and shown her a picture of a tree, but he felt like he'd just waterboarded an old lady.

He sat on the edge of the bed, utterly defeated. As though he had to solve a murder where the only witness was the victim's dog, and to crack the case, he would first have to have to teach the dog how to speak.

He took his phone back and put it in his pocket. He

tipped the leftover food and rubbish into the takeaway bag and put the plate and the cutlery in the other bag. He put his mother's uneaten Sunday sandwich in his coat pocket, shaking a few crumbs onto the plate first, like a parent on Christmas Eve after eating Santa's mince pie. He straightened the two pictures on the wall, knowing his mother would move them back again after he'd left. He stood last year's Christmas and birthday cards back upright on the dressing table. Asha had scribbled out the names of the charities on the backs of the cards because Harvey's mother had thought the cards meant her son had cancer or Parkinson's disease.

"Are you going on holiday again?" his mother asked, watching him putting his coat on.

"No, Mum. I'm going home. I'll be back next week."

"That will be nice. I can cook something."

She picked up the headphones and was trying to put them on. Harvey helped her. He reset the volume on the television. He took his phone out and stood at the end of the bed.

"Say cheese, Mum."

She smiled, and he took her picture. The headphones were so large on his mother's head. She reminded him of someone, but he couldn't think who; a superstar DJ or the child of a racing driver at the Grand Prix perhaps. He took another picture. He gathered everything together and said goodbye.

On the way to the lift, an email arrived. There was new activity on his video channel. Harvey clicked on the link.

"Do you review shoes?" – Jess86

When Harvey walked towards the Wildways office, he thought about asking Asha for advice about his mother. He could tell her about the family tree. Asha would know what to do. But the office door was closed.

Harvey took the plate and the knife and fork back to the dining lounge. He'd forgotten to get a pen to sign in and out of the visitors book. There was nothing to prove he'd ever been there and that he wasn't a terrible, neglectful son. On the way through the gates, he considered the latest comment from Jess86 asking if he reviewed shoes. Harvey was sure, based on what he'd overheard in the Castle staff canteen and on the shuttle bus every day, and from his seven years of stacking the shelves of an enormous retail store and knowing the quantity and the range and the number of shelves required and the frequency with which he had to restock them, that it wasn't men who were particularly interested in shoes.

As he waited for the care home gates to open he realised who his mother had reminded him of in the big headphones. It wasn't a DJ or a child at the Grand Prix. A few nights ago, Harvey had watched a news report on the trial of an ageing war criminal. Even though he was accused of some horrific atrocities, Harvey had found himself feeling sorry for him. The grey-haired old man behind the courtroom glass looked so sad and confused as he listened in obvious bewilderment to the evidence against him, via an interpreter through a large pair of headphones. No, your mum is a Nazi war criminal.

7

On the way home, Harvey had the unshakeable feeling his dad was in the Fusilier. He was convinced he was sitting on his usual stool at the bar, sharing a joke with the landlord or selling a vehicle logbook to a tourist. If Harvey didn't at least go into the pub and check, he would spend the rest of his life thinking that he'd missed him. And besides, Harvey really didn't want to go home yet. The only thing waiting for him there was mess. And not just the usual flattened cardboard boxes and bubble wrap, and enough blocks of white polystyrene to build an igloo. And not the DVDs, the video games, the comics and sci-fi magazines, left on the sofa, the sideboard, and piled up like Jenga on the living room carpet (When Harvey was at home, he never managed to put anything on shelves.). Apart from the usual mess – the shredded cardboard, the pink pasta shapes and the polystyrene peanuts, the void fill as it was called – there was a new mess, a more abstract void that needed filling. Harvey thought a quick drink and the company of a few local strangers might help somehow.

He walked between the same two old men who were smoking outside the pub earlier. They were standing on either side of the pub door like bouncers. Harvey felt like he might be expected to tip them. One of the men viewed him with cowboy film suspicion. Maybe his dad had once sold him a stopped-watch or some counterfeit perfume. If there was a family likeness between Harvey and his father, the man might have noticed it. Harvey nodded to the two men as he went through the door.

It was like stepping back in time. In the quarter of a century since he'd last been in the pub, it had barely changed. The tables and chairs, the sticky red carpet and the flock wallpaper. It was all so familiar. The pub looked the same as it had when Harvey was eight or nine years old. He knew if he touched the raised floral pattern on the wallpaper, it would give him goose pimples up and down the back of his neck. The Fusilier was so intimidatingly empty that Harvey almost walked straight back out again, but the barman caught his eye, and so Harvey went up to the bar and ordered a drink. He asked for a pint of Guinness, because it was what his father used to drink. Harvey wasn't sure he'd known that until he walked through the door. His sense of recall seemed heightened by his surroundings. If he stayed in the pub for long enough, and drank enough Guinness, maybe he'd remember what his dad looked like.

Harvey had never had Guinness before. It took ages for the barman to pour it. He even had enough time to walk away and serve another customer halfway through. While the barman was gone, the two old men from outside came back in. They climbed on to two high stools next to Harvey. One man did so with such difficulty that Harvey instinctively reached out to 'help'.

The barman returned to pour part two of the Guinness. Harvey paid him and went as far away from the bar as possible. He stood next to the jukebox and looked at the songs on offer. Queen, Dire Straits and Wham! The music in the Fusilier hadn't changed in a quarter of a century either. Harvey ran his fingertips along the numbers and letters and had two different muscle memories of selecting 'K7'. The first memory was a Kit Kat Chunky from the vending machine in the foyer of The Castle. He wondered if the pub sold chocolate. If Harvey owned a pub, they'd sell chocolate.

The second 'K7' muscle memory was 'Peggy Sue' by Buddy Holly. His dad would put the coins in the Fusilier jukebox and tell Harvey which songs to choose. One would always be 'Peggy Sue'. It was a song Harvey's dad used to sing all the time. Because Harvey's mother's name was Margaret, and Peggy – for some reason – was short for Margaret.

'K7' on the Fusilier jukebox was now the official 2006 England World Cup song. It may be the one thing in the pub that had changed. Harvey allowed himself the romantic notion that his father had returned at some point in the last twenty-six years and asked if he could take the Buddy Holly record away with him.

'K8' on the jukebox was still 'Peggy Sue Got Married'. If Buddy Holly hadn't died so tragically young, maybe he would have written more Peggy Sue songs and Harvey would have a better idea about what had happened between his parents.

His dad had his own name song, too. 'Terry' by Twinkle. The lyrics were about a man dying in a motorcycle accident. Harvey laughed to himself thinking about that. Maybe all pop songs were prophetic. Perhaps life was its own musical. Harvey couldn't remember his dad ever having a motorbike, though, just lots of different cars, sometimes a different one every week.

He flicked through the songs on the jukebox. 'Terry' wasn't there but 'Cathy's Clown' was. That was Harvey's mother's sister Cathy's song. Harvey remembered his mother saying that the clown was Cathy's estranged husband, Stephen. He always thought she was saying Cathy's *strange* husband.

The barman cleared some empty glasses from the table next to the jukebox. He looked at Harvey's Guinness. He'd hardly touched it.

"It doesn't work," the barman said. He nodded at the jukebox.

"Oh, right. Thanks. I was just looking at the songs," Harvey said.

The barman looked at the Guinness again. Harvey made a show of taking a large swig. It had already miraculously started to taste better than when he'd started drinking it.

The barman went away, and Harvey continued browsing the jukebox songs. There was still an extensive rock 'n' roll section. 'L3' (a plain chocolate Bounty in The Castle vending machine) was 'Long Tall Sally'. That was Cathy's daughter Sally's song.

Sally was five years younger than Harvey. They were both only children, and when they were growing up they'd taken on the roles of big brother and little sister. Harvey took Sally to the swimming pool and the cinema. He pushed her on swings and spun her around on roundabouts. He buried Sally's Barbies in the garden and let her bury him up to his neck in the sand on Bantham beach.

Sally and Auntie Cathy had gone to live in New Zealand around the time that Harvey's dad had died for the first time. His death had probably taken the sting out of them leaving, and Harvey hadn't thought about Sally for years. But now he suddenly missed her, as though she'd only just left for the airport.

Harvey had written to Sally shortly after she'd emigrated. He'd been taking part in a pen pal project at school and had written letters to a boy in Germany named Henry, who didn't reply once. When the project was over, Harvey had stolen a few sheets of the blue airmail paper and written to Sally in New Zealand. He told her about his new school, describing the building and the food in great detail, because he couldn't think of anything positive to write about any of the people there. He filled every bit of available space on the thin blue paper. Drawing a border of spaceships and aliens and colouring in the dots above all the i's and the j's. He sealed the letters and gave them to his mother to add Sally's new address in New Zealand and take them to the post office to buy the correct stamps. Harvey didn't expect Sally to write back, because she was too young, but he enjoyed writing to her anyway. He knew how thrilling it was to receive something in the post with your name on.

Harvey selected 'Long Tall Sally' on the broken jukebox and imagined the song playing. He couldn't actually remember how it went. He took his phone out and searched the internet for 'songs containing the name Harvey' and found a country and western song from 2013. The lyrics were about a man who dies and is brought back to life four minutes later. Harvey felt like he was being catfished. His phone pinged loudly. The barman looked over at him. Harvey turned the ringer volume down.

He put his Guinness on the top of the jukebox next to a black plastic ashtray. He stood on tiptoes to see if there were any dog ends left behind from before the smoking ban. The image of his father's face may have been melting like an out-of-season ice hotel, but Harvey had a vivid memory of him smoking. It was probably what killed him. Harvey opened his video page to read the new comment. He was pleased that it was Jess86 and not just somebody calling him a fat bastard.

"What's a troll hunter?"

Harvey had forgotten he'd asked if Jess86 was a troll hunter when he was in the Bay of Bengal. He certainly hadn't expected a reply. He drank some more Guinness and replied.

"There was this Scandinavian who hired a load of kids who were good with computers to track down trolls on social media. They'd confront the trolls on live TV. The main guy was called the Troll Hunter."

Harvey didn't usually use the word 'guy'. Surely it was a little late to start thinking about appearing cool for Jess86. She – or he, *it,* Harvey still didn't know for sure – had already seen him stammering and blinking his way through at least four different unboxing videos. They knew he wasn't cool. He finished his Guinness and went up to the bar. He ordered a lager and asked the barman if he had any crisps.

"Cheese and onion, salt and vinegar or plain?"

Harvey chose cheese and onion and asked if there was a password for the Wi-Fi. The barman seemed put out by the request. He shook his head, sighed and walked away. Harvey waited, unsure whether the barman had gone to get the Wi-Fi code or if he'd just gone. He took a sip of the lager. It tasted weird after the Guinness. Not better or worse, just weird. The two old men on barstools were staring at him. He nodded hello and stared at the carpet. It was difficult to tell what was pattern and what was dirt. The pub didn't look like it had ever been properly cleaned. There were probably a few of his dad's cigarette butts trodden deep into the filthy carpet. Harvey imagined the Fusilier as a rich source of King DNA. His presence in the pub was only adding to it. The barman returned and gave him a small strip of paper.

"Don't download any films," he said, and from his expression it was clear the barman wasn't joking.

Harvey thanked him and went and sat at the table next to the jukebox. He logged onto the Wi-Fi, opened his video page and clicked on Jess86's name. A new window opened, showing their profile. They had only signed up to the website ten days ago. So far they hadn't uploaded any videos, created any playlists or favourited any video channels. Apart from the comments and thumbs-ups for Harvey's printer and headphones unboxings, Jess86's only other activity had been two more positive thumbs – one for Harvey's unboxing of a games console and another for his review of the phone he was looking at now. Harvey took a swig of the lager and opened the crisps. His phone pinged.

"Are you in Scandinavia then?" Jess86 said.

"No. I'm in a pub. In between Devon and Cornwall. Do you know it?"

"I don't know. What's the pub called?"

"Sorry. I meant do you know Devon and Cornwall?"

"I know. I was joking. I must apologise for being sarcastic. I've just spent the whole day working with small children and I forget to switch off sometimes."

Jess86 didn't say whether she – Harvey had decided

Jess86 was definitely female – knew Devon or Cornwall or not. He wondered whereabouts in the world she was. Would it be weird to ask?

"I haven't been to this pub for years," Harvey said. "I'm sure some of the same customers were here the last time I came."

"When was that?"

"A very long time ago. I used to come here with my dad."

"Who are you with in the pub now?"

Harvey considered saying he was out with 'a few mates'. But instead he said, "I'm on my own. I'm sort of drowning my sorrows."

"I am sorry to hear that. Do you mind if I ask why?"

What a relief it would be to tell somebody the whole story. Even a complete stranger. *Especially* a complete stranger. Harvey could say anything he wanted to Jess86. He could be as candid as he liked with no real consequences. They could be best friends in just a few clicks and strangers again in a few clicks more. As fast as the broadband speed would allow. And the Fusilier broadband was insanely, bafflingly, fast.

"My dad died," Harvey said. He felt a heavy weight had been lifted from his shoulders. He finished his lager to celebrate.

When Jess86 didn't reply, he presumed he'd shared too much, too soon, too fast. Curse this speedy Fusilier broadband.

The barman came over and took his empty glass away. Harvey would either have to leave or buy another drink. He still didn't feel like going home yet. If he never went home again it wouldn't matter. Life would go on without him. The central heating would switch itself on and off twice a day, the television would record his favourite programmes. The fridge would defrost itself, and a plug-in air freshener would fill the living room with fresh summer meadows every four hours. Even his computer was only ever half asleep, still collecting emails and downloading software updates. Megan's family tree would still be there at the top of the front page of the bookmarked genealogy site. Dragging the PDF onto the desktop hadn't removed it from the website. Neither had printing the family tree or filming himself printing it. If Harvey dragged the PDF to the trash folder, deleted the email, emptied the trash, took a hammer to the hard drive and blew the house up, Megan's family tree would still be on the internet. The genealogy website would carry on emailing it to hundreds and thousands of amateur genealogists with the same surname as Harvey and Megan. The death of his father was just more clickbait now.

Harvey went to the toilet. He stood at the urinal, reading the graffiti on the wall, looking for clues that his dad had been there – 'TERENCE KING WOZ ERE' and a date perhaps. Harvey looked for cigarette butts in the urinal. He was swaying because of the drink and had to put his hand on the wall to steady himself. The wall was sticky. He didn't usually use public toilets because it still reminded him of school. He couldn't stand at a urinal without expecting to be pushed forward by one of the Lyon brothers.

Harvey washed his hands in the cold water of the Fusilier's sink. He looked at the blank rectangle on the wall, where a mirror once hung. The contraceptive vending machine next to a machine dispensing disposable toothbrushes made him feel inexplicably sad. The hand-dryer didn't work so he wiped his wet hands on his jeans and went back to the bar. He ordered another Guinness and two bags of crisps. The barman asked him which flavour he wanted.

"Salt and vinegar and plain, please."

"Are you collecting the whole set?"

The barman knew him too well. Harvey asked him if he knew anyone named Terence King.

The barman shrugged. "I don't think so."

"He was known as Terry," Harvey said. "He was my dad. He used to drink here."

"I've only been here for a year. What did your dad look like?"

The barman was asking the wrong person. It was too embarrassing to explain, so Harvey said it didn't matter. He paid for the drink and crisps and the barman said he'd bring the Guinness over when it was poured. Harvey went back to his table. While he'd been away Jess86 had posted another comment.

"I'm really sorry."

Harvey couldn't remember what either of them had said to make her sorry. He scrolled back through the comments to the one where he'd told Jess86 his dad had died. It occurred to him that he'd also told as many as three billion other people as well.

"It's OK," Harvey said. "It's funny actually. You know when you hear that a famous person has died and you don't know how to react because you thought they were already dead? It's a bit like that."

"I don't understand," Jess86 said.

Harvey started typing a reply. The barman put the Guinness on the table and Harvey covered his phone with his hand until he was gone.

"I thought my dad died 26 years ago and then I found out from a family tree on the internet that he'd been alive all that time. Until he actually did die this year."

It looked like the onscreen description for a guest on a daytime tabloid talk show. Or the lead story in one of the real-life magazines the girl with the tea trolley left in his mother's room.

"What?!" Jess86 said. "No way! How old were you?"

"I was eleven when I thought he died the first time."

"And you had no idea he'd been alive since then?"

Harvey would have assumed that what had started out

as an exchange of comments about – what was it again? – a printer? noise-cancelling headphones? – would have ended a long time ago. But Jess86 kept the conversation going, asking him more questions. And Harvey was more than happy, and now more than drunk enough, to keep answering them.

"No," Harvey typed into his phone. "For the last 26 years of my life I thought he was dead."

"How did you find out he died?"

"This time or the first time?"

"Both"

"It's a long story."

"There's nothing on telly."

Harvey told Jess86 he'd joined a website to research his family tree and they sent him regular emails, informing him there were members of his family who wanted to share their information.

"But it's never my actual family," Harvey said. "Just some stranger with the same surname as me. The website will have sent the email to loads of other people called King as well, hoping some of them will click the link and see their advertising and sign up to their website. When I got the email, I thought it was just more of their clickbait."

"What's clickbait?" Jess86 said.

"It's a teaser bit of information and a link, to tempt you onto a website."

"I've not heard of it before."

"It was the dictionary word of the year a few years ago."

"There's a word of the year?!!?"

Someone dropped a glass and for a moment Harvey thought Jess86 was in the Fusilier. He looked around at the few customers in the almost deserted pub. The two old men at the bar, the barman, another old man who may have been asleep, and a middle-aged couple who'd barely spoken to each other since Harvey had arrived. None of them looked like the Jess86 Harvey was imagining.

Another comment arrived.

"If it's a computer thing I wouldn't understand," Jess86 said. "I'm surprised I'm managing to type this actually. The four and five-year olds I work with are more computer literate than I am. The computers at work only let us type in Comic Sans."

"No way!"

"Sorry. Joking again. I don't even know what Comic Sans is. And I'm not at work. It's eight-thirty in the evening. School's out!"

Harvey smiled. He looked at the time on his phone. It was eight-thirty where he was as well. He opened the web browser and typed: 'Countries in the same time zone as the UK'. Jess86 was either in the UK, Mauritania, Western Sahara, Saint Helena, Senegal or Togo.

"So, you're sure this latest email from the family tree website was genuine?" Jess86 said. She wasn't giving Harvey enough time to reply now. "It definitely isn't clickbait. Is that what you're saying?"

"Yes. The link led me to a family tree compiled by a distant relative in Canada. I don't know her. It's really detailed. You should see it. I suppose you have. When it was coming out of the printer in the unboxing. It was the date on her family tree that told me my dad had died this year and not 26 years ago."

"It's not a mistake?"

"That's what I thought at first. But I looked it up and found the official death record."

"Do you mind me asking something?" Jess86 said.

"What?"

"Is your mum still alive?"

"She was the one who told me my dad was dead," Harvey said, wishing he'd used locked caps. "The first time he died I mean. When I was eleven."

"I see."

Jess86 was managing to follow things so easily that

Harvey thought she might be taking notes. She was probably just not as drunk as he was. He'd almost finished another pint and was starting to feel nauseous.

"It was my mum who I was compiling the family tree for," Harvey said. "As a present for her. I was going to frame it and everything."

"Perhaps your mum wanted you to find out about your dad."

"You don't understand," Harvey said. "My mum didn't *ask* me to compile the family tree. If that's what you mean. It was going to be a surprise for her. A surprise for her. Rather than for me. I wanted her to remember who her family were. She's not well. I won't bore you with the details. The thing is, I can't think why she would have lied about my dad dying in the first place. Why would anyone do that?"

"And your mum knew your dad died this year?" Jess86 said.

Harvey almost dropped his phone. Now he really did feel sick. When he'd been to the care home earlier, he'd tried asking his mother about the first time his dad had died. But he hadn't told her about the second time, his father's *actual* death. His mother didn't know!

"It's complicated," Harvey typed, thinking the understatement would be the end of it. Staring at his phone was making him feel dizzy.

But Jess86 wasn't satisfied. "What do you mean by complicated?"

It was just too complex a question to answer in the comments section of a video sharing website. Perhaps if he explained some of his mother's health issues, Jess86 would understand his predicament. What should he tell her? What was currently the boss of his mother, the migraines or the vertigo? The aphasia or the mini strokes? The small vessel disease?

"My mum forgets things," Harvey said. "I don't know

what she remembers and what she doesn't. It makes it really hard to ask her about the past. And she gets her words mixed up as well. She might say that she needs eat instead of saying she's hungry. She sometimes refers to me as her man instead of her son. I told you it was complicated."

"There's a boy at work whose first language is Greek," Jess86 said. "He's learning English as an additional language and he gets his words mixed up in a similar way to your mum. He'll call his cousin his sister for example."

"My mum called me her brother once," Harvey said. "She hasn't got a brother by the way."

"Has she got any sisters?"

"She's got one. But she lives in New Zealand."

Harvey looked around the pub. The middle-aged couple and the sleeping man had gone, and it was just Harvey, the two old men and the barman left. It was definitely time to go home. He picked up his phone.

"How old is your mum?" Jess86 said as though she was trying to stop him from leaving.

"Old."

"How old?"

"Seventy."

"That's not old."

Harvey wondered if Jess86 *was* eighty-six.

"She does actually seem more like a child sometimes I suppose," Harvey said. "We've watched Shrek four times because she really loves the donkey."

"Oh, I adore that film," Jess86 said. "What are you going to do next?"

"What do you mean, next?"

"You have to find out what really happened to your dad surely. Ask your mum."

"Like I said, it's really not that simple."

"But you do *want* to know? Don't you?"

"I suppose so," Harvey said. "But apparently it's best not to ask people with dementia too many questions."

"Your mum you mean? You didn't tell me she had dementia."

Harvey thought he had. He needed to sober up. He needed to go home.

"Someone at my mum's care home told me I shouldn't ask her a lot of questions," Harvey said, not mentioning Asha by name, as though Jess86 would think he was cheating on her. "If I was to ask you if you want a cup of tea for example," Harvey said, repeating word for word what Asha had told him. "Before they can answer you, they'll first ask themselves other questions. Have they had a cup of tea not long ago? Does this person make a nice cup of tea? Would they prefer a cold drink? Will they need to use the toilet if they have a cup of tea?"

Asha had told Harvey that he could go through such supplementary questions really quickly, too fast to even notice he was asking himself questions at all, before he arrived at the simple answer as to whether he wanted a cup of tea or not. Harvey's mother, however, would look back at her recent memories related to tea, and she'd find nothing there. She would have to look further and further back in her mind, until she was in the nineteen-fifties or sixties, and then she'd start asking herself further questions. Is this person offering to make me a cup of tea having a cup too? Will they be put out by having to make one especially for me? And she could end up confused and wonder, who is this person asking if I want a cup of tea?

Harvey pressed send on his long reply and stood up. The whole pub shifted an inch to the left.

"What's your mum's care home called?" Jess86 said.

"Wildways. The staff call it the Wild West. Why?"

"Oh right. Nothing really. My friend's dad is in a home down there. I thought it might have been the same one."

"Is it?"

"No. But listen. This is what you should do next. You should use the information you already have to find out more. Do you know when your dad was born?"

"Yes."

"And you know his name right? And you know when he died?"

"*Both* times he died."

"Order a death certificate."

8

When Harvey left the Fusilier, he was so drunk that he started walking in the wrong direction. He didn't realise until he saw the lights on downstairs in the front room of his old house, the same room where his mother had told her lie. A silver car was parked in the carport. It would have ruined the grass his dad had laid if the new owners hadn't already dug it up.

Harvey and his mother had moved out of the house, and into a smaller, cheaper one on the other side of the village, just before Christmas, the first Christmas without Harvey's dad. A man named Phillip had hired a van and helped them move. Phillip was a chef and arrived in the van still wearing his checked work trousers. He had long hair and a big moustache. Harvey could remember him more vividly than his own father. Although he might have been getting him confused with the chef from *the Muppets*.

It had taken a few van trips to decanter their old house into their new one. When there was nothing left but echoes and light bulbs, Harvey's mother closed the front door and broke a fingernail picking the key off of her key ring. She was about to post the key through the letterbox, when Harvey asked, "What about Dad's grass?"

"What do you mean, Dad's grass?"

"The grass me and Dad laid."

"We can't take grass with us, Harvey."

"Why not?"

"What would we do with it? There's no garden at our new house. We can hardly dig it up and lay it in the front room. And even if we wanted to, the garden spade is already at our new house."

"What do we need a garden spade for if we haven't got a garden?"

"Oh, Harvey. Can we talk about this later? I'm exhausted. And Phil is going to cook for us."

"Who's Phil?"

"Oh, please don't do this, Harvey."

"Is *Phil* moving in to our new house, too?"

"Don't be silly. He's just going to cook us something nice for dinner. He's going to plumb the electric cooker in."

"You don't plumb an electric cooker in."

"Don't be difficult, Harvey. It's been a long day."

"What's he cooking?"

"I don't know. Would you like me to ask him for the menu?"

"Yes, please."

Phillip made rigatoni arrabiata that evening (It was funny what Harvey could remember.). His sticky toffee pudding was delicious, even if Harvey would never have admitted that at the time.

After dinner, Harvey's mother and Phillip were chatting and laughing loudly in the living room of the new house. Without carpets, it sounded like they were onstage at Wembley Stadium. Harvey was sulking in the kitchen, reading a comic and fiddling with the controls of the cooker Phillip had fitted. He changed the time on the clock, opened and closed the oven door and turned the hobs on and off, watching them glow orange and change back to black. He placed his hand on the smallest hob, like it was a saucepan of beans, and he screamed, as much in surprise as pain. He hadn't realised quite how hot it would be. It wasn't even orange.

Harvey's mother rushed into the kitchen and she screamed, too. She hugged Harvey and held his hand under the cold tap, looking desperately around the kitchen at the unpacked cardboard boxes, trying to remember what the right thing to do was – put butter on the burn, bandage it or let the air get to it. Phillip, who was used to dealing with burns in the kitchen at work, didn't panic. He tipped the leftover muscovado sugar he'd brought for his delicious sticky toffee pudding out of a cling film bag. He turned the bag inside out and wrapped it around Harvey's hand. Then Phillip drove Harvey and his mother to the hospital in the hire van. Harvey sat in the front between Phillip and his mother, who consoled and reassured her injured son, while he licked sugar from the bag wrapped around his burned hand.

Harvey couldn't remember ever seeing Phillip again after he'd driven them back home from the hospital. His mother dated two other men after Phillip, who Harvey could remember. David designed wedding cakes, and there was a man named Al who came to the house a few times. Harvey liked Al, because he always brought sweets. He owned a confectionery factory. Harvey wondered if his mother had been trying to find a suitor for her son, as much as she was looking for a new companion for herself. He imagined her compiling a wish list.

~~The Swedish chef from the Muppets~~
~~Mr Kipling~~
~~Willy Wonka~~
Bertie Bassett
Colonel Saunders

Harvey must have missed his dad that first Christmas in their new house without him, but he couldn't honestly remember. He did remember the Christmas before. That was the year his mother was in hospital, the same hospital where Harvey's burn was dressed. She was recovering from an operation. Harvey had woken up on Christmas Day to find there was no pillowcase full of presents at the end of his bed. That was the year Harvey realised that Santa wasn't his dad. It might have also been the Christmas when he had the feeling that his presents had come from underneath somebody else's tree.

9

Harvey ordered a death certificate when he got home from the pub. He should have waited until the morning or at least until he was more sober. Hopefully he'd ordered one for the right Terence King. He put two pizzas in the oven and went upstairs to search for family photographs. He looked in bedroom drawers and cupboards, on top of wardrobes and under beds. In his mother's room he felt like a burglar. For as long as he'd been filming himself and posting the videos online, Harvey had been convinced there were hidden cameras and microphones everywhere. It was the reason he filmed all his unboxings on a camera not connected to the internet rather than using his webcam, which he kept permanently covered up with a Hitler moustache of black electrical insulation tape. He'd recently upgraded his video camera to a 'high definition, ultra-compact, low noise, lightweight handycam'. The unboxing of the new camera had been the last thing he filmed using his low definition, bulky, old camcorder. The poignancy of that particular unboxing was appreciated only by Harvey, and perhaps by the unwanted old camcorder itself.

In his mother's wardrobe Harvey found the *Doctor Who* scarf his mother had knitted him for his twelfth birthday. It was the year after his father's first death. Harvey had a party but he didn't want to invite any of his 'friends', and so it was just him and his mother, who catered for a small army anyway, making sausage rolls and sandwiches, quiches, miniature hamburgers and a cheeseboard. What twelve-year old has a cheeseboard at their birthday party?

Harvey and his mother played party games, pinning the tail on a picture of a donkey taped to the fridge and passing parcels back and forth between each other. Every time the music stopped, Harvey would unbox another present, one of them was the scarf. It was supposed to be the same as the scarf Tom Baker wore in *Doctor Who*. The colours weren't right and there were too many stripes, but Harvey wore it for the rest of the day. Twenty-five years later, and the scarf was still so long that he had to wrap around his neck three times to stop himself from tripping over it.

He went downstairs to the kitchen and, using the end of the scarf as an oven glove, he took the two pizzas out of the oven. He put them on a plate, went into the living room and sat on the carpet in front of the sideboard.

There were three wide drawers at the centre of the sideboard and a cupboard at either end. It was a long piece of furniture, almost taking up the length of the wall. It had been the last thing to leave their old house in the back of Phillip's van. Phillip had decided, using his outstretched arms for measurement, that the sideboard required a van trip all of its own. Harvey had waited in their gutted old house, while his mother went with Phillip and the penultimate van-load of furniture and boxes to their new home on the other side of the village.

Harvey lay on the bare floorboards, with his head underneath the sideboard and ate a Mars bar (His mother had swanned off in a van with her new friend, but she had at least left Harvey with one of his old ones.). His mother and Phillip were gone for almost an hour and Harvey was soon bored. He opened one of the sideboard cupboards and started folding himself inside. It was a snug fit but he managed it. When he heard Phillip's van pull up outside, doors opening and his mother's voice, and then Phillip's, Harvey decided to stay inside the cupboard. His mother was laughing loudly. Shouldn't she still be in mourning? Harvey gripped the edge of the cupboard door with the tips of his fingers and pulled it closed. He listened for the key in the front door and footsteps in the hall, and then in the living room.

"Where the hell is he?" Phillip said, with an impatience he wasn't entitled to.

"Harvey?" his mother called up the stairs. "Are you up

there?" and then she was back in the living room. "He's not upstairs, Phil. He's probably gone to the shops."

"He eats too many sweets, you know," Phillip said. "You have noticed he's overweight."

There was no answer from Harvey's mother and he feared he was about to discover how she spoke about him when he wasn't there to hear. Instead, she called out his name again, this time in the kitchen. Phillip was still in the living room, muttering to himself. Harvey hated him.

"He's not in the garden," Harvey's mother said. She was back in the living room. "I don't know where he can be." Not for one second did she believe her fat son could fit inside a cupboard.

Harvey's leg had started to cramp up, but he didn't want to come out yet. He imagined Phillip and his mother carrying the sideboard out to the van and driving all the way to their new house with him still inside. He hoped Phillip got the heavy end.

The living room was silent, but Harvey thought his mother and Phillip were still there. Were they actually kissing? His mother's husband was dead and her son was missing, probably kidnapped by serial killers or witches, and she was making out with the Swedish chef from *the Muppet Show*.

When Harvey couldn't stay in the cupboard any longer, without serious injury, he opened the door. The living room was empty. He found his mother and Phillip in the back garden. Phillip was smoking a pipe. His mother asked Harvey where he'd been and he said he'd been to the sweetshop. Phillip looked so pleased with himself for having been right about that.

Harvey finished the first pizza and took a bite out of the second. He pulled out the bottom sideboard drawer. It was heavy but the action was smooth. Harvey felt he could trust the drawer not to collapse in his hands. Unlike all the other furniture in the house, the sideboard clearly hadn't come from The Castle. It was well-built, held together with proper mortise and tenon, and dovetail joints. The cupboard doors wouldn't fall off their hinges every time they were opened.

Harvey dragged the heavy drawer onto the carpet. He went through the utility bills, faded receipts and various instruction manuals for household appliances, long since retired and taken to the recycling centre. In the middle drawer there was a tennis-ball-sized rubber band collection and a pile of his mother's old recipe and cook books. The closest she came to cooking nowadays was drowning her chicken chow mein in soy sauce every Sunday. How must it have felt, for someone who used to love cooking so much, to live in just one room with no cooker, not even a kettle? When Harvey ran his care home, he'd put kettles and cookers in every room. He should probably never be allowed to run a care home.

In the top drawer of the sideboard Harvey found his birth certificate. For a moment he thought it might be his dad's death certificate. How typical it would be, to find it twenty minutes after paying £14 for a new one. At the bottom of the drawer there was a box of liqueur chocolates. It was unheard of for chocolates or sweets to survive uneaten in the house for longer than a day. There was something of the Holy Grail about the long box of foil wrapped miniature chocolate bottles. There was no sell-by date on the box, which was perhaps an indication of just how past that date they were. Harvey unboxed them anyway. He tried a whisky one. It was foul.

Harvey ate the two Cointreau chocolates and moved onto the two sideboard cupboards. In the one on the left, there were two LP records – *Buddy Holly Lives - Twenty Golden Greats* and John Lennon's *Rock and Roll*. Both albums had versions of 'Peggy Sue' on. It was impossible not to read something into his father leaving only those two records behind. Harvey took the Buddy Holly record out of the sleeve. It was warped. He sniffed it like it was a fine cheese or a cigar. He wished there was something he could play it on.

In the right-hand cupboard, Harvey found a cardboard box. It filled almost the whole cupboard. He dragged it out onto the floor and went through the spaghetti of SCART and phono leads inside. He took out five three-pin plugs and some old audio cassette tapes. The tapes were all unused and still wrapped in cellophane. Except for one. He read the handwritten label: *The Harvey King Show. Episodes 8 and 9.*

Before his dad died for the first time, Harvey used to record television chat shows and replace the interviewer's voice with his own. Sometimes he'd ask his guests different questions, to make them appear confused or simple. There'd been no internet to upload *The Harvey King Show* to, and so no one called him a fat prick or gave him the thumbs-down. There were a few awkward guests, of course. Perhaps a footballer would turn up drunk or a Hollywood superstar would only answer questions with monosyllabic grunts, but as Harvey was in control of the stop and record buttons, they were never really a problem. *The Harvey King Show* ran for two series, ending with a special non-celebrity episode, when Harvey interviewed his parents. Like the records, he had nothing to play the cassette on. But the idea that he might have found the captured voice of his father was exciting. He put the cassette on the sofa with the two records.

When he found a photo album in the cardboard box, he was almost too nervous to open it. He sat on the sofa and wiped the dust from the leather-look cover. He ate a Grand Marnier liqueur for courage and turned the first page, expecting to see a picture of his dad looking back at him. He thought he'd at least find a few mysterious blank patches, like the space where the mirror once hung on the wall of the Fusilier toilets. But the photo album was completely and disappointingly empty of photographs. Not even half a torn-edged picture of his mother on her wedding day, gazing longingly to her side.

In between the last two pages of the photo album, there were five small sheets of paper. The paper was wafer thin and pale blue, with a darker blue and red border on one side, and the words 'par avion' in the corner. The writing paper was its own envelope, and the envelopes were all sealed. There were no addresses or stamps on any of the sealed airmail letters, just two words, written in the same hand as the labels on the cassette: 'To Sally'.

Harvey sat on the sofa, with his unplayable tape and records, and the unsent airmail letters. Every time he searched for answers, he found more questions. He finished the liqueur chocolates, biting off the ends and tipping the sticky liquids down his throat until he felt sick. He sat and stared at the empty sideboard cupboards. He held his arms apart like a tape measure and wondered...could he…still?

10

Harvey had a thumping headache. The clatter of till beeps and shop floor infomercials was deafening, and every time he took a breath, Harvey tasted a cocktail of Guinness and Grand Marnier, Cointreau and cherry brandy. His whole body ached. The Castle shelves were either too high or too low. He could still feel the scarf he'd slept in, like a rash on the back of his neck. He felt sick and sorry for himself and just wanted to be left alone. And Jess86 just wouldn't leave him alone.

"Did you order the certificate?"

It was midday and Harvey was in the goods lift, bringing a new delivery of furniture up from the basement: a leather sofa, a bookcase, a nest of tables, three televisions and a standard lamp. John Chalmers said that, in London or Padstow, the lift would be a one bedroom flat and "Twats would pay a thousand pound a month for it". Midway between the basement and the ground floor, Harvey forced the inner concertina gate open, causing the lift to shudder to a stop. Anyone calling it now would presume it was in use or the door had been left open by mistake again.

Harvey told Jess86 he'd ordered the certificate. He told her it hadn't been easy because he was so drunk and that he'd wrecked the house, unsuccessfully looking for a picture of his dad. He decided not to mention that he'd also searched online for anyone using the name Jess86. Harvey had looked on Facebook and Twitter, LinkedIn, Instagram, Pinterest, Tumblr and Reddit, searching for 'Jessica' and 'Jessie', and for 'Teachers called Jess'. But all he could find were the thumbs and comments underneath his unboxing videos. Jess86's entire online presence revolved around him. Harvey didn't tell Jess86 he'd eaten a whole box of antique chocolate liqueurs either, shortly before he'd managed to get himself stuck halfway-in and halfway-out of a cupboard.

"Don't you think it's strange that there are no photos of my dad?" Harvey typed into his phone, his fingers shaking with hangover tremors.

"Perhaps you didn't have a camera," Jess86 said.

Perhaps they didn't have a camera. It was a thought that had never crossed Harvey's mind. Everyone photographed everything nowadays. Holidays and weddings, birthday parties and mealtimes. People took selfies in the bathroom and at funerals, smiling in the foreground of terrorist atrocities. Harvey had his own video channel, where he filmed himself opening boxes. The idea that there were no photographs simply because none had been taken had been too preposterous for him to even consider.

"When are you next going to see your mum?" Jess86 said.

"I'm going after work."

"Where's work?"

"The Castle."

"A castle?"

"*The* Castle. It's a medieval retail store."

"Not the big pink castle the plane crashed into?"

"How do you know about that?"

"I must have seen it on the news."

"I didn't know it was on the news."

"Did you work there when the plane crashed?"

"No. I've heard stories about it though. A two-seater plane coming in to land at the nearby airfield lost power and sliced through the guy rope attached to the advertising blimp. It took the tip off one of the turrets. According to John who works in the warehouse, it was our nine eleven."

"Wow."

"John also claims the deflated blimp was found in a garden centre in Surrey and the person who discovered it had looked for a tag to see who they needed to contact to claim their prize."

"Is that true?"

"Nothing John says is true."

"What do you do at the castle?"

"I stack shelves," Harvey said, regretting not calling himself a produce and commodities facilitator. Or a stock replenishment officer, like it said on his name badge.

"What sort of things do you put on these shelves?"

"Lots of things. You name it."

"Perfume?"

"Yes."

"Hats?"

"Yes."

Harvey tried to guess which product Jess86 would say next and decided on shoes, but she'd obviously grown bored with that game.

"Do you live near the castle?" Jess86 said.

"Quite close. I live in Whynot St. Peter. I know right, eat your heart out New York." Harvey wondered if Jess86 lived in New York. If he kept casually naming places, maybe he'd eventually find out where she was.

"I'm sure it's a lovely village," Jess86 said.

"It's actually a small town now. It's got a leisure centre, a skate park and a Wikipedia page," Harvey decided to seize the opportunity, "Where do you live then?"

"Scotland. Edinburgh. We've got our own castle too."

"Does it have a teacups ride and a Food Court of King Arthur?"

"We've got Arthur's Seat."

"What's that?"

Jess86 didn't reply for quite a while. Harvey had been between floors for ages. Somebody would surely be looking for him soon. The furniture would be missed, even if he wasn't.

"Arthur's Seat is the main peak of the group of hills in Scotland which form the majority of Holyrood Park," Jess86 said.

"I'll have to look it up."

She didn't reply this time, either because she had nothing else to add, or because of a loss of interest or Wi-Fi signal or a flat phone battery or because the pips had gone at the school where she worked, or any number of other reasons.

Harvey took Megan's family tree out of the pocket of his jeans. He unfolded it and smoothed out the creases on top of the nest of tables – a tree on top of a nest, he thought. The world really is topsy-turvy. He pushed a piece of Blue Tack onto each corner of the back of the paper and stuck it to the screen of one of the three display televisions in the lift. He pulled a string on the standard lamp, sat back on the leather sofa and pretended he was on television. He was in the back of a posh car paid for by the BBC, on his way to Rome or Paris, to meet an expert in a library, where he'd find out about his mysterious ancestry. Harvey leaned forward and looked at the hyphen between his father's dates of birth and death, and he thought about the years the hyphen represented. Where had his dad been in that time, and what had he been up to?

Harvey couldn't stop thinking about why his father hadn't attempted to make contact in all that time. He hadn't written a letter or phoned. He could have emailed or sent a text message. The longer his father had had to communicate, the more means there would have been for him to do so. Sure, Harvey and his mother had moved to a new house, but only as far as the other side of Whynot St. Peter. It might be a town now, but it was still small. His dad could have stood outside the Fusilier and called out Harvey's name. He probably would have heard him.

Harvey imagined the expert on television, turning the dusty page of a huge book with a white-gloved hand, inviting Harvey to read aloud from it.

"Selfless acts of...What's that word? It's difficult to read the handwriting."

"Heroism. Your father's selfless acts of heroism."

The camera would zoom in on Harvey's face, and the show's director and the rest of the television crew would wait for him to cry, so that they could pack up and go to the pub.

11

When Harvey arrived at Wildways, his mother was asleep. He couldn't be sure at first, because she was wearing a large pair of men's sunglasses. Harvey stood and watched the almost imperceptible rise and fall of his mother's chest. Her breathing was shallow enough to make him think about reaching for the panic alarm by the side of her bed. He also considered leaving and coming back later. Harvey knew how precious deep sleep was to her.

Before his mother had moved into the care home, Harvey used to hear her in the bedroom opposite his, turning over and over in her bed, searching for the sweet spot, a quiet spot, trying to alter the acoustics inside her skull by hiding under the duvet or the pillow, moaning and groaning to herself, desperate for just one good night's sleep or for the morning to come so she could stop trying. For the last year or two before his mother moved out, her nocturnal moans and groans had been Harvey's tinnitus.

With one eye on his slumbering mother, Harvey picked up her handbag. He popped it open and looked inside. He didn't know what he was expecting to find – a third family tree, with another completely different and conflicting date perhaps? He performed a quick fingertip search of the bag's contents, moving the balled-up tissues to one side to reveal an old red lipstick and half a packet of Extra Strong Mints. There were two door keys in the bag, on a 'Visit Cornwall' key ring. And the television remote control was in his mother's handbag. Harvey had recently covered all but three of the buttons with masking tape. He'd written *ON/OFF*, *LOUDER/QUIETER* and *CHANGE CHANNEL* next to the three remaining buttons with a felt tip pen. He probably could have taped over the rest of the buttons as well, because the television was rarely switched off, and when it was on, it was permanently set to the same quiz and game show repeats channel. Harvey closed the handbag. The familiar click of the closing clasp brought back memories of pocket money and a craving for pick 'n' mix. It also woke his mother up.

"Is it today?" she said. Harvey guessed she meant Sunday.

"No, Mum, it's Monday. Whose sunglasses are those? I haven't seen them before."

"Do you want me to go in the shop?"

"No thanks, Mum. Listen. I've brought something."

12

Phantastic Retro Personal Cassette Player and Recorder

"This will be my first ever live unboxing in front of an audience. Of one. That's you, Mum."

Harvey took the small box out of the carrier bag and put it on top of the chest of drawers. He used the point of a biro to slice through the Sellotape and opened the box. He took out the warranty and the instructions booklet and put them to one side.

"I don't think we'll need these," he said, taking out a small pair of earphones. "Where are those headphones I bought you, Mum?"

Harvey looked around the room. He found the headphones on top of the wardrobe. He reached up to get them and hooked them around his neck like a stethoscope. He took the old fashioned looking personal cassette player out of its box and removed it from the plastic sleeve.

"This is the Phantastic Retro Personal Cassette Player and recorder. It's got a built-in microphone, earphones with mini jack and a detachable belt-clip. It's powered by two AA batteries, or via the three-volt DC power output – neither of which are included. But luckily…" Harvey took two batteries out of the carrier bag and held them up to show his mother.

Even though she was wearing huge, dark sunglasses, Harvey could tell his mother was even more entranced by his live performance than when she watched his unboxings on video. Harvey_King351 from the television *was in her room!*

Harvey opened the back of the cassette player and inserted the batteries. He closed the compartment and pressed the play button to check the cassette player hadn't been damaged earlier.

When he'd taken the box down from the top-shelf in

the Electronics and Audio department, Harvey hadn't properly fixed the brake on the high-wheeled stepladder. And as he reached out, the ladder had started to move away beneath him. The sound of Harvey and the cassette player crashing to the ground brought staff from all over the store, as though there'd been a coded announcement informing them of a shoplifter. Harvey was offered tea from a flask and someone brought him a chair. Tissues, cotton wool and plasters seemed to materialise from nowhere, but presumably from the shelves. He would probably have to account for their absence later.

When it was clear Harvey hadn't lost consciousness and nothing was broken, just a small L-shaped cut to his forehead and a superficial dent in the cassette player's box, everyone went back to work. Harvey thanked them for their concern, even though it had felt as much like bullying as when, last Christmas, his secret Santa gift had been a fridge alarm that said, 'Step away from the snacks fatty!'

Harvey took the old cassette tape out of his coat pocket and put it into the machine and pressed rewind, which seemed to take forever. If he was filming the unboxing, Harvey would have made a joke about that. He plugged the large headphones into the cassette player. He put them on and pressed play. The theme music surprised him. He'd forgotten *The Harvey King Show* had a theme tune, even if it was just taped from *Parkinson*. Harvey adjusted the volume, took the headphones off and walked over to his mother. He gently removed her sunglasses.

"Where did these come from, Mum?"

She didn't answer and Harvey put the sunglasses on the bed. He picked up the headphones and held them open above his mother's head. She moved away a bit.

"They hurt his sounds," she said, meaning *her* ears.

"They were actually supposed to help with that, Mum." Harvey moved the headphones closer to his mother. She grimaced a little but allowed him to put them on her head.

Harvey pressed play on the cassette player and watched his mother's expression, at first blank, then bemused, and finally breaking into a broad smile.

"That's you," she said loudly.

Harvey nodded. She looked delighted, astonished even, that Harvey could be inside the cassette player and stood in front of her at the same time.

"Malcolm and Wise?" she said.

Harvey nodded. "Malcolm and Wise."

"You are talking now," she said and pointed at Harvey.

He put the cassette player on the bed next to his mother and sat down to watch as she reacted to his old interview with Morecambe and Wise. After about ten minutes, from the disappointed look on his mother's face, he could tell the interview must have ended. He removed the tape from the machine, turned it over and rewound it to the start of side two. He checked the volume again and caught a bit of his young voice. For a second he thought the tape was playing too fast. It sounded like him, but him on helium.

Harvey was surprised to hear that he stuttered his name in the introduction. He'd always believed his stammer began when his dad died for the first time. He put the headphones back over his mother's head and watched her reactions again. He wondered whose voice she was listening to – his, his mother's own voice, or her husband's.

Harvey hadn't had enough time to listen to the tape before playing it to his mother and he tried to recall what he'd talked to his parents about in the interview. He probably would have asked them about their favourite television programmes and films and whether they had any hobbies. But once the tape was playing, just by watching his mother's face, Harvey started to remember certain things they'd spoken about over a quarter of a century ago. He may have had to allow his imagination to fill in the detail, but otherwise, he remembered it all.

His parents had told him where they'd first met, both of

them laughing and turning to look at each other, deciding who should answer. They told Harvey about a dinner and dance that was held in a club they were both members of. They'd eaten dinner and then they'd danced together, to three songs in a row. They later held their wedding reception in the same club. They were married in the middle of the summer, but it rained.

Harvey watched his mother. Did she know who she was listening to on the tape? She'd recognised Harvey's voice, and Eric's and Ernie's, but did she recognise Harvey's father's voice, or even her own? Would listening to the tape remind his mother of the day it was recorded, and would she too remember what was being talked about on the recording? There was every chance she thought she was listening to a radio show that her son was the star of, in the same way she thought his videos were television shows. She couldn't stop smiling though. And Harvey forgot that he was supposed to be angry with her. He'd forgotten about his unsent airmail letters to Sally.

From his mother's reaction to the tape, Harvey was sure his parents had been happy together. He couldn't remember a time when they weren't. It must have taken something truly awful to force them apart, so awful that his mother had wished her husband dead.

Harvey's mother's smile changed to a frown and he knew the interview had ended. He gently removed the headphones and opened the cassette player. The tape had been chewed-up and was stuck inside the machine.

13

The next day Harvey unboxed a record player. He fashioned a handle using parcel tape and carried the box to the care home like a small suitcase. On the way, he stopped to post a comment to Jess86 about *The Harvey King Show* and how it seemed to have triggered a memory for his mother.

"Maybe I should record a new episode of *The Harvey King Show*, with my mum as the guest," Harvey told Jess86. "I could be a bit tougher with her this time. More Frost/Nixon and less Parkinson/Rod Hull and Emu."

He told Jess86 he hadn't listened to the tape himself yet, and she asked him if he was mad. He explained how the tape had got stuck inside the cassette player and he'd tried to take the back of the cassette player off, but there were no screws. It was glued together and Harvey didn't want to force it open and risk further damaging the tape. In a way, he was pleased the tape had got stuck. Because even though hearing his father's voice might help him remember what he looked like, he worried it might spoil the memory of watching his mother listening to the tape.

"That cassette is like an aide memoire," Jess86 said, and before Harvey had time to Google what that meant, she posted another comment, "Héy! How do I put an accént over the é in memoire? I can't séém to typé an accént over the é in memoire."

Harvey laughed. He stopped outside the Fusilier and put the record player down. He needed to use both hands.

"I havé no idea Jéss86. You'ré thé téachér."

"I teach five-year olds. It's all sound buttons and Bee-Bots at the moment."

"What are Bee-Bots?"

"They're programmable robots. We use them with the children at work."

"Is it wrong that I'm excited by the idea of programmable robots? You should unbox one. Do they come in a box?"

"Film myself?!? No way Harvay. I told you, I am no good with technology. I wouldn't know where to start."

"It's easy. Film it on your phone. Or use the camera on your computer."

Harvey didn't tell her the camera on *his* computer was covered in electrical tape.

"There's a camera on my computer??!!" Jess86 said.

Harvey laughed. "Film something. It's easy."

"But I can't stand the sound of my own voice," Jess86 said.

"You don't have to speak."

It was hard to believe Jess86 didn't know there was a camera on her computer. She must have been joking, unless there was something about herself that she didn't want to share. Harvey found himself wishing a squint onto Jess86, a twitch or a lazy eye, some imperfection that would make her more like him.

"Give my love to your mum," Jess86 said. "And don't be too hard on her. I think she was just trying to protect you."

"Protect me from what?"

There was no reply. The conversation ended there, unfinished, as usual, and, as far as Harvey was concerned, most definitely to be continued. He scrolled through their recent exchange of comments. Once again, he'd forgotten which video the comments were under or that they were even on a video sharing website.

He walked through the village, thinking about what Jess86 had said about not liking the sound of her voice. He copied the comment into a text-to-speech app, turned up the volume on his phone and switched between the automated voice options, but the voices were all American, and Harvey didn't think Jess86 was American. She lived in Scotland. Not that that necessarily meant she was Scottish.

When Harvey went through the Wildways gates, he bashed his shoulder because he didn't wait long enough for them to open. Jess86 had boosted his ego enough to make him feel two stone thinner. He entered the door code and signed the visitors book, thinking about the phrase 'aide-mémoire'. Maybe Jess86 was French. Jess quatre-vingt six. Harvey copied her comment about not liking her voice into Google Translate. He played the resulting phrase in his phone's text-to-speech app.

"Je ne peux pas supporter d'entendre ma voix."

Asha came out of the dining lounge with an armful of towels.

"Pard*on*?" she said, in a mock French accent.

Harvey awkwardly stuffed his phone into his pocket and picked up the record player.

"It's not Sunday already, is it?" Asha said, not stopping. "Good news, by the way. Your mum had lunch in the dining lounge today."

Harvey looked confused.

"She isn't a Dalek after all," Asha said. "For now, at least."

Asha walked through a door on the other side of one of the communal lounges. All the communal rooms at Wildways had two doors, as though the care home had originally been built to stage a West End farce. Harvey walked along the corridor, 'Brimful of Asha' was playing inside his head, but he was thinking about Jess86. He took the lift up to the first floor, walked along the corridor, took his shoes off and knocked on his mother's door.

14

Auraltastics 3-Speed Stereo Turntable with Built-in Speakers

"This is the Auraltastics 3-Speed Stereo Turntable with Built-in Speakers. Not the best turntable on the market. But if you just want to play some old records and aren't too worried about having the greatest sound quality, it's more than sufficient."

The record player was made from thin plastic. It was coloured to resemble teak or mahogany, but it was very lightweight. Most of the weight had been in the box and the packaging. Harvey felt like a fool for carrying it all the way from work without unboxing it first. He plugged the record player in, watched with interest by his mother.

He took the Buddy Holly record out of its sleeve and placed it on the turntable. He switched it on. The warp in the vinyl was more pronounced when it was turning. Harvey watched the record rise and fall. The rainbow colours on the label were almost hypnotic. His mother stared at Harvey, observing his every move, listening to his sales patter.

After a few horrible-sounding misses, Harvey placed the needle at the start of the second song. Formerly 'K7' on the Fusilier jukebox, and a Kit Kat Chunky in the foyer of The Castle. He stopped his commentary and let the music do the talking. The rolling drums, the guitars, and then Buddy Holly's voice like hiccups. It was as though Harvey's dad was in the room. What was going through his mother's mind right now? It was a question Harvey had asked himself countless times before. But what about right now? How powerful was music? Harvey's mother didn't sing along or jump up from her bed and start jiving around the room, but she didn't throw her handbag at the record player either.

"He took it," his mother said.

"What's that, Mum?"

"He took it."

"Who, Mum? Who took what? Do you mean Dad? Did Dad take it? What did he take, Mum?"

She seemed to be searching for the words. Harvey didn't say anything. He waited while she collected her thoughts. She was miming something, turning her finger in circles.

"You know," she said. "The thing. Our house one."

Harvey thought she was miming stirring something. A saucepan? Soup? A roundabout? She pointed at the record.

"Do you mean the record player, Mum?" Harvey said. "Did Dad take our record player?"

His mother nodded.

'Peggy Sue' finished and the next song, 'Words of Love', started. Harvey let it play. He posted a comment to Jess86.

"There were no photos because we didn't have a camera and there was no music in our house because *HE TOOK THE RECORD PLAYER!*"

"What are you doing?" Harvey's mother said.

Harvey looked up from his phone.

"Just talking to a friend."

"A girlfriend?"

"Mum. Please. I'm nearly forty."

"Are you married?"

"Am I *married*?" Harvey laughed. "I think I would have told you."

"Can I come to the wedding?"

"What wedding? There isn't…I'm not getting married, Mum. If I do though, you'll definitely be invited. You'd have to come downstairs though. I'm not getting married in the occupational therapy room while everyone gets their toenails cut."

How Harvey would have loved to be able to tell his mother that, yes, Jess86 was indeed his girlfriend. He'd love to turn up on a Sunday with a bag of Chinese food and a hat catalogue. Even if he was deluded enough to think it was a genuine possibility though, Harvey was sure if he brought his virtual relationship with Jess86 into the real world, it would never survive.

Four years ago Harvey had joined an online slimming group. He was a lurker at first, reading everyone else's exercise and dieting tips but not contributing any of his own. Eventually though, he felt brave enough to join in with the weekly weight loss updates. The mildly competitive nature of the updates helped Harvey lose enough weight for a woman on the shuttle bus to comment how well he was looking. If he stuck with it, Harvey thought he might lose enough weight for people to ask him if he was ill.

One of the slimming group's more prolific posters, Charlotte, became quite chatty with Harvey. When she found out she lived less than half an hour's drive from him, she suggested they meet.

Charlotte picked Harvey up after work and they drove to a restaurant where they had a nice meal – kormas and jalfrezis, bhajis and Peshwari naans – Charlotte adding up the calories of everything on the menu, using an app on her phone. After the meal she drove Harvey home. She said she'd really enjoyed herself and looked forward to seeing him again.

A day or two later, on the thirteenth page of a thread about quinoa, Harvey found Charlotte discussing a date she'd been on with 'a creepy guy with a really irritating stutter.' Egged on by others on the forum, Charlotte said she didn't like to bad mouth anyone, but she just didn't like fat guys. Harvey left the slimming group. Within a month he'd put back all the weight he'd lost. The whole whirlwind romance, from his first posted comment when he'd lied about his true weight, to Charlotte fat shaming him, was no doubt still online. Like Megan's family tree, it would remain on the slimming website or in its cache or archived by the Wayback machine until the end of time.

Harvey knew he could never risk bringing his relationship with Jess86 into the real world. Like the salvaged shipwreck of his father's face, away from keyboard, the relationship would disintegrate.

Harvey tidied his mother's room, stacking the teacups and yoghurt pots, moving around the room, accompanied by Buddy Holly's music, as he picked things up and put them back where they belonged, wondering where some of them had come from. There were always things in his mother's room that he didn't recognise. Men's cataract sunglasses, small mantelpiece ornaments, maybe a single glove or a shoe, like there was a fox loose in the care home. There was a vase of flowers on the hostess trolley beside her bed.

"Who gave you the flowers, Mum?"

"The girl."

"That was nice of her. Much better than those horrible magazines she gives you."

"They smell," his mother said.

"Nice, I hope," Harvey said, sniffing the yellow flowers.

'Oh Boy' kept skipping, so Harvey lifted the needle. He turned the record over and played 'Peggy Sue Got Married'. He hoped what he was doing wasn't cruel. If he did manage to rebuild his mother's memory and bring her husband back to life, Harvey knew he would immediately have to kill him again.

When 'Bo Diddley' played, his mother started humming and tapping her fingers on her thigh. 'Brown Eyed Handsome Man' was a smash hit, too. If only Harvey could remember what colour his father's eyes were, let alone whether or not he was handsome. Harvey looked in the bathroom mirror, uncertain what colour his own eyes were. Green. The last song on the record, 'Wishing', played. When it ended, his mother applauded. Harvey almost punched the air.

15

Harvey left his mother in high spirits. Both him and her. He was looking forward to his next visit. Thinking about which aide-mémoire he could unbox. If he saw Asha, he was going to tell her what he was doing. He would tell her about the family tree and his father's two deaths, and how he was using objects to repair his mother's memory. Maybe Wildways would introduce a similar scheme for the other residents. They could call it the Harvey Method.

The office door was open, and the care home manager, Glenda, was sitting behind the desk. Asha was sitting opposite her. Glenda asked Harvey if he had a minute for a quick chat.

"Could we have the room please, Asha?" Glenda said, as though she was in an American drama about politics or big business. Asha stood. She half-smiled at Harvey and walked off in the direction of the dining lounge.

"Come in," Glenda said. "Close the door so we can have a bit of privacy. Take a seat."

Harvey sat down. Glenda sorted through some forms on her desk. Harvey looked at her eyebrows. They appeared to be drawn on. They made him feel nauseous for some reason, like when he read a book in a moving car. He looked around the office, reading the motivational witticisms printed on fluorescent post-it notes and stuck to the wall, and the sombre looking thank-you cards pinned to a notice board behind Glenda. Harvey presumed the cards were from the loved ones of deceased Wildways residents.

There was a wall planner next to the notice board. Harvey wondered what the red and blue spots represented. On the square for next Wednesday, the word *FUNERAL* was written in green pen. Harvey looked back at Glenda. Her eyebrows seemed to have moved higher up her forehead, as though she'd quickly erased and redrawn them when he wasn't looking. The back of Harvey's neck was burning.

He couldn't help feeling he'd done something wrong. He thought he was in trouble, maybe for bringing Chinese food in or for playing Buddy Holly records too loud.

Glenda finished sorting through the forms on her desk. The desk was from The Castle. Particleboard and oak veneer. It was very heavy. The goods lift had noticeably dropped when Harvey and John Chalmers had taken the same model of desk up to the shop floor a few months ago. Perhaps it was this actual desk. Glenda looked up at Harvey, her eyebrows were back in the position they were in when he'd first entered the office. Her whole face said, 'professionally empathetic'.

"I won't keep you long," she said. "I know you usually come on Sundays when I'm not here. I wanted to catch you while I had the opportunity. Basically, I need to ask a couple of questions about your mum."

"Is it the sunglasses?" Harvey said. "I don't know who they belong to."

"Sunglasses?" Glenda said, her eyebrows going full-on quizzical, before relaxing and almost disappearing over the top of her head. "No. I wanted to speak to you about whether or not you would want Margaret to be resuscitated or not?"

"Is she ill?" Harvey said. He knew there were a lot of things wrong with his mother, but he'd never considered any of them life-threatening. Whatever was wrong with her had always seemed more abstract.

"Oh, no," Glenda said, with a half-smile. "There's absolutely no cause for alarm. It's more of a precaution, really. And it's always better to get these difficult, and often highly emotional, decisions out of the way in advance, rather than in an emergency. Don't you think?"

Harvey looked at the pen Glenda was holding. It was one of those pens with four different ink colours. They sold them at The Castle. Glenda had the pen set to green. Harvey thought of the word *FUNERAL* on the wall planner.

"If the time comes when your mum's body gets weaker and her heart stops," Glenda continued, "would you want the paramedics, or A and E, to try to restart it? A lot of people find everything involved in trying to artificially restart a heart once it's stopped can be an undignified, and even quite a violent, experience."

Harvey tried to get the picture out of his head of paramedics hammering on his mother's chest and singing 'Nellie the Elephant'. He didn't want that as an ear worm.

"There is no hurry, of course," Glenda said. "If you'd prefer to go away and think about it, that is perfectly fine."

"What do you think is best?" Harvey said.

Glenda put the pen down and steepled her fingers together. Harvey was terrified she was about to start praying.

"Resuscitation might be painful and traumatic," Glenda said. "And it may actually make your mum's condition worse. If I'm honest, although I have to tell you that it might prolong her life, it would almost certainly not improve the quality of it. As I say, it is best to have this conversation now. But it really doesn't mean we've given up on Margaret. Please don't think that."

Harvey looked around the office and down at his hands, looking for answers in the paper cuts. The way Glenda had said 'restart her heart', it made it sound like she could turn his mother off and on again.

"How do you feel about it all?" Glenda said.

"If you think it's best," Harvey said.

"Do not resuscitate?" Glenda said, eyebrows raised, as though she was asking him if he wanted chocolate powder on his cappuccino.

Harvey nodded. Glenda wrote something on the form. Black pen.

"And the other thing is," Glenda said, "it's probably best to kill two birds with one...Sorry. Appalling choice of words. But if Margaret can no longer feed herself, would you want her to be tube fed?"

"Tube fed?"

"Yes. It sounds so horrible, doesn't it? We do have to ask though, I'm afraid. There is every likelihood that at some point your mum will forget how to swallow, and a decision would need to be made whether or not to feed her by tube."

"What do you think is best?" Harvey said again, passing the buck to Glenda. His stomach grumbled. He put a hand on his belly to muffle the sound, trying to divert the gas along his alimentary canal to somewhere more secluded and soundproof.

"Well, there can be complications," Glenda said. "She might try to pull the tube out for example, and that can lead to infections. I certainly wouldn't want to go through it myself. It may never be an issue, of course."

Harvey's stomach grumbled again. It groaned and bubbled like a meth lab. Like a wood pigeon on the top of a chimney. It sounded so loud in the quiet office. He hoped to God it didn't lead to a fart. Glenda's eyebrows had moved again. She looked at him and smiled her best sympathetic, empathetic, understanding, pragmatic and professional, all-purpose smile. Harvey couldn't help thinking – *What about Chinese Sundays?*

He told Glenda that he wouldn't want his mother to go through any unnecessary pain or suffering. Glenda smiled and wrote something on the form. She clicked the pen from black to red, to signal the meeting was over.

Harvey thanked her, even though it felt like the two of them had just conspired to kill his mother. He picked up the record player and left the office. He walked along the corridor in a bit of a daze. Asha was sitting at a table in the empty dining room. She was looking at her phone.

"Everything okay?" she said.

"Yes, thank you." He'd just left a planning meeting for his mother's demise, but otherwise everything was just dandy. "Can I ask something?"

"Yes, of course," Asha said. She put her phone down to give him her full attention.

"Do you think it's possible to remember some things from the past but forget other things, even if they happened at the same time?"

"Do you mean, is it possible for your mum to do that?"

Harvey nodded. "Could she pick and choose what she remembers, and what she forgets?"

"Like a sort of selective memory?"

Harvey nodded.

"I'm not an expert," Asha said.

"Oh, I'm sorry."

"No, no, that's okay. You should really talk to Glenda though. She knows a lot more than I do. I don't think there are any hard and fast rules, though," Asha said. "In my very limited experience, short-term memory loss is quite normal for people like your mum. It tends to be long-term memory that remains."

"Does it make a difference if the memories are good or bad? Is it easier to remember good things than it is to remember bad things?"

"Hmmm. You should definitely talk to Glenda," Asha said. "I'll only say the wrong thing."

Harvey said he would ask Glenda next time he visited. Although right now he'd be happy if he never spoke to Glenda ever again.

"See you on Sunday?" she said.

Harvey nodded and Asha went back to her phone. From the look on her face, Harvey thought she might be reading a YouTube comment from somebody she liked.

He signed out of the visitors book and held the door open for a man pushing an elderly woman in a wheelchair. The bottom half of the woman's leg was missing and the top half heavily bandaged. Harvey wished his mother had something that could be bandaged. An illness that was visible or removable, like a gammy leg or cataracts. The man said thank you, for holding the door open. Harvey couldn't help feeling a little envious of him.

16

For the whole of October, The Castle would be haunted. Every day Harvey would refill baskets with more rubber bats and plastic spiders, fangs, fake blood and glow-in-the-dark skulls. There was a promotion on in the DVD department for *Halloweens* one to ten and also for the twelve films in the *Friday the 13th* franchise. Royalty free cover versions of *Monster Mash, Ghostbusters* and *Thriller* would play all day on a loop over the public-address system. At weekends, children could have their faces painted like Frankenstein and carve their own Jack-ò-lantern out of a pumpkin.

Harvey, meanwhile, was haunted by his own ghosts. Even though he could hardly remember what his father looked like, he saw him everywhere. He cropped up in crowd scenes in films and in the studio audiences of television shows. Harvey thought he saw his father on a news report about the royal family and standing behind the goal on *Match of the Day*. He even thought that he saw him, very late one night, animated and killing an alien in a video game.

Harvey's memories, such as they were, had become unreliable and confused. He was remembering things that had happened when he was eight or nine as though they'd happened yesterday, and yet, more recent events felt so vague, that if they'd happened at all, it was as though they'd happened to someone else.

He had dreams about his father. One dream felt more real than some of his memories. He dreamed his dad was climbing into a green car. The boot was too full to shut properly, and so he'd tied a length of rope to the handle of the boot and wrapped the other end around the heavily-laden roof rack. The backseat of the car was piled so high with his dad's belongings that he couldn't see through the rear window. He wouldn't have seen Harvey and his mother on the doorstep in tears. It was only a dream, but the sense of his father leaving in a hurry felt real.

And then Harvey remembered something that had happened about three years ago. He'd seen a man in the village who he'd mistaken for his father. Harvey had nothing else to do and he'd started following him. At the end of the road, the man turned the corner. Less than ten seconds later, Harvey turned the same corner and there was no sign of the man. The road was a longish one, and straight, with no buildings on either side. The only logical conclusion was that as soon as the man had turned the corner, he must have started running and then escaped through the park.

Harvey had thought nothing more of it at the time. But what if it had actually been his father? So desperate not to face his son that he literally ran away? What if his dad was on his way to their new house, but when he'd seen Harvey, he'd panicked? Once Harvey had entertained that idea, he thought about what could have spooked his father enough to make him run away. It could have been guilt, of course, or embarrassment for not coming sooner. But what if it was the sight of his little boy, grown up into such a big man? What if Harvey had repulsed his father? He couldn't help thinking that, if the tables were turned, he would have reacted in exactly the same way.

Harvey tried picturing the back of the escaping man's head, before he'd disappeared around the corner. He went for a lunchtime haircut at The Castle's hair salon, and when the hairdresser held a mirror up behind his head, Harvey looked for a family likeness. To be honest, he wouldn't have been able to recognise the back of his own head. If the hairdresser had shown him a picture of a coconut, Harvey would have been none the wiser. After the haircut, he walked through the Home Furnishings department, hoping to catch his reflection in one of the mirrors and mistake himself for his father.

He thought about the way the man was walking before he'd disappeared. Whether his hands were in his pockets or held awkwardly down at his sides. Was he carrying anything? Did he have a present for Harvey or flowers for Harvey's mum? And what did the man's body language say? Was his walk a walk of confidence or shame? Was he stumbling over his own feet in a blind panic to get away? Was it clear from the way the man was walking that he'd already made the decision to run? Harvey tried mimicking the man's stride and became so aware of putting one foot in front of the other that he had to sit down in a display kitchen until walking was a natural, unthinking act again.

On Sunday Harvey went to see his mother. They ate Chinese food and Harvey did his best to not imagine his mother having hers fed to her via a tube. They watched *Toy Story 3* and an old unboxing of a video game steering wheel. Harvey's dad had left very few of his belongings behind and Harvey had run out of aide memoirés.

Every day Jess86 asked at least twice whether the death certificate had arrived. Harvey sometimes felt like it was her father who'd died, and he was the one who was helping her out. Jess86's interest in Harvey was still so alien to him that he found it hard to accept it for what it was. Every time she posted a new comment, he expected it to be the one that asked him for his bank details or led him to a virus or a Rick Astley video.

The death certificate arrived on Harvey's birthday, like a novelty card from beyond the grave. He picked the manila envelope up from the doormat as he was leaving for work and put it in the pocket of his parka without opening it. The shuttle bus would be leaving the leisure centre an hour earlier than usual, to get everyone to work in time for the breakfast huddle, and Harvey was already late.

On the first Monday of every month the entire Castle workforce would assemble on the shop floor for the breakfast huddle. At any other time, it seemed like maybe fifty or sixty people worked there, and Harvey was always surprised to see three hundred people, all gathered together in their uniforms, like an army preparing to invade Argos.

This month's motivational huddle speaker was assistant manager Alison. Twenty years ago, as Harvey counted down his final days at St. Peter and Paul Community College, a careers adviser came to the school. She asked everyone in Harvey's class what they were going to do when they left school. They all said they were going to be doctors and lawyers, pop stars and astronauts, fire fighters, formula one racing drivers and actors. Craigthony were both going to be footballers. Alison declared her intentions to become the first female Pope. When it was Harvey's turn, he'd shrugged. "I'll stack shelves or something."

Everyone laughed, but within a week of leaving school Harvey's ambitions were already fully realised, as he stacked his first shelf at the small grocery shop at the end of his road. From there, Harvey worked his way up the canned food chain, from mini-market to supermarket and, eventually, out of town hypermarket. In his twenties, Harvey was like a shelf-stacker mercenary, a price gun for hire, or 'hand operated labeller' as he had to refer to it in today's PC world – which was another shop he'd briefly stacked the shelves of.

Alison stepped onto the breakfast huddle podium to address the crowd of Castle employees. In her head she was probably stepping through the window of her papal apartment overlooking St. Peter's Square, rather than onto one of those small plastic steps used by small children to help them reach the toilet.

"Good morning, guys," Alison said. "Are we all here?"

"I'm not," John Chalmers said.

"Thank you, John. Helpful as ever."

Pope Alison told everyone to give themselves a round of applause for all their hard work in September. She read out a list of new products and the old stock that needed a big push to make room for those new products. There were the usual messages of thanks from the shareholders, before Alison announced two retirements and a pregnancy in the Garden department. "Not actually *in* the Garden department," she joked, to muted laughter. "And we have two birthdays." Alison consulted the back of her hand. "Markus Catrosky on the tills and Harvey King from stock replenishment."

"I'm not giving him the bumps!"

"Thank you again, John," Alison said. "Happy birthday, Markus and Harvey."

Even though Alison had just addressed Harvey twice by name, and despite it being written on her hand, and on the badge on Harvey's fleece, Alison didn't recognise him from school, just as she hadn't recognised him on any of his previous birthdays, or at any other time in the seven years they'd both worked at The Castle.

Harvey zoned out while Alison talked about targets and goals. He was thinking about the manila envelope in his pocket. He was concerned that opening it might lead to an anticlimax. He also worried it would mean the end of his correspondence with Jess86. Above all, Harvey wasn't ready for that to end.

"For exceptional September sales," Alison said, "this month's Queen – *spoiler alert* – or King is...And I hope I'm pronouncing this right, Agnieszka from Perfume! Come on up, Agneiszka."

A heavily made-up young woman shuffled forward, and Alison stepped down from the podium to make way for her. Alison placed a gold plastic crown on Agnieszka's head and gave her a matching gold plastic badge. There was a round of applause, and cups of coffee and doughnuts were distributed. Ten minutes later, the paper cups and the empty cake boxes were cleared away, the toilet step was removed, and three hundred Castle employees dispersed, leaving only a sticky sugar-covered floor and a shy Polish girl in a cheap crown as the only evidence they had ever been there.

At lunchtime, Harvey went to three different outdoor concession stands and bought a baked potato, a side order of curly fries, a Müller corner, two cream doughnuts and a can of Diet Coke. He carried them to a bench table on the stretch of grass above the miniature railway station.

The train below was building up a loud head of steam. Harvey couldn't see a single passenger in any of the carriages, and there was no one waiting on the platform. Each carriage had been decorated for Halloween with fake cobwebs and plastic spiders. When the train passed through a tunnel, a witch would cackle and a glow-in-the-dark skeleton would appear to come back to life as the passing locomotive blew it about.

Sending the train on the mile and a half journey empty might have seemed like a waste of steam and effort, but it always left on time, every half an hour in the summer and once an hour in the winter. Seven days a week, 364 days a year, empty or full, come rain, hail or shine, the Castle steam train always left on time. As though Mussolini was in charge of the timetable.

Harvey had been on the same train with his father. They'd sat in the first of seven open-sided wooden carriages, so close to the engine that Harvey could have reached out and pulled a lever and caused a miniature train crash. He'd watched the driver, operating the controls, tooting the loud whistle and leaning out of the side of the train, because he was allowed to. Harvey had been particularly fascinated by the train driver's thick Elvis sideburns. They looked so fake that they must have been real.

It was Christmas when Harvey rode the train. The same Christmas his mother was in hospital for her operation. In the second of the railway's three tunnels the train had stopped. The tunnel was covered in tinsel and lit with fairy lights. 'Jingle Bells' played through a crackly speaker hanging from the tunnel roof. A member of staff dressed as an elf, directed the passengers along the fake-snow-covered platform to Santa's grotto. The children met Santa and were each given a present. Harvey still had the Jabba the Hutt playset that Santa had given to him in the tunnel that day. He remembered such a lot of detail about the train ride. But once again, he couldn't actually picture his father sitting next to him on the train. He started to think that all his memories of his father weren't his memories at all. They were stories that his mother had told him *about* his father. And how could Harvey ever trust anything she had to say?

The steam train left the station and Harvey took the manila envelope out of his coat pocket. He couldn't put it off any longer. He held the envelope up to the light, trying to see though the address window on the front. His hands were sweaty and shaking as he opened the envelope, his tongue darting in and out of his mouth as he picked away at the glue. He removed a delivery note and put it on the table.

Now the certificate had arrived, Harvey realised how much he'd come to accept his father's original cause of death. He wasn't sure he was prepared for something different. He cleared his throat, as though he was about to announce Best Actress in a Supporting Role at the Oscars, and he unfolded the death certificate.

He read the names of the death registration district, the sub-district and the administrative area at the top of the certificate. All of them were close to where Harvey lived and worked. That didn't make sense. He decided to ignore it for the moment. An administrative error. The date on the certificate he already knew of course, but it was good to have it confirmed on such an official looking document. As much as Harvey worshipped the internet, there was nothing like a hard copy.

The 'place of death' on the certificate was a hospital

so close by that, if it wasn't for the trees, Harvey would have been able to stand on the bench seat and see it. His father's occupation was listed as 'Retired'. Retired from what? The cause of death was 'Small cell carcinoma of the bronchus'. Harvey thought that was lung cancer. So, it *was* the smoking. His father's 'usual address' on the death certificate was in Whynot St. Paul, which was so near to where Harvey lived that it made him feel physically sick. But not as much as the 'Name and surname of informant' – 'Andrew King. Qualification: Son.'

17

Hammersmyth Zoom42 12 x 25 Rubber Armoured Binoculars

Harvey took the lift up to the top floor of The Castle. He went past the offices and a row of old filing cabinets next to some boxes of vending machine coffee powder. Someone had arranged some pink toilet rolls in the shape of The Castle. Harvey went through a door next to the toilets and climbed four steel steps to the roof.

He sat on an upturned plastic crate on the roof, sheltering from the wind behind one of the turrets. He used the small box he was carrying to sweep the cigarette butts and spent matches away from the ground in front of him, and then, with a Stanley knife he'd borrowed from the warehouse, Harvey cut the seal on the box.

He took the binoculars out and practised focusing the lenses on the car park below. He looked at the steam train, the maze, the fun fair, the boating lake and the adventure golf, just beyond the car park. He adjusted the zoom some more and took in the surrounding countryside and landmarks, the electricity pylons, the wind turbines in a row on the horizon like children's windmills, and the hospital incinerator chimney.

Harvey hadn't noticed before, how much the brown section at the top of the white chimney made it look like a giant filter-tipped cigarette. He wondered how much of his dad had gone up in smoke at the hospital, or at the crematorium just beyond. He could see the crematorium and the cemetery through the binoculars. He was having trouble believing his father might have ended up there. The idea that Harvey might have a brother named Andrew, who visited the grave, leaving fresh flowers and bagging any dog mess, made him want to jump off the roof.

He hooked the binoculars around his neck and took

the death certificate out of the manila envelope. The certificate was like a coded map of the surrounding view. The hospital where his father had died. The cemetery or the crematorium where he might have been burned or buried, and the street where he'd last lived. His father's 'usual address'. Whynot St. Paul was just to the north of Whynot St. Peter. Harvey knew that, but he wasn't sure which direction north actually was. *Never eat Shredded Wheat,* he said to himself. Which direction was Never? He pointed the binoculars at what he'd always thought was the group of white cluster homes and link houses where he lived. He adjusted the lenses again and looked beyond, half expecting to see Andrew King staring back at him through his own pair of binoculars in Whynot St. Paul.

Harvey trained the binoculars on the farms and the fields between the Whynots. He could see sheep and grazing cattle. He watched a plane land on the small airfield. The grass surrounding the runway looked too perfect. Too green. Like a Subbuteo pitch. Harvey watched another plane taxi and take off, following its flight path through the binoculars until he lost sight of it and was staring at the pink turret just a few inches away from him.

Last night, Harvey searched online for the plane that had crashed into The Castle. He looked for news articles or videos, Google images or any kind of mention. Soon, his browser was full of other recommended crashes, near misses, wobbly take-offs and spectacular emergency landings that he might also enjoy. Video suggestions stacked up in his sidebar like an airport runway during bad weather. He scrolled down the thumbnail list of aircraft exploding in mid-air, huge passenger jets flying dangerously low over tourist beaches, and a microlight landing on the White House lawn.

There were movie recommendations in his sidebar as well as the videos – *Battle of Britain, Tora! Tora! Tora!, Snakes on a Plane*. And songs. 'I Believe I Can Fly', and 'Leaving on a Jet Plane', which was a song by Peter, Paul and Mary. Harvey had never heard of them before. He wondered if they were a local band and there used to be a third village called Whynot St. Mary.

After a long search, Harvey eventually found a short report on the Castle air crash. It hadn't really been a crash at all, and not even that near of a miss. The plane hadn't hit the guy rope holding the blimp in place, and the balloon hadn't then flown away, let alone landed in a garden centre in Surrey. The two-seater light aircraft had actually missed the turret by a good ten feet or more. The pilot hadn't needed to heroically steer the plane away from the families at the fun fair or on the boating lake, as John Chalmers had always claimed. No wonder it had taken Harvey so long to find anything about it online. He was surprised it had even made the local news, let alone the national news that Jess86 had seen in Scotland.

Harvey laid the death certificate out in front of him. He placed the binoculars on the corner, to stop it from blowing away. He took out his phone and located the most recent comment from Jess86.

Underneath it he typed, "I've got the death certificate. He died this year from small cell carcinoma of the bronchus. Which is lung cancer. I looked it up and it's also called oat cell carcinoma. It's usually caused by smoking and it's rare for somebody who had never smoked to develop it, and I think my dad smoked a lot. Apparently one in three people with the condition live for at least a year after being diagnosed, while fewer than one in ten live for at least five years. I don't know which one of those he was. There's something called a usual address on the death certificate. Although I can't think of anything usual about it, because it's really, really, REALLY close to where I live. I looked the address up on Google Maps. I counted the numbers on the front doors and I think I know which house it is. It looks very small. I don't know if he was still alive when the picture was taken. Don't you think it's weird that I could be looking at his house on a computer, and he might still have been alive inside when the picture was taken? There's a newsagent next door to the house and the sign above it says they sell confectionery, greetings cards and tobacco. Tobacco. That probably didn't help with his small cell carcinoma of the bronchus. And it's stupid but I just can't stop thinking, if he lived so close to a shop that sells greetings cards, why didn't he ever send one to his son? Oh. And finally. Guess what? I've got a brother. His name is Andrew."

Harvey pressed send and put his phone down on the death certificate. He picked up the binoculars and looked for his mother's care home. How was he possibly going to explain this latest cluster of bombshells to her? He wished he could make paper planes out of the death certificate and the family tree and launch them from the roof of The Castle, so the wind would carry them to the care home, and he could leave his mother to work it out for herself.

He imagined the two paper planes, sailing in formation over the car park and then along Castle Road, strafing the animal sculptures and statues in the trees below, before turning onto the B-road and then the A-road, dipping under the bridge with the graffiti on that said: *GRAM FJG 4 EVER*. Harvey had passed under the bridge thousands of times without any idea of the graffiti's meaning.

The paper planes would continue their flight, passing over Harvey's old house, and then his new one. It would fly on through the village, passing the leisure centre, the Bay of Bengal and the Fusilier, scattering the two old men smoking outside and scaring the ducks in the park. The planes would then make their final descent, flying through his mother's open window, landing on her bed like origami carrier pigeons.

His phone pinged. He exchanged it for the binoculars on top of the death certificate and read Jess86's new comment.

"What are we going to do next?"

Jess86's apparent lack of interest in any of the shocking detail on the death certificate, choosing to simply move on to the next step, would have annoyed Harvey, if he wasn't so flattered that she considered them a 'we'.

"I don't know," Harvey said. "It's never like this on television."

"What would they do on television?"

"I don't know. What do you think they'd do?"

"I think they'd go to the address on the death certificate."

"Then what?"

"Knock on the door and say, hello Andrew, I'm your brother."

"But I don't even know if he is my brother or if he even lives there."

"Knock on the door then and find out."

"I don't want to rush into it. What if I don't like what I find?"

"Imagine never knowing though. Wouldn't that be worse?"

"I'm beginning to wonder if not knowing would be *better*."

"Really? Seriously? I would *have* to know. It would drive me insane otherwise. I'd be wondering what Andrew was like. What he looked like. Whether there was a family resemblance and so on."

"I did tell you I can't remember what my dad looked like didn't I?"

"Even more reason to go to Andrew's house."

Harvey watched two cars almost drive into each other in the car park below. A herring gull landed on the turret opposite. It had a sausage roll in its beak. Life carried on as normal.

"I suppose I should have guessed where my dad was living," Harvey said. "It's a local joke I've heard a million times. About how people from Whynot St Peter don't die, they just move to Whynot St Paul. Do you know I can practically see his house from here?"

"Where's here?"

"On the roof at work."

"Be careful. Don't fall off. Remember bad things come in threes."

Harvey wasn't sure what the other two bad things were. There was so much going on and all of it seemed bad. He couldn't remember everything he'd told Jess86. Had he told her about falling off the ladder at work? Was that one of the bad things? And what was the first of the three things? His dad dying? Or was that both of the two other bad things?

"I can see the hospital where he died as well," Harvey said, looking at a trickle of smoke at the top of the incinerator chimney.

"Well then. You should go there first. Go to the hospital. That's what they'd do on television. And then you should go to his house. I'm actually at a hospital myself at the moment."

Don't die, Harvey almost typed. Don't die Jess86. He thought about small cell carcinoma of the bronchus, small vessel disease, and mini strokes, none of them really felt small or mini. He was too scared to ask Jess86 why she was in hospital.

"I'm here with one of the pupils," she said, and Harvey hated himself for feeling so relieved. "Another teacher had noticed this little boy looked a bit pale. He was actually turning blue. He was asked if he felt ill and he said that he did. Kids will do that if you ask them leading questions. One thing led to another and we rushed him to hospital, where it turned out he was wearing new jeans and the blue dye had come off on his hands and he'd rubbed it on his face. Isn't that hilarious?!"

"It sounds like an urban myth."

"Urban myths have to start somewhere. I'll take a picture

if you need proof."

Make it a selfie, Harvey thought. Photobomb the boy in the new blue jeans.

"Oh, and I almost forgot," Jess86 said. "Happy birthday."

"How did you know it was my birthday?"

"I've seen your family tree remember. You printed it on the internet. You should probably delete it or at least pixelate the date out. Before someone steals your identity."

Harvey told her he never used his real date of birth online. He used Harrison Ford's birthday instead. Jess86 didn't reply. It was probably the end of her lunch break or he'd frightened her off by talking about *Star Wars*. He looked at the time. His lunch break was over too. He put the death certificate back in the envelope, re-boxed the binoculars, and returned them to the shelf he'd borrowed them from.

18

Harvey chose a birthday card, with a picture of Luke Skywalker on the front, and a badge attached to it that said *Jedi Birthday Boy*. After work Harvey went to Wildways. He gave his mother the card and put the wooden tray on her lap and handed her a pen. She looked at the pen and the card, unsure how they were somehow connected, maybe wondering why there was no Chinese food on the tray.

"You need to sign the card, Mum," Harvey said.

It took a long time, but she started writing, slowly and deliberately. When she was finished, she held the card out to Harvey. He put it in the envelope, licked and sealed it, returned it to his mother, and immediately took it back again.

"Thanks, Mum."

Harvey put the pen behind his ear and the tray on the floor. He sat on the chair at the end of the bed and opened the envelope. He took the card out and put the empty envelope in the pocket of his parka. His hand brushed against the other envelope in his pocket, the one containing his dad's death certificate. Harvey opened the birthday card. His mother's writing looked like she'd tried to disguise it by using her non-writing hand.

Harvey read it out aloud, "'My son to happiness birthday'. You've signed my card like Yoda, Mum. Very much I thank you, Mother."

He pinned the badge to his work fleece and put the card on the chest of drawers with last year's Christmas cards.

"Have I got any brothers or sisters, Mum?" he asked, not expecting an answer.

"You're his brother," she said.

"I'm your son, Mum. Have I got any brothers? Did you and Dad have any other children?"

"She's gone. My sister."

"I know that, Mum, but not your sister. Not Auntie

Cathy. I mean my brothers or sisters."

"I feel worse for both of you."

"Both of who? Who do you feel worse for, Mum?"

"You. And his sister's child."

"Sally? Do you mean Sally? You felt bad for Sally and me? Why's that, Mum?"

She didn't answer. What, if anything, was she trying to tell him?

"Did I have any brothers though? Did Dad have a son called Andrew?"

"*You're* his son," she said. It was exasperating. There was a knock on the door and Asha walked in carrying a cake, shielding the flame of a single candle and singing 'Happy Birthday'.

Harvey blushed. He stood up and was surprised when his mother started singing along with Asha. She sang in a high-pitched voice, with a vibrato he'd never heard before. She sang all the words, and in the right order. Singing apparently had the same miraculous effect on her aphasia as people were always telling Harvey it would have on his stutter. Harvey did not sing. Not even in the shower.

When his mother reached the penultimate line of the song, Harvey was relieved that his name wasn't the one lyric she didn't know. Asha put the cake on top of the chest of drawers and gave Harvey a knife.

"Save a bit for me," Asha said, and Harvey had to mentally reduce the size of his planned slice, to leave a less incriminatingly large hole in the cake when he took it down to Asha later. He asked Asha how she knew it was his birthday.

"Margaret told me."

Harvey watched Asha leave the room. He didn't want to look at his mother because he thought it might make him cry. And then he realised it was too late. Two tears chased each other down his cheek, like raindrops on a window. He wiped his face on his sleeve and turned to face his mother.

"You remembered my birthday, Mum."

"It's today," she said, as though he was the forgetful one. She pointed at the cake and at the still-burning candle. Harvey blew it out. If his mother asked him what he'd wished for, he wouldn't have known where to begin.

19

Harvey took two days off work. He went to the hospital first, the place of his birth and of his father's death. There was a sort of messy symmetry about it all. It was also the same hospital where a nurse had dressed his burned hand, and where his mother had spent three weeks before moving into Wildways.

It was while she was in hospital that a doctor had suggested she might be better off somewhere else other than at home, somewhere she could be better cared for. A social worker had agreed, telling Harvey the council would even pay the majority of the care home's costs, but in the end, it was up to Harvey to decide whether his mother should go home or not.

For three weeks he'd been alone in the house, staying up all night playing video games in the living room and watching *Doctor Who* marathons in his pants, eating cold pizza for breakfast and ice cream straight from the tub. While his mother was in hospital, Harvey brought more and more of his bedroom downstairs to the living room, frequently falling asleep on the sofa, fully-clothed and with a game controller in his hand.

He did his best to not let his current idyllic bachelor lifestyle influence his decision. He told himself he was doing what was best for his mother and not what was best for himself. But when the taxi from the hospital had turned towards the electric gates and she'd turned to him and said, "This isn't my home," he felt like the most selfish son alive. A year later and he still couldn't leave Wildways after visiting his mother without feeling at least a little guilty.

Harvey bought a coffee and an iced bun in the hospital cafeteria and found a place to sit down. The cafeteria was on the ground floor, which was mysteriously named 'Level 4'. It occurred to Harvey that when he was visiting his mother in the Medical Assessment Unit on Primrose ward a year ago, Andrew might have been just three floors above on Thistle ward with his father – *their* father.

Harvey watched a seemingly never-ending stream of sick and injured, cured and incurable, medical staff and visitors coming and going through the main entrance of the hospital. The mix of visitors and staff, and the patients milling around in dressing gowns and slippers, gave the cafeteria the appearance of a hotel lobby during a fire drill.

Harvey wondered if he might see G. Walker MBBS, the doctor who'd certified the cause of his father's death. He had no idea what G. Walker looked like or even if they were male or female. He'd searched for them online but all he found was a long unfathomable medical essay attributed to them. He did now know that MBBS stood for Medicinae Baccalaureus, Baccalaureus Chirurgiae though, even if he had no idea what it meant.

If Harvey did miraculously recognise G. Walker MBBS – perhaps he'd see it on their ID badge or catch their reaction to their name being paged over the hospital public-address system. He imagined himself asking G. Walker MBBS whether his dad had suffered or not. He pictured the doctor breaking into a smile, shaking their head and then staring wistfully into the distance, before chuckling to themselves, as they recalled what a character Harvey's father had been.

G. Walker MBBS would tell Harvey that his father had been the talk of the hospital, playing card games with the other patients late into the night, running a sweepstake on who would be the next patient on the ward to die, hustling right up until his last breath. "D'you know something, Harvey?" G. Walker MBBS would say with a wry smile. "I think your father cheated at cards. And yet sadly, he couldn't cheat death."

G. Walker MBBS would wipe away a tear. Their name would be called, and they would have to rush off to save a life. Before the doctor left, Harvey would ask for a quick selfie, so that he could share it with Jess86.

Harvey finished the coffee and the iced bun and went outside to get some air. It had started to rain and he pulled the hood of his parka up. Through the tunnel of the coat's snorkel he watched patients and hospital porters seeking shelter for their cigarettes. Harvey thought about his dad, standing in the rain outside the hospital, naked but for a cotton gown with *Property of Devon and Exeter NHS Foundation Trust* printed on the front, with one hand on a wheelie pole attached to an IV drip, and the other holding a cigarette. With nothing left to lose. An ambulance arrived with its blue lights flashing, but in no obvious rush, and Harvey left the hospital and headed for the cemetery.

20

Harvey walked through the cemetery gates just as a large funeral arrived, and he found himself in the awkward position of walking faster than the long procession of slow-moving vehicles. As hard as he tried not to, he was soon overtaking the cortège. He removed the hood of his parka, in lieu of a hat, and looked directly ahead, so as not to catch the eye of any of the mourners. He counted the cars as he passed them, wondering if his father had been so popular that his cortège had made people late for work. As he neared the front of the procession of cars, Harvey prepared himself for the inevitable *DAD*, spelled out in ironic forget-me-nots on the top of a coffin. But when he was parallel with the lead hearse, he saw the word: *GRANDDAD*. He almost double-took with the realisation: if his dad had another son, then why not grandchildren too?

The funeral procession stopped outside the chapel, and Harvey carried on into the cemetery. There didn't appear to be anyone else around. Not living at least. If it was dark, Harvey would have been scared. He actually found it quite peaceful.

As he looked at the graves, he had the same feeling he'd had at the hospital. What the hell was he doing there? What did he hope to achieve? He had no idea where to start searching for his father's grave, or if it was even there.

The rain stopped at last, and the sun came out, creating a rainbow over the cemetery. Harvey considered taking a picture, but it felt too disrespectful, almost as disrespectful as the rainbow itself, like a Hawaiian shirt at a wake. Harvey wished he'd brought flowers. Not just to put on his father's grave, but so he didn't feel so much like a gate-crasher.

He unzipped his parka and walked along the paths between graves, looking for the newer stones, ignoring any with worn-off inscriptions or those overgrown with weeds.

He turned right at the end of one row of graves and started along the next. He thought of the cemetery as a huge shop. The paths between graves were the aisles, the graves were the shelves. Gravediggers were shelf-stackers. At the end of one of the aisles, there was a massive gothic gold monument, towering over everything else in the cemetery. That was The Castle.

Harvey didn't know if the monument was a mausoleum or a family tomb. It may have been an ornate public toilet for all he knew. It had a pitched-roof, with four sides meeting beneath a spire at the top. The monument was made from the whitest stone and the shiniest marble. There were fresh flowers in front of it. It was clearly cared for regularly. In an arch under the roof at the centre of the monument, there was a gilt bronze statue of a man. Harvey's heart raced as he walked closer to the monument. Anything was possible, because he knew nothing. A monument erected in honour of his father! When he was close enough to read the inscription on the plaque, he was surprised how disappointed he was to find out it was a shrine to a Victorian philanthropist who died in 1890.

After searching the cemetery for almost two hours, Harvey had found a number of dead Kings – James King, Muriel King, Suzanne King and George Kinge – but none of them were his father. Every time he saw anything close to his name-sake, he felt a rush of adrenalin, followed by anti-climax. The gravestones were like clickbait, dating back as far as the eighteenth century. With more than half of the cemetery still to search, Harvey was exhausted and starving and decided to give up.

When he walked back past the chapel, the funeral cortège from earlier was gone. The doors to the chapel were wide open and classical music was playing quietly to an empty room. Harvey wondered what music had played at his dad's funeral. He really hoped it was 'Terry' by Twinkle.

21

The first people Harvey saw the next morning were the two old men outside the Fusilier. The pub wasn't open for another three hours, and Harvey might have felt sorry for the men if he didn't envy them. Standing outside a closed pub first thing in the morning was no worse than switching a computer on at five a.m. to continue a game of *Scrabble* or *Grand Theft Auto*. The old men really weren't that different to Harvey or the hundreds of thousands of people checking their Facebook and Twitter feeds before they got out of bed. Meeting outside the Fusilier every morning was the two old men's social network. But at least theirs happened in real life.

Harvey waited until he was out of their earshot and resumed rehearsing what he was going to say to Andrew if and when he answered his front door.

"Good morning, Andrew. I'm your brother."

"Andy. Now, don't get alarmed."

"*Whassup*, bro?"

Harvey took out his phone and typed, "I'm on my way. Wish you were here."

He didn't know when Jess86 would read his message. Maybe not until she got into work. In Comic Sans on the staff room computer. One of the other teachers would see it and ask, "Who's Harvey_King351? Is he your boyfriend?" And Jess86 would say no, even though the wallpaper on her computer – a screen-grab of Harvey unboxing a desktop printer – suggested otherwise.

Without Jess86's encouragement, Harvey doubted he'd be walking to Whynot St. Paul at seven in the morning. Without Jess86 to motivate him, Harvey would still be in bed or asleep on the sofa after drifting off playing Xbox. He checked his phone. Less than a minute had passed since posting his message. He had no idea what time the school day began in Scotland. He always saw children on their way to school when he was walking to the shuttle bus in the morning. That wouldn't be for at least another hour yet.

When Harvey saw the schoolchildren, especially at the start of September, dressed in their perfect new uniforms, he knew whose PE bags were going to be thrown over a wall by the end of the day. Harvey recognised the victims and he wanted to at least warn them.

There were hardly any cars on the roads. Nobody to thank for driving carefully through the village. Harvey walked past the the sign, past the care home, staring at the ground, in case he saw his mother up at her window. He had the feeling he was setting out on an adventure. It felt selfish to not at least *invite* his mother along.

In the trees and hedgerows birds sang their dawn chorus. Butterflies landed on wildflowers with the same names as hospital wards. Everything was green or brown, except for the hay bales shrink-wrapped in black plastic and the occasional white face of a cow staring at Harvey through a five-bar gate.

Considering he lived in the middle of so much countryside, unless it was from the window of the shuttle bus, Harvey rarely saw any of it. His mother lived even closer to the countryside. He remembered how she used to love walking aimlessly into the woods with him. Picking wildflowers and making daisy chains, crossing a stream if they came across an unexpected shallow point. It must have been frustrating for his mother to be able to see so much greenery from her window and not be able to touch it. The view from her window was little better than a painting. A screensaver. Harvey decided he would have to take her out when all this – whatever all this was – was over.

Harvey couldn't remember ever going into the woods with his father, but he did have a vague recollection of going to the park with him. He remembered tearing bread into the smallest possible pieces, to prolong their time together by the duck pond, his dad clearly wishing he was somewhere else, constantly checking his watch while Harvey chased after a ball, as though it was his dad's turn to reluctantly exercise the family dog.

Shortly before the 'WELCOME TO WHYNOT ST. PAUL, PLEASE DRIVE CAREFULLY' sign, the countryside ended and the new-builds and show homes of Whynot St. Paul began. The further Harvey walked into the village, the older the buildings were, as though he was travelling back in time. When he reached the far side of Whynot St. Paul, the houses would be neither new nor old. That was where his father had last lived, the 'usual address' on his death certificate. It had taken Harvey less than an hour to walk there. That was how long it would have taken his father to come and visit. He could have driven it in five or ten minutes.

Harvey stopped close to his father's house. There were no obvious signs that anyone was at home. No smoke billowed from a chimney and there were no lights on. Of all the insane and unthinkable things that had happened recently, Harvey found the notion of his father having chosen the pretty curtains at the window above the front door as almost the hardest to believe.

He walked closer to the house – if that's what it was – it looked more like half of a house, a slice of house. The whole building wasn't a lot wider than the front door. It looked like it had been built in the last available plot of land left, an architectural afterthought squeezed in between the newsagent on one side and a much larger house on the other. Harvey had seen it online, but the house was different in real life. Harvey's stomach turned with nerves. He contemplated going back home to eat breakfast and watch a film.

He was very close to the house now. If anyone looked out of the window, they'd see him. His heart raced at the thought of that. He walked past the house and into the newsagents.

It was more of a small supermarket. Similar to the one Harvey had stacked the shelves of after leaving school. He pictured his dad coming in to the shop every day to buy a newspaper and a pint of milk – another twenty cigarettes. Harvey looked at the row of newspapers and wondered if his dad had been a Mirror or a Mail reader. Was the milk his father bought full-fat or semi-skimmed? Maybe he was lactose intolerant, like Auntie Cathy. How different might Harvey's life have been if he'd inherited a food allergy from his father? He looked at the comics with the free toys taped to the front and tried to not think too much about his dad buying Andrew *The Beano*.

Harvey walked around the shop, pretending to browse. There was a sign above the counter that said: 'Sorry no cheques.' The shop probably had to put the sign up after one too many of his dad's cheques had bounced. The man behind the counter smiled and Harvey felt obliged to buy something. He looked at the chocolate bars, moving a Twix from the Mars bars pile and putting it back in its rightful place. Even on his day off, he was Harvey King from stock replenishment. He picked up a small bag of Maltesers and swapped it for a larger family bag. He looked up at the smiling shopkeeper, standing in front of a wall of cigarettes and tobacco, the man complicit in the death of his father, who he was about to give money to.

Outside the shop Harvey opened the Maltesers. He looked at the thin building next door. Apart from feeling so anxious about who he would find behind the front door, Harvey was aware it could signal the end of his search. And he wasn't quite ready for it to end yet. In a way, Harvey had hoped to find the house bulldozed or boarded-up, on fire, anything to keep Jess86 logged-on and interested.

The front door of the house opened. Harvey panicked. He took his phone out and pretended to answer it, spilling Maltesers onto the pavement like a burst necklace.

"Hello," he said into the phone and started walking past the house. "Yes, of course. I can get there by ten."

Out of the corner of his eye, Harvey saw a man – Andrew? – walking up the garden path and through the gate. He stopped for a moment and appeared to kick something. A Malteser? Harvey angled his phone and flipped the camera to selfie-mode. He took a photograph. He made a show of completing his fake phone call and exaggeratedly pretended to realise he'd forgotten something. He pirouetted and walked back in the direction of the thin house and the newsagents, following Andrew – it *had* to be him. As he went past one parked car and then another Harvey wondered if any of the cars had belonged to his father, not that he thought any car had ever truly belonged to his father.

Andrew walked with purpose but without appearing either hurried or late. He had a confident swagger that Harvey was instantly envious of. He found himself trying to echo Andrew's confident stride. Why had his brother inherited their father's cool walk instead of him? Andrew was wearing earphones. Harvey was desperate to know what music he was listening to. Maybe it was an audiobook or a podcast. A hypnosis tape – *How to Walk with Confidence*.

Harvey thought Andrew was in his mid-twenties. *My little brother*. All the things they could have shared: piggybacks and bear hugs, Snap instead of Patients, non-computer chess, Conkers, pallbearing their father's coffin. As Andrew's big brother, Harvey would have taken him fishing, teaching him to how cast-off, even though Harvey had never had the slightest interest in fishing before. He would have boosted Andrew over high walls and carried him on his shoulders inside a long raincoat as a practical joke or to purchase alcohol.

He followed Andrew to a large pub on the outskirts of the village where he stopped in an empty car park. Harvey crouched down behind a recycling bin and pretended to tie his shoelace. Two women arrived in the pub car park. They spoke to Andrew as though they knew him. Harvey adjusted his crouch to stop himself falling over and to get a clearer look at Andrew's face. He was chatting with the two women, with an air of relaxed confidence that Harvey could only dream of. Andrew put his hand in the pocket of his coat and took something out. He made a gesture to the women as though he was offering them something. And then he did something that, for Harvey, was like a blow to the head. His amnesia was instantly and miraculously cured. Andrew lit a cigarette. The shipwreck was restored. The picture of Harvey's father was complete.

A bus stopped next to the pub, blocking Harvey's view. When it drove away, Andrew and the two women were gone. Andrew's cigarette was still smoking on the ground. Harvey stood up and watched the bus pull away into the distance. It was white with an orange stripe along the side. It had no number or named destination. But Harvey knew exactly where it was going. It was identical to the bus he rode to work and back every day.

ANDREW

22

Harvey closed his eyes and imagined the road surface and all its signs and markings underneath him. He could feel the tarmac change from smooth to gritted beneath the shuttle bus. Like a blindfolded kidnap victim, he counted the raised joins where the sections of road met. He knew when the bus was about to slow down for a speed camera. He could smell the strawberries on sale by the side of the road. He counted down their arrival in time with the signs – *strawberries in 500 yards, strawberries in 250 yards, strawberries in 100 yards, STRAWBERRIES!*

There was an imperceptible change in the air pressure coming from the twisty vents in the ceiling of the bus when it passed under the high trees at the start of Castle Road. The gentlest of breezes tickled Harvey's hair. No one else on the bus, except maybe Bob Carpenter, would have noticed.

The bus went by the petrol station and Harvey could smell the diesel spilled on the forecourt. There was a new detergent in the car wash. He knew what the man cleaning the petrol pump had eaten for breakfast: bacon and eggs, brown sauce and tea – two sugars.

Harvey felt the dead-eyed stares of the animal sculptures and statues that hid in the trees on both sides of Castle Road as the bus passed them by. Deer, goats, cows, squirrels, badgers, foxes and – not native to the area (from Totnes, according to John Chalmers) – a unicorn.

The shuttle bus crossed the trickle of a man-made stream. The journey was almost over, but Harvey didn't open his eyes yet. *Use the force, Harvey. Use the force,* the toy koi carp called out to him from the stream. After a few more twists and bends and an incline barely steep enough to roll a marble down, the shuttle bus stopped in the car park and Harvey opened his eyes, in perfect time with the bus doors.

He waited for everyone to leave, checking to see if Andrew was a passenger, and then Harvey walked to the front of the bus.

"Can I ask you a question?" he asked Bob Carpenter.

"Knock yourself out."

"Are there a lot of these buses? Is there a whole fleet of them, I mean?"

"A fleet?" Bob said, with a little laugh. "A flotilla, maybe. Definitely less than a fleet. We've got a few smaller minibuses. Some eight-seaters. But if you mean big ones like this?"

Harvey nodded.

"Five," Bob said.

"Do they go anywhere else? The big buses. Apart from here?"

"There are some up north."

"North Devon?"

"Leeds. Why do you ask?"

"Oh, nothing. I saw one yesterday and wondered where it was going."

"Like this one?"

Harvey nodded.

"In that case, it was either going here or leaving here," Bob said. "Those are the two destinations. I could drive blindfolded."

"I sometimes close my eyes and imagine the journey." Harvey realised how ridiculous that sounded. But Bob didn't seem bothered. Harvey thought he might have been serious about driving the bus blindfolded.

"Are there only three big buses that come here though?" Harvey said.

"That's right."

"Oh. Okay. Thank you…I don't suppose you know someone called Andrew King?"

Bob shook his head. "Is he a relative of yours?"

"I think so."

"Are you still doing the family tree then?"

Harvey nodded. "Actually, I've got a picture of him."

He held his phone out to Bob and showed him the photo he'd taken of Andrew leaving his house.

"That's you," Bob said.

Harvey looked at the photo. "Oh sorry, right. Behind me. He's the one opening the gate." Harvey pinched and stretched the phone's screen until Andrew's face filled it. The increased size removed any detail. Bob squinted his eyes and tilted his head.

"It's quite a blurry picture," Bob said.

Harvey thanked him. He put his phone in his pocket. He had another thought. "How about Terence King? You don't know him, do you?"

"I used to know a Terry King. Years back, though," Bob said.

"How many years?" Harvey practically yodelled with excitement.

"Oh, at least ten. He used to drink in the Rams."

"Is that a pub?"

"The big one, up the road," Bob pointed in no obvious direction. "Is he a relative of yours as well?"

"He was my dad," Harvey said. It felt like he was confessing to alcoholism or drug addiction at a meeting. "Did you know him well?"

"Not really. He was just someone in the pub. Now that I think of it, I'm sure he owes me twenty quid," Bob laughed. "How is he? Shit. I'm sorry. I've just realised you said, '*was* your dad'."

"It's okay," Harvey said. "He died a long time ago."

He thanked Bob, said goodbye and, after checking the other buses for Andrew, he caught up with the last of the stragglers crossing the drawbridge.

Harvey spent the morning looking for Andrew. He looked for him in the Music department, in Household and Kitchen, and the Furniture department. He checked the Garden, Electrical, and Toys and Games departments, where for a moment he thought he'd found Andrew. But the man with his face painted like a skull was a Polish man named Mateusz.

Harvey moved through the store, hoping to find Andrew demonstrating a new cooking gadget, or handing out samples of ham and cheese on cocktail sticks in the Food Court of King Arthur. He walked back and forth along the line of checkouts at the front of the store and checked the toilets.

At lunchtime Harvey joined the queue in the staff canteen, leaving without buying anything after he ascertained Andrew wasn't there. He went outside and bought chicken and chips, corn on the cob, coleslaw and a Diet Coke from one of the concessions. On the way through the foyer he'd stopped to look at the framed photograph that hung on the wall above the penny-squashing machine. It was a picture of the entire Castle workforce, taken on the first Monday of last February. It was the last shot the photographer had taken, and he'd asked everyone to shout 'Castle!' and to put their hands in the air as though it was graduation day. Pope Alison was doing jazz hands at the front and centre of the photograph. John Chalmers was on the right-hand side, with his hands stuffed stubbornly deep in his pockets. Harvey was next to John in the picture. But there was no sign of Andrew.

Harvey ate his lunch outside at his usual bench table. He answered a comment from Jess86, asking him whether he'd managed to meet Andrew.

"Not exactly," Harvey said. "But I followed him."

"Where to?"

"Through the village where he lives."

"Did he see you?"

"I don't think so."

"Where exactly did you follow him to?"

"To a pub car park. He got on a bus."

"Did you get on too?"

"It wasn't that kind of bus."

"What kind of bus was it? Mystery? Magic?"

"What's the mystery bus?"

"From Scooby Doo."

"That's the Mystery Machine. It was a shuttle bus. The same as the one I get to work. I think he must work here too."

"At the big pink castle?"

Harvey nodded, as though Jess86 was there with him.

"I've spent the whole day unsuccessfully looking for him," Harvey said.

"Maybe he was driving the bus he got on."

"Definitely not. It arrived in the pub car park after he did."

"Ghost bus?"

Harvey wasn't in the mood for Jess86's jokes. The whistle sounded on the steam train in the station below and he watched it move slowly away. The driver leaned out of the side of the engine, because he was allowed to. His face emerged through the steam from the train's two chimneys and from the smoke coming from his cigarette. Harvey couldn't type the words into his phone fast enough.

"I think I've found him."

23

Harvey left his lunch on the bench table – that's how seized by the moment he was. He walked across the short patch of grass and jogged down the steps to the station. At the bottom of the steps he pushed open the gate and walked onto the platform. He followed alongside the slowly departing train, increasing his pace to overtake the carriages one at a time, like he'd tried so hard not to do with the funeral cortège. The train picked up speed and Harvey was now the one being overtaken. He waited until he was next to an empty carriage and jumped on board the moving train, like it was a ski-lift. Once he'd caught his breath, his first thought was how small the carriages were, or how big he'd become since he'd last been in one. He felt like he was sitting in a tiny chair at an infant school parents evening.

Now he was on the train, Harvey realised that, unless he climbed out onto the carriage roof and made his way to the front of the train like James Bond, the journey itself served no real purpose. He could have simply waited for the train to return to the station and confronted Andrew then. With nothing else to do, Harvey did his best to sit back on the hard-wooden-seat and enjoy the scenery.

The steam train made its way up the hill, its puffing increasing and quickening as Harvey's slowed and settled. The train passed the children's fun fair and the maze that nobody had ever quite managed to get lost in, before circling the edge of the boating lake and entering the first tunnel.

When Harvey had last been on the train, there were no boats on the lake. Today, there were a dozen assorted fibreglass pedaloes and rowboats, all unoccupied and moored to the shore. Years ago, during a particularly cold winter at The Castle, the water had frozen solid and staff had skated on the lake. Or at least according to

John Chalmers.

The train circled the perimeter of the overspill car park. Harvey could see the shuttle buses. He thought he saw Bob Carpenter, chatting with another driver. After a short incline, the train passed through the second and longest of the three tunnels, where Harvey had once met Santa. A witch cackled and a glow-in-the-dark skeleton flew towards Harvey, almost hitting him in the face. It was the least scary part of the journey.

After a further ten minutes, the steam train exited the final tunnel and Harvey could see the cars out on the main road. There was one last bend and then Harvey could see The Castle, standing proud on the top of the hill, always the centre of attention.

The train pulled into the station and Harvey stuck his head out of the side of the carriage. He could see Andrew doing the same from the engine at the front. When the train had fully stopped, Harvey climbed out onto the platform. He was a bit unsteady on his legs, which had more to do with his sudden dash down the steps earlier or the thought of meeting Andrew than it did the thrill of the sedate choo-choo ride he'd just been on.

Harvey quickly considered and reconsidered what he was going to say. For once, stammering wasn't his greatest concern. He still needed to find the right words, but for different reasons. If the only way out of the station hadn't been at the end of the platform, he might have run away. But with no other way out, there was no choice other than to walk towards the front of the train, where Andrew had started uncoupling the engine.

"You need a ticket."

It was a shock hearing Andrew's voice for the first time. From just those four words, it was clear he'd picked up more of the local accent than Harvey. Had their father's accent been strong? Harvey would have to add that to his long list of questions.

"There was no one in the ticket office," Harvey said, pointing back at the small padlocked garden shed next to the station entrance. "Can I pay you now?"

Andrew looked put out by the request. He was the driver not the conductor. Harvey paid him for his ticket. He was so determined to not touch Andrew's hand that he dropped the coins on the ground. A pound coin rolled off the platform, towards the tracks. Andrew put his foot on the coin to stop it. He picked it up and put it in the pocket of his anorak. The anorak was the same shade of blue as the boiler suit he was wearing underneath. The anorak was jacket-length and had no hood and Harvey found himself distracted, wondering whether the length and the lack of a hood still qualified it as an anorak.

Andrew was wearing a cap and had a red paisley bandana tied around his neck. Harvey didn't know if it was his official train driver's uniform, a costume even, or if they were Andrew's own choice of clothes. Harvey envied him for working at The Castle but not having to wear an ugly pink fleece with a logo above his name.

Before Harvey had the chance to say anything else, Andrew had climbed back onto the uncoupled engine and started driving it the short distance to the end of the line. Harvey walked along the platform beside the engine, until Andrew stopped it on a turntable and climbed down. When he saw Harvey was still there, he sighed.

"You don't want an actual physical train ticket, do you?" Andrew said. "For a souvenir or something? We haven't got any left. You could come back tomorrow. See if there are any then."

Andrew put both hands on the side of the engine and started pushing it until it was turned 180 degrees and facing back the way it had just come from. Harvey stayed where he was, watching the simple operation. So that's how they do it, he thought. Andrew took a half-smoked roll-up from behind his ear. He put it in his mouth but didn't light it, as though the cigarette was just another part of his costume.

"This is going to sound strange," Harvey said. "But I was compiling my family tree a while ago and one of the websites I used for my research sent me a family tree. It was from someone else in my family. My distant family."

Andrew nodded without looking at Harvey. Not really listening. He climbed back on board the engine.

"Anyway," Harvey continued, "to cut a long story short, I found out my dad had been alive when I thought he wasn't."

"Is that right?" Andrew said, still not making eye contact, no doubt used to strange people who liked to be around old trains talking to him.

"It was a bit of a shock, to be honest," Harvey said. "I ordered a copy of my dad's death certificate to make sure it wasn't a mistake…And that was when I found out he had a son. My dad did. Apart from me, I mean. I suppose I should have asked you this question first. Is your name Andrew?"

Andrew looked at him for the first time. '*Brown Eyed Handsome Man*', Harvey would think much later.

"Why?" Andrew said.

Harvey held out his hand. "My name's Harvey."

Andrew looked at Harvey's outstretched hand but he didn't accept the handshake. He opened the throttle of the uncoupled engine and it started moving slowly away on the opposite rails to the rest of the stationary train. The engine disappeared out of sight behind the carriages and only the chimneys were visible, blowing clouds of steam over the carriage roofs, as it passed them by on the adjacent track. Harvey walked along the empty platform. He sat on the wooden bench next to the rear carriage that would depart on the next journey as the front carriage.

A few minutes later the engine reversed back into the station and stopped next to Harvey. Andrew climbed down. He appeared more resigned than surprised to see

Harvey still there, probably readying himself for questions about the type of engine, the size of the wheels, or the capacity of the chimneys.

Andrew sat down on the floor of the front carriage with his legs dangling over the edge, his heavy black boots on the platform. He removed his cap and pushed his hair back. He relit his roll-up with a Zippo lighter, using a single, seamless movement that almost made Harvey scream.

"Dad," Harvey started, and then corrected himself. "*My* dad used to do that with his lighter."

Andrew looked at his Zippo. "Is that right?" He put the lighter in his pocket.

"He smoked a lot when I was a child," Harvey said.

Andrew did his best to ignore him.

"This is going to sound a bit mad," Harvey said. "But I think my dad was your dad too."

Andrew picked a bit of tobacco from between his teeth.

"I think we're brothers," Harvey said. He lifted the front of his fleece and held it out to show the badge, like a footballer celebrating a goal. "We've got the same name." He sounded like a small child.

Andrew looked like he might laugh.

"Are you related to Martin Luther King as well?" Andrew said. "How about B.B. King? Stephen King?" He stared into the distance. Harvey thought he was trying to think of other famous people named King.

"Billie Jean King," Harvey said, helpfully.

"Who's he?"

"She's a tennis player."

"Never heard of her. I suppose she's your sister then, is she?"

"I'm sorry. I didn't really explain myself very well, did I? I was researching my family tree–"

"Yes," Andrew interrupted. "You already said. He blew out a thin stream of smoke.

"Can I ask?" Harvey said. "Did your father pass away

this year?"

Andrew stood up. "Is this some sort of joke?"

"His name was Terence King," Harvey said. "My dad's name was Terence King."

Andrew looked around, as though he was expecting a crowd of hysterical workmates or friends to appear and shout *Gotcha!*

"Do you know someone called Megan in Canada?" Harvey said. He fumbled around in his coat pockets. The manilla envelope had slipped inside the lining. He hated his coat. He managed to eventually retrieve the envelope. He took the family tree out and offered it to Andrew, trying to stop his hand from trembling.

Andrew looked at the piece of paper in Harvey's hand. He seemed to consider it for a few seconds, and then he took it. Andrew's hand, Harvey couldn't help noticing, was as steady as a bomb disposal expert's.

"I think you were the one who registered the death?" Harvey said, mixing up the family tree and the death certificate in his mind.

Andrew didn't seem to notice. "Where did you get this?"

"Online. On the internet. A relative in Canada compiled it. Megan."

"And you're saying that you're one of these people on here, are you?"

Harvey said yes and then corrected himself, "I mean, no. I'm not actually on it. Neither are you. It only goes as far as my…*your* dad."

Andrew moved towards Harvey. Harvey flinched. He thought Andrew was going to hit him. Instead he gave him back the family tree and took the now tiny cigarette out of his mouth.

"Why did you come here?" Andrew said.

"To talk to you. I'm sorry. It must be a bit of a shock. I realise that. I've been through similar feelings myself. And I know I probably seem like a nutter, but I've been looking for you ever since I found out you existed. Sorry, that makes it sound like you're an alien or something." Harvey grinned at his own attempt at a joke. Andrew remained stone-faced.

"I knew you worked here somewhere," Harvey said. "I looked everywhere. And then I just saw you. I couldn't believe it. From up there." He pointed in the direction of the steps and at the bench table above.

"Do you work in the shop?" Andrew said.

Harvey nodded. "I stack shelves."

It had never sounded quite so much like nothing before. So little like something. Not a suitable job for a big brother at all, especially when his little brother was a train driver, right up there with astronaut and fire fighter.

"I saw you get on the bus yesterday," Harvey said. "That was how I knew you worked here."

"What bus?"

"The shuttle bus." Harvey pointed again, this time in the direction of the car park.

"You're starting to freak me out, mate," Andrew said. "You saw me get on the bus where exactly?"

"Near your house."

"Near *my house*? Dude, have you been *following* me?"

Harvey didn't think anyone had ever called him dude before. He wanted to laugh.

"No," Harvey said. "Well, yes. I was *sort* of following you. But I already knew where you lived."

"How the hell do you know where I live?"

"It was on the death certificate."

Andrew shook his head. He held the cigarette dog end between his thumb and first two fingers, like a darts player taking aim, and flicked it over the roof of the train. Harvey ducked. Andrew climbed on board the engine. He opened the throttle and pulled the whistle. Harvey looked up at the station clock. The next journey wasn't for another four minutes yet. The empty train started to move. Andrew looked back at Harvey.

"I think you should probably fuck off, mate."

Of all the fairy-tale reunions that Harvey had imagined – the embrace, the handshake, the high-fives, the laughter and tears, the reminiscing, the joshing, the fishing trips, the chess games and table tennis tournaments – Harvey hadn't considered this one. Even though he now realised it was perhaps the most obvious and understandable one.

24

Harvey stopped the lift between floors and took out his phone.

"He didn't believe me!"

He leaned against the wall of the lift, staring at his phone like a watched pot. Communicating via the comments thread on a video sharing website had such obvious limitations, one of them being any sense of urgency, especially as, unlike Harvey, presumably Jess86 hadn't set up her phone and her computer to alert her of any new activity. She'd be busy, teaching a class or marking homework. If five-year olds even did homework. Harvey knew so little about her, especially considering how much she knew about him.

If only he could send her an email or a text message. A correspondence he could open with *Dear Jess86* or even a simple *Hi* or *Hello*. The video comments they'd been sharing with each other had no beginning or end. With the benefit of hindsight, an email would have been a better way for Harvey to introduce himself to Andrew. A letter would have come as less of a shock. A huge blimp attached to the roof of a massive pink castle would have been better than Harvey's clumsy confession on the station platform. What must Andrew have thought of him?

Harvey looked at his reflection in the dirty mirrored wall in the goods lift. When he'd seen Andrew coming out of his house for the first time, Harvey had tried to kid himself that he hadn't noticed the main difference between them. He made himself believe that it hadn't been his very first thought.

Andrew was thin. As thin as the slice of a house he'd just walked out of. More importantly, Andrew was thin*ner*. Andrew was chalk. Harvey was cheese. Cheese and biscuits, cheesecake, cheese string and cheese straws. Harvey was chocolate and doughnuts, burgers and chips, family bags of

Maltesers. Maybe if he'd grown up with his father, instead of with his mother, Harvey would look more like Andrew. The glaringly obvious physical difference between the two men must have made what Harvey was saying to Andrew sound even more ridiculous than it already was.

Harvey checked his phone again. Nothing. He shut the lift gates and pressed G. When his phone pinged, he pulled the gates open again with such force that he felt the recoil all the way up his arm.

"What happened?" Jess86 said.

"I went to the station where he works and told him about the family tree."

"What did he say?"

"He told me to f***off."

"Typical."

"What do you mean typical?"

"Why did he tell you to fuck off?" Jess86 not using asterisks shocked Harvey a little. She was a teacher of small children, after all.

"I presume he thought I was mental," Harvey said.

"Did he believe you?"

"Would you have?"

"He might have known it was true, but he just didn't *want* to believe it."

"I don't think so. I'm going to have to leave my job now. I can't stay here anymore."

"You're overreacting. Did you show him any proof you were related?"

"I showed him the family tree but he's not even on it. I'm not on it. I'm an idiot. What was I thinking?"

"Haven't you got anything else you could show him? Some proof?"

"What? A birthmark you mean, or a tattoo?"

"There must be something else."

In real life they would have been shouting this exchange at each other instead of typing and waiting, typing and waiting.

"There's the death certificate, I suppose," Harvey said. "I could show him that. But it still proves nothing. Apart from me being some kind of identity thief or madman."

"How about a birth certificate then?"

"I haven't got his birth certificate."

"*Your* birth certificate," Jess86 said. "It will have your name on it *and* your dad's name."

"It's in the sideboard!" Harvey said.

"Describe this sideboard."

"It's just a sideboard. Long with drawers and cupboards. Very well made. Why?"

"Nothing. What was Andrew like?"

Harvey wanted to say that Andrew was 'cool', and how he was just like his dad – *their* dad.

"He's thin," Harvey said.

"Is that it?"

"I mean, he's not fat like his brother."

"You're not that fat."

Harvey would have been entitled to feel patronised because Jess86 had watched all of his videos, and unless she had the screen resolution on the wrong setting, she knew exactly how big he was. Unless, of course, she was even bigger. Maybe Harvey was 'not that fat' in the same way he wasn't that fat compared to Bob Carpenter. In all of Harvey's unsuccessful lucid dreams about Jess86, he hadn't entertained that as an option. Jess 86 stone. Harvey hated himself for wondering how that might negatively affect the way he felt about her, how he might be no better than Charlotte from the slimming website

"You need to go back," Jess86 said.

"I really don't think that's a good idea."

"You have to. You can't just leave it. Not after you've come this far."

"But I actually thought he was going to hit me."

"There you go. Proof. Brothers famously don't get on."

"Isn't that an urban myth?"

A few minutes passed.

"Cain and Abel," Jess86 said. "Gomez and Fester Adams." She'd obviously Googled 'famous brothers who don't get on'. "Liam and Noel Gallagher."

"We *were* both wearing anoraks," Harvey said. "At least I think we were. If a coat doesn't have a hood does it still qualify as an anorak?"

"What material was it made of?"

"Anorak material. It was quite short though."

"How short?"

"Like a suit jacket."

"Is this Andrew's anorak or yours?"

"His."

"You can ask him when you go back and see him."

25

Harvey found his birth certificate in the sideboard. He resisted any further temptation to climb into either of the cupboards. He took a photo of the certificate and uploaded it to his computer. He opened Megan's family tree and copied all her names and dates onto his own version, watching his new family tree blossom with new cousins, second cousins and cousins once and twice removed. He added Andrew, leaving his date of birth blank. Harvey's family tree was now bigger than Megan's. He knew virtually no one on it.

He decided to try and forget about his family for a while. He microwaved a jacket potato and put *Return of the Jedi* on. But he couldn't relax. He kept thinking about the steam train journey and Andrew swearing at him. He stopped the film and opened his video channel on his computer. He read back through the most recent comments. Harvey had been so involved with Jess86 that he'd been neglecting his other fans. There were hardly any new comments. It was strange, but he almost missed the badmouthing and fat-shaming.

Harvey stared at his computer, moving the mouse around, feeling like he'd finished the internet. He uploaded the latest pictures he'd taken of his mother and added them to the slideshow. He experimented with different musical accompaniments, to see how it affected his mother's mood. The theme to the *Benny Hill Show* produced the most satisfying results. Harvey turned the volume up and watched the slideshow three times. He plugged the record player in and ran the slideshow with a Buddy Holly accompaniment, hoping to capture in the slideshow the same spark he'd seen light up his mother's eyes when he'd played the record to her.

Harvey left the record playing and went into the kitchen. He made some snacks – cheese and biscuits, pickles, ice cream and microwave popcorn, and restarted the film. He was still too restless to enjoy it though, and found himself looking for something to unbox, but there was nothing. If he ordered something online, how quickly would it get to him? The next day? An hour? He could order a drone and get it delivered by a drone. He could film the drone arriving and make that the start of the unboxing. He hadn't seen that done before.

Harvey looked at the latest videos from some of the other unboxers he followed. He wondered how it would feel to type a nasty comment. He clicked on a professional looking video of a man reviewing a PlayStation game. It had over a million views, and enough upward thumbs for one negative thumb to pass by unnoticed and without hurting anyone's feelings. Harvey's real thumb hovered over the onscreen virtual thumb for a full minute. But he was unable to cross over to the dark side. He supposed he was always going to be one of the good guys. Even if that good guy was, what someone on his channel had once called, 'A fat Jar Jar Binks'. Harvey went back to the sofa. He started *Return of the Jedi* one more time. And then he remembered something.

26

1983 Star Wars Return of the Jedi Jabba the Hutt Playset. Poseable figure, with hookah pipe, dungeon, throne, leash, and small Bib. Fortuna figure. Brand-new, Unused, Unopened, Undamaged. Sealed, in its Original Packaging.

Harvey imagined three billion gasps of horror all over the world, as he broke the seal and tore at the cardboard like a deranged puppy, as he unboxed the unboxable. Every rip and tear further devaluing the contents of the box, transforming something highly-collectable into the children's toy that Father Christmas had given him in a train tunnel all those years ago.

27

Harvey waited in the car park after work. He had an envelope, containing his birth certificate and a print out of the updated family tree. He'd also brought a gas bill, thinking proof of address might somehow convince Andrew he was genuine, even though the bill was in Harvey's mother's name.

When Andrew entered the car park, Harvey tried reading his body language. He looked for gritted-teeth or balled-fists. Andrew had a cigarette in his left hand and was holding his anorak in his right. The anorak, if indeed it was an anorak, was slung over his shoulder like an afterthought, held in place by his index finger, hooked through the label inside the collar. He looked like James Dean. Every time Harvey saw Andrew, it was a little harder to believe they could possibly be related.

Andrew didn't break his stride when he saw Harvey, as though he'd already forgotten all about him. When he was close enough to throw a punch, Andrew stopped. He pinched the end of his cigarette between his thumb and forefinger and put it behind his ear like a carpenter's pencil. Harvey almost told him to be careful not to burn himself. He desperately wanted to be Andrew's big brother.

Harvey pushed the large envelope into Andrew's hand, not letting go of it himself.

"There's a copy of the family tree in there," Harvey said, "and my birth certificate and a utility bill. Take them home and think about it. There's no hurry. Take as long as you want. And if you don't want to see me ever again afterwards, I promise you, you never will."

Harvey had practised the speech in his head. It actually sounded surprisingly less laughably melodramatic out loud than he'd expected. He let go of the envelope, relieved that it didn't fall to the ground. He turned his back on Andrew and walked off into the car park and boarded the shuttle bus. Bob Carpenter said hello and Harvey nodded. He couldn't speak. He sat down near the back of the bus and waited for his heartbeat to slow down. He was shaking. He didn't dare look back to see if Andrew was reading the family tree or looking at his birth certificate, or if he'd thrown the envelope in the bin.

Harvey watched the other passengers board the bus. They were taking so long. Come on, *come on*. Harvey's leg had started to shake now. He put a hand on his knee to stop it, but his hand shook, too. The bus from Whynot St. Paul was parked alongside the St. Peter bus, but Harvey hadn't noticed Andrew get on yet. He closed his eyes, wishing Bob would shut the doors and start the engine. He wanted Andrew to take the envelope home and give himself enough time to read everything and think it through. In spite of the bravado of Harvey's speech, the last thing he wanted was to have to be true to his promise to never see his brother ever again.

There was a knock on the bus window and Harvey opened his eyes. Andrew gestured for him to get off the bus. It didn't seem like it was a threatening gesture, more of a *come hither* than a *step outside*. Harvey got up and made his way through the passengers standing in the aisle of the bus.

"Forgotten something?" Bob Carpenter said, as Harvey went down the steps.

"I won't be a minute."

"We're off soon."

"I'll *get a cab*." The irritable authority in Harvey's voice surprised him. It looked like it had surprised the bus driver, too.

Harvey walked across the car park and found Andrew sitting on a wall, rolling a fresh cigarette.

"You said that if I didn't want to see you ever again I never would?" Andrew said when Harvey was close enough to hear. "We work about fifty-yards from each other. How's that going to work exactly?"

"We've lived pretty close to each for long enough, without bumping into each other up until now," Harvey said.

Andrew put the finished roll-up behind his ear. He held up the gas bill as though it required explanation. Harvey remembered his mother had told him once that his dad had fixed the meter at their old house so it ran backwards. Maybe Andrew had never seen a gas bill before.

"Is Mrs. King your wife?" Andrew said.

"My mum."

Harvey watched anxiously while Andrew studied his documents, as though he was checking his papers at a border crossing. In spite of the cold, Harvey was sweating. He pulled the collar of his fleece away from his throat to let some air in. He wanted to sit down, but the only available space was on the wall next to Andrew.

"How do I know you didn't forge all of this?" Andrew said.

"Believe me, I thought the same thing when I first saw the family tree. But then I couldn't think of a reason why anyone would bother doing that to me. So, what reason could I have for forging it for you?"

"A scam," Andrew said. "A joke?"

"Honestly, It's not either."

"What do you want then?"

Very good question. What *did* Harvey want?

"I don't want anything," Harvey said.

"There's no money. No family heirlooms."

"Really, I don't want anything like that. I just want to know…the truth, I suppose."

Andrew turned his head away and stared up at The Castle. Half a minute passed.

"My sister told me my dad had another family." Andrew said.

Harvey thought he'd misheard.

"Wait…What?...He's got a *daughter*?"

Andrew nodded. "I think she tried to find you once."

Harvey was still trying to absorb this latest information, carrying out mental topiary on his family tree. Did he have a sister as well? Is that what Andrew was telling him? Or a stepsister?

"But she didn't find me?" Harvey said.

"I don't think so. It wasn't something we ever talked about, though. Me and my sister didn't get on. We still don't talk a lot now. The funeral was the first time we'd spoken in years."

Andrew's sudden apparent acceptance of the situation had taken Harvey unawares. He'd been expecting more of a struggle before reaching this point.

"What was the funeral like?" Harvey said. "Sorry. That's a stupid thing to ask—"

"Quiet," Andrew said. He sounded almost bored talking about it. "Just Dad, my sister and Dad's tobacconist."

Harvey didn't know if he was joking about the tobacconist. Maybe it was the same man Harvey had bought Maltesers from.

"Mum and Dad separated when I was ten," Andrew said. "I stayed with my dad, and my sister went and lived with our mum."

Harvey was probably reading too much into anything and everything that Andrew said, but he couldn't help noticing he'd said, '*my* dad' and yet, '*our* mum'.

The doors of their respective shuttle buses closed. Harvey asked Andrew if he needed to go. Andrew shook his head. He clearly needed answers too.

"Did my…your dad, ever say anything about me?" Harvey said.

Andrew shook his head. "Maybe he thought I was too young to understand."

"Not later on though? He didn't mention me at all?" Harvey could hear how self-centred he sounded, but he had to know.

"Perhaps he forgot," Andrew said. It was an idea that was crushing for Harvey.

"Didn't you ever wonder about us, though?" Harvey said. "After your sister told you that you had this other family?"

Andrew shrugged. "It is what it is."

What did that even mean? C'est la vie? Que sera sera? Shit happens? *What* was what *what* was?

The two shuttle buses left the car park in convoy, leaving behind a smell of exhaust fumes and an uncomfortable silence. Andrew took the roll-up from behind his ear. He lit it and inhaled deeply, holding the smoke for five seconds. When he exhaled, Harvey realised it was a spliff. Andrew offered it to him, and Harvey didn't know if declining the spliff would be the equivalent of not eating monkey brains in an *Indiana Jones* film.

"I don't smoke," Harvey said.

Andrew laughed. "Are you sure we had the same dad?"

They watched the two buses, turning right on the other side of the car park and then left, the sound of their engines rising and falling, as the series of short bends leading to the main road brought them closer and then further away, until they couldn't be heard at all.

"Now what?" Andrew said.

28

They shared a cab back to the Whynots. Andrew had to go past Harvey's house in St. Peter to get to his house in St. Paul, so it made perfect sense to share. Once they were in the cab though, Harvey would rather have cartwheeled home blindfolded. The close proximity between him and Andrew on the backseat of the cab, led to an intimacy that they didn't know each other well enough for yet. With Andrew sitting next to him in such a confined space, Harvey felt like he had a neon sign flashing the words *FAT BROTHER* on and off above his head. Andrew must surely have been having similar thoughts. Harvey leaned into the door, to stop their knees from touching. He was sure Andrew was doing the same thing on the other side of the cab.

And what was it about getting into cars that rendered people so speechless? For the whole journey, they barely spoke. And Harvey had so much he desperately needed to say. He'd been planning for this moment. He'd dreamed about it. He was going to ask Andrew where he was born, when he was born, was it in the same hospital as him? The hospital where their father died.

Where did Andrew go to school? Did he stay on and go to university? What did he study there? Had he taken a gap year? Where did he go? Harvey wanted to know about all the Father's Days he'd missed, all the birthdays and Christmases. He wanted to know whether their dad had taken Andrew to the park and the zoo. Had they gone to the fair together and to football matches? Had they travelled abroad, on surfing and skiing holidays? Had their dad taught Andrew how to swim and to ride a bike? Harvey had so much to ask Andrew. But instead, he sat in total silence, staring out of the cab window, wishing the journey was over. When he saw the lights of the leisure centre, he told the driver he could walk the rest of the way from there.

Harvey gave Andrew more than half of the fare and asked him if he wanted to go for a drink sometime. He noticed the cab driver in his rear-view mirror, arching his eyebrows.

"We're brothers," Harvey told the cab driver.

Andrew gave Harvey a look, but at least he didn't deny it.

As soon as the cab had driven off, Harvey took out his phone and told Jess86 everything that had happened. He typed it in a long comment under his Jabba the Hutt unboxing. The video had already picked up a record amount of negative feedback. Around eight p.m., Jess86 replied.

"Did he pay towards the cab fare?"

"We paid half each. Why?"

"Just wondered. Did he believe you?"

"He said he sort of knew already. His sister told him."

"What happens now?"

"I'm going to meet him tomorrow after work to talk about it. Did you see what I just said there? He's got a sister. *I've* got a sister. My life's turning into an episode of The Waltons."

"Where are you meeting?"

"We're going to a pub, but we're meeting at the train station first."

"Very Brief Encounter."

"Let's hope not."

":-)"

Harvey left work, full of doubts. He thought the whole thing was a huge mistake. Andrew had had twenty-four hours to think, to study the documents Harvey had given him and to reach his own conclusions. What if he'd decided that, yes, they were related, but so what? Maybe Andrew didn't want or need a new half-brother in his life.

Harvey went down the steps and walked along the

station platform. There was a young family in one of the carriages, but all the others were empty. Andrew was leaning into the engine, stoking the firebox, filling the water jacket, polishing the pistons or one of the things Harvey had read about on Wikipedia last night. Andrew stood up and wiped his hands on a filthy looking rag. He walked towards Harvey.

"I've still got one more trip to do," Andrew said. He seemed to be in a friendlier mood than yesterday. He gave Harvey his envelope back. "I've edited your family tree for you."

Harvey took the family tree out of the envelope. Under his name, Andrew had written his date of birth. Harvey swallowed the lump in his throat. If they were on television, this would be where the uplifting music would go. He made a mental note of Andrew's birthday – was he twenty-six or seven? – and gave him back the family tree.

"You can keep it if you like," Harvey said. "I've got the original."

"You sound like a blackmailer," Andrew said. Harvey reassured him he wasn't.

Andrew rolled the family tree up and put it into the deep trouser pocket of his boiler suit. He checked his wristwatch. It was an old fashioned looking, silver-coloured watch, with a matching strap. It had probably been bequeathed to Andrew by their dad. A watch that he'd won in a card game or slipped from an unsuspecting wrist during a handshake in a pub. Andrew climbed on board the engine. He looked back at Harvey.

"Are you coming?"

"*Me*?" Harvey said. "Up there?"

Andrew nodded. Harvey hesitated and then shrugged. "Okay."

He crossed the narrow platform and climbed onto the engine. Andrew opened the throttle, tooted the whistle and the train started moving.

For the first minute of the journey Harvey didn't speak. It wasn't like the uncomfortable silence they'd shared in the back of the mini cab, even though they were just as close to each other. Harvey couldn't speak because he was too excited. Nervous, but excited. Once he'd realised the speed of the train was unlikely to throw him out and into the sidings, Harvey relaxed.

"How did you get this job?" he said, raising his voice above the noise of the steam and the clickety-clack of the wheels.

"I applied for it."

Harvey laughed. "Right. Of course."

"Seriously though, I've always liked trains."

Harvey nodded. He did *not* want to stack shelves anymore.

"The last time I went on this train was with Dad," Harvey said, forgetting he'd been on the train just yesterday. "To see Father Christmas."

"I bet it's a lot different now?" Andrew said.

"Completely," Harvey said. *So different.* He imagined competition winners and bucket-listers with not long to live might have been allowed to ride up front with Andrew before, but he doubted it had meant quite as much to any of them as it did to him right now. When the train approached the first tunnel Andrew asked him if he wanted to sound the whistle.

Harvey turned to look at him. "Seriously?"

Andrew nodded and Harvey pulled the cord. He could have sworn the train picked up a burst of speed, as though he'd activated the turbo charger. At the end of the ride, Harvey climbed down onto the platform. He stood and watched Andrew uncouple the engine and then followed alongside it to the turntable at the end of the track.

"Give us a hand with this, will you?" Andrew said.

Harvey stepped cautiously over the rails.

Andrew laughed. "It's a steam train. You won't get

electrocuted."

He told Harvey to put both hands on the side of the engine, and together they pushed it around on the turntable. When it was facing in the opposite direction, Harvey stepped back onto the platform and Andrew drove the engine the short journey along the tracks, so it was ready for its first trip the next morning. As the engine disappeared behind the stationary line of carriages, the whistle tooted twice. Harvey decided it was definitely for his benefit. His brother was letting him know he was still there, like a bird reassuring its young in a nearby nest.

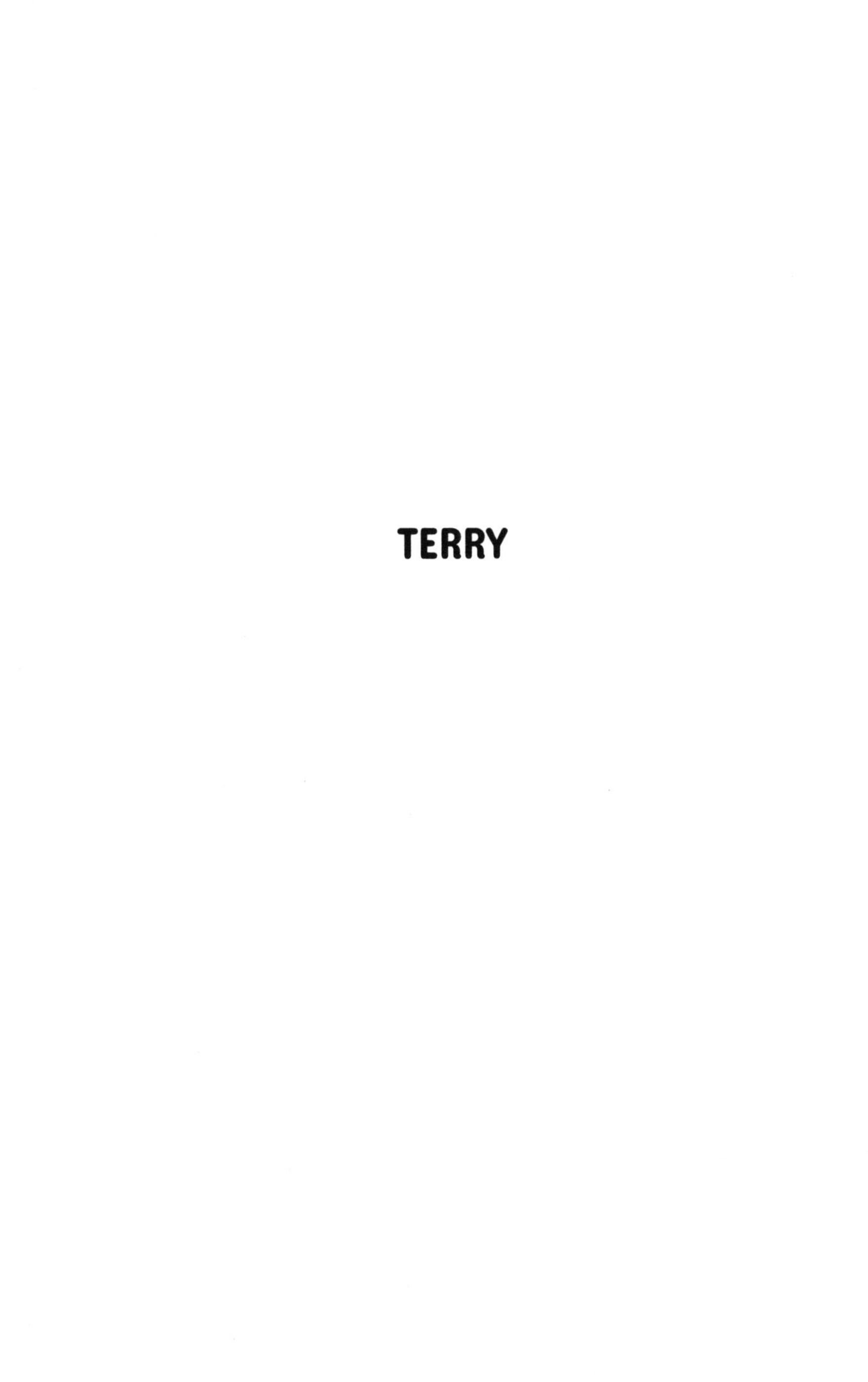

TERRY

29

Andrew's earliest memory of his father was of him not being there. He was four years old and the whole family were supposed to be going to Disneyland Paris. They were all at the station, Andrew, his sister and their mother, but his dad didn't turn up. The three of them went to Disneyland anyway. They took the train to London and another train to Paris. They were Andrew's first ever proper train journeys. He claimed to remember the make and model of both trains. All the time he was at Disney, Andrew thought his dad would still turn up. On the rides and in the restaurants, when Andrew was eating his Mickey Mouse shaped-pizza and when he was watching the Main Street Electrical lights Parade, every time Andrew saw one of the enormous Disney characters, he asked his sister or his mum, "Is that Dad?"

"No, that's Mickey Mouse."

"Is that Dad?"

"That's Goofy."

For three days, Andrew was convinced his dad was there, wearing a costume, looking for the zip.

"Where was he?" Harvey asked.

Andrew shrugged. "He was away a lot."

Harvey had been with Andrew for an hour. It was like digging up a time capsule. On the walk to the Ramshackle – the pub that Bob Carpenter had called 'the Rams' – Harvey realised the years he'd missed out on with his father hadn't been all fun fairs and football matches after all.

In the years between his two deaths, their father had been almost as absent for Andrew as he was for Harvey. He had to travel further and further away from home to make any money, driving across the country to new pubs and hotels. Travelling fifty or sixty miles to sell a car stereo, staying overnight in cheap bed and breakfasts or sleeping in his car. All the things their dad had once bought and sold in pub car parks could be found just as cheaply on eBay or Amazon or bought in pound shops and variety stores like The Castle. Every time Harvey had put a cut-price toaster or a budget TV onto a shelf, he'd been unwittingly contributing to his father's downfall.

"Did he ever go straight?" Harvey said.

Andrew laughed. "Straight?"

"I mean did he ever get a normal job?"

"He delivered leaflets for a pizza restaurant for a while."

It was the saddest thing Harvey had ever heard. Don Corleone collecting shopping trolleys at Lidl.

Andrew said that he and his sister were 'shared out' between their parents, along with everything else in the house. Andrew's sister went to live with their mother and Andrew stayed in the thin house in Whynot St. Paul with their dad. Andrew said the house went back a long way and wasn't quite as tiny as it appeared from the front. He told Harvey that after his mother and sister had moved out, his dad, who'd been away for so much of his life, was suddenly there all the time, rarely getting up from his armchair.

It was a depressing story, and Harvey already knew it wasn't going to have a happy ending. Andrew told him how long his father had been in hospital, and the different treatments the doctors had tried. None of the romantic deathbed scenarios Harvey had dreamed up were true. His father hadn't scammed the other patients with sweepstakes and card games. Andrew couldn't remember meeting a doctor named G. Walker MBBS.

Harvey was almost in tears, but Andrew seemed totally nonplussed by it all. Perhaps he'd told the story before, enough times for it to have lost its potency. Harvey didn't admit to feeling sad. If Andrew, who'd spent so much more time with their father, wasn't upset talking about his death, Harvey didn't feel he was entitled to be upset about it either.

After two or three drinks in the pub, the two men were relaxed enough in each other's company for casual observers to presume they'd known each other for a long time. Andrew told Harvey all about himself. He wasn't married and was 'between girlfriends'. His sister was six years older than him and she never let him forget it. Andrew didn't have any children to add to Harvey's family tree, but his sister had a daughter.

Andrew had been to the same school as Harvey and had been taught by some of the same teachers. He'd had a better time at St. Peter and Paul Community College than Harvey, enough to want to stay on for two extra years. When he left school, Andrew studied engineering at college. He once ran a half-marathon without any preparation or training and came thirty-ninth out of three thousand runners. On his eighteenth birthday, he had an allergic reaction to a bee sting, ending up in hospital, where he was told he could easily have died. He showed Harvey the EpiPen he carried with him. He had no pets but preferred dogs to cats. He hated clowns and circuses and didn't think animals belonged in zoos, with the exception of geese. He'd once been attacked by a goose.

Last year Andrew had won three thousand pounds on the lottery. On the same day he almost choked to death on a peanut. He'd spent his winnings on a train journey across Norway. Andrew said he could never remember which was gross and which was net, he only ever ate the top half of hot cross buns, because 'that was the best bit', and he didn't own a television!

Andrew showed Harvey a scar on his arm from an 'uncoupling incident' and his two tattoos – the Santa Fe Super Chief train on his right arm and the Mallard steam locomotive, 'still the fastest steam train in the world', on his left calf. Harvey had no scars or tattoos to show him in return, other than the tiny *Loser* cut on his forehead from falling off a stepladder at work and the almost invisible childhood burn scar on the palm of his hand.

Andrew asked Harvey if he was married or had children.

"There is a girl I met online," Harvey said. "She lives in Scotland."

"What's she like?"

"She seems nice. Quite funny."

"Seems? You make it sound like you haven't met her yet."

"I haven't. And when I say I met her online, I don't mean on a dating website. It was in the comments section of a video sharing website."

Andrew raised his eyebrows. "What kind of video sharing website?"

"Probably not the type you're thinking of," Harvey said. But then found telling Andrew about his unboxing videos equally embarrassing.

"Can I see one of your videos?" Andrew asked.

"They're not very good."

"I don't care."

"Maybe later."

"What does she look like? The girl you *met* online?"

Harvey smiled.

"Shit," Andrew said. "You haven't even *seen* her, have you? She could be a man. An old man."

"Or a robot."

"Operated by an old man. What's her name? This…*girl*. Do you even know her name?"

"Jess86."

"Eighty-six?"

Harvey nodded.

"Double-barrelled," Andrew said. "She must be posh." He waved his empty glass in the air. "Another?"

Harvey was already quite drunk but said yes. He didn't want Andrew thinking his big brother was a lightweight.

While Andrew was at the bar, Harvey watched the queue of people piling food onto plates. It was all-you-can-eat carvery night. Four types of roast meat sizzled in fat and juices, while fifteen types of steamed and roasted vegetables congealed in metal serving trays beneath huge brass lamps. On a table next to a fizzy-drinks machine dispensing free refills, there were four gravies and various colour-coded sauce bottles.

Andrew came back from the bar and put two pints of lager on the table.

"I'd like to apologise on behalf of my people," Harvey said, gesturing towards the all-you-can-eaters. "I bet with a half-brother like me, you're glad you didn't end up with a whole one."

"You're not that big."

"Yeah, sure. Compared to what?"

Andrew pointed at the food queue.

They observed the enthusiastic diners for a while. Commenting on their choice of leisurewear and the different techniques they used to cover as much of their plates as possible. One woman carefully placed a boiled potato on the top of her Buckaroo of food. When it didn't collapse, they quietly cheered.

"Was Dad like me or like you?" Harvey said.

"What do you mean?"

"Did he look like me or you? Was he Laurel or Hardy?"

Andrew shrugged. "I never really noticed."

"Seriously? You have a very casual outlook on life, you know. I think perhaps you smoke a bit too much of the..." Harvey searched for the correct and most up-to-date word – dope, weed, grass? – and decided on "hashish". He stammered so much saying it that it sounded like he was about to sneeze.

"Don't take it the wrong way," Andrew said, "but a little bit of hashish might help with your stutter."

Harvey shook his head. "No thank you."

"You'll never know until you try it. You don't even have to smoke it. I could make you a cake."

"I see what you're trying to do," Harvey said. "Tempt the fat man into taking drugs by hiding them in his food. My mum used to do that. Crush pills and mix them up with ice cream or Angel Delight to make me take them. But no. Really. Thank you. But I'm afraid I'm one of those boring people who'll never take drugs."

"What do you do if you've got a headache?"

"That's different."

"Why?"

"Because they're legal drugs."

"Cannabis is legal in twenty-three states of America."

"We're not in America." Harvey looked at the queue of food enthusiasts in their sweatpants and baseball caps. "Despite evidence to the contrary. No. Thank you. I prefer my drugs in a box with a list of ingredients and possible side-effects on the side."

"People use weed medically all the time," Andrew persisted. "To relieve the symptoms of multiple sclerosis, HIV and Crohn's disease, tinnitus and tics. Stammers. My dad, *our* dad, tried it."

"He *did not*!"

Andrew nodded. "When he was feeling sick from the chemotherapy."

When Harvey pictured his dad smoking a spliff it didn't seem so unbelievable. It was just another form of cigarette, after all.

"Did it work?" Harvey said.

"A bit."

Harvey's attention was suddenly drawn to someone in the food queue.

"Oh my God. Don't look. Jesus Christ. Shit. I think I know that man."

Andrew turned his head to look at the food queue. "Which one?"

"Don't *stare*. The one spilling peas onto the floor. Standing under the *Go KING SIZE for a fiver* sign, which I personally find a bit insulting by the way. King size, indeed."

"Who is he?"

"I'm not a hundred per cent sure," Harvey said. He studied the man piling food onto his plate. He'd changed a lot. He looked less feral than when Harvey had last seen him. His face had settled down, and although he still had a skinhead haircut, it was no longer through choice. "It's weird seeing a twin on his own," Harvey said. "But I think it's either Anthony or Craig Lyon. They used to bully me at school."

Andrew turned his chair fully around to get a proper look.

"What did he do to you?"

"Just stuff," Harvey said. "It's actually funny seeing him in a dinner queue after all this time. Him and his brother used to stand in the school dinner queue. One of them would hold their hand down at their side in the shape of a circle. If I looked at the circle the other brother would punch me."

"And *that's* him?" Andrew said. "*Him*?"

It was true. It *was* hard to believe the man currently shovelling turkey on top of beef, pork and gammon could have ever been capable of bullying anyone. He seemed to be exhausted just from the effort of standing up and collecting food. He was puffing and panting like a dog trapped in a hot car. There were visible meat sweats dripping down the sides of his red cheeks. He looked like a disgraced MP.

"Him and his brother made school a living nightmare for me," Harvey said. "The thing is, he's really changed. I mean...He's fat. But more importantly...He's fatter than me. I don't think I've ever experienced schadenfreude quite like it." Harvey looked around the pub. "I wonder if his brother's here and whether he's the same. Can you have one fat and one thin twin?"

"You should go over and make a circle with your hand," Andrew said. "If he looks at it, I'll come over and punch his face in."

"We're better than that," Harvey said, even though the idea thrilled him.

"I'm not," Andrew said.

"Leave it," Harvey said. "Don't feed the trolls."

"I reckon he's doing that well enough for himself."

They both laughed.

Anthony or Craig Lyon finished filling his dinner plate. He picked up a bowl, already loaded up with apple pie and custard with his other hand.

"*Quick,*" Harvey said. "He's coming over."

"Shall I trip him up?"

"*No.*"

"I'm going to spit in his custard."

"*Don't.*"

Craig or Anthony walked by. He went through the door leading to the adjoining bar.

"You should have said something," Andrew said.

"If he comes back for more food, I will."

"If you don't, then I definitely will."

They drank and chatted for a while. Harvey couldn't stop thinking about Craig or Anthony. He kept looking over at the door to the other bar. When Andrew took out a magazine to show him a picture of a train, he was glad of the distraction.

"That's the Rossiya," Andrew said, pointing to a train with red white and blue stripes down the side like squeezed toothpaste. "Next month I'm going on the Trans-Siberian Railway, from Moscow to Vladivostok."

"How long will you be gone?" Harvey said, his voice went up in pitch at the thought of losing his brother so soon after finding him.

"Six days on the train once I get there. I go from London to Belgium first, and from there, I go to Germany and Moscow. I spend a day in Moscow and then I take the train to Vladivostok. I'm going on a ferry to South Korea and

Japan. I'll spend some time there." Andrew stood up. "I'm going outside for a cigarette. Do you want to come?"

"I'll stay here," Harvey said. "It'll give me a chance to catch up with you." He gestured at their respective beer glasses. Andrew's was empty, Harvey's still half full.

"I meant go to Russia," Andrew said.

"*Me* go with *you*?" Harvey couldn't believe Andrew was asking him to join him on the Trans-Siberian Railway, as casually as when he'd invited him onto the miniature steam train ride around the boating lake and back.

"I can't leave my mum," Harvey said.

Andrew shrugged. He went outside to smoke. When he came back he was carrying two large vodkas. Harvey reluctantly followed his lead and drank the shot in one. He slammed the empty glass on the table and the whole room spun. When it stopped spinning, Harvey took his phone out and showed Andrew the slideshow of his mother.

"She's got small vessel disease and vascular dementia," Harvey said.

"I believe you," Andrew said. "You can't leave your mum."

"I know, but seriously. She's also got aphasia. Or aphonia. Basically, she speaks in riddles a lot of the time. She wrote my last birthday card in Yodic."

"What's that?" Andrew said.

"You know. How Yoda talks."

"I see, said the blind man." Andrew put Harvey's phone down on the table.

"Have you got any photos of my dad, sorry, our dad?" Harvey said. "If he'd walked in here now, before I'd met you, I don't think I would have recognised him."

"I'm sure you would have."

"I don't think so."

"I'm pretty sure there's a box of photos somewhere at home," Andrew said. "My sister's got most of the family ones. But she left the pictures of me and Dad. If I can find them, I can bring them to work if you like."

"That would be great," Harvey said. "When I was trying to imagine his face, the harder I tried the more difficult it was. I couldn't remember what colour his eyes were or if he was tall or short. Was he fat? Was he thin? Did he have a moustache?"

"Is this a game?"

"It's just some of the stuff I've allowed myself to obsess over. Did he go grey? Was he bald? What do I have to look forward to?"

"He had a moustache for a while," Andrew said.

"What kind of moustache?"

"What kinds are there?"

"I don't know. Handlebar, horseshoe, Salvador Dali. Lando Calrissian."

"What's Lando Calrissian?"

"*Who*. He's from *Star Wars*."

"Oh right. It was just a normal moustache. The top lip kind. I think he grew it for the wedding. And he did go grey, but not bald. Not until he started the chemo, at least."

"Of course," Harvey said. "I'm sorry."

Andrew shrugged. "It is what it is."

"Hang on," Harvey said. "Whose wedding?"

"Dad's."

Harvey stared at him, open-mouthed.

"You didn't know my mum and dad were married, did you?" Andrew said.

"I didn't even know mine were *divorced*. I thought he was dead. *Why would I think he was divorced*? I think I'm going to need a minute or two to come to terms with this latest bombshell."

"It was only a small wedding," Andrew said, "if that makes you feel any better."

Andrew stood up and went to the toilet, leaving Harvey shaking his head with disbelief. For years he'd believed his mother was a widow. Somehow, her being divorced seemed worse. Andrew came back.

"Do you think he left my mum to be with yours?" Harvey asked him. "When did they meet?"

"I don't know."

"You must have an idea though."

"Me and Dad didn't really discuss things like that. Remember, I didn't even know you existed, until you got on the train yesterday."

"The day before yesterday. So, you don't know why my mum would have told me my dad, *our* dad, had died?"

Andrew shook his head. He waved his empty glass. "I think it's your round, H." He pronounced it 'Haitch', using up the spare letters he'd dropped earlier from the beginning of the word 'erb', which he pronounced with what he probably thought was a West Indian twang but made him sound more West Country than he already was.

Harvey stood up. He had to lean on the table to balance himself.

"I think I should go after this one," he said.

Trying to keep up with Andrew's drinking was a mistake, especially on an empty stomach. Harvey was in a pub on an all-you-can-eat night, and he hadn't eaten a thing. He went to the bar and bought a drink for Andrew and four packets of crisps. He took them back to the table and split the crisp packets open for sharing. It was a new concept for him.

"What the hell is this?" Andrew said, holding his phone up to show Harvey a picture.

"It's Jabba the Hutt," Harvey said. The picture was actually a paused video, and it wasn't on Andrew's phone, it was on his.

"Is that a hookah pipe?" Andrew said.

"Trust you to focus on that. Can I have my phone back, please?"

"Looks like a bong. Who's Jabba the Hutt?"

"Jabba Desilijic Tiure. Hutt gangster and crime lord.

He's a member of the Grand Hutt Council."

Andrew looked at him blankly and something unthinkable occurred to Harvey.

"You haven't *seen Star Wars*?"

Andrew shook his head.

"Not *at all*?"

Andrew shook his head again. Harvey's incredulity quickly turned to possibility.

"You'll have to come round to my house and watch it," Harvey said, excitedly. "We can watch all the films. We'll watch them in the Machete Order. We'll start with Episode Four, then we'll move on to Five, then Two, then Three and, finally, Six. We can leave out Episode One, because it doesn't really add anything to the story."

"I can't wait. Explain it all to me again."

Andrew's sarcasm was no match for Harvey's enthusiasm. "The first film is Episode Four, then comes Episode Five, after that we'll watch Episode Two and then Three and, finally, Six. We won't bother with Episode One because it doesn't add anything to the story. I've confused myself now. I must be drunk." Harvey ran through the viewing order in his head and then explained it all again. "And then there are the new ones, of course."

Andrew asked him to explain it just one more time. They were both really laughing now. Andrew may have thought he was winding Harvey up, but he would have been perfectly happy to talk to him about *Star Wars* until the pub closed or was demolished and developed into luxury apartments.

"I wish I could live my life in Machete Order," Andrew said, exhausted from laughing so hard.

"What do you mean?"

Andrew didn't answer. He gave Harvey his phone back.

"By the way," Andrew said, "I knew there were a lot of dicks on the internet, but I didn't realise they were all on your website. Some of the shit they say to you on there.

Arseholes. I've replied to a few of them for you."

Harvey looked at his phone. "*What?*"

He scrolled and clicked between unboxing videos until he found Andrew's comments. He'd replied to three different people, telling them he was going to hunt them down and destroy them, even if it took him the rest of his life.

"But they'll *think you're me*," Harvey said. He was mortified, thinking of the possible repercussions. He could simply delete Andrew's comments, of course. And it was unlikely anyone would have seen them yet. But Harvey knew already that he never would delete them. Any fallout would be worth it for the way Andrew defending the family name had made Harvey feel.

Harvey suddenly felt lightheaded and excused himself. He stood up, wobbled a bit and went to the gents. He went into a cubicle, closed the door and leaned against the wall, waiting for everything to stop moving. After a while, he heard someone else come into the toilets. He thought it might be Andrew. Harvey opened the cubicle door and went to the sinks to splash some water onto his face. In the mirror he saw the back of a large man, standing at the urinals. It was Craig or Anthony Lyon. Harvey wondered which brother it was. Maybe it was both of them. Maybe Craig had eaten Anthony, or vice versa, to finally fully become Craigthony.

Harvey looked at the man's reflection in the pub mirror. If this chance meeting had happened in the toilets of St. Peter and Paul Community College, Harvey would have been desperate to make his escape before Craigthony turned around. But now he couldn't seem to leave. He wanted to stay and speak to whichever Lyon brother it was. He wanted to ask why the brothers had chosen to make his young life such a misery. What made them trip him up on the stairs and put fireworks in his school bag? Why did they whip the back of his legs with a wet towel and throw his trousers in the swimming pool? What was the point of the Circle Game? Harvey had often fantasised about meeting his bullies in later life. But unless a high score on *Kung Fu Panda* on Wii counted, he hadn't yet mastered martial arts to the level he'd always planned for that encounter.

Craig or Anthony seemed to piss for ages. All those free fizzy-drinks, the four gravies and the colour-coded sauces. Harvey decided he'd count to five. If Craig or Anthony hadn't turned around by then, he would leave. One. Harvey thought about the trolls on his video channel. Two. Fat pig stutters bad. Three. Poor little Harvey. Four. Craig or Anthony farted loudly and zipped up his fly. Before he had time to turn around, Harvey pushed him into the urinal.

30

The cab home couldn't have been more different to the awkward and silent one they'd shared the previous day. When Andrew had stopped laughing and slapping the seat, and when the cab was far enough away from the pub for Harvey to be certain they weren't being chased by Craigthony, they talked, Andrew enthusing about the Trans-Siberian Railway and his trip to Russia and Harvey doing his best to convince his brother how much he was going to enjoy their *Star Wars* marathon when he returned.

Yesterday's cab had taken them to Whynot St. Paul via Whynot St. Peter, tonight's would go past Peter to get to Paul. When the cab pulled up outside his house, Andrew asked the driver to wait, while he ran in to get something. He was gone for a long time. Harvey started to feel sick. He opened the cab window. The cold night air worked wonders. When Andrew came back, he passed a small wooden box through the open cab window to Harvey.

"Photos," Andrew said.

Harvey had been expecting something larger, a shoebox maybe. Instead, it was an old cigar box, deep enough to contain twenty or thirty photos at the most.

"I got you this as well," Andrew said. He passed a plastic Tupperware container though the window.

"What is it?" Harvey asked.

"Something for later. I made it myself."

Andrew patted the back of the cab, like a cop dispatching an ambulance to the hospital. The cab pulled away from the kerb. Harvey closed the window and looked at the two boxes on his lap. He lifted the lid on the Tupperware container. Inside there was a small plain looking cake and a folded sheet of A4 paper. Harvey took the sheet of paper out and unfolded it. He held it up to what little light there was in the back of the cab. Something was written in ballpoint pen. It looked like a list, but it was too dark in the cab to read it. Harvey put the piece of paper back in the Tupperware container, closed the lid and put it on the seat next to him.

He lifted the lid on the cigar box and saw his father for the first time in twenty-six years. He was washing a car, either green or blue. His dad was wearing a white shirt, the sleeves were rolled up and his tie was tucked into the front of the shirt. He looked like a politician visiting a hospital ward. There was a cigarette hanging from his bottom lip and the tell-tale bulge of a packet of another twenty in the front pocket of his shirt. The car he was washing was the only clue to Harvey's dad's age. It looked like a car from the 1990s. Without better lighting though, Harvey couldn't be sure. He thought his dad looked happy in the picture, though. He certainly didn't appear to be heartbroken or consumed by a dreadful guilt for whatever it was he might have done in the past. He looked like a man washing his car.

The second photograph in the box was more recent and more upsetting. His father was a lot older. He'd aged so rapidly in the turn of a single picture. Harvey thought he might already have been ill when it was taken. Maybe he knew he was dying.

Harvey went through the rest of the photographs, about twenty in total, taken at different times, and obviously with different cameras. They weren't arranged in any noticeable order – not chronologically or by size or the camera used. It was like looking at the slideshow of his mother in that respect. His father ageing, and then growing younger again, his hair straight and short, and then almost shoulder length and curly. His dad looking healthy, and then sick, and then well again. Slipping in and out of remission.

In one photograph his father was sitting in an armchair. Harvey remembered he used to own a large table-top lighter. It was in the shape of a sail boat. His dad called it his 'indoors lighter'. To Harvey, it had seemed like the heaviest possible object that could be held in the palm of his hand. His father's initials – his first, middle and last names, Terence Albert King – were engraved on the side of the lighter – 'T.A.KING'. Taking. It was probably his dad's idea of a joke. The flame of the lighter was always too high and his dad would adjust it by turning a wheel at the bow of the boat. He'd always forget about it, and the next time he used the lighter, the flame would be too high again. Harvey's dad used to let him fill the lighter from a tube of butane gas. He would also be allowed to empty his dad's ashtray. It stood on a stand as high as the armchair. Harvey would push the button at the centre of the ashtray, like he was starting a spinning top, and the ash would disappear inside. His dad called Harvey his 'smoker's apprentice'.

Andrew was in a few of the photos. Harvey wished he was still in the cab to act as a guide, to answer his questions – *Where is that? When was this taken? Who took this one? Do you think he looks like me there?* There was one photograph that Harvey wasn't expecting to find in the cigar box. Andrew couldn't have known it was there or he would have mentioned it. It was a passport photo of Harvey sitting on his dad's lap. They were both pulling funny faces. Harvey must have been seven or eight years old in the picture, and yet he already looked overweight. He'd always had a very clear timeline of events. His dad had a heart attack, his mum overfed him, and he got fat. The photograph didn't make sense.

The last picture in the cigar box, though, that one really knocked Harvey for six. It had been taken on a beach. It looked like Bantham beach, where Sally had buried Harvey in the sand when he was eight and she was five. Harvey's dad was holding the camera at arms-length to fit everyone in. Taking a selfie long before it was dictionary word of the year. It looked like a sunny day but it was windy as well. Andrew's mother was holding her hair in place, her hand almost covering the streak of white hair that ran in her family. A lorry drove by and filled the cab with enough light to see the photo clearly. How happy they all looked together: Andrew, Sally, Auntie Cathy, and Cathy's new clown – Terry.

31

Harvey asked the cab driver to stop opposite Wildways. He paid the fare and immediately threw up at the side of the road. He leaned against something metal, a telephone junction box or something, and sat down on the grass verge with his head between his knees. He was either sweating heavily or he was crying.

Harvey pulled his coat sleeve over his hand and wiped his mouth and looked up at the windows of the care home. Ever since his mother had moved there, Harvey had worried about the day she would no longer know who he was, and now he wasn't really sure himself. *Your Auntie Catherine is going to live in New Zealand.* He could hear his mother saying it to him like it was yesterday. *Your Auntie Catherine is going to live in New Zealand.* It sounded so much like a euphemism that it was almost funny. His mother hadn't killed her sister in the way she'd killed her husband, but she had banished her to the most distant place on earth she could think of.

Harvey recovered slightly and opened the cigar box, hoping it might have been a drunken hallucination or a trick of the headlights from passing traffic. But it was most definitely Auntie Cathy in the photo. He threw up again. The vodka burned his throat.

What must it have been like for his mother to decide to choose never to see her sister again? Having already lost her husband? *I feel worse for both of you,* Harvey's mother had said recently. *You. And his sister's child,* she'd said. Was that Sally? And *where was* Sally? Presumably not quite as far away as Harvey had always believed. Maybe there'd been no need for airmail paper. Even as drunk and disoriented as Harvey was, it all made such perfect sense to him. The timing, his dad 'dying', Cathy and Sally 'emigrating'. Andrew's age. Had Cathy been pregnant with Andrew when Harvey had last seen his aunt? He tried to picture her with a bump or wearing loose-fitting dresses and eating mad food.

He pulled himself up from the verge and, when he could see straight, he started walking. He zigzagged past the house where he used to live. Where his dad had fixed the gas meter so that it went backwards, where Harvey had helped him lay new turf, and where his dad had cheated on his mum with her sister. It was like a story from one of his mother's real-life magazines. *My Brother's Mother is my Mother's Sister!*

The last, stubborn customers were leaving the closed Fusilier. The landlord held the door half-open, ready to shut it again before they managed to slip back in, like zombies or floodwater. Outside his house, Harvey took his phone out. He typed frantically, as though his battery was about to run out.

"My mothet is my Auntie Cathy!!£ My sister is mu cousind."

He struggled to get the key in the front door and didn't make it upstairs or even as far as the sofa. He lay down on the living room carpet and fell asleep, still wearing his coat and shoes. It was the worst night's sleep he'd ever had. It was fitful and seemed to go on forever. His head was pounding and his stomach growled. All night he heard noises. Burglars and intruders, mice tapping out S.O.S. messages behind the bedroom wallpaper, working on their mouse novels on their tiny mouse typewriters. Tap-tap. Click-click. Chickerty-chick. Ant novelists, beetles writing blogs, cockroach keyboard warriors and woodlice trolls.

Harvey turned around to face the bedroom wall, but it wasn't there. Where was the bedroom wall? Where was he? The ants were knitting now. Clack-clack. Knitting socks for centipedes. *Doctor Who* jumpers for wasps. The sound of chopsticks and castanets inside Harvey's skull, keeping him awake. Magpies warning other magpies, a feather stuck in a bicycle wheel, hailstones falling on the metal roof of a post office van. Tap-tap. Changing pitch now. A low hum. Like the fridge they used to have. His dad had brought it home in the middle of the night. The sounds in Harvey's head more persistent and rhythmic. Thrumn-thrumn. Like an all-night drum and bass party two streets away. Was this what it was like for his mother every night? Were these the kind of noises in her head?

The long night finally ended with a dream. Harvey dreamed he was looking at photographs in the back of a cab, before being sick on the grass outside a care home. What was the point of dreams if they were nothing more than diary entries? Not even a unicorn or a Wookiee to remind him he was asleep.

At seven a.m., after going upstairs to the bathroom and retching for ten minutes, Harvey came back downstairs. He took his parka and shoes off and sat on the sofa. He switched on the TV and watched the breakfast news, hoping for an earthquake to put everything into perspective. He rang work and left a message to say that he'd picked up a stomach bug and wouldn't be in. He switched his computer on. There was still no answer from Jess86. He wished he had something to unbox to get her attention. And then he remembered Andrew had given him two boxes.

He sat on the sofa and lifted the lid of the plastic Tupperware container. He picked the cake up and sniffed it. It smelled like the sweetest cake ever. He put it back in the container and unfolded the piece of paper.

INGREDIENTS:
200 grams of baking flour
60 fluid ounces of milk
2 eggs
180 grams of sugar
180 grams of cannabutter
Icing sugar

FOR THE RELIEF OF:
Stammers:

DIRECTIONS FOR USE:
Take one slice to make you feel relaxed and happy or to give you the giggles or become very talkative. It can make you more aware of your senses and even give you the sensation that time is slowing down.

POSSIBLE SIDE EFFECTS:
Can cause feelings of anxiety, suspicion, panic and paranoia. May cause light headedness, feeling faint and slight nausea. This is called a whitey. And may make you feel really hungry. This is known as 'the munchies'

Harvey stuffed the piece of paper back in the Tupperware container and slammed the lid closed. He was already experiencing anxiety, suspicion, panic and paranoia and he'd only opened the box.

He went over to his computer and Googled 'What is cannabutter?' He looked at the images of something green that looked like pesto-flavoured ice cream. '*Cannabutter is a butter substitute, used in cannabis-infused recipes*', Harvey read. He looked up 'cannabis-infused recipes.' That led him to delicious-looking banana breads and scrumptious carrot cakes. He found recipes for cannabis doughnuts and potsicles, cannabis cupcakes, airy-fairy cakes, kooky cookie cakes, canna-pancakes, pot-corn, chocolate space brownies, canna-berry sorbet, cannabis pumpkin and apple pies, served with cannabis ice cream or covered in canna-custard.

Harvey read three different online chats about the pros and cons of eating marijuana – or cannabis, weed, grass, pot, ganja. The posters on the weed websites seemed to have more words for cannabis than Eskimos had for snow. There was a point in every debate where the discussion would be side-tracked by a comment along the lines of – 'Don't cook it dude, smoke it!'

Harvey read the same claims that Andrew had made in the pub about medical cannabis being legal, or at least decriminalised in many countries, including twenty-three states of America. It could apparently help to relieve symptoms of multiple sclerosis, HIV, Crohn's disease and tinnitus. Harvey followed links from stoner websites that took him to cancer message-boards and to multiple sclerosis and tinnitus sufferer support groups. Switching back and forth between the medical and pothead chatrooms, he noticed the desired goals of one were similar to the symptoms and side-effects from the other.

Harvey watched three videos showing 'The effects of eating space cake'. In one video a man fed a piece of cake to his aggressive dog and the dog stopped barking. In another clip, a woman laughed hysterically at nothing for three minutes. One man filmed himself eating a lump of hash cake and then scored 180 in a game of darts. Without the cake he could barely hit the board. Harvey closed all the browser windows, deleted his search history, cleared the cache, and shut his computer down.

He picked up the cigar box. He thought about his dad smoking a cigar to celebrate his wedding to Auntie Cathy, the birth of Andrew or the sale of a cut-and-shut Nissan. Harvey cleared a space on the living room carpet. He sat down and opened the box. He laid the photographs out in front of him, sorting them into what he thought was chronological order. He began with the passport photo of himself and his dad pulling faces. Next to it he placed the picture of his father sitting in an armchair. He was still relatively young, not a lot older than Harvey was now. The object on the arm of the chair wasn't his dad's indoors lighter after all, just an indistinguishable ornament or paperweight.

Fourth in the sequence of pictures was the kind of

photograph Harvey had expected to see in the album he'd found in the sideboard. It was the left half of a torn wedding photo. His dad was dressed in a suit and tie, with a white flower in his buttonhole. Judging by the width of the jacket's lapels and the size and shape of the shirt collar, Harvey guessed the bride missing from the other half of the photograph was his Auntie Cathy, rather than his mother.

He put the picture of the whole family on the beach next in the sequence. Andrew looked about seven years old and Sally was in her early teens, six or seven years older than when Harvey had last seen her. Harvey's dad had his arm around Auntie Cathy's waist in the photograph. They looked so happy together. Harvey was reminded of how happy his parents had seemed during their interview on *The Harvey King Show* – even though he still hadn't actually listened to the tape.

By the afternoon there was still no response from Jess86. Harvey gave the thumbs-up to all her comments to try and get her attention. He needed to talk to somebody. The void in the house had never felt so in need of filling. He went through the fridge and the kitchen cupboards and put together an indoor picnic of biscuits, Jaffa cakes and millionaire shortbread. When he'd eaten it all, he was still hungry. The fridge was empty. Harvey needed to go shopping but didn't feel up to leaving the house yet. He sat on the sofa and removed the lid from the Tupperware box. He took out the list of ingredients and side-effects, quickly replacing the lid. The smell stayed in the room. The cake seemed to be saying *EAT ME, HARVEY*. The cake knew his name.

Harvey took the cake out to the kitchen, and with a sharp knife he cut a small slice. He put the cake in his mouth and held it there, not intending to chew. He was reminded of how he used to challenge Sally to eat sugar-covered doughnuts without licking her lips. It was as impossible as when they'd tried folding a piece of paper more than seven times. Harvey bit into the cake. It was delicious. He couldn't stop chewing and then he swallowed.

Harvey finished the slice of cake and sat on the sofa waiting for something to happen. Five minutes passed without any noticeable effects. Ten minutes went by, then fifteen, half an hour. A full ninety minutes passed without Harvey feeling psychotic or hallucinating Beatles lyrics. He reread Andrew's handwritten list of side effects. He wanted to phone him but didn't have his number. He couldn't actually recall Andrew having a mobile phone.

He switched the television on, found the sci-fi channel, and immediately started to worry the combination of science fiction and drugs might do something to his mind. He turned the television off and started up his computer. He listened for a while to the comforting hum of the hard drive and the dust crackling on the static of the monitor screen. He updated his apps, tidied the computer's desktop and emptied the trash. He did the same with the kitchen bin. When he was outside, he heard a siren. He went back indoors and spent the rest of the night waiting for Andrew's drugs to take effect or for the police to kick his front door in.

When he woke the next morning, Harvey wasn't aware of having felt any effects from the cake while he slept. He had woken with a warm feeling all over his body, but that may have been because he'd left his electric blanket on. He wondered if Andrew might be playing a trick on him and the hash cake was a placebo hash cake. A cake. As he was getting out of bed, Harvey realised there had been one unusual thing. He was undressed and upstairs in bed with the electric blanket on and yet he had no recollection of ever leaving the sofa.

He got dressed, went downstairs, made a coffee and considered what to do with the leftover cake. He could eat it, of course. He was certainly hungry enough. Or he could take it to the park in the Tupperware box. Throw the cake in a bin or leave it in the bushes. But he remembered John Chalmers had told him about drug dealers in London, hiding their crack cocaine supply in people's front gardens. Squirrels had eaten the crack cocaine and their stomachs had exploded. Harvey didn't want to be responsible for that. He decided to return the remaining cake to Andrew. He wrapped it up in the list of ingredients, put it in the Tupperware box, and hid the box at the back of the fridge behind a low wall of leftover soggy lettuce and soft tomatoes.

32

Just after five o'clock, when the Bay of Bengal opened, Harvey bought Chinese food and walked to the care home. His mother's door was open. She was sitting on the edge of the bed, staring out of the window. Harvey walked over and stood by her side. He looked at her reflection in the window. She'd put make-up on. In the way a child or a chimpanzee might.

"Mum?" Harvey said, but she didn't seem to hear him. He looked for toilet tissue in her ears. She appeared so calm that he didn't want to disturb her.

Her handbag was on her lap and she was wearing her overcoat. Where did she think she was going? She finally turned to look at Harvey, examining his face. Would this be the day when she didn't know who he was? Or did she notice something different about her son? Could she tell that he knew the truth, or at least the insanity he now presumed was the truth? She redirected her gaze to the window.

"What is it, Mum?" Harvey asked. "What are you looking at?"

"Can I have one of those ones, please?" his mother said.

Harvey followed his mother's eyeline. It was already dark outside. There were solar-powered lights flickering in the garden next door.

"What, Mum? The fairy lights in the garden you mean?"

"No," his mother said. "The low ones."

Harvey looked again. "The wind turbines? You can't have a wind turbine. What do you...Bungalows!" Harvey said, like Archimedes in the bath.

His mother smiled. "I hate steps."

Harvey laughed. "Do you want me to ask if there's a room free on the ground floor again?" he said, knowing that whenever a room at Wildways did become available, the reason why was invariably the same. For his mother to be free from stairs, somebody had to die first. Glenda needed to use her green pen if Harvey's mother was to get her bungalow.

"Are you going to take your coat off, Mum?" Harvey said. He closed the curtains. There was a cushion on his mother's lap. It had a picture of Donkey from *Shrek* on and looked brand new.

"Whose is this, Mum?" Harvey went to remove the cushion. His mother hugged it to her chest.

"Shall I take the cushion for now, while you have your dinner?" Harvey said. "I've got Chinese."

His mother released her hold on the cushion. Harvey put it on the chair and helped her out of her coat in his usual hands-off way.

"Shall I be mother?" The same jokes every Sunday.

Harvey dished up the food and took the plate over to his mother. She held the plate while he picked up the wooden tray and put it on her lap.

"Ready?"

His mother put the plate down on the tray. He gave her the knife and fork, and then she seemed to be stuck. She was holding the cutlery as though she'd forgotten what it was for. Harvey looked at his mother, on pause.

"Sorry, Mum," he said, realising he hadn't given her the soy sauce. "I forgot the sauce." He'd broken the sequence. It was like removing a bulb from a string of fairy lights. Harvey took the bottle out of his coat pocket, flipped open the lid and gave it to his mother. He put the fresh newspaper on the bed, open at the crossword page.

"I've left the difficult clues for you."

Harvey plugged the laptop into the television. He chose an old video at random. A wireless modem. It was one of his earliest unboxings. He would have liked to be able to say that his naive presenting skills in the video had improved vastly in the months and years since, but really, he knew they'd peaked from the start. He pressed play and sat down to eat.

"Mum?" he said, looking up from his food. "You don't need to tell me anything. I think I know. He broke your heart, so you broke his. Literally."

They ate their Chinese food, watched four old unboxing videos and *Finding Nemo*, and then Harvey washed his mother's plate up and tidied the small room. He took a photograph to add to the slideshow. He tried to make everything feel normal, for both of them. That was what he needed right now. To go back to their routine.

When he left, Harvey returned the real-life misery magazines to the lounge downstairs and took the Donkey cushion along to the office. Asha was there with Rupert. He was the only male member of staff at Wildways. Harvey had heard him being referred to as 'Rupert the Bear' but only ever by Rupert himself, hoping his nickname would catch on. Harvey knocked on the open office door.

"I'm sorry to bother you," he said. "But I think my mum's been taking things from one of the other rooms again." He held the cushion out to Asha.

"Oh no, that's hers," Asha said. "Your sister brought it in."

"I haven't got a sister," Harvey said.

"I'm sorry," Asha said. "I just presumed." She turned to Rupert. "Who was the girl who brought the cushion in for Margaret?"

"The *girl*?" Harvey said.

"I thought she was your sister for some reason," Asha said. "Your mum was very happy to see her."

Rupert nodded his agreement.

"Did she bring flowers as well?" Harvey asked, doing his best to sound calm while his brain played pinball with his thoughts.

"She did bring flowers, actually," Asha said. "I got her a vase for them. Is everything all right?"

"Did the girl have a Canadian accent?" Harvey said.

"I don't think so. She sounded English to me. Did you speak to the young lady visiting Margaret, Rupert? Was she Canadian, do you know?"

"I don't think so," Rupert looked at Harvey. "Is your sister Canadian?"

"I haven't *got a sister,*" Harvey said. What was it with this place that made simple enquiries so frustratingly complicated? "Did she say what her name was?"

Asha shook her head. "Are you sure everything is all right?"

"I need to go back upstairs," Harvey said. "I forgot something."

He didn't wait for the lift. He didn't take his shoes off or knock on the door. He burst into his mother's room and walked over to the bed. She'd opened the curtains again. Harvey closed them. A curtain ring shot across the room. He took the beach photograph out of his coat pocket and held it in front of her. He refused to be disarmed by her smile.

"Who's that, Mum? Who is that in the picture?"

Harvey held the photograph closer to his mother's face, like a referee with a red card. He was breathing heavily from the stairs and the corridor. If he had a heart attack, an actual bonafide heart attack, it would serve his mother right. She looked at the picture, studying it for no more than a second, before pointing at the people in the picture one by one.

"The girl. Terry. Terry's boy. Terry's friend."

33

In the lift Harvey looked at the photo of everyone on the beach. He was gripping it so tightly there was a crease through his dad's face. He looked like he was laughing. Harvey almost tore it into shreds. His mother knew about Andrew, and Sally had been to the care home to visit her. It was Sally who gave his mother the Shrek cushion and the flowers. Her room suddenly seemed decorated with such obvious clues.

Harvey left through the fire exit. He didn't want to have to explain his erratic behaviour to Asha. He wasn't sure he even could. If he ever came back, he'd ask her for more details about Sally. He'd find out how often she'd visited. He'd ask Asha to get Sally to leave her phone number if she came again.

When Harvey got home, he checked his computer. There was still nothing from Jess86. Andrew threatening the trolls had resulted in some particularly obnoxious insults, but there was nothing from the one person Harvey could share everything with.

He started to think his computer had become sentient. It had been his closest and only companion and confidant for a very long time. They'd played games together, killed aliens, defeated the Nazis and won intergalactic wars. They made a great team. And Harvey's computer had always made an effort for him. Updating its image and appearance, improving the way it performed the tasks he expected of it. Was it possible the computer was jealous of Jess86? Because of all the attention she'd been getting? Could Harvey's computer have deliberately tried to sabotage his relationship with Jess86 by hiding her correspondence? Harvey went through the hundreds of spam emails he'd accumulated, and then a different, more rational thought occurred to him. It was so hidden-in-plain-sight, it had practically been invisible.

He read back through Jess86's comments. All of her questions about Harvey's mother. Wanting to know her name and her age, where the care home was, and what it was called. Harvey read his own comments. He'd told Jess86 that he'd watched *Shrek* with his mother. He'd told her how much his mother liked the donkey.

Harvey found his Jabba the Hutt unboxing video and, beneath all the insults and death threats from *Star Wars* fanatics, he typed, "Jess86. Have you been to see my mother?"

He read Jess86's comments again, switching between different unboxings to locate them all. He read her comments where she'd suggested he should use the information he already had to find out more. Jess86 told him to order a death certificate. She seemed more interested in his family than he was. Harvey typed, "Are you Megan?"

He carried on reading and rereading Jess86's comments. She'd been so keen for him to find Andrew. She said it would drive her insane not knowing what he looked like. She pretty much ordered Harvey to go to Andrew's house, and once he'd found Andrew driving the train, and after Harvey had spoken to him and told Jess86 that it hadn't gone well, she'd convinced him to try again.

And how had Jess86 known all about the plane crash at The Castle? The plane crash that had been so insignificant that Harvey had to search for ages online to find any mention of it. And what about Jess86's reluctance to video herself? Blaming her shyness and her lack of computer skills, when her liberal use of emoticons and knowing how to type an accent over an e contradicted that.

Jess86 had described Andrew's initial negative reaction towards Harvey as 'typical', as though she'd been expecting it. And she'd suggested that Andrew might have known he had a brother, but he 'didn't want to believe it.' Jess86 had asked if Harvey's mother had any sisters. She'd told Harvey to give his mother her love. It hadn't seemed odd at the time. But now Harvey was questioning everything about Jess86. Was she even a teacher? Did she live in Scotland? He looked at their exchange of comments about that.

"Whereabouts in Scotland do you live?"

"Edinburgh. We've got our own castle too."

"Does it have a teacups ride and a Food Court of King Arthur?"

"We've got an Arthur's Seat."

"What's that?"

"Arthur's Seat is the main peak of the group of hills in Scotland which form the majority of Holyrood Park. Happy birthday by the way."

Harvey typed 'Arthur's Seat' into Google. The very first entry that came up said: 'Arthur's Seat is the main peak of the group of hills in Scotland, which form the majority of Holyrood Park.' Word for word what Jess86 had said.

And what about her wishing Harvey a happy birthday?

"Oh, and happy birthday by the way."

"How did you know it's my birthday?"

"I've seen your family tree remember. You printed it on the internet."

Harvey was shaking as he located Megan's original family tree on his computer. He already knew what he'd find. Or rather what he wouldn't find. Harvey knew his birthday wasn't on Megan's family tree, because *he* wasn't on Megan's family tree. He typed a third comment, "Sally?"

SALLY

34

Bad things didn't come in threes. They came in ones and twos, in fours and fives. Now and again or all at once, surfacing after a long period of calm, like activated sleeper cells. It wasn't even always clear which things were bad and which things might turn out to be blessings in disguise. But right now, Harvey felt as though enough bad things had happened to him to fill an entire magazine. The caption on the daytime tabloid talk show – if it would even fit across the screen – would be too absurd to possibly be true.

I thought my dad died twenty-six years ago and then I found out from a family tree that he'd been alive all the time, until he died this year, and then I found out I had a brother who works at the same pink castle as me and his brother's mother is my mother's sister, and I fell in love with a girl online, and then I found out she's my cousin.

Harvey didn't want to think too much about what might have motivated his side of the conversations with Jess86. He didn't want to think about how it might have appeared to her either. If he had been chatting his cousin up all this time, was that the way she saw it? Harvey read back through some of his comments. With all of her encouragement and cajoling, if anything, it looked like she was grooming him.

He sat in the living room, staring at the computer until it sent itself to sleep. He touched the keyboard to wake it again. Over and over he refused to let the computer sleep, his fingertip tapping the spacebar whenever the screen began to dim. Jess86 would have to reply eventually. Hopefully not with the question: 'Who is Sally?' Harvey was so convinced it was her, it would be difficult to talk to Jess86 again without thinking he was talking to his cousin.

Her reply came late on Monday morning. Harvey was helping John Chalmers and a zero-hours temp unload yet more Halloween stock from a truck at the rear of The Castle.

There was no mock-medieval pink cladding at the back of the building and the true age and form of the structure was clear to see – the ugly metal frame, the steel lintels and the grey breezeblocks. It was like an undressed Tower Bridge – an unboxed Castle.

John Chalmers and the temp unloaded the stock onto a high-sided trolley and Harvey wheeled the trolley to the goods lift. When the truck was empty, the temp dropped a box of plastic masks and fancy-dress costumes. For the next ten minutes, John Chalmers chased the poor boy up and down the corridor. He was wearing a Michael Myers mask and waving a rubber knife. John didn't chase Harvey. He didn't goad him into participating. John Chalmers knew Harvey wasn't 'game for a laugh'. He didn't go out for a drink on Friday nights with his work colleagues or join in with any of their quizzes, sweepstakes or lottery syndicates. While John chased the temp, Harvey stood on his own waiting for them to finish, like a gooseberry in a goods lift. He was watching a video on his phone.

35

Bee-Bots Rechargeable Floor Robots

She was in an office. There was at least one desk. A teetering pile of exercise books threatened to topple over from the desk onto the floor. She appeared in shot, coming from the left-side of the room. She looked into the lens of what Harvey guessed was a webcam, and she spoke quietly, either not wanting to be overheard or because she didn't want to disturb the others in the room.

"Hi," she said to the camera. And Harvey knew she was talking to him. Not the other three billion people who might be watching. "Today I'm going to unbox some Bee-Bots."

Her hand covered the screen and then the computer seemed to fly. As Harvey followed it across the room, he realised it must be a laptop which she'd picked up and was carrying. The picture settled and she was now sitting on the floor. She folded her legs to one side. Her hair was short and parted on the right. Her hair was darker than it was when she was six or soon after that, when the photograph on the beach was taken. She was still bouncing about like she'd drunk too much Tizer.

There were other voices in the background. Harvey had caught a glimpse of an older woman sitting behind a desk when the laptop flew by, and there was a man in the background. Harvey could only see the lower half of his legs. He was wearing scuffed brown brogues and one of the laces was untied. His socks were the same shade of brown as Sally's skirt, which was speckled with cream-coloured bits of wool and looked like the inside of a Toblerone.

She was sitting on a grey mat. At her side there was a smallish box. She removed the lid and pulled out some cardboard packaging and then removed the Bee-Bots. There were six of them, round and yellow, with black stripes and smiley faces. They were arranged in a circle in some sort of plastic hive. Harvey had focussed solely on the bot aspect up until then. He hadn't realised they would be part bee as well. The way the round, yellow and black, cartoon-like bees were arranged in a circle reminded Harvey of the radiation hazard symbol. Sally removed one of the bees from the hive and placed it on the mat next to her.

"The Bee-Bot is a programmable floor robot," she said. "It's a great educational tool for teaching directional language and simple programming for small children. The buttons are clear and easy to understand. They're rechargeable in the docking station." She gestured to the docking station that Harvey had been thinking of as the Bee-Bots' hive. "I've charged this one up already," Sally said, "so that I can show you a few of the simple things it can do. I'm going to make him go forwards a couple of times and then he'll turn. First, I select forward. Two times." She pressed the forward button on the top of the Bee-Bot twice. "Then I press turn." She pressed the turn button. "And then I press go."

She pressed the go button. The Bee-Bot moved forward a few inches and then stopped. Its eyes flashed, and it beeped three times like a lorry reversing. Then the Bee-Bot started moving again. It stopped, flashed its eyes and beeped, then it turned a half circle.

"There are various different floor mats available," Sally said. "Streets and so on, and I've got to go now because those are the pips you can hear."

She looked into the lens of the webcam and smiled. The video ended abruptly. Harvey pressed pause on his phone. His next video suggestion feed was probably already full of other Bee-Bots and similar educational toys. He started the video from the beginning again and noticed a daily tear-off calendar on the wall behind Sally showing today's date, like a kidnapper's proof-of-life photograph.

36

Harvey wanted to give the Bee-Bot video the thumbs-down. Not because the video itself was so terrible. It was far from technically proficient, it was poorly-lit and the camera work was a bit of a disaster. And it needed editing. But there was no denying it had a naive beginner's charm to it. And Sally was great, of course. She had a natural, effortless onscreen presence that, with all Harvey's experience and hours of practice in front of the mirror, he could only dream of. But it was everything else that Harvey wanted to give the thumbs-down to. In particular, how he'd been made to feel like such an absolute chump. Allowing himself to be so easily duped and manipulated by his six-year-old cousin.

While he thought about registering his dislike for the video, Cuttin8Clive_09 beat him to it. By the time John Chalmers and the exhausted-looking temp had returned to the goods lift, there were four negative thumbs under the Bee-Bots video. Harvey checked his phone all morning, watching the thumb count rise. At eleven o'clock, while he was emptying the last of a high-sided trolley of Halloween items into a large wire basket, the first comment was posted.

"Don't give up the day job little girl." – Swizzel359

Followed shortly after by Davetheave9ger: "I want this bich would push my buttons."

And then Doctoroffuk: "With short hair you look like a boy. More likely dyke I fucken bet."

The comments continued. They were increasingly vicious and spiteful. The greater the numbers piling on to have their say about Sally's harmless Bee-Bot video, the more emboldened the anonymous posters. It became a game of one-upmanship – and Harvey was certain they were all men – to see who could say the most offensive thing. People were joining in without even watching the video. Not realising that his words were almost identical to

Sally's very first comment defending him, Harvey typed, "Leave her alone, you morons."

He wrote a second comment, "Sally. Change the settings of the video to unlisted and tell me when you've done it."

Harvey put the last of the rubber snakes into the wire basket and pushed the empty trolley to the lift. He shoved it inside with such force that it crashed noisily against the opposite lift wall. He slammed both sets of gates closed behind him and pressed *B*. As soon as the lift started to move, Harvey pulled the inner gate open, forcing a sudden stop. He sat on the floor of the empty trolley and waited for Sally to reply.

"I think I've changed the settings," she said.

"We'll soon know if you haven't."

"What did Andy tell you?"

"Nothing."

"How did you find out?"

"He gave me some photos. One of them had you and Auntie Cathy in it. I thought it was a nightmare. It *is* a nightmare. And then they told me at the care home that my sister had been visiting my mum. Obviously, I haven't got a sister have I. That was you wasn't it?"

":-) I'm sorry. I should have told you. I was about to. Going to see your mum was a spur of the moment thing."

"Did you give her the cushion and the flowers?"

"Yes."

"And the magazines?"

"What magazines?"

"Those horrible magazines about baby eating snakes and holidays from Hell."

Harvey had hoped the ugly magazines would cancel out Sally's pretty flowers and the comfy cushion. He was angry with Sally. He wanted to stay angry with her.

"Why did you do all this to me?" he said. "Why didn't you just tell me who you were?" It had never been more frustrating to be on a website that didn't allow italics.

"I had to find you first. Even Mum didn't know where you lived. I had looked for you before but you'd moved. And Dad refused to ever discuss what had happened. Andrew didn't even know. Unless Dad had told him. But I honestly doubt that. When Dad died, I spoke to Andy about it again. About you and your mum. But he said he wasn't interested. I thought I should try a bit harder to find you and Margaret. I could introduce you to Andy and get our mum and your mum to talk to each other again. It sounds madder written down but it made total sense at the time. After Dad died, I know Mum really missed her sister. She was grieving more for your mum than she was for her husband. And Dad died without resolving things with Mum. I didn't want the same thing to happen between her and Auntie Margaret. I searched for you online and found your videos. Even though you'd changed a lot, I was sure it was you. But I wanted to be definite. Before I said anything stupid. And then I read what all those idiots were saying about you, and I just couldn't help myself."

"You let it carry on for so long after that though," Harvey said. "Why? You must have been sure it was me at some point."

"I didn't want to make a fool out of myself."

"Instead of making one out of me you mean?"

"Is that what you think? Oh God, I'm sorry Harvey. That was the last thing on my mind. I know I should have come clean sooner, but remember I had no idea that your mum had told you Dad was dead years ago. I didn't know that until you told me yourself. I'd always assumed you just didn't want anything to do with him before. I didn't want to interfere."

"Seriously? *SERIOUSLY?*"

"You know what I mean. I was worried you wouldn't be interested. Like Andy wasn't. And I really did try telling him about you, Harvey. He said he was too upset to talk about it. I suppose he did take Dad's death a lot harder than me. Which is maybe understandable because he'd spent so much more time with him than I had. And I always forget that Dad wasn't my actual dad."

"It does sound weird. You calling him Dad," Harvey said. "The last time I saw you he was your Uncle Terry."

"I know. Mad eh. Even when I was small, I remember it being strange that your dad was now my dad too. I suppose we're more willing to accept things for what they are when we're kids."

"Like when your mum tells you that your dad's had a heart attack you mean? Were you *ever* going to tell me who you really were?"

"Yes of course I was. But then it was all going so well and I thought I'd wait until you met Andrew first. I didn't want to jinx things. And Harvey. I hate to admit it, but I was kind of enjoying it. I thought you were too. You *were* enjoying it, weren't you?"

Harvey couldn't admit she was right.

"It is what it is," Harvey said.

"Is that Andy you're quoting there? God, that drives me mad when he says that. He's still like a moody teenager sometimes."

"Does he know about any of this?" Harvey said.

"No way. And I knew he wouldn't stumble onto it online. He hates the internet. He hasn't got a computer, Harvey. I know I just said he's like a teenager, but he's also like an old man. Or maybe not old, but a man from the past. With his steam trains and his roll-ups and so on. He uses phone boxes for Christ's sake!"

"But you're not on the internet either," Harvey said. "I couldn't find you on social media."

"I'm not on social media. Hardly any of the staff at work are. The parents would only use it to share their criticisms of us. The grown-ups can be more childish, and worse bullies than the children. Just look at those morons on your video page."

"And yours now," Harvey said. "You shouldn't have encouraged them."

"I tried my best to ignore them. But we're family."

"You make us sound like the mafia."

"Lol. What did Andrew say when you saw the photo of us all?"

"He wasn't there. I was in a cab on my own," Harvey said. He suddenly had an awful memory of telling Andrew about Jess86 in the pub. At the very least, he was sure he'd implied she was his girlfriend.

"Well, I suppose my stupid brother's ruined things as usual," Sally said. "I wanted you to meet each other and instantly bond. Although, maybe not quite as instantly as you did!! You should feel incredibly honoured about that. I thought that once you'd met, Jess86 could disappear and Sally would come to see you, or ring you up or something. I would have got your address from Andrew and maybe written you a letter." Harvey thought about the unsent airmail letters he'd found. "What did you think of my video by the way?" Sally said.

"It wasn't bad for a first effort. Where did you film it?"

"The staff room."

"So, you really are a teacher then?"

"*Like* a teacher you mean? Yes."

"In Edinburgh?"

"Nearer to Bristol. I picked a place a long way away from you. I think I thought the distance would make it all more believable somehow."

"You should have said New Zealand. Why the name Jess86?"

"Jess is my cat's name."

"And eighty-six?"

"The year I was born."

It had been hidden so clearly in plain sight it was practically invisible.

"I thought you might be a robot," Harvey said.

"?"

"The eighty-sixth model of the Jess robot. I came up with some acronyms. Jupiter Experimental Synthetic Series Eighty-six was my favourite."

"Are you disappointed that I'm not a robot?"

"A little."

":-)"

"As you're just my cousin now, I think I can tell you. I really hate emoticons."

":-(And hey, what do you mean *just* your cousin?"

Harvey heard the clicking sound of someone calling the lift.

"I wish I hadn't used my real name for my video channel," he said. "I should have called myself The Unboxinator or something."

"I wouldn't have found you so easily then."

"I actually thought you were Megan," Harvey said. "Do you know her?"

"No."

"Are you sure?"

"Of course, I'm sure."

"You can't blame me for thinking it was you. You're looking for me and I find Megan's family tree at almost exactly the same time. It's a bit of a coincidence don't you think?"

"That's all it is. A coincidence. Dad's death must have been a catalyst. It triggered all these life-changing events all across the globe. That small world everyone's always banging on about."

"I definitely know about that," Harvey said. "Your brother drives a steam train just yards from where I stack shelves."

"*Our* brother."

The person calling the lift was getting impatient. The persistent clicking was like Morse code. Harvey thought he heard John Chalmers call his name.

"I have to go," Harvey said.
He pulled the lift doors closed and pressed *B*.
"So, what happens now?" Sally said.
"What would they do on television?"

37

They met by the boating lake. Like spies. Harvey took a longer lunch break, and Sally phoned in sick and drove down from Bristol. He watched her walking towards him and felt incredibly nervous. He worried he might stammer uncontrollably, which was ridiculous. It was only Sally. When she was close enough, Harvey held out his hand, but Sally wrapped her arms around him. Harvey was sure she was trying to see if she could still make her fingertips meet behind his back, just like she used to do when they were kids. He breathed in to make it less of an impossibility. He couldn't remember the last time he'd been so close to another person.

"You've changed so much," Sally said.

"Got fatter, you mean."

Sally shook her head and tutted, because what else could she say that couldn't be interpreted as either patronising or a lie?

All of Harvey's anxiety leading up to meeting Sally, planning what he was going to say, rehearsing his lines, worrying that offline he'd be struck dumb or incoherent, like a silent movie star failing to make the transition to talkies – all those fears were ill-founded. They simply picked up the conversation from where they'd left it, and not even where they'd left it online the day before, but twenty-six years ago, when Sally was six and Harvey was ten.

They sat on a wooden bench facing the boating lake.

"Have *I* changed?" Sally said.

"I thought you'd be taller. And longer."

Sally looked confused. "Why's that?"

"Don't you remember the songs? Yours was 'Long Tall Sally'".

Harvey told her about 'Peggy Sue', 'Terry' and 'Cathy's Clown', but she didn't remember. Harvey started to wonder if he'd imagined the whole thing.

"I did think of something funny about our names yesterday, though," Sally said. "Jessica and Harvey are both fictional rabbits."

If Harvey had still been talking to Jess86, he would never have picked her up on her mistake. In case she thought he was a nerd or mansplaining. But it was only Sally now. Harvey could be as nerdy and pedantic as he liked.

"Jessica Rabbit wasn't a rabbit."

"Yes, she was."

Harvey shook his head. "Nope. She was Roger Rabbit's human wife."

"Are you sure?"

"Definitely."

Sally thought it through. "She would still be a Rabbit though. With a capital R. Like you're a King and yet you don't wear a crown and you don't..." She turned her head to look at the pink building behind them. "I was going to say you don't live in a castle but—"

"I don't *live* here," Harvey said. "Did you get a chance to speak to Andrew?"

Sally sighed. "I'm afraid so."

"What did he say?"

"After he stopped swearing, you mean? He went all silent and rolled a jazz cigarette. I should probably point out that I didn't actually see any of this, as I was talking to him on the phone. But I recognised the sounds. Or the *lack* of sounds."

"Is he angry with me?" Harvey said.

"With you? *No way,*" Sally said. "Andy likes you. He flipping loves you, which is high praise indeed because he hates pretty much everyone else. Andy doesn't like people. He likes *things*. Trains and weed. That would be the title of his autobiography. Anyway, luckily for you, he's holding me completely responsible for not telling him about you before, even though I did my best to do exactly that.

But that doesn't seem to count. Oh, and he's angry with Mum, of course. He seems perfectly fine about his dad having a complicated affair, but his mum doing the same is somehow indefensible to him. Like I said, he's very old fashioned. An unreconstructed man. That's volume two of his autobiography."

Sally had mentioned Andrew's autobiography enough times for Harvey to wonder whether he might actually be writing one.

"When we were younger," Sally said, "Andy always used to say that it wasn't fair that I had a brother and he didn't. It was supposed to be a joke. But now, after he's actually had a brother for less than a week, I've suddenly told him I've got *two*. He's jealous."

"Actually, I think you're still my cousin," Harvey said. "I'm not your brother."

Sally thought for a moment. "Oh yes," she laughed. "That was an argument I didn't need to have with Andy, wasn't it?"

"He told me you didn't get on with each other," Harvey said.

"That's an understatement. But it's nowhere near as bad now that we're both older. Now we're technically grown-ups. Especially since we don't live together anymore. Growing up in the same house together was a nightmare. Especially when Mum and Dad had started arguing, too, and me and Andy chose sides."

Sally recounted details of some of her more eventful childhood fights with Andrew. Like the time when he hit her with a cricket bat, or when she'd needed stitches in her arm because he'd whipped her with the hook on the end of a fishing line. Harvey winced at the thought, but he also wanted to know if Andrew had ever gone fishing with their dad.

"He seemed so laid back in the pub," Harvey said.

"Like a land mine."

"Is that why you needed me? To break the...is it *good* news? Bad news? Did you need me to break *the news* to him?"

Sally shook her head. "If you hadn't told me you were in a pub drowning your sorrows when I first contacted you, I would have just asked you if you were my cousin or not. I would have told you who I was. I wasn't really thinking how Andy fitted into it at all at the time. But it was so easy to get swept up by the thrill of the chase. I developed this mad idea that we could fix your family tree together. And we'd all live happily ever after. One big, happy family. Both our mums would get their sisters back. Maybe it would even bring me and Andy closer together. Heaven forbid. I honestly did want to come clean with you, Harvey, but you kept making all these discoveries. You made it all too bloody enjoyable."

"I am sorry," Harvey said, attempting sarcasm. "Would you like me to have pretended I hadn't seen the photo of you all together on the beach, so you could have had a bit more fun?"

"Ah yes, *the photograph,*" Sally rolled her eyes. "*Spoiler alert.*"

"I've got it with me." Harvey gave her the cigar box.

"Cigars?" Sally said. She opened the box.

"Andrew said it was just you, him and a tobacconist at Dad's funeral. Was that a joke about the tobacconist?"

"No, the tobacconist was there," Sally said. "But so were a few of Dad's friends from the pub. And the tobacconist's wife."

"I probably misunderstood what Andrew meant."

"He more likely exaggerated. Do people actually still say tobacconist?"

"You did say Andrew was old fashioned. Why didn't your mum go to the funeral?"

"Because she thought Auntie Margaret might be there."

"But Mum didn't even know he'd died."

"I know. And I did try telling my mum that. But she seemed to think Margaret might have read it in the papers."

"Was it in the papers?"

Sally smiled and shook her head. She took the photos out of the cigar box and flicked quickly through them, as though she'd seen them all before, only pausing to answer Harvey's questions – *Where's that? When was this taken? Who took this one? Do you think he looks like me there*? He had the feeling that looking at the pictures of his dad irritated Sally. Maybe they reminded her of a time she'd rather forget. She reached the torn wedding day photo.

"I didn't even know my mum and dad were divorced until Andrew told me Dad had remarried," Harvey said. "He tried to make me feel better about it by saying it wasn't a big wedding."

Sally looked up from the photograph. "Did he tell you it was in Las Vegas?"

"You're joking."

Sally shook her head. "Elvis impersonator and everything. Also torn out of the photograph."

Harvey couldn't believe it. "He married my mum at the registry office in Plymouth. It rained. Did it rain in Las Vegas?"

"Not unless it was part of the hotel's theme."

"Were you there?" Harvey said.

Sally nodded apologetically.

"I would have liked to go to Las Vegas," Harvey said. "He never took us anywhere."

"Why don't you go now?"

"I can't leave my mum."

"I could go and visit her while you were away," Sally said.

"I'll think about it," Harvey lied. "Did you know Andrew's going to Russia?"

Sally looked at him, open-mouthed. "*Is he*?"

"On a train that looks like a toothpaste tube," Harvey

said. It felt great to finally know something everyone else didn't already know. "He's going to Japan as well. He asked me if I wanted to go with him."

"He hasn't told me or Mum about any of this," Sally said. She shrugged. "Still. My offer stands for Andy's train trip too. If, for some insane reason, you *really* want to go on a long train journey with my brother, I'll take care of Auntie Margaret."

"Maybe when I get back from Vegas."

"I'm serious," Sally said. She closed the cigar box and sat back on the bench, with her hands clasped behind her head.

"Some of my earliest ever memories are at this place," she said. "I'm not technically saying that it's crap now. But I think I must remember it differently."

They watched a young couple swapping places in a rowing boat. The boat rocked from side to side as they stepped awkwardly past each other. Harvey and Sally both sighed with disappointment when neither of them fell overboard.

"You brought me here when I was a little girl." Sally said.

"Did I? By myself?"

"Mum was here as well. She worked in the shop."

"I don't remember that. What did she do?"

"She worked on the tills. Do they still have tills?"

Harvey said yes, not sure if she was joking or not.

"And do they still have the animals at the back of the shop?" Sally said.

"The Kingdom of Pets. Yes. There are hardly any animals there though. It's more of a kingdom of empty cages."

"I didn't like it," Sally said. "It was cruel. And it stunk of poo. I felt especially sorry for the birds. Imagine being able to fly and having to spend your life in a tiny cage in a shop shaped like a castle."

"There's still a myna bird there," Harvey said. "It's not

for sale though. It's more of a customer attraction. Do you remember John Chalmers who I told you about? My boss. The one who said the plane crash was 'our nine eleven'?"

"I'd seriously like to meet this guy. He sounds like a right catch."

"Be careful what you wish for," Harvey said. "Anyway. John has spent the last six months trying to get the myna bird to swear. Apparently, he swore at a customer last week."

"The bird did or John Chandlers?"

"*Chalmers*. And it was the bird that swore."

"What did it say?"

Harvey wasn't sure if it was because Sally was a teacher or because she was his six-year old cousin, or both, but he found he couldn't repeat the myna bird's swear words in front of her.

"Shall we go for a walk?" Harvey said.

They got up from the bench. Sally took their picture with her phone.

"What happened to your forehead?" she said.

Harvey traced the L shaped scab with his finger. "An aide memoiré fell on me."

He gave Sally the full tour of the Castle grounds – the children's fun fair, the eighteen holes of adventure golf and the twenty food concessions. The fair was deserted apart from a few members of staff. Sally said she felt like the Sultan of Brunei.

"What if we get lost?" she asked, as they walked through the entrance of the maze.

"We won't."

Harvey asked Sally what his father was like. "Was he a bad man?"

"How do you mean?

"I wondered if he turned to more serious crime. Andrew was quite cagey about it."

"No one likes a grass," Sally said, tapping the side of

her nose with her finger. "But no, he wasn't really bad. Not Hitler bad. But then, I suppose it depends on whether you think there's such a thing as a victimless crime or not. As far as I know though, he didn't ever walk into a bank with a sawn-off shotgun or mug an old lady. Whether that makes him a good person or a bad criminal, I don't know. I probably wouldn't buy him a T-shirt with World's Best Dad printed on. But you already know that, of course, him living so close and not bothering to contact you all those years."

"We sell those T-shirts in the shop," Harvey said. "World's Best Dad. I think he did try and contact me once, by the way."

Harvey told Sally about the time he thought he'd seen his dad in the village, how he'd followed and lost him.

"What would you have done if you had caught up with him?" Sally said.

"I've thought about that a lot lately. I think it would have been unbearably awkward. For both of us. We would have been like complete strangers again after such a long time. What would you have done? In my position?"

"I would have grabbed him by the lapels and asked him where the bloody hell he'd been. I'd want pocket money, backdated, with interest. I would have rugby tackled him to the ground—"

Harvey laughed. "Perhaps if I hadn't been so unfit I might have caught up with him."

"Hmmm. I think you're presuming he would have been fit enough to escape."

Harvey wondered if she meant because of the cancer.

"I've been wondering if he'd come to make peace with the world before he left it," Harvey said. "Does that sound romantic or stupid?"

Sally said of course it didn't sound stupid. They turned a blind corner, heading deeper into the maze.

"Are you sure we're not going to get lost?" Sally said.

"More people get lost in the shop. After a Pensioners' Bonanza they always find at least one old lady the next morning wandering around in a daze in the Haberdashery department, trying to find the way out."

"That's a joke, right?"

"Apparently, it did happen one year, according to John anyway."

Harvey told Sally about the Pensioners' Bonanza. There were two every year, one in the summer and one in the winter. For two days a year, everything in the store was reduced by 20% for local senior citizens. Coaches would ferry customers in from surrounding towns and villages, and many more arrived in sheltered housing car pools and on care home minibuses. There were always arguments at the Bonanzas. Fights would often break out between customers who were well into their seventies and eighties. The St. John Ambulance would be on stand-by in the car park all day, and the police were frequently called. Black Friday was tame by comparison. Since her sixtieth birthday, Harvey's mother had never missed a Pensioners' Bonanza. Harvey remembered how she'd return home afterwards with armfuls of carrier bags, buzzing with excitement and stories, as though she'd been to the circus or for a day at the races. Harvey told Sally that because of his mother's phobia of stairs and her general confused state, he doubted she would make the upcoming Winter Bonanza. Sally offered to take her in her car. Harvey said maybe.

They continued through the maze, going nowhere in particular but never actually lost. The big pink castle was always there on their horizon, preventing them from losing their bearings.

They talked about Christmases when they were children and all the food Harvey's mother used to make. Sally reminded him about running races on the beach and the time he'd filled his pockets with stones and his trousers fell down as a result. If going to the pub with Andrew was like digging up a time capsule, walking through though the maze with Sally was like hitting a piñata full of memories with a big stick.

"I used to love firework nights at your house," Sally said.

Harvey said he was surprised she was old enough to remember.

"Remember, remember, the fifth of November," she said. "You always had the biggest fireworks at your house, and your mum made tons of food, baked potatoes and soup. I remember the soup."

"Do you remember how we used to go out the next morning to look for used fireworks?" Harvey said.

"I do. I still like the smell of bonfire night, and how it always seems to be foggy for two days before and afterwards."

"Dad used to say it was the smoke from the previous year's bonfires and that it took exactly one year to circulate around the globe. I don't know why I've suddenly remembered that. And I expect it was nonsense."

"He certainly loved a bonfire."

"I used to help him collect things to burn for weeks before," Harvey said. "He'd turn up on the fifth of November with a load of illegal and dangerous looking fireworks. And he'd light them with his cigarette lighter, never at arm's length, not following the firework code, often with a lit cigarette in his mouth."

"You had such a realistic looking Guy Fawkes one year that I thought you were burning a real man," Sally said.

"I always felt like there was an element of the destruction of evidence to Dad's bonfires, so who knows?"

"We didn't have any fireworks after my mum and dad split up," Sally said. "Mum always hated them. She still does. Every bonfire night we have to keep her indoors like a cat."

Harvey told Sally that once his dad was gone the

fireworks stopped in their house, too. It sounded daft but Sally knew what he meant.

"I've just remembered," Harvey said. He stopped walking and put his hand in his coat pocket. He fished around in the lining for a while and pulled out the airmail letters he'd found. He gave them to Sally. "They're a bit late."

Sally read his childish correspondence. She read his descriptions of his school building and the food. She looked at his drawings of spaceships and aliens.

"My mum told me she'd post them to you," Harvey said.

Sally looked for an address or any stamps on the letters.

"She didn't post them," Harvey said, "obviously. I do wonder why she kept them, though."

"I think she was always planning on telling you," Sally said.

"Telling me what?"

"Everything."

"What? And *she just forgot*?"

"It can't have been easy for her. She was only trying to protect you."

"You sound very sure of all this," Harvey said.

"She told me."

"She *told* you? When?"

"When I went to see her at the care home."

"But how?" Harvey said. *Semaphore*? he wanted to say. *Telepathy*? Some form of blink once for yes, twice for no arrangement?

"She just told me," Sally said.

"Why the hell didn't she just tell me?"

Sally replied with a look that said, *duh,* and Harvey realised Sally was saying, his mum hadn't told him she was protecting him... *because* she was protecting him.

"I found the letters in the sideboard," Harvey said.

"The one you used to hide in?"

"How did you know about that?"

"You used to do it when we played hide and seek."

"I don't remember that."

"I used to think you'd vanished," Sally said. "It scared the shit out of me."

"I tried again," Harvey said. "To fit in the sideboard. When I was looking for photos."

Sally laughed.

"I thought I'd never walk again," Harvey said. "I almost called the fire brigade." Sally was really laughing hard now. Harvey laughed too. "I was wearing an incredibly long scarf at the time, which really didn't help."

They left the maze, both still laughing, and started walking towards the train station. They talked about some of the things that had happened since they'd last seen each other, all the places they'd been to and so on. Harvey had so little to share that he was tempted to make something up. He didn't even have an imaginary internet girlfriend any more.

Sally told him she was married and had a four-year old daughter called Molly.

"Like the song," Harvey said. Sally claimed to not know it. She asked Harvey to sing it, but he flatly refused.

He took out his phone. "It's on the Fusilier jukebox. I think 'Good Golly Miss Molly' and 'Long Tall Sally' are by the same singer."

Harvey was pleased when he found both songs were by Little Richard. Sally stopped abruptly. She put a hand on Harvey's shoulder to stop him. Sally stared at him, with her mouth wide open.

"Oh my God, Harvey."

"What?"

"Richard is my husband's name."

"Seriously?"

"And he's only five-foot tall."

"Shut up."

"Oh," Sally said. "Wait a minute. My mistake. His

name's Bruno. He's six foot one." Sally laughed and started walking. Harvey looked at his phone.

"*Don't* look up 'songs with Bruno in'," Sally said.

Harvey stifled a laugh.

"What is it?" Sally asked.

"Nothing."

"Seriously. What's so funny? Come on," she adopted her severe school teacher voice, "I've got all day, Harvey King. Nobody's going anywhere until you tell us all what's so funny."

"It's just that Bruno sounds like another made up name. Is his surname Eighty-Six as well?"

"It's Lucas, actually," Sally said, sounding offended. "He's Portuguese."

Harvey wasn't sure if any of that was true. He would have to wait until he met Bruno to find out. He presumed they'd meet. He was particularly looking forward to meeting Sally's daughter.

"Where would Molly fit on the family tree?" Harvey said. "Is she my niece?"

"Your second cousin," Sally said but she seemed unsure. "Actually, I think she's your first cousin once removed. You can call her your niece if you like, though. She's definitely going to be calling you Uncle Harvey. By the way, there was something I've been meaning to ask you."

"Oh no," Harvey said. "What is it now? No more revelations, *please*."

Sally paused dramatically. She looked him firmly in the eye.

"Do you think I should buy the headphones?"

Harvey tutted.

Sally sighed. She looked at her watch. "I suppose we can't put it off any longer. Let's go and see my stupid brother."

"*Our* stupid brother."

38

On the steps down to the station, Harvey was as anxious as when he was about to meet Andrew before going to the pub. They'd ended up getting on so well, but they had both been pretty drunk, and Harvey was worried this latest revelation about Sally might have reset them back to being strangers on a train.

There was a family on the platform. On the surface at least, they looked like the perfect nuclear family: a mother, a father, one boy and one girl. The full set. But who knew? Maybe the mother and father were actually sister and brother, and the children were somebody else's kids. They were waiting for the next train. It was there but not ready for them to board yet. Harvey looked at the station clock. The train was going to be late. He thought there might be something wrong with the engine. Or maybe it was the clock that was wrong. He checked his phone and ruled out a broken clock. The father of the nuclear family saw Harvey's work fleece and approached him.

"We've been waiting for fifteen minutes," the man said.

"I don't work here," Harvey told him.

The man looked accusingly at the logo on Harvey's fleece.

"I work in the shop," Harvey explained. "Not on the train. Wait a minute."

Harvey walked along the platform to the front of the train. He looked in the engine and then back at Sally and called out with some alarm, "He's not here."

"That's what I've been saying," the nuclear father shouted back.

"Do you think he's gone to Russia already?" Sally called out unhelpfully.

Now that Harvey thought about it, he hadn't heard the whistle or seen the train passing by the boating lake or the maze earlier. He walked back along the platform to where Sally was standing. She was talking to the mother of the nuclear family. He overheard Sally joking about a 'replacement miniature bus service.'

"Where do you think he is?" Harvey asked her.

Sally shrugged. "I don't know. But the Fat Controller isn't going to be happy."

The nuclear father looked at Harvey, probably because Sally had said 'Fat'.

Harvey suggested they check the ticket office. He walked there with Sally. She knocked on the door. Harvey showed her the padlock. The shed was locked from the outside.

The nuclear father was arguing with the nuclear mother, or his sister, his second cousin or whoever. The nuclear fallout. Sally said to Harvey, loud enough to be overheard a mile away, "Those children should be at school."

They went back up the stone steps. Harvey looked for Andrew in the nearby toilets, and they went to see if he was at any of the food concession stands. Harvey wanted to stop and buy food for the journey. He didn't know if he was actually going anywhere, but something told him he was.

In the car park, Harvey asked Bob Carpenter if he'd seen Andrew.

"The train driver you were arguing with?" Bob said.

Harvey nodded, turning to Sally, "We weren't arguing."

Bob said he'd seen Andrew yesterday but not since. Harvey thanked him and they checked the other buses, speaking to the drivers. There was no sign of Andrew.

"Where do you think he is?" Harvey said to Sally.

"Where's his car?"

"I didn't know he had one," Harvey said, surprised. "He gets the bus to work."

"Hmm." Sally said she'd drive around for a bit and see if she could find him. Harvey wasn't sure if she meant drive around Devon and Cornwall, drive around the grounds of The Castle or just the car park.

"I'm sure he'll come back," Harvey said.

"I've taken the day off work and come all the way down here," Sally said. "I'm not making a second trip because he's run away like a big kid."

She started walking through the car park, away from the shuttle buses.

"I'm coming too then," Harvey said.

"Don't you have to be back at work?"

"I doubt anyone would notice I was missing. I was in the same class at school as the assistant manager and she hasn't recognised me in seven years."

"What if today's the day she does?"

"What, because I'm a more striking presence when I'm not there, you mean?"

Sally rolled her eyes. She said she would drive to Andrew's house and see if he was there. Harvey insisted on going with her.

"If they do miss me at work," he said, "I'll say I had to leave in a hurry. I'll say it was a family emergency."

"I don't think it's quite that," Sally said.

They walked to the far side the car park. Harvey tried to guess which car Sally's would be. She stopped next to a dirty hatchback. It was the car Harvey would have picked.

"You'll have to excuse the mess," Sally said, opening the door. She leant in to dismantle a child seat and threw it into the back. The floor of the car was littered with sweet wrappers and crisp bags. It reminded Harvey of home. He climbed into the front passenger seat and pushed a takeaway coffee cup away with his foot. Sally said he would probably want to move the seat back because Molly had been sitting there. Harvey adjusted the seat, but not as much as he really needed to. In the same way that he'd taken a smaller slice of birthday cake so Asha didn't think he was greedy.

On the way to Andrew's house they stopped at the Ramshackle. Harvey looked in the three bars and the men's toilets. He was terrified that Craig or Anthony might still be in there, stuck in the urinal.

Sally was getting more and more irritated that she'd arranged to meet Andrew and he hadn't been there. Harvey thought her irritation was the reason for her erratic driving. Harvey held onto his seat as she overtook another car in the inside lane.

"If this was a television show," Harvey said as they drove past the cemetery, "Andrew would be in there talking to a gravestone."

Sally slammed on the brakes and pulled a sudden right turn across the middle of the road. She drove in through the cemetery gates. Harvey almost broke a fingernail, gripping his seat so tightly.

"Dad was cremated," Sally said. "But there's a bit of him in the memorial garden. We should check. Just in case."

Harvey looked at her. "A *bit* of him?"

"Ashes."

Sally parked the car and they walked into the cemetery, following the same path Harvey had taken – yesterday? The day before? He'd lost all track of time. It could have been a year ago. Sally said the huge gothic monument at the centre of the cemetery looked like a mini Albert Memorial. She'd recently taught her class about it for some royal anniversary or other. The crayon interpretations of the monument were still up on the classroom wall.

"It's nearly two hundred feet high and took ten years to build," Sally said. "It cost ten million pounds in today's money. Queen Victoria never stopped mourning for Albert, you know. She wore black for the rest of her life and kept all Albert's rooms exactly as they were when he was alive, changing the towels and putting hot water in the rooms every day." She sounded like a tour guide. "It's funny, don't you think, that Victoria built a massive Albert Memorial directly opposite the Royal Albert Hall, because she wanted her husband's name to be remembered. Can you imagine how horrified she'd be if she knew his name *had* been remembered, but for a slightly different reason?"

"What do you mean?"

"*Prince Albert*?" she said.

When Harvey realised what Sally was referring to, he felt his face redden. It wasn't what he wanted to be talking to his six-year old cousin about, and definitely not in a graveyard. He just hoped she hadn't told her pupils the same thing. They walked through a leafy archway into the memorial garden. Harvey was about to meet his father at last.

He saw Andrew first, standing at the far side of the memorial garden. Andrew turned his head and looked at Harvey and then he saw Sally. His eyes were bloodshot and Harvey thought he'd been crying. And then Harvey smelled the sweet aroma, sweeter than all the roses, lilies, orchids and chrysanthemums in the memorial garden. Andrew had been smoking a joint.

Later on, Harvey would have time to reflect on what a peculiar family reunion he'd found himself at the centre of. His stoner half-brother, his sister who was actually his cousin, the remains of his twice-dead father, and a woman with a white stripe in her hair, who looked so much like Harvey's mother, he had an instant craving for Chinese food.

CATHY

39

Auntie Cathy had always been the quieter sister. Seeing her again, it all came flooding back to Harvey. Cathy was her own aide-mémoire. Harvey's aunt used to be scared of the dark. She was also scared of thunder and lightning and spiders. Auntie Cathy, who used to jump with fright at the slightest unexpected thing. Harvey remembered how he and Sally would sneak up on her when she was doing the washing up or reading a book. They could scare the living daylights out of her with a boo or a popped paper bag.

Cathy used to have a red shopping bicycle. It had small whitewall tyres and a basket on the front. She drank Lucozade from a bottle wrapped in orange cellophane, even when she wasn't ill. When it rained, Cathy disappeared under one of those transparent plastic umbrellas shaped like a mushroom. It had big googly eyes on it. In the summer she used it as a parasol.

Cathy was always softly spoken, almost talking in whispers, and often behind her hand or with her head turned slightly away or angled down like Princess Diana. People called her 'Chatty Cathy', in the same ironic way John Chalmers sometimes called Harvey 'Slim'.

Seeing his aunt in the aptly named memorial garden, it was impossible for Harvey to think of her as a home-wrecker anymore. This softly spoken woman, who was scared of fireworks and who'd been allergic to nuts and dairy, years before it became a thing. It was Harvey's dad. He was the home-wrecker. Destroying marriages and taking an axe to family trees. Harvey's father was the lumberjack.

Andrew stubbed his cigarette out with the heel of his shoe and put the dog end behind his ear.

"What the hell are you doing here?" Sally asked him.

"We came to see Dad's memorial," Andrew said.

It was a grand description for the sad looking rose and

laminated index card with 'Terence A. King' printed on it. Harvey presumed the 'bit' of his father was buried in the earth beneath the rose. He had an almost overpowering urge to dig his hand into the soil.

"I thought we'd be back in time to meet you," Andrew told Sally. "The traffic was bad."

Sally shook her head. "There are some pretty irate passengers waiting for you in the station."

Andrew shrugged.

"You'll lose your job," Sally said.

"I'll say it was a family emergency."

Hang on a minute, Harvey wanted to say. 'Family emergency' is *my* excuse.

"I've come a long way to meet you today, Andrew," Sally said. "It was going to be a nice day. You've sort of ruined it now."

Andrew shrugged again. He was trying to appear nonchalant, but he wasn't as confident or cool as he'd been on the train or in the pub with Harvey. His older sister was clearly the boss of him.

"And why have you brought Mum here?" Sally said.

"Because she wasn't at the funeral."

"That isn't anything to do with me, if that's what you're implying. She didn't *want* to come."

"I thought you'd be pleased," Andrew said. "You told me you wanted to unite the family."

"Yes, but now you've just made things unnecessarily awkward."

Andrew said he was sorry, but in the most unapologetic and insincere way. He took a tobacco pouch out of his pocket.

"I can't believe you're doing that in front of Mum," Sally said. It was the first time she'd acknowledged her mother's presence in the memorial garden.

"She doesn't mind," Andrew said. "Do you, Mum?"

Auntie Cathy wasn't listening. She'd been staring at

Harvey. Looking him up and down as though he was familiar, but she wasn't quite sure why yet.

"You're fatter," she said at last.

"*Mum!*" Sally said.

Andrew laughed.

"It's all right," Harvey said with a smile. "I am. A *lot* fatter."

His aunt's say-what-you-see honesty was refreshing. The kind of non-malevolent bluntness he usually had to go to the doctors for.

"How is Margaret?" Cathy said.

Harvey thought about how long his aunt had waited for the opportunity to speak to someone who could provide the answer. Unfortunately, he wasn't sure it was him. Harvey took out his phone. He found the slideshow of his mother and gave the phone to Auntie Cathy. He showed her where the play button was and she started the slideshow. The *Benny Hill Show* theme tune started playing. Loudly.

It might not have been appropriate for the memorial garden of a cemetery, but to Harvey it seemed like a more fitting tribute to his father than a wilting shrub and a laminated index card with his name on. A better monument to his father even than the gothic marble and bronze cock ring, towering over all the other gravestones like The Castle, would have been. He switched the sound off on his phone and gave it back to Cathy. She sat on a stone bench and watched the slideshow of her sister.

"We could go and see her if you like," Harvey said, not thinking of what the possible consequences might be.

40

Harvey got his funeral cortège, Andrew's Renault Clio and Sally's Volkswagen Golf. Harvey went with Andrew. His compact modern car, with its metallic purple paintwork and Bluetooth MP3 player, was so at odds with the man behind the wheel, with his hand-rolled cigarettes and love of steam trains, that Harvey thought Andrew must have stolen the car. He found himself avoiding touching anything for fear of leaving fingerprints.

Andrew didn't drive as slowly as he'd promised Sally he would. He took turnings without indicating and sped up at amber traffic lights. Even with Sally's poor driving skills, Harvey wished he'd chosen to go with her instead.

"I bet you regret ever starting your family tree," Andrew said.

Harvey thought about everything that had happened in the relatively short period since Megan's family tree had arrived on his computer. He'd been catfished by his cousin, found a half-brother he didn't know existed, and been reunited with an aunt he thought lived in New Zealand and presumed he'd never see again. He'd ridden in the engine of a steam train, sounded the whistle, been in a low-speed car chase and taken drugs. He was now on the way to some sort of intervention at a care home.

"She'll be talking about me, you know," Andrew said, when he saw Harvey checking behind them for Sally's VW.

"But aren't you talking about *her*, just by saying that?" Harvey said, sending Andrew into a silent sulk.

"I tried a bit of your cake," Harvey said, to break the silence.

"How was it?" Andrew said.

"It tasted nice, but I didn't really feel anything, to be honest. I was a bit more relaxed than usual I suppose, and I had no recollection of going to bed."

Andrew turned to look at him, causing the car to swerve

a little to the right. Harvey gripped his seat, leaving fingerprints in the upholstery.

"Exactly how much did you eat?" Andrew said.

Harvey held his thumb and forefinger barely apart. "About that much."

Andrew smiled. The car swerved again.

"Can you keep your eyes on the road, please?" Harvey said.

"Did it help with your stammering?" Andrew said.

"I don't stutter when I'm on my own. I don't even know if it's possible. Like trying to tickle yourself. Or strangling yourself."

"Have you tried strangling yourself?"

"Hasn't everyone?"

Andrew looked at him again. The car swerved. Harvey closed his eyes.

"If you want any more cakes," Andrew said, "just ask."

Harvey opened one eye. "Can you make one without the drugs?"

"I'm a chemist, Haitch. Not a baker."

"It's just up here on the right," Harvey said, pointing at the Wildways gates.

Andrew turned into the short driveway. He leaned out of the window and pressed the button to open the gates and drove through. Sally and Cathy arrived just behind. They parked the two cars on either side of the Wildways minibus. Harvey got out of Andrew's car. He watched to see if Andrew wiped the door handles. He was a little disappointed when he didn't.

After Sally had finished telling Andrew off for not waiting for her, Harvey entered the care home door code. Everyone followed him in and he signed them into the visitors book. It felt good to be leading for a change, the one who knew the way. Maybe that was why Andrew had taken his mother to the cemetery. To be in charge of something. They walked along the corridor to the office and Harvey introduced everyone to Asha. He asked her if they could use the large lounge on the first floor.

Cathy was understandably nervous about meeting her sister for the first time in twenty-six years. Harvey hoped he hadn't made a terrible mistake bringing everyone to the care home. He did his best to hide his own doubts by reassuring Cathy that everything would be fine. He showed everyone into the lounge and they sat in an assortment of armchairs. Harvey made more preparatory excuses for his mother. He warned everyone she could be hard to understand and had difficulty communicating, sometimes using the wrong words. They all told him it didn't matter.

Harvey went along the corridor. He looked at his mother's door picture, touched it for luck, took his shoes off and knocked.

His mother was thankfully dressed and in a good mood. She said hello and asked if it was Sunday already.

"No, Mum. You're having dinner downstairs today. But before that, you've got some visitors. They're in the lounge. Do you want to come along and see them?"

"Where?"

"Just along the hall. Do you need to use the bathroom first?"

"I went," Harvey's mother said, and without questioning who her visitors might be, she picked up her handbag.

"You don't need your bag, Mum."

His mother opened the handbag and put the television remote control inside.

"You definitely don't need the remote control."

She clicked the bag shut.

"Okay," Harvey said. "Bring your bag. Are you ready?"

His mother opened the wardrobe and started going through her clothes.

"We're only going to the lounge, Mum. You won't need your coat."

She looked out of the window at the grey skies and the

drizzle falling on the hill farms in the distance. She took her coat off the hanger.

"How about I carry it for you, just in case?" Harvey said, taking the coat from her.

They finally left the room and walked slowly along the corridor. Harvey's mother held tightly onto his arm, as though they were crossing a rope bridge over a ravine. Her coat was slung over his other arm. His mother wasn't wearing shoes.

"He left," she said.

"Who left, Mum?"

"In the car. A long time away."

"Dad? You mean Dad left?"

"He did a bad thing."

"I know."

"Very bad. He smoked too much as well," Harvey's mother said.

"He did, didn't he? Like a chimney."

Harvey went into the lounge first, followed by his mother. Everyone stood, as though the Queen had arrived, handbag and all. She looked around the room. She didn't appear angry or confused or frightened. She didn't even seem particularly surprised to see everyone there.

"Do you know who this is, Mum?" Harvey said.

His mother gave an almost identical answer as when he'd asked her who was in the family beach photograph. Quite matter-of-fact, as though everything was completely normal, with just one person missing from the picture.

"The girl, Terry's boy, my friend."

Harvey was about to tell her that Cathy was actually her sister, but he realised 'my friend' was exactly what she'd meant to say.

Cathy had been so anxious about this moment that she'd avoided it for twenty-six years. But now it was happening, she couldn't hold herself back. Cathy stepped forward and hugged her sister, repeating over and over that she was sorry.

"You're higher," Harvey's mother said.

Cathy laughed through her tears, "Actually, I think you're shrinking, Margaret."

Harvey's mother was looking over Cathy's shoulder at Andrew, the only one in the room not in tears.

"Terry's boy," she said. "He's the same."

Cathy stepped away from the embrace with Harvey's mother and turned to look at her son, the living, breathing aide-mémoire of his father and the husband to both her and her sister. It was such a complicated monkey puzzle of a family tree. Harvey had thought he'd be jealous of Andrew for being the one to take after their father, but he wasn't. In spite of all her problems, he would rather be like his mum.

"Why don't you sit down, Mum?" Harvey said.

Cathy helped her sister into a flowery patterned armchair – both hands on, Harvey noticed – and then she sat herself down on a plain green chair next to her sister.

"It's nice here, isn't it, Margaret?" Cathy said.

"I like the puddings. There's no view."

Cathy looked out of the window, at the trees and bungalows, the tidy back gardens, the windmills and the fields and farms – a horse was grazing in the fine rain on the top of the hill.

"It's better than the view from my house," Cathy said. "I live opposite a wastewater works." She pinched her nose. "It stinks to high heaven as well."

Just like Harvey and Sally, the two sisters seemed to pick up from where they'd left off. Whether that was because everything bad that had happened between them was all water under the bridge now, or maybe because Harvey's mother wasn't aware there'd ever been a bridge, Harvey didn't know. But when he considered all their lost and wasted years, he couldn't help feeling this could all have happened a lot sooner.

Cathy continued to sing the care home's praises. She liked the wallpaper and the carpet and the comfortable chair she was sitting on. She said Asha seemed nice and another member of staff who'd said hello to her in the corridor was nice, too. She liked the way it smelled like a real home and not a hospital or a charity shop. Cathy mentioned the wastewater works where she lived again.

Harvey was so happy to hear his aunt echoing many of the positive things he'd told his mother about Wildways when he was trying to convince her – and himself – that it was best for her to move in.

Harvey's mother pointed at Harvey. *"My son,"* she declared.

"He's a lot bigger than when I last saw him," Cathy said.

Harvey frowned. "None taken."

"He makes me Chinese dinners and shows me cartoon films," Harvey's mother said. "He's very good."

"And you're very lucky," Cathy said. She looked at Sally and Andrew. "We're both very lucky."

There was the sound of rattling cups on saucers in the corridor and the squeak of a wheel.

"The girl with the tea trolley," Harvey's mother announced, apparently now name checking everyone in the room. The girl with the tea trolley said hello. She was surprised to see such a crowd.

"Do you want tea, Margaret?" she said.

Harvey watched his mother's face, thinking about what Asha had told him, wondering what complicated equations were going through her head. Was she trying to work out if she'd had a cup of tea recently? Did the girl make a nice cup of tea? Would she prefer a cold drink? Would she need to use the toilet as a result of having a cup of tea? Asha had said that if she couldn't find answers in her short-term memory, she'd need to look further back in time. Harvey imagined his mother's whole life flashing before her. Meeting a man at a dinner and dance and dancing to three songs with him. Getting married on a rainy day, the birth of her son, her sister and husband having an affair, her sister being banished to New Zealand. Would she have to go through all of that, just for the sake of a cup of tea?

"Can my friend have one as well?" Harvey's mother said, pointing at Cathy.

The girl with the tea trolley looked at the other three people in the lounge.

"I'm not sure there's enough tea in the urn for everyone," she said.

Harvey and Sally said they didn't mind going without and the girl poured tea for Harvey's mother, Cathy and Andrew. She had just recognised Andrew from school. She asked him how he was and told him she was working at the care home for the experience and she was training to be a nurse. There was nothing like being in a room with a teacher, a nurse and a train driver to make Harvey feel so much like a shelf-stacker. The girl's name was Caroline, and Harvey knew that 'Sweet Caroline' would be in his head for the rest of the day, or at least until he next saw Asha.

Caroline asked everyone if they wanted milk and sugar and Cathy said she couldn't drink milk. Harvey thought of some of the food he wouldn't have eaten if he was allergic to dairy: cheese and butter, cream, crème caramels, custards and profiteroles, éclairs and biscuits, ice cream, but it just made him hungry. He'd been so caught up with everything else that he hadn't eaten since breakfast.

Caroline put two cups of tea on a small table between Harvey's mother and his aunt and gave another cup to Andrew. Harvey asked her if she'd take a photograph of the whole family together. He thought she raised a quizzical eyebrow. With the exception of the two women with the Dickie Davies hair, as a family group they were as mismatched as the armchairs.

They all grouped together around Harvey's mother.

"Say cheese," Caroline said.

"Teas," Harvey's mother said, and they all laughed.

Harvey took Sally and Andrew downstairs to the small garden at the rear of the building, leaving his mother and aunt in the lounge. They had a lot to catch up on. Their voices could be heard all the way along the corridor. Harvey would often hear his mother, still chatting away to herself or to the television before he arrived or after he'd left. It was nice to hear the television answer back for a change.

MARGARET

41

Five Chinese Sundays passed, a breakfast huddle assembled and dispersed and Mateusz from Toys and Games, who'd spent most of October with a skull painted on his face, was crowned King of The Castle. Halloween was over at last and Christmas had arrived. Tinsel and fairy lights hung from trees and bushes and along both sides of the drawbridge. A reindeer had joined the other animal statues in the trees on Castle Road and the pumpkins outside the main entrance had been replaced with Christmas trees. A one-eyed mechanical Santa, more terrifying than anything on show during Halloween, waved his broken arm at customers when they walked through the foyer. For two insufferable months, 'Walking in the Air' and 'Simply Having a Wonderful Christmastime' would play on the public-address system, sending Harvey almost round the bend as he filled shelves with novelty jumpers and greetings cards, advent calendars and Christmas crackers. Every morning he'd wake up covered in glitter.

Harvey had been on the shuttle bus sixty-eight times since the family reunion in the Wildways lounge. He'd said hello and goodbye to Bob Carpenter 136 times and ridden the steam train next to Andrew twice. Until the end of December, the train would stop in the tunnel so that children could meet Santa, just as it had when Harvey was a child. In the first week of November, a boat caught fire on the lake. Arson was suspected and the lake was closed until an investigation was carried out. The lake reopened two days letter. No investigation had taken place. At the fun fair, the teacups had been repainted, and still no one had managed to get themselves lost in the maze.

Harvey updated his family tree. He moved Auntie Cathy so that she was next to his father, who now had two wives. The displacement left his mother without a sister, and Cathy as an only child, so Harvey moved Cathy back beside his mother.

He'd thought about Andrew being both his cousin and his half-brother and wasn't sure where to place him on the family tree. Did one relative supersede the other? Like in a game of Rock, Paper, Scissors or a hand of cards? Was half a brother better than a full cousin? Harvey added Molly to the tree, and Sally's husband, Bruno, who Harvey hadn't found any songs about. Harvey posted the family tree online.

A week later, he received a web message from Megan in Canada. She was thrilled to discover a whole new branch of her family she'd previously known nothing about. Harvey replied. He said that if Megan was ever in the UK, they should meet up. Secretly though, he hoped she would never take him up on the offer. He was happy with the family he already had.

Shortly after posting the family tree online, a brand-new one appeared on Harvey's computer. Megan had found another distant half-cousin. His name was Rufus. He lived in, of all places, New Zealand. Harvey updated his tree once more and printed it onto three sheets of paper. He taped them together and added fruit and leaves, apple blossom, and a myna bird, perched on the tip of a branch. He drew and coloured everything in by hand – no apps, no tools or drop-down menus. He used felt-tip pens his mother had bought at a summer Pensioners' Bonanza five years ago and had sat unused in the top drawer of the sideboard ever since.

Harvey had been spending less time online. He hadn't unboxed anything since October apart from a 1:76 scale model of the Castle steam locomotive that they sold in the store. It was made of thin plastic, with no moving parts. The wheels were so flimsy that one of them broke off when Harvey was taking the train out of its packaging. He was disappointed to find no tiny model of Andrew inside the engine.

Andrew would be on a different train now, somewhere between Moscow and Vladivostok. Harvey imagined him with a big Russian beard like Rasputin, flecked with bits of tobacco and breadcrumbs and with a line of borscht at the bottom of the beard, like the soil on a returned Castle spade. Andrew would have already made a lot of friends on the train. He'd be playing cards and knocking back vodka shots with the off-duty guards in the restaurant car, or sharing a doobie with backpackers from Amsterdam, blowing the smoke out of the train window and into the snow-covered countryside while icicles formed on his beard. A fur Soviet Army hat, with the flaps deployed, would keep Andrew's ears warm.

In the weeks following the family get together at Wildways, Harvey had seen Andrew quite often. Usually just in passing at work or in the car park as they got on or off their respective shuttle buses. Yesterday, Harvey was eating his lunch at his usual table above the station. He'd waved to Andrew, forgetting there was a different, temporary driver turning the engine around on the turntable while he was away.

Not long before Andrew went to Russia, Harvey was surprised to see his car driving through the gates of the care home. Andrew had been to see Caroline. She was now his girlfriend. Harvey felt like Cilla Black. Bringing everyone together. Andrew and Caroline, his mum and Auntie Cathy. He was the human Void Filler. That could be his new YouTube name.

There hadn't been enough time to watch *Star Wars* with Andrew before he left for Russia. Their Machete marathon would have to wait until he returned. Harvey was in no real hurry, to be honest. He'd actually been having second thoughts about the whole idea, thinking it might be better to have a brother who'd never seen *Star Wars* rather than one who didn't like *Star Wars*.

Harvey had only seen Sally twice but they communicated

all the time, by email and on the phone. Sally often sent Harvey photos. They arrived without accompanying messages as attachments on his phone, like emoticons. Or they came with just a simple title or phrase, like the picture Sally had taken of the two of them together at the boating lake – 'When Harvey met Sally'. Harvey replied with, "Have you actually *seen* that film?!"

Harvey had spoken briefly on the phone to Molly. Her mother coerced her into saying, "Goodbye, Uncle Harvey." One time, Harvey rang Sally's home phone and Bruno had answered. He sounded very nice and was perfectly friendly, but Harvey had stammered quite badly. He hadn't rung Sally's house phone after that, in case Bruno answered again. Sally rang Harvey at six in the morning one Sunday, just to inform him that an anorak was a hooded jacket.

The Bee-Bot video was still Sally's only unboxing. She'd threatened to delete the video, in case one of her pupil's parents saw it and Sally 'went viral'. Harvey told her that, unless she changed the privacy settings, nobody except him could see the video. He suggested she should leave it online for future generations to find and for Molly to look at when she was grown up with children of her own. It would be like watching a quaint home movie from the olden days Harvey said. He'd watched Sally's unboxing video a few times himself, usually when his cluster home was in need of void fill.

Auntie Cathy came back to Wildways two weeks ago for Harvey's mother's birthday. She arrived with Sally. They brought flowers and a cake and sang 'Happy Birthday', Harvey's mother joining in, singing happy birthday to herself. His mother had had her hair cut especially. She showed everyone her pedicured toes.

Cathy had written a letter to her sister every single week. Harvey's mum was so pleased to receive something in the post. Harvey read the letters to her and helped her write replies, translating her Yodic into English or leaving it as it was.

Harvey had visited his mother at least twice a week since the family reunion. Apart from the usual Chinese Sundays they'd also shared a fish and chip Friday and a pizza Tuesday. Some evenings there was no theme or food involved at all. They'd sat and watched cartoons and reruns of Harvey's unboxing videos, which were now rotating as often as the quiz and game shows on his mother's TV. Harvey would always make a point of talking about Cathy, Sally and Andrew when he was visiting his mother. He never mentioned his father.

There were eighteen new pictures of his mother in the slideshow. 'Brimful of Asha' had been in Harvey's head, on and off, for most of November. He'd even plucked up enough courage to mention it to Asha. She told him she knew the song but had always thought it was called 'Roomful of Asha'. Harvey wanted to say that any room she was in would be full of Asha. But of course, he didn't.

On the penultimate Chinese Sunday of November, Harvey was washing his mother's plate in the bathroom. He dried the plate on a bathroom towel and put it in a carrier bag and came back into the room, leaving the bathroom light on. The hum of the extractor fan might help his mother sleep, but he expected it would keep him awake, like the idling car engine of his neighbour's car outside his bedroom window at five o'clock every morning.

"Shall I take that?" Harvey said, picking up the paper napkin from his mother's lap. He wrapped the cake crumbs inside the napkin and put it in his jeans pocket with his own parcel of crumbs. "Shall I put the card on the windowsill with the others?"

His mother gave him the birthday card from Cathy. She kept it in her handbag with the remote control and the Extra Strong mints. The family photo that Caroline had taken was in her handbag as well. It was badly creased, and stained with tea and cranberry juice. It was the third copy of the photo Harvey had printed for his mother. It was a great picture, even though Harvey had his eyes closed and he looked so huge. He doubted he would ever truly be happy with a photograph of himself. He put Cathy's birthday card on the windowsill and closed the curtains. He felt the radiator. It was warm. He didn't know if it was heating up or cooling down. It was like trying to determine the direction of the tide by its position on a beach.

"You've got glitter in your hair, Mum," Harvey said. "It must be from Cathy's card."

He lightly brushed the glitter from the top of his mother's head with his fingertips. Harvey couldn't remember having ever touched his mother's hair before. He'd always expected the white streak that parted her hair to feel different. Coarser, like an old toothbrush or the pattern on the wallpaper in the Fusilier.

Harvey moved the clothes his mother had chosen for the morning from the back of the chair. He put them onto hangers and hung them over the top of the slightly ajar wardrobe door. He went over and switched the big light off. The only light in the room now was from the muted television and coming through the crack in the bathroom door. The television screen flickered every time there was a marked change in the brightness or colour. Harvey knew it would keep him awake in the same way the idling bathroom extractor fan would.

He sat down on the armchair. It was more comfortable than the room's smaller chair but still only really designed for waiting rooms and hospital visits. Not a chair to get too comfortable in. With the uncomfortable chair, the noise of the fan and the flicker of the television, he didn't expect to get much sleep. He pulled the blanket that he'd borrowed from the newly empty room next door up and over his knees and tried not to think about the reason for the room being empty. He put the Donkey cushion behind his head. His mother was watching his every move.

"It's good you're come," she said.

She didn't ask him why he was still there or why he'd turned the big light off and why he was sitting down with a blanket over his knees.

"I've got nothing else to do," Harvey said. He hadn't intended it to sound so callous.

He pulled the blanket up to his chest.

"How are you feeling, Mum?"

"Hungry."

Harvey nodded. He didn't know which cliché was responsible for his mother's hunger, the short amount of time that had passed since eating Chinese food or the munchies from the hash cake.

42

Harvey slept surprisingly well. He had a proper dream, even if it did take place at work. The shop was deserted and all the lights and tills were switched off. Harvey was in the Kingdom of Pets. He was breaking open all the cages and hutches, releasing guinea pigs, gerbils, hamsters and long-eared rabbits into the wilds of Household and Kitchen. Watching them wreak havoc in Home Furnishings and Haberdashery. There were lovebirds and finches nesting in the fake trees of the Garden department, and a cockatoo was perched at the top of a children's slide in Toys and Games, where a myna bird was recording swearwords into a programmable plush replica of itself. Harvey was about to take a sledgehammer to the wall of aquaria to release the fish when he woke up.

Harvey knew that feeding one's elderly mother cannabis-infused cakes would, at best, be frowned upon by society and was probably, in fact, most definitely, illegal. But it seemed to have worked just as well on his mother as the hum of a television game show repeat, an extractor fan, or an open window on a rainy day. He never would have thought the sound of somebody else snoring could be so reassuring and pleasurable to listen to.

Harvey sat and watched his mother's shallow breaths. They didn't seem strong enough to produce a single snore. Andrew had told him about the last moments of their father's life. He'd sat by his hospital bed for three days, waiting for his breathing to change dramatically or stop. Andrew said that every time there was a sharp intake of breath, with no subsequent exhalation, he felt like time had stood still. Andrew found himself holding his own breath, not breathing out again until his father did. Harvey certainly didn't envy Andrew that. When the moment had come for their father to take his last breath, Andrew had been downstairs in the hospital's pocket W.H. Smiths, getting change to buy a cup of hot chocolate from the vending machine.

Harvey's mother stirred. She said something indecipherable and opened her eyes. She didn't seem at all surprised to see her son sitting there, maybe thinking he was always there, like the television and the hum of the bathroom extractor fan. Perhaps Harvey was being too modest, and the cake didn't deserve all of the credit for his mother's good night's sleep – and he still had his suspicions that the only cannabis in the Tupperware box was the word on Andrew's handwritten list of ingredients. He definitely hadn't felt any effects from the cake himself, other than the munchies. But when had Harvey *not* had the munchies? For his mother though, perhaps it was her son's presence in the room that was the real miracle drug.

When she was fully awake, Harvey helped his mother get dressed, turning his back while she put on the frock she'd chosen. She put a thick grey jumper over the frock and a blue cardigan over the jumper, and then she put on her winter coat. Less than a year ago, so many layers would have meant she was too tightly packed into the coat to be able to move. But she'd lost enough weight since then for there to still be room for another two jumpers. Harvey's mother *was* shrinking. Harvey supposed he already knew that. But it had taken his mother's sister to see her for the first time after a twenty-six-year absence to notice quite how much she'd changed.

They walked together towards the lifts. Already the sounds of breakfast television from the other rooms filled the corridor. Harvey's mother held onto him but not tightly like she was on a rope bridge over a ravine this time. Instead, she hooked her arm through the teapot handle of Harvey's arm, as though he was a gentleman escorting her home from the opera. Harvey pressed the button to call the lift and they stood and watched the illuminated display change from *G* to *1*. There was a ping and the doors opened, captioned by a recorded female voice. Harvey led his mother into the lift.

"Doors closing," the female voice said.

"Thank you," Harvey's mother replied.

It only took a few seconds for the lift to travel a distance that was probably only about as far as the lift's height, but the journey felt a lot longer as Harvey worried she might panic. The lift shook as it arrived on the ground floor.

"Doors opening."

"Thank you."

Opposite the lift there was a row of wheelchairs, lined up like bicycles outside a large city railway station. Harvey chose one and tested it, pushing it backwards and forwards as though it was a shopping trolley. He helped his mother into the wheelchair, placing her feet on the footrest and fastening the loose-fitting seatbelt. He hooked the noise-cancelling headphones over the handles of the wheelchair and pushed his mother along the corridor. As they passed the office, Harvey heard a radio playing quietly and a woman's voice talking on the phone. If he'd been certain it was Asha, he might have knocked and told her where they were going. Perhaps he would have asked her if she wanted to come with them. At the front door he signed himself, and for the first time ever, his mother, out.

They walked through the village, passing the park and their old house, seeing no one at all except for the occasional dog walker, early-riser or insomniac. Harvey couldn't recall a time when he'd walked past the Fusilier without seeing anyone outside, either reluctantly leaving late at night or queuing for their first drink of the day.

They left the village and headed out onto the A-road, where it was a lot busier. The wind was stronger and colder. Harvey checked his mother was warm enough. He offered her his long Tom Baker scarf, wrapping it around her quite a few times so it didn't get caught in the wheels of the chair. His mother hadn't stopped talking since leaving

Wildways. He couldn't hear what she was saying because of the traffic and the wind, but he said yes and no and really, every now and then, so that she wasn't talking to herself. His mother was clearly glad to be outside. As they walked under the bridge with the *GRAM FJG 4 EVER* graffiti on, a passing motorist honked his horn, as though Harvey and his mother were striking nurses.

Harvey took his phone out and checked the time. Everyone would be in early today, getting everything ready for the Winter Bonanza. By the time Harvey and his mother crossed the drawbridge, everyone would be too busy to notice them, and even if they did see Harvey, without his fleece and name badge, he'd be invisible. Harvey looked across the busy road and pushed his fringe out of his eyes. With the early morning sun rising behind it, The Castle actually looked quite beautiful.

❖

ACKNOWLEDGEMENTS

Thank you Holly, Marc, Chris, Neil and Mark Reynolds for early reading and encouraging. Thank you Mark Reynolds for the amazing cover art and the disintegrating Saturns and to Nathan Eighty for the book's interior design. Thank you Richard Anderson, Matt Ingham, Adam Velasco, Ricky Martin and everyone at Cherry Red. Thank you Michael Cobb for putting my commas in the right place(s). Thank you Nicola Barr. Thank you Jonathan, Justine and Karen at the Bookseller Crow. Support your local bookshops. Thank you Emma Ollington. Thanks Les and Tim. Thank you Becca Lockley for advice on police procedurals. And of course, thanks as ever to Jacqueline.

When writing 'A Godawful Small Affair' I did my best to get the astronomical details correct. If there are mistakes, I will say in my defence that the story is told from the viewpoint of a ten-year-old boy living on a council estate in Brixton, rather than a fifty-five-year-old particle physicist at the CERN institute. So obviously, all mistakes are deliberate. There were two books that were invaluable during the writing of 'A Godawful Small Affair'. 'Apollo' by Zack Scott, published by Wildfire, and '100 Things to Know About Space' by Alex Frith, Alice James, Jerome Martin, Fredrico Mariani and Shaw Nielsen, published by Usborne.

ABOUT THE AUTHOR

J.B. Morrison is the author of six novels and two memoirs. His books have been translated into eight different languages. In 2015 his fourth novel *Frank Derrick's Holiday of a Lifetime* won the 'Best Older Person's Character in a Book, Film, TV or Radio Drama' in Gransnet's Older People in the Media Awards. As Jim Bob, J.B. Morrison was the lead singer with chart-topping, Glastonbury headlining, indie pop superstars, Carter The Unstoppable Sex Machine. He continues to write and perform music. J.B. lives in London and watches far too much television. He hopes to one day be successful enough to not have to write his own 'about the author' blurbs.

Other titles available from

A Plugged In State Of Mind: The History of Electronic Music
Dave Henderson

All The Young Dudes: Mott The Hoople & Ian Hunter
Campbell Devine

Arguments Yard – 35 Years Of Ranting Verse And Thrash Mandola
Atilla The Stockbroker

Best Seat In The House: A Cock Sparrer Story
Steve Bruce

Bittersweet: The Clifford T Ward Story
David Cartwright

Block Buster! – The True Story of The Sweet
Dave Thompson

Burning Britain: A History Of UK Punk 1980 To 1984
Ian Glasper

Celebration Day: A Led Zeppelin Encyclopedia
Malcolm Dome and Jerry Ewing

Children of the Revolution: The Glam Rock Encyclopedia
Dave Thompson

Death To Trad Rock: The Post-Punk fanzine scene 1982-87
John Robb

Deathrow: The Chronicles Of Psychobilly
Alan Wilson

Embryo:- A Pink Floyd Chronology 1966-1971
Nick Hodges And Ian Priston

Fucked By Rock (Revised and Expanded)
Mark Manning (aka Zodiac Mindwarp)

Goodnight Jim Bob:On The Road With Carter USM
Jim Bob

Good Times Bad Times - The Rolling Stones 1960-69
Terry Rawlings and Keith Badman

Hells Bent On Rockin: A History Of Psychobilly
Craig Brackenbridge

Independence Days - The Story Of UK Independent Record Labels
Alex Ogg

Indie Hits 1980 – 1989
Barry Lazell

Irish Folk, Trad And Blues: A Secret History
Colin Harper and Trevor Hodgett

Johnny Thunders: In Cold Blood
Nina Antonia